FAITH

a novel by

Karin Coddon

This novel is dedicated to my mother.

The very definition of the real becomes: that of which it is possible to give an equivalent reproduction. The real is not only what can be reproduced, but that which is always already reproduced. The hyperreal.

Jean Baudrillard

Chapter 1

January 1999

It was a slow news day.

The President and Congress were deadlocked over aid to Bosnia, health-care, and the future of Social Security. The Republicans were proposing yet another independent prosecutor to investigate campaign finance misdeeds. And a current nominee to the federal courts had failed to pass some Southern senator's personal litmus-test on Affirmative Action.

In Washington, it was business as usual.

Ideology made the sexy story, but in reality, the good stuff was happening on both sides of the aisle. Senators elected on Born-Again platforms fucked little girls -- and boys; pro-choice, pro-feminist congressmen did the same; the handful of women invited into the club decided a greater good was done by staying silent, forging friendships, and bartering favors.

And then there were the Stepford-women, those smiling, big-haired, political "girls" who, regardless of age (which seemed to range from twenty-two to seventy), invariably snagged featured spots on "Geraldo" and "Internight" and "Politically Incorrect," tittering and mincing in their miniskirts as they espoused family values.

"It all makes me sick -- just goddamn sick," muttered Jessica Anders, "legal correspondent" for CNN's "This World Today," talking back to the TV as she threw herself together in the master bedroom of her Georgetown townhouse. In truth, she was really more annoyed to be dragged away from her six-month-old son Jordan in order to provide pat commentary about a run-of-the-mill-execution. Right, fine, she was the in-house anti-death-penalty person, and God knew she was paid handsomely for it. But a dozen serious scholarly opinions against death felt expendable when the sun was easing up and a cranky baby was insisting *Just ME!*

She looked like hell as she dashed downstairs to catch the CNN limo designated to take her to the studio for the death-watch. She hadn't had time to wash her thick mane of ash-blonde hair, and so she'd swept it back carelessly in a loose ponytail. Her pale blue eyes were circled, but the makeup folks at the studio could easily conceal the jagged crescents. She glanced over her notes as the limo sped downtown. Though half her mind was on Jordan, and another quarter on the remnants of her shattered marriage to Gregg, the details of this particular execution still chilled her. Darryl Jones, convicted of a brutal murder at fifteen, was now twenty-one, apparently reconciled with "the Lord," a model prisoner willing to waive any possibility of parole. Yet he admitted to the torture-murder of his thirteen-year-old girlfriend; having caught her *in flagrante delicto* with another boy, he'd wrenched her away and slowly, horribly, beaten her to death with a claw-hammer, until her brains had spilled out through her ears. The other boy, perhaps by the grace of God, had lived to testify against Darryl Jones.

It probably would not have garnered national headlines had Jones not been black, and the victim and her would-be defender been white.

As a mike was affixed to the front of her sweater and powder was dusted across her face, Jessica was already straightening up, awaiting a sound-bite. Hands kept adjusting and readjusting lights, and a director admonished her to attend to the bright camera light when it shone her way. A video monitor allowed her to view the show, which originated in Atlanta.

On the screen the host, a decent, deadpan career news guy named Paul Duncan, was somberly introducing the show, happily with no Geraldo-esque melodramatics. As

Duncan explained the specifics of the impending execution, the camera cut to a live-feed from Angola, Louisiana. Outside the death house, an all-too-familiar congregation was massing. Proponents of the death penalty hooted and waved incendiary signs: "AN EYE FOR AN EYE!" "WHAT ABOUT THE VICTIMS???" "FRY THE NIGGER!" The camera jerked away from the jeering frat boy bearing the last message, and turned to a small, somber group of protesters, silently holding hands. It zoomed in on a particular figure, a petite black woman with huge, sad eyes and a rosary clasped between her hands joined with a pair of others on either side. A simple headdress identified her as a Catholic nun.

"That, of course," Paul was saying, "is Sister Cordelia Marie Davis, perhaps this country's preeminent activist against the death penalty, as well an advocate for many other controversial social causes."

Cut back to Duncan in the Atlanta studio. "I'd now like to introduce my fine panel. Here with me in Atlanta is Beverly Wallace, trial attorney and supporter of the death penalty." Beverly, a smartly dressed woman with a fashionable bob, smirked.

Though Jessica had been on a dozen of these TV panels with Beverly, she could never get over how the woman could bring herself to grin and giggle when discussing capital punishment. Maybe it was just nerves. They'd finally met face-to-face at an ABA conference last year, and Jessica was surprised by Bev's genuine warmth and intelligence, the former of which just didn't seem to come over on TV.

"In our Washington studio, defense attorney and professor of law at Georgetown University, Jessica Anders. Jessica assisted in putting together the appeal for Darryl Jones."

The little light was on, so Jessica nodded grimly. "Good morning, Paul."

The other panelists were a very famous criminal defense attorney from Texas whom Jessica used to admire terribly until running into him at an ACLU function and discovering he was an incorrigible letch; and Reverend Charles Ingraham, a grandstanding right-wing televangelist who hadn't even deviated from his Baptist brethren's selective mercy to plead for the life of Karla Faye Tucker a couple years before.

Jessica bit back a grimace. She was in sorry company indeed when Bev Wallace was the sole panelist she could personally stomach.

Happily, Paul asked Jessica first to weigh in with her opinion. "The execution of Darryl Jones is a textbook example of everything that's wrong with capital punishment," she said, even as she noticed the little clock imposed on the corner of the screen, ticking off second-by-second the ten-minute countdown to Jones's extermination. Christ, what was this, a basketball game?

But she continued. "You have a minority defendant without sufficient monetary resources to retain top-flight counsel --"

Bev broke in. "Jessica, what about the victims? This man was convicted of a horribly brutal crime. You're obscuring the issue by playing the race card."

Randall Casper, the famed lawyer, responded. "Bev, it's been statistically proven that when the victims are also black, the defendant is less apt to get a one-way ticket to the big house."

The three started bickering, talking over each other (as they were encouraged to do), then a seemingly bemused Paul Duncan interrupted. "All right, cool down, people. Reverend Ingraham, the Bible says an eye for an eye, right? Yet here we see Sister Davis, a respected death-penalty opponent, leading prayers to the governor to spare that man's life. How does that jibe?"

Again, the screen returned to the scene in Louisiana, and a close-up of the nun, her lips moving in prayer.

"Well, lemme say this first," replied Reverend Ingraham in his syrupy Virginia drawl. "Sister Cordelia's not even a right representative of her own Church. How many times has the Vatican had to reprimand her about her liberal stands on abortion and homosexuals?"

"You're changing the subject," Jessica snapped. "The Pope -- not to mention human rights organizations world-wide -- condemns the death penalty, Reverend."

"All the same, the American people overwhelmingly favor capital punishment," rejoined Bev in that smug way she apparently deemed to be her "pundit" manner. "Like it or not, it's the law of the land --"

"Wait a minute, wait a minute," Duncan interrupted excitedly. "Something's going on."

Jessica watched the monitor switch back to the crowd outside the death house. People were swarming wildly and shouting. Had a riot between the pros and antis broken out? Uniformed cops were shoving through the mob. Someone outside of camera range was weeping shrilly.

The camera zoomed in on CNN's on-site reporter, Ken Gianelli. "This is incredible, Paul," he said breathlessly into his mike. "Someone's been shot. Who it was and how bad it is I can't tell ... " Behind him, state troopers mobilized, pushing people back. A siren wailed in the distance.

For once, Paul Duncan's ordinarily loquacious panel fell unanimously silent. Jessica could only watch the screen in horror as Ken Gianelli managed to waylay a sobbing woman. "What happened? Can you give us any idea of what happened?" the reporter pressed.

"He ... he shot her," the woman stammered. "Thank God some big guys wrestled him down right away ..." Distraught, she looked right into the camera. "When's all this killing going to stop?"

Now an ominous blue ribbon reading "SPECIAL BULLETIN" bordered the bottom of the screen. Jessica's heart was thumping. "Christ, who shot whom?" she snapped at the monitor.

Paramedics bearing a stretcher hastened past Ken Gianelli. The sobbing woman was no longer with him. He seemed to be listening intently to news he was hearing through his ear-piece. "Paul," he said, "we've just received an unconfirmed report that an as yet unidentified male did indeed shoot Sister Cordelia Marie Davis. No word on her condition. The young man has been taken into custody."

Jessica blenched as if she herself had been shot. Tears streamed down her face. A technical director gave her a box of Kleenex, and asked if she would be able to stand by to offer commentary in half an hour or so. Obviously, Paul Duncan's regular format had been suspended in lieu of continuing live coverage from Louisiana.

She nodded shakily, asked for a glass of water.

It seemed like the longest day of her life, longer even than the day, two months before, that Gregg told her he was in love with someone else. Maybe because then, the shock had been so acutely personal, her anger and grief so cleanly focused. They'd been married for twelve years, since the day after she graduated from Boalt law school. She'd met him while interning at Legal Aid in Berkeley. Gregg had been everything she wanted to be herself: dedicated, idealistic, a true advocate for the poor and marginalized. True, the debts they'd both accrued in law school rather quickly caught up with them, and he'd taken a job at a big prestigious firm in San Francisco while she worked first as a D.A., then, for the ACLU. She developed a specialization in appellate work; when Gregg was transferred to his firm's New York office, she took a year off to get her L.L.M at Yale. When the offer to teach at Georgetown arose, Gregg seemed as happy as she. He'd grown up in Maryland, and still had connections in D.C. He easily joined another big firm as a lateral partner.

The last two years, their lives, both professional and private, seemed to be going so well. The brouhaha surrounding the Texas execution of Karla Faye Tucker had led CNN to Jessica's expertise on the legal implications of the death penalty, and she'd been a regular consultant since. Between teaching and playing talking head every week or so on TV, her schedule had finally relaxed to the extent that having a baby at last seemed feasible. Gregg had been as thrilled as she about the pregnancy. Basketball fanatics, they named their little boy Jordan after Michael, thinking themselves oh-so-original until a whimsical essay in *Newsweek* informed them that thousands of couples across the country were doing the same.

Had Gregg, despite all of his progressive posturing, simply followed that age-old male tendency to lose sexual interest in his wife the moment she became a mother? Had he grown threatened by her increasing visibility on cable television? Or was it something far more mundane, the gradual, insidious souring of a marriage for no reason, for every reason, that had made the vivacious flight attendant on United's New York shuttle so suddenly irresistible to him?

And yet tonight, it felt trivial, even selfish, to dwell on the dissolution of her marriage. It was past ten by the time she got home. Thank God for Vicky, her tireless nanny. Jessica changed into her pajamas and bathrobe, then, cradling a slumbering Jordan in her arms, she settled down in front of the TV and automatically, started to channel surf, keeping the volume low.

None of the Big Three was running special reports, but cable was more than picking up the slack. She watched herself dumbly on a show taped earlier, talking so calmly and coldly about "the culture of violence" engendered by capital punishment, the "lynch mob mentality" that thirsted for vengeance, not justice, and that had apparently incited a twenty-five year-old high school drop-out to gun down a good, even saintly woman quietly protesting an execution. Almost lost in all the reportage was the fact that Darryl Jones's death by lethal injection took place after only the briefest of delays.

On another channel was another televangelist, trying to fend off another abolitionist's charge that today's tragedy demonstrated exactly what was so immoral about the death penalty. A panel on MSNBC was discussing the possible influence of race on this morning's horrific incident; after all, not only Darryl Jones, but Sister Cordelia had been black, while the alleged assailant, one Brad Lefebvre, was white. Jessica

remembered that awful sign wielded by one of the pro-death people: "FRY THE
NIGGER."

She clicked off the TV. Adjusting the blanket around Jordon's downy head, she
whispered, "What do you say, kiddo? Want to move to Sweden?"

The vast majority of Americans had awakened that day without the slightest idea a
poor black man named Darryl Jones was scheduled to die in the Louisiana death house.
Only a few more had ever heard of Sister Cordelia Marie Davis, and many of those who
did held rather negative impressions. The nun's tireless opposition to the death penalty
irked most people, and her work among welfare mothers and drug addicts was seen as
bleeding-heart do-goodism at its most quixotic and anachronistic. And wasn't she the one
the Pope was always trying to rein in for saying abortion should be a matter of
conscience, not of law?

But by evening, there was hardly a household -- a household with a television, that
is -- that didn't know almost everything about the Louisianan nun's life and death. Born
forty-six years before in Baton Rouge, Cordelia Davis had dedicated her life to God and
to service from childhood on. She'd taken the veil at twenty, risked her life as a
missionary in Central America, where she'd incurred the wrath of the Reagan
administration for her criticism of U.S. policies in Nicaragua and El Salvador. The
Vatican, already antsy about the spread of "liberation theology" among Catholic
missionaries in the region, arranged for Sister Cordelia to be summoned home to New
Orleans.

But Sister turned out to be just as irrepressible a "soldier of Jesus," as she liked to
put it, domestically. Snippets from a 1995 60 Minutes interview were shown almost
incessantly, in which the doe-eyed, soft-spoken nun decried the forces of intolerance and
bigotry against "all God's children, be they black, white, yellow, red; be they heterosexual
or homosexual." Another segment of the interview showed Ed Bradley accompanying

Sister Cordelia to an AIDS hospice, where she comforted the afflicted and embraced an emaciated young Haitian man ravaged by lesions.

Yet some of the murdered nun's more controversial acts were glossed over: her heated 1996 denunciation of "welfare reform" as immoral and punitive to the poor; her participation in peaceful demonstrations against the Gulf War; her passionate eulogy at the funeral of a Jewish abortion doctor slain by a "pro-life" clinic bombing. No, tonight, even Sister's fiercest critics were praising her as a saint, a martyr to the cause of non-violence that she carried on in Jesus's name. The President issued a statement mourning her tragic death, and vowing swift reprisal for her killer. An emissary from the Vatican spoke for the Holy Father, asserting that she "died, as she lived, in the Holy Spirit," and urging that her death might be the last sacrifice in the movement to end capital punishment. Friends on the left likened her to Dorothy Day, founder of the Catholic Worker. Friends within the Church called for her beatification. And political and theological enemies deigned to honor her as a woman of principle and Christian love, one even insisting the nun was a model of "personal responsibility," just in case any viewers mistook the faint praise for an endorsement of Sister Cordelia's beliefs.

In a matter of perhaps twelve hours, it was as if Americans had suddenly decided they couldn't get enough of Sister Cordelia Marie Davis. Live coverage of her death -- on cable, anyway -- continued long past midnight.

Just after six a.m., Jessica received a call from the CNN producer. "Can you be at the studio in an hour?"

She groaned. "Sorry. I have to teach at nine."

"OK, how about two? This thing's big, Jessica. We're planning live coverage of the funeral on Saturday. Will you be available?"

"If Sonny Bono's funeral merited live coverage, I guess I should be reassured that Sister Cordelia's does. Sure."

Within fifteen minutes, she got another call, this time from MSNBC. Could she be part of this evening's "Internight" panel?

It was strange, she mused as she showered, even a little sick. Would any of these media organizations, much less television viewers, give a damn about Sister Cordelia if her murder had not occurred on live TV? She squeezed her eyes shut as she raised her face to the driving spray of hot water and lathered suds into her hair. She was too cynical to hope that the media circus might result in a genuine public debate on the merits of capital punishment. No, in two weeks, another celebrity would die or be arrested, another lurid allegation would emerge about some eminent politician, another conspiracy theory would arise about Diana or O.J. or those rich people in Boulder who murdered their beauty-queen little girl. And producers would be on the phone to round up pundits from the ever-expanding pool of telegenic "experts" whose claim to fame was a tangential involvement in some previous feeding frenzy.

An awful thought: what if they were all Kato Kaelins who just happened to be blessed -- most of them, anyway -- with a modicum of intelligence?

Dressed in a blue silk blouse and gray Donna Karan pantsuit, her hair clean and fluffy from blow-drying, Jessica went downstairs to the kitchen, where Vicky was feeding Jordan in his high-chair. "Here, let me," Jessica said, taking the jar of mash from the nanny.

"Want some toast?" Vicky offered, pouring Jessica a cup of coffee from the Braun.

"No, I'll have half a bagel at work." She spooned mashed bananas into Jordan's gurgling, Cupid's bow little mouth.

Damn if he didn't already look like Gregg.

In her Constitutional Law class, all the students wanted to talk about was Sister Cordelia, but the Socratic method had a way of keeping them on point. After class, Bobby Carroll, editor of the Law Review and one of her favorite students, approached her at the lectern. He was a tall, good-looking African-American man whose social activism Jessica admired. He'd worked three years for Operation PUSH before deciding to enter law school. Jessica thought he had a great shot at a judicial clerkship.

"I'm organizing a candlelight vigil in memory of Sister Cordelia and against the death penalty," Bobby said.

"I'll be there. When?"

"Tomorrow night." He drew in a sharp breath. "I don't know how you did it. Keeping it together all day yesterday on TV."

"You know what, Bobby? I don't either." She shoved her lecture notes into her briefcase. Then, afraid she'd sounded too brusque, she added, "It was almost like the way you're forced to react when you're a parent. You're a complete wreck, but you've got to put on a brave face for the kid's sake."

Bobby smiled grimly. "That's some high opinion you have of the good folks out in television land, Professor!"

"Actually, the kid in question was me." She managed a feeble wink. "You see, Bobby, I'm not really a pundit, I just play one on TV."

That afternoon, she was not CNN's lone D.C.-based legal analyst. To her mild irritation, she was joined in the studio by Caroline Bruckner, a young woman Jessica regarded as a "lawyer" in only the strictest sense of the word. Where Bruckner had gone to law school was anyone's guess, and by her own giddy admission, she'd never practiced. Rather, she was a full-time consultant for a conservative lobby called the American Family Institute. Less officially, she was a member of what Jessica and Gregg had long referred to as the Bimbo Brigade, a mysterious cabal that seemed to provide a veritable assembly-line of vacuous, leggy blondes to spout off against Democrats and feminists on any cable talk show -- and there were plenty -- that would have them on. Caroline Bruckner was among the worst offenders, constantly flipping her waist-length tresses and outright snickering when another panelist attempted to correct one of her endless factual errors or misstatements of the law.

Unlike Bev, who came off as smug and snooty onscreen but was actually charming in person, Caroline was just as smarmy and supercilious when the camera was averted.

The two women greeted each other politely, but that was about it.

Jessica was rather offended that Bruckner had been invited to opine about the murder (now the media was calling it "assassination") of Sister Cordelia in the first place. What could she possibly have to offer other than right-wing platitudes about the sanctity of gun ownership and the ostensible irrelevance of the death penalty to the crime that had claimed Sister's life?

So of course, when the moderator, this afternoon CNN's more confrontational Owen Shawn, solicited Caroline's opinion, Bruckner responded with an exaggerated roll of her heavily mascara'd eyes. "You know, Owen, I'm just worried about this rush to judgment -- if I can use that term without invoking the master snake oil salesman."

Jessica had to interrupt. "Ever heard of Mark Lane's book on the Kennedy assassination? Cochran didn't coin that phrase, and I'm not even sure Lane did, but it's about time somebody set the record straight."

"Now, now, Jessica, let's not drag Kennedy into this," coaxed Shawn, for all that he was famous for provoking shouting matches between panelists.

"What I was saying," Caroline asserted, "was that it makes me sick to see liberals trying to exploit this tragedy to further a partisan political agenda whose ultimate aim is to deprive law-abiding Americans of their Constitutionally-guaranteed right to bear arms."

"That's simply idiotic," Jessica snapped, knowing that Owen encouraged open shows of rancor. This was no show, either. "'The right to bear arms in a well-regulated militia' is a heck of a lot different from allowing every Tom, Dick, and Harry to wield a personal firearm. Right-wingers like Ms. Bruckner are indirectly responsible for the climate of vigilantism that led to Sister Cordelia's murder, and I'm not afraid to say it!"

Bruckner, of course, had giggled all the way through Jessica's stern diatribe, a reaction conveyed via satellite on a split screen.

Owen Shawn simply mugged as they wrangled, as if he were a bemused kindergarten teacher trying vainly to arbitrate a dispute between two five-year-olds wrestling over a coveted box of Crayolas.

A pinstriped civil attorney in New York tossed in his two cents. "Professor Anders has a point, but I think she's oversimplifying. Once we start limiting the free exchange of ideas in the name of a greater social good, we're talking censorship."

A shaggy-haired radical defense attorney in San Francisco, Dave Steiner, joined the verbal fray. "Professor Anders is not talking about limiting the free exchange of ideas, and you know it!" he thundered. "She's talking about a concerted effort on the part of the extreme right to trick Americans into thinking that gun ownership has anything to do with personal freedoms! And as for the death penalty, we've known for years it isn't a deterrent, but yesterday's events in Louisiana proves beyond any doubt it actually promotes violence and killing!"

Again, Caroline Bruckner was rolling her eyes and snickering. Jessica, stone-faced, said, "That's exactly right. What happened yesterday was as inevitable as it was tragic." But secretly, she wanted to hug Dave, one of her best friends from Boalt Hall. His fire-and-brimstone bluster still made her want to cringe, and God knew, he'd rubbed his share of judges the wrong way. But he wore his heart on his sleeve, and had never sold out. After all this madness blew over, she'd have to give him a call, see how he and Roberta and the kids were doing.

Owen -- as was his wont -- was playing devil's advocate. "Look," he said, gesticulating with a pencil in "exasperation," "this is a crazy world. There are a lot of nuts out there, guns or not. This guy who shot Sister Cordelia was clearly a nut. So was Hinkley. So was the guy who shot John Lennon."

"You're making an excellent case for stricter gun control, Owen," Jessica said acidly.

"You're missing his point," Caroline Bruckner sighed. "Guns don't kill people -- people do. Look at O.J.! This guy in Louisiana might have rushed at that nun with a steak knife -- oh, but that's right, you liberals are all vegans, aren't you. You'd be happy to ban cutlery, too. And why stop there? People slip and die in the shower all the time -- next thing, you'll have us all stinking and politically correct, just like the French!"

Owen chuckled. "Uh-oh, Caroline, we're gonna get letters on that one."

The show cut to a break. Jessica felt vaguely ill. If she had any integrity at all, she decided, she'd pull a Dan Rather and storm out of the studio. It wasn't simply the reactionary views and condescending, unprofessional attitude of Bruckner that were getting to her. She was used to it, and usually even relished the opportunity to spar with so wrong-headed an opponent as Caroline, because Jessica knew she'd always win. No, tonight was different, and the recognition that they were making entertainment out of a genuine tragedy sickened her as never before. Why? She'd commented dispassionately on any number of brutal murders, grotesque injustices, and executions. Maybe it was having witnessed -- via live video feed -- the murder of Sister Cordelia. Sister Cordelia Marie Davis, a woman she'd never met but had profoundly admired. A woman whose faith and compassion actually made Jessica wistful for the mysterious yet strangely comforting Catholicism of her own childhood. The Catholicism she'd drifted away from, nominally because of the Church's medieval positions on birth control and abortion. But her alienation wasn't purely a matter of principle. Somewhere along the line she'd started to doubt. Maybe doubt began the first time, in junior high, the boy she really liked stood her up, with no excuses, for a date she'd been anticipating for weeks. Maybe doubt was cemented further by philosophy classes at UCLA; her intellect could wrap around and grasp Hegel and Marx and Sartre and Foucault, whereas Augustine and Aquinas and Kierkegaard seemed exquisite, masterful examples of wishful thinking.

And maybe when her difficult, beloved mother died ten years ago of congestive heart failure undiagnosed by a doctor she'd seen that very day, doubt dissolved into stark certainty.

She and her brother Steve, now a film critic for a San Francisco newspaper, saw to it that Mama had a funeral Mass.

It was the last time she'd set foot in a Catholic church.

Since Jordan's birth, Steve good-naturedly pestered her to have the baby baptized. "I want to be a godfatha," he teased, in his best-worst-Seinfeld-doing-Brando. At thirty-eight, Steve was two years' Jessica's senior, but still the poster-boy for the Peter Pan Syndrome, dating one neurotic, "sensitive artist" female after another. Jessica told him to mind his own family values. When she and Gregg split up, Steve abruptly quit badgering her about baptizing Jordan. Holy water or not, he'd told her quietly, he considered himself his nephew's godfather.

They were back on the air. The last thought she had before resuming her role as Jessica Anders, the legal expert she played on TV, was that her faith and her marriage had withered away in nearly identical manner, terminal until one decisive, traumatic blow put the patient out of its misery.

Chapter 2

Sister Cordelia's hometown of New Orleans rose to the occasion of national, and in some cases, international, notoriety. Ordinarily the country's undisputed mecca of wanton carnival and drive-thru daiquiri stands, home to Mardi Gras and the Sugar Bowl, voodoo queens and streetcorner jazz, New Orleans showed itself capable of staging an appropriately somber, if typically baroque, theatre of mourning. Reporters, often accompanied by camera crews, interviewed tourists in French Quarter bars, pilgrims who'd journeyed across the continent to say goodbye to Sister Cordelia, and here and there, sincerely devout Catholics and grieving African-Americans who'd known all along of Sister's good works and commitment to social justice. The occasional, callous redneck remark was carefully edited out of "special reports," except on Italian TV, which had no stake in showing the world a grieving America unriven by the racial divide or moral quandary of the death penalty.

Jessica had heard this from one of the CNN technical people, and she wished heartily she'd taken the time to study Italian, instead of French, to fulfill her undergraduate language requirement. At the last minute, the network had decided to send her and another analyst -- a prominent theologian from Washington's Catholic University -- to New Orleans for live, on-site commentary on Sister's funeral, along with their chief correspondent. Thank God Gregg had been available to take Jordan (and the faithful Vicky) for the weekend. He'd actually told Jessica he was proud of her work on TV, proud she was standing up for a woman they had both admired.

She'd thanked him stiffly. Only residual Catholic guilt kept her from telling him to go fuck himself.

It was macabre, even surreal, the way the Sister Cordelia story continued to grow. Almost like a crazy strain of cancer, the germ had taken hold the morning the nun had been murdered on live television, had metastasized to become a raging national disease. *Better her than Sonny Bono*, Jessica repeatedly reminded herself, but she still felt ghoulish, vaguely complicit in whipping the country into a collective frenzy that seemed to have little to do with what the nun had accomplished, what she had stood for. The Vice-President was due to attend the high funeral Mass at St. Louis Cathedral, as were delegations from Rome, France, and each of the tiny Central American countries to whose needy Sister had ministered.

Jessica had dashed from the Georgetown Law School vigil, held in front of the Lincoln Memorial, to the incongruously monikered Ronald Reagan National Airport, where she caught a plane to New Orleans. On the short flight, she reviewed notes and struggled not to beat herself up over leaving Jordan, if only for a weekend. He'd been cranky this morning, a little sniffily; would Gregg know enough to monitor his temperature, his appetite? It took a martini and the knowledge that Vicky, who'd been with Jordan from the day they'd brought him home, would be there to soothe the raw ends of Jessica's nerves.

She arrived in New Orleans just after eleven, early for the Big Easy. A harrowing cab-ride transported her from Kenner to the French Quarter and the majestic, appropriately rococo Monteleone Hotel on Royal Street. A handful of faxes awaited her, all from CNN, advising her as to the schedule and logistics of tomorrow's coverage. The funeral was due to start at three p.m.; she needed to be at the makeshift headquarters, at the riverfront Hilton, by noon for makeup and briefing.

A porter insisted on carrying her overnight satchel and garment bag up to her fourth floor room. "You here for Sister's funeral, Miss?" he asked morosely.

She fumbled for a couple of bills. "No -- I'm on vacation," she lied. She knew her lie was transparent; it was splashed across her face. But she just didn't want to get into it.

After he left, she unzipped the garment bag, removed the black Calvin Klein gabardine jacket and matching sheath, and hung them up carefully. Luckily, the January weather was moderate, in the low sixties, for she hadn't brought a coat. She'd flown out of D.C. in her usual travel gear -- wool sweater, jeans, and Nikes --

Shit!

She'd forgotten dress shoes! "Oh, I'm going to be a sight tomorrow," she said aloud, imagining the lean tailored lines of the Calvin Klein suit "complemented" by a worn pair of Air Jordans. Her mind worked frantically. She'd been to New Orleans a few years before, for the ABA; wasn't there a mall nearby, on Canal Street, where she could possibly secure for herself a pair of plain, black serviceable pumps?

She flipped through the "Guest" book in the room, and assured herself that Canal Place was only a few blocks away.

She'd get up early tomorrow, and dash over to Saks for a simple pair of Bally's. One could never have too many pairs of Bally's.

Listen to yourself, you goddamn hypocrite. Caroline Bruckner also probably thinks one can never have too many pairs of Bally's.

Jessica winced as she tried to muffle the inner reproach. She needed to cut back on these stupid TV legal panels; she was starting to internalize the sniping, opposing voices.

"Room service," she said aloud, decidedly. She found a menu, chose a cup of seafood gumbo, a cheeseburger, and glass of white wine. She scanned the push-buttons on the phone, then pressed "5."

"Sorry, Mrs. ... Anders," came an apologetic voice. "Room service stops at eleven. However, we do have a restaurant next door that serves until one."

"Forget it," she said, almost amused. "It's my fault -- this is New Orleans. Nobody orders room service here."

She tossed on her jacket, rode the elevator to the grand, chandeliered lobby. She glanced a moment or two toward the bar; she could probably get peanuts or pretzels if she ordered a cocktail. She decided against it. This was, after all, New Orleans, and it seemed a shame to waste her one night in a hotel bar, not when she was only a block away from Bourbon Street.

At the corner of Bienville and Bourbon, she bought a spicy, steaming hot dog from a vendor's kitschy red stand. As she ate the hot dog, doing her best to avoid spilling mustard on herself, she observed the hurdy-gurdy unfolding against a backdrop of nightclubs, bars, souvenir stands and porn shops, most housed in historic stone and stucco buildings with their characteristic lacy iron grillwork balconies. Live blues, jazz, and Cajun music strained against canned pop hits from humbler bars and the random saxophonist blowing a sultry melody on the sidewalk. Yellow neon letters above the Royal Sonesta's oyster bar Desire seemed as much motto as literary allusion. Rollicking tourists guzzling Hurricanes from eighteen-ounce plastic cups staggered down Bourbon in Mardi Gras sweatshirts. Mounted police kept a watch over the revelry astride nervous, nostril-flaring horses. Across the street, Jessica saw a bull-necked teenager in a Denver Broncos T-shirt reel out of a topless club, take one wobbly step before vomiting what looked to be a gallon of nauseous, half-digested slop into the gutter.

Revolted, Jessica tossed her half-eaten hot dog into a trashcan. Maybe she should've stayed at the Monteleone bar after all. It wasn't just the guy puking his guts out; the Quarter's carnivalesque atmosphere, no more Bacchanalian than usual and downright tame compared to the revels of Mardi Gras or even New Year's Eve, tonight struck her as ghoulish.

The liveried doorman back at the Monteleone smiled at her pleasantly. "Gettin' a little chilly out there, ain't it?"

She hadn't even noticed, but she just nodded and headed for the dark, slowly revolving Carousel Bar. Before her first stay at the Monteleone for the ABA, she'd never even heard of a revolving bar that was street-level; the notion seemed quaint, almost absurd. On the other hand, the rooftop revolving bars at the Westin in Toronto and the Bonaventure in L.A., despite their dramatic skyline views, tended to give her vertigo. She'd come to consider the designer of the Carousel Bar an architect possessed of uncommon good sense.

Though the night was early by New Orleans standards, only a handful of other patrons -- all looking like serious media types with their notes and cell phones -- hunched over tables in the soothingly dark room. Not eager to engage in any shop-talk, Jessica took a seat at the bar. She ordered a glass of Cabernet, and found herself inordinately pleased by the bowl of "party-mix" the bartender brought her along with her drink.

"Y'all stayin' here at the hotel, Miss?" he asked casually. He was a weathered bear of a man with a slow drawl and that uniquely Southern courtliness that not even the most ardent feminist could mistake for condescension. A nametag pinned to his neat black vest identified him as "Kip."

"Yes, I am. It's a great old place. Much better than those Leviathans over on Canal Street."

He seemed to take the compliment personally. "Now, didn't you hit the nail on the head! The Sheraton, and the Marriott, and the Hilton, and the Westin -- they all got the feel of a giant, brand-spanking-new airport to me."

It felt oddly comforting to have a bona fide meaningless conversation. It seemed she hadn't had one in years. "You should see the J.W. Marriott in D.C. It's like a self-contained metropolis -- it's got everything but gridlock and muggings."

Kip chuckled. "That where y'all are from, Washington?"

"I'm afraid so." She prayed he wouldn't start grilling her about Sister Cordelia.

"Just don't get me started on all those politicians," he grinned, setting a cocktail napkin in front of a newcomer two stools down. "Crooks, all of 'em, both sides of the aisle." Then he caught himself. "I beg your pardon, Miss, for all I know you're an important lady senator -- "

She laughed. "Let me assure you, I have absolutely no aspirations to political office."

Assured he hadn't offended, the bartender then turned to the other customer. "What can I bring you, sir?"

"Gin and tonic."

Absently, Jessica glanced over. A tall man of slim athletic build, around her own age, in a suede jacket and Levis. Shaggy black hair, olive skin. Dark, impatient eyes. Great cheekbones. In fact, one of the better-looking men she'd seen in quite a while. Half-embarrassed by her own fleeting shallowness, she reverted her eyes to her wine glass.

The stranger lit up a cigarette. "Do you mind if I smoke?" he asked.

Jessica was momentarily startled, at first not realizing he was addressing her. "Oh," she said, recovering. "Not at all. I quit myself three years ago, and second-hand smoke makes me sort of pleasantly nostalgic."

"I guess I brought my smoking paranoia with me from L.A., where you're better off shooting heroin into both arms than lighting up a Marlboro in a neighborhood dive."

Kip brought him his drink.

The man lifted his glass to Jessica. "Cheers," he said in patent irony.

So he wasn't in town either just for a vacation.

He took a sip of his drink, then set the glass down and extended a hand over the empty stool. "I'm Alex Trujillo. Nice to meet you."

She shook his hand cool from having clutched the icy gin and tonic. "Jessica Anders."

"Yeah, that's what I thought. That must mean you're here for the same reason as I am."

The dreaded subject had been raised, but his demeanor -- cynical and no-bullshit, even a little brusque -- served, oddly, to put her at ease. (It didn't hurt, either, that he was great-looking, she had to privately admit.) "The whole thing's so bizarre," she said slowly, shaking her head. "After it's all over, I've got to really sit down and think things through."

She hardly noticed him ease over to claim the stool right next to hers. "What's there to think about?" he carped. "A great little lady had the fucking misfortune to be blown away on national TV. Bingo -- it's a quote, unquote, Event." He took another gulp from his glass. "Makes me damn proud to be a member of the media."

"Television?"

"Haven't stooped that low yet. Nah, I write for the L.A. *Times*. Supposedly specializing in Latino affairs. They sent me out here because Sister Cordelia's been a saint for years in the barrios."

"Especially in California, I'm sure," she said, sipping her wine. "I remember how she raked that idiot Wilson over the coals about that awful anti-immigrant bill."

"Prop 187," he confirmed. "See, that's the problem. To that community -- my community -- her death really does mean something. It's more than just the flavor of the day for MSNBC."

"You're really hard on us, you know that?" She motioned to the bartender for another glass of wine. "Unfortunately, I tend to agree with you."

"Put that on my tab, amigo," Alex instructed Kip.

"Absolutely not," Jessica said.

"Look, don't think of it as a sexist display of Latin *machismo*. I'm just assessing myself a fine for being an obnoxious asshole."

"Hmm. In that case . . . "

"Seriously, Jessica, sorry about bashing what you do. I must have seen that clip of you a dozen times -- the one when that sonofabitch shot her. I thought you did a hell of a job."

A kind of melancholy had fallen over him; it was clear he wasn't merely flattering her. "Tell you what," she said, trying to lighten the mood. "Let me bum a cigarette from you and pay for your next drink. Then we'll be square." She slipped a Marlboro Light out of the pack on the bar top.

Her ploy worked. "That's right, make me responsible for your falling off the wagon," he said, smiling and proffering his lighter. "Besides, you strike me as one of those lawyers itching to file a monster class-action suit against Big Tobacco."

"And you strike me as the kind of muckraking journalist drooling to write an expose of how the industry specifically targets minorities," she teased back, taking a deep drag. It made her a little light-headed, reminding her of how she used to savor, like the headiest of drugs, that first smoke after a long, nicotine-deprived plane flight.

She was flirting without realizing it. For had she realized it, she would have been appalled by herself, and then, awkward and self-conscious, mentally calculating precisely how many years had elapsed since she'd cast even a sideways glance at a man other than Gregg.

Their conversation took a decidedly less philosophical turn. They talked basketball. He was a huge Lakers fan, and chided her about her loyalty to the Washington Wizards.

She conceded that the Wizards had the stupidest team name in all of pro sports, but reminded him of the indelicacy of continuing to call a D.C. team the Bullets. She confessed that she and her soon-to-be ex-husband had named their infant son after Michael Jordan, and happily, Alex didn't pry about the specifics of the break-up. He offered little about his personal life, but he didn't wear a ring. However, she respected his privacy and knew better than to make any assumptions.

They talked about California, of its problems and allures. Though born and bred in Los Angeles, Alex had gone to Stanford, and shared her appreciation of the fierce beauty and chic urbanity of the Bay Area. When he asked her how her brother Steve could stand working for a paper as mediocre as the *Chronicle*, her answer was succinct: "San Francisco." But she got her comeuppance when, turning the tables on him, she wondered how he could abide living in L.A. "Easy -- the *Times*."

Then all of a sudden, it seemed, it was after two, and they were the last ones in the bar. Not that Kip, the garrulous bartender, was rushing them; he maintained a discreet post at the far end of the bar, tallying receipts.

Despite his earlier promise, Alex insisted on paying the entire tab. "Cool it. I'm on an expense account -- wouldn't you rather stiff the Chandlers than Ted Turner?"

"Ted Turner hasn't run CNN for years."

"OK. You can buy me dinner at the Commander's Palace tomorrow night, and send the bill to Time-Warner."

Reality returned with a thud. She was at once conscious of the dull throbbing between her temples after three glasses of Cabernet. "I have an eight o'clock flight back to Washington," she said, as they strolled out of the Carousel Bar. Funny how the entire time, she'd never noticed the structure revolving. He asked for no elaboration, but she offered one anyway. "This is the longest I've ever been away from my kid."

To her mild disappointment, he shrugged, as if it were no big deal. "In that case, maybe we'll run into each other tomorrow during Disneyland on Ice."

He walked her to the elevator but made no move to get in the car with her. "I'm gonna hit Al Hirt's over on Bourbon and see what's going down."

"Oh, the advantages of being in the print media -- you don't have to worry about looking human the morning after." She fumbled in her purse. "Here's my card. If you're ever in D.C., give me a call."

He pocketed the card without looking at it. "I probably won't be, but who knows? Maybe this Sister Cordelia thing will turn out to have 'legs.'"

"I doubt it," she sighed. "Goodnight, Alex. Thanks for the drinks."

She reached out her hand, which he pressed rather than shook. "'Night, Jessica. Don't beat yourself up too much over all this bullshit, OK?"

Then he released her hand, the elevator door slid shut, he was gone, and she was alone.

Overnight, barricades were erected around Jackson Square and majestic, Gothic-style St. Louis Cathedral. Platforms to accommodate media crews and their equipment blocked pedestrian access to St. Peter and St. Ann Streets between Chartres and Decatur. NBC, and its cable-sisters CNBC and MSNBC, had somehow managed to secure the prime site of the "overview," the small, raised concrete park between Jackson Square and the muddy Mississippi, a spot where on an ordinary day, tourists brought their cameras and their beignets from nearby Cafe du Monde for far more innocuous, personal photo-ops.

Though Sister Cordelia's convent was actually located just outside of the city, in Metairie, city planners had deemed a full-scale funeral procession unfeasible, given security interests, traffic, and the unpredictable nature of New Orleans weather in January. The archdiocese had made an extraordinary gesture, allowing Sister Cordelia's body to be housed temporarily at the old Ursuline Convent, only a few blocks away from the Cathedral in a southeastern corner of the Quarter. The serene, austere white convent, with its high scrubbed walls and exquisite garden, was now closed to sightseers and would be until the end of the month, the bishop decreed. It was not simply that the local Church hierarchy appreciated the symbolism of sheltering the body in the convent, the oldest French colonial building in the region, dating back to 1734. They also understood the logistical sense the site made, both from a civic and media perspective. The cortege would take a tidy, L-shaped route: one block south on Ursulines, then four blocks west on Decatur to Jackson Square and the Cathedral.

Because of the relatively short distance from the convent to the church, many of Sister's devoted followers were complaining that they were being excluded from honoring her in death. Charges of racism circulated; was New Orleans afraid of showing the world that a majority of Sister Cordelia's Louisiana acolytes were African-American? Fearing unrest, the city and archdiocese made a few hasty concessions. Bleachers would be put up along Decatur Street and in Jackson Square, just so long as room was still made for the media, with giant TV screens providing coverage of the funeral Mass itself. And, almost more importantly, Sister's coffin would be open, that the whole world might not forget for a moment that Cordelia Marie Davis was not only a holy woman, but a black woman.

Her assassin had shot her through the heart; the bullet would still be lodged there had not the coroner removed it, at the D.A.'s request, for evidentiary reasons. Her killer had left her lovely face intact, an image to be admired and mourned by what was predicted to be a huge television audience.

Despite her fatigue, Jessica had slept poorly. She might as well have accompanied Alex Trujillo to the jazz club, for all the repose abstaining had afforded her. By the cold, drizzly light of morning, she felt she'd made an utter idiot of herself last night. She vowed not to think about it, about how she'd laughed and bantered and on cue, spilled her soul, as if to demonstrate to him she was indeed a woman of substance.

And she found she missed Jordan terribly, ached for him, in fact. Before leaving her hotel room, she made herself phone Gregg. "I don't want to get into anything," she told him flatly. "How's Jordy? Does he still have the sniffles?"

Gregg knew better than to press matters. "He's fine, Jessie. He hasn't even sneezed. He's just been playing with his bunny and acting like an all-around happy camper."

"Put Vicky on the phone."

Vicky, sweet-tempered as always, confirmed Gregg's report. "He's doing great, Jessica. Gregg's spoiling him rotten, but Jordy isn't exactly complaining. Stop worrying. We'll see you tonight."

More or less appeased, Jessica showered and dressed, clomped over to Cafe Beignet in her chic Calvin Klein ensemble and hightop Nikes for a *cafe au lait*. Royal Street seemed unusually quiet, even for a Saturday morning. Sipping her buttery, chickory-flavored coffee, she walked slowly toward Canal, pausing here and there to admire antique armoires and bric-a-brac in the windows of closed curio shops.

At Walgreen's, she stopped to buy a cheap umbrella and (hating herself) a pack of Merits. Damn Alex! Damn her own foolishness! Well, she'd smoke a few today, then toss out the rest at the airport. No way was she going to subject Jordan to second-hand smoke.

She smoked a couple of cigarettes on her way to Canal Place, where she atoned for her venality and bought a pair of plain, ninety-eight-dollar pumps at Saks. The leather was cheap and cardboardy, and her feet would be eligible for federal disaster relief should she wear them for more than an hour's sitting, but she was commenting for CNN, not running the Boston Marathon.

She resolved to dump the shoes along with the cigarettes in a handy trash receptacle at New Orleans International.

At the riverfront Hilton, the CNN producer promptly informed her of a change in plans. "We don't think it's appropriate for a legal analyst to be commenting directly on a funeral," he said.

She read between the lines: in short, no one at MSNBC was doing it. "Fine. How soon can you get me to Kenner and the airport?"

"No, no, no, Jessica, don't get me wrong," the producer said with a nervous laugh. "Father Finnerty will offer commentary while the procession and funeral are happening.

You we want inside the Cathedral to report after the service is over. You're Catholic, right?"

"Recovering," she said acidly. "But Lee, I'm not a reporter, for Christ's sake, I'm a lawyer. Why put me in the church?"

Lee looked miserable. "Gianelli's got food poisoning. Or so he says. Shit, this happens every time we come to New Orleans. Next time we have a breaking story, I hope it's in fucking Salt Lake City."

"Michael Jordan got sick from the pizza there."

Lee snorted. "Yeah. I buy that about as much as I do that Gianelli ate a bad bowl of gumbo. You game, Jessie?"

"Whatever."

Mass, she was thinking. All that goddamn standing and kneeling. If there was a God, He was indeed vengeful, laughing at her for thinking herself virtuous for buying cheap Brazilian shoes.

They briefed her, powdered her, and credentialed her. A CNN security crew escorted her through the swarms of mourners amassed in Jackson Square. Despite her uneasiness about media exploitation, she was moved by the faces of genuine sorrow she saw. Black people, white people, nuns in old-fashioned wimples and veils. Many were crying, and most held flowers and candles whose flames flickered weakly against the steady drizzle.

She thought of what Alex said: *To this community -- to my community -- she really did mean something.* To these people, nameless and uncelebrated assembled in Jackson Square, Sister Cordelia meant something, too. They weren't simply extras in a real-life, media-spawned blockbuster that both CNN and MSNBC were currently titling "Murder and Martyrdom: The Life and Death of Sister Cordelia."

Even with her CNN credentials, the Secret Service agent at the door of the Cathedral triple-checked her, uttering terse comments into a walkie-talkie before he nodded and admitted her. She wasn't terribly surprised. The Vice-President's attendance at the funeral was somewhat controversial, given the administration's pro-execution stance. Just two nights before Jessica had hotly debated Caroline Bruckner over the propriety of the Vice-President's appearance at the funeral in an official capacity. "It sends the wrong message," Bruckner had snickered. "Why should a death penalty opponent's funeral deserve more acknowledgment than the victim of a drug-related killing?"

Out of habit, Jessica dipped her fingertips in a marble holy water font and blessed herself. The Vice-President had yet to arrive, but most of the front and center pews were either occupied or reserved. Incongruously, it reminded her of the time, years ago in New York, that she and Gregg had gone to see *Cats*.

She claimed a space in the last row of center pews, on the end. Few others back here seemed to be mourners; likely they were media voyeurs themselves. She cast her eyes upward, lingered over the stained-glass saints, the stations of the cross, the dizzying beams and gilt and sacred murals above her.

I wish . . .

The half-formed thought would remain incomplete. The Vice-President and his delegation were entering. A single Secret Service man genuflected briefly, and Jessica bit back her amusement. The Vice-President was escorted to a pew directly in front of the altar, the altar adorned with "PEACE" banners made by local schoolchildren and grand vases and wreaths of flowers fragrant enough to scent the entire cathedral. Above the array, the carved figure of Christ crucified hung in still indifference.

More luminaries were shambling in. The Italian ambassador, and the Vatican assembly. The archbishops of Managua and San Salvador. The first lady of France. Representatives from Amnesty International, the ACLU, the NAACP, the Southern Poverty Law Center. TV cameramen, poised on the far right and far left aisles of the cathedral, were actually doing their best to be unobtrusive.

And then a familiar voice whispered at her elbow. "What's a nice girl like you --?
"

She smothered a smile with her palm. "Don't. We're in church."

Alex, his press-pass dangling from the pocket of his leather jacket, eased into the
pew beside her. "It's insane out there."

"I thought the people in the square seemed incredibly sincere."

"I'm not talking about the square. The procession's begun. People are wailing and
carrying on and trying to hurl themselves on the hearse."

Tears stung her eyes. "Christ, that's ... sick." She knew he wasn't alluding to the
dignified, sincere mourners with their candles and flowers outside. It was people -- no,
leeches -- determined to seize upon their proverbial fifteen minutes, maybe even some of
the same swaggerers and frat-boys she'd glimpsed last night on Bourbon Street hooting
mindless obscenities and puking on their shoes.

All to get their fucking faces on TV.

"C'mon, Jessica, don't cry," Alex urged quietly. "Look, here comes the Harlem
kids' choir."

Through bleary eyes she saw them, sweet and solemn in their gold-and-white
robes. Darling and delicate their perfect black skulls, their huge, serious eyes. Who the
hell did she and Gregg, and the multitudes of well-heeled white people, think they were,
naming their babies after Michael Jordan as if that merited a plaque in the Civil Rights
Hall of Fame?

The boys' choir began a sonorous, heartbreaking *Ave Maria*, and her heart broke
accordingly. She wept, not just for Sister Cordelia and all the little black boys who had
about as much chance of "being like Mike" as she did of being like Mother Teresa, but
also for Mama, who didn't have to die so stupidly, for herself and Gregg and the failure of
their marriage, for her lost faith, that made her fear all the more for the world Jordan was
inheriting.

She shuddered with sobs, barely aware that Alex's arm clasped her shoulders tightly. "C'mon, c'mon," he whispered. "Wake up, woman, they're bringing in the coffin."

She struggled to compose herself. After all, she had a job to do.

He was either wrong, or had deliberately misled her. The monsignor, resplendent in his gold and white alb and miter, was following the solemn processional of the Book and cross down the Cathedral's center aisle. A ritual that had always moved her, despite its patriarchal implications. She found a Kleenex in her purse and dabbed her eyes.

"I'm OK," she mouthed to Alex, without looking at him.

Then came the pallbearers, hoisting the casket on their broad shoulders. They were all male, of course; mostly black; a couple wore the collar of the Catholic cleric. They gently lay Sister's coffin before the altar.

Even from the back of the Cathedral, Jessica gasped at her first true glimpse of the nun's waxen face. Gowned in a simple navy dress and plain crepe veil, Sister Cordelia seemed a hauntingly beautiful mannequin. The rich mahogany skin, high cheekbones, full, generous lips might as well have belonged to a pretty doll, stripped of the animating force of those wide, passionate dark eyes.

Jessica had chosen not to view her mother's body. Steve had, and he'd told her that it had helped: "I knew for sure Mom was really gone." Still, Jessica had never regretted her decision. Looking at the nun's lifeless body, she knew she'd done the right thing.

The priest, hands folded in prayer, stepped up to the microphone at the center of the altar. "The Lord be with you."

Automatically, Jessica, and Alex, and most of the people in the Cathedral, responded: "And also with you."

Sister Cordelia sat up.

Amid gasps and even a few random screams, Sister nonchalantly swung her legs around and lithely hopped down from her white-satin-lined casket. She fell to her knees and blessed herself before the altar, where even the priest gaped, dumbfounded.

Then Sister Cordelia faced the shocked congregation. "The Lord raised Lazarus from the dead," she spoke in a clear, no-nonsense contralto that those who knew her recognized as her own. "In His infinite mercy, He has seen fit to raise me." She turned again to face the cross. "Not my will, but Thine, be done!"

Tears streamed from those famous dark, round eyes.

And then wild, joyous shrieks burst forth in the Cathedral. Sister's longtime followers swarmed about her, laughing and hugging her and each other, even while the Secret Service jockeyed to shove them back. Somehow Sister managed to emerge from the throng, stepping back onto the altar. She addressed the ashen Archbishop quietly, and though the church fell silent, not even those in the front pews were able to tell what she was saying. He blessed her, then took her arm and led her away into the sacristy, out of sight of the world's incredulous eyes.

A handful of people -- Sister's followers, a few particularly aggressive reporters -- started to rush the altar, but the rector serving Mass along with the Archbishop raised a warning hand. "This is the House of God," he said sternly, though even he looked a bit surprised that his words were uniformly obeyed.

The Cathedral remained hushed, now the only sounds muffled sobs throughout the congregation. Father, plainly improvising, spoke again. "The Mass will proceed, in celebration of the miracle God, in His infinite love and mercy, has seen fit to bestow on us. Praise be to You, Lord Jesus!"

Now most of the media in attendance rushed toward the Cathedral's great double doors, to report first-hand what millions of television viewers had witnessed telegenically, some to camp behind the church, from where Sister Cordelia would sooner or later have to exit.

Jessica was shell-shocked, genuinely fearful she had lost her mind. The last few minutes had seemed to whiz by at a manic fast-forward rate, and yet to have stretched out for an eternity. She was ice-cold and her knees trembled.

She was on the verge of fainting, and Alex saw as much. "We gotta get you out of here," he said softly. He glanced over his shoulder at the bottle-neck of journalists pushing their way out the doors. "Damn."

"Alex," she said in a shaking voice little more than a whisper. "What the hell just happened?"

"Looks like we may have either just witnessed the hoax of the century, or an honest-to-God resurrection."

Chapter 3

Outside in Jackson Square, near-riot conditions prevailed. Spontaneous choruses of "We Shall Overcome" broke out from joyous believers. Smaller factions of skeptics were just as passionate, chanting "BULL SHIT! BULL SHIT! BULL SHIT!" as if razzing the visiting team at a college football game. Throughout the square reporters clutched head-sets and spoke into mikes, while minicam operators struggled not to be jostled by the mob or by suddenly ubiquitous police trying to impose order. The rain had stopped an hour before, but the sky was still swollen and the air damp and oppressive.

The talking heads and their frantic producers were flabbergasted at their various sites. Directors kept close watch on the Mass, on the chance Sister Cordelia would reappear. MSNBC had corralled a true believer and a skeptic, and the reporter was doing his best to promote an impromptu debate. CNN had already hooked up via satellite a well-known conspiracy theorist in Wyoming.

Jessica, still supported by Alex's arm, finally made her way out of the Cathedral. "I've got to get to the Hilton," she said, aghast at the madness out in the square.

"Lotsa luck," Alex rejoined. "It'll take you an hour to walk two blocks in this mess."

But CNN's Ann Magee, accompanied by a cameraman, was pushing over to where Jessica and Alex stood on the steps of the Cathedral. "Tell her to fuck off," Alex urged *sotto voce*. "You're in no condition to --"

"It's my job, remember?" she snapped. "Stop treating me like a goddamn damsel in distress!"

"OK, lady. You wanna pass out on international TV, it's no skin off my fucking back."

But, to her annoyance, he remained by her side as a breathless Ann Magee reached her. "Here's our own legal correspondent Jessica Anders," she panted into her mike. "Jessica, you were actually inside the church when this phenomenal event occurred. What was it like?"

Jessica leaned into the mike, and out of habit, looked into the camera. "Ann, it's almost impossible to describe the moment that Sister Cordelia apparently arose from the dead. I'm still having a hard time believing what just happened." Now she was playing "Jessica Anders, legal correspondent," and she felt her composure return.

"I notice you use the word 'apparently,'" Anne said. "Did you have any sense, Jessica, that might indicate a hoax?"

"I'm a lawyer -- I have to wait for the facts to come in before I can make that evaluation. Instinct and common sense tell me that there must be more than meets the eye to what we all just saw inside the Cathedral."

By this time they were all but shouting over the clamor in the square. Ann asked Jessica something about the appearance of the nun's "body" as the casket was borne in.

Jessica hadn't made out the entire question, but she answered as best as she could. "I don't have a great deal of experience with dead bodies, but yeah, she looked pretty much deceased to me."

"It's crazy down here -- back to you, Paul," Ann said, and the minicam lowered.

Jessica glanced around. Alex was gone. Good. She'd obviously convinced him she was pro enough to recover her equilibrium, no longer requiring his knight arrantry.

CNN had arranged for a police escort to transport her to their makeshift headquarters at the Hilton. There, she found the producers, directors, and anchors operating in crisis mode. It was going to be a long, long night.

While the makeup woman touched up her powder and eye-shadow, Jessica called Gregg on the cell phone. "Looks like I'm going to be hung up here for a while. I'm hoping to catch a red-eye, but more likely, I'll leave first thing tomorrow morning."

"Jesus Christ, Jessie. I'm still reeling. Who do you suppose was behind it? Has Rome resorted to smoke and mirrors to attract recruits?"

"I have no clue. Maybe it's somebody's idea of the perfect millennial practical joke. Look, we'll talk when I get back. Kiss Jordy for me, OK?"

Ten minutes later she was miked up and seated behind a long desk along with Paul Duncan and Father Joseph Finnerty, professor of theology at Catholic U. The satellite analysts were (once again) televangelist Reverend Ingraham, a spokeswoman for Atheists of America, and a former federal prosecutor now in private practice in L.A.

Currently, Paul Duncan was listening to Ann Magee's latest report from Jackson Square. "Paul, as you know, the Mass ended about five minutes ago. The crowd here in the square is still holding fast, waiting for some sign of Sister Cordelia."

"Tell me, Ann, can we expect the Archdiocese to be issuing any kind of statement in the immediate future?" Paul asked.

"We haven't heard anything, Paul."

"Thanks, Ann. We'll check back with you a little later." He then re-introduced Jessica, "now here with us in our New Orleans studio. Jessica, I've been wanting to ask you: as a lawyer, how would you go about trying to tease out what actually happened inside St. Louis Cathedral this afternoon?"

"Well, the first thing I'd want to see would be the coroner's report and go over that with a fine-tooth comb. Sister Cordelia was ostensibly killed by a single gunshot wound to the heart. Maybe it was a lesser injury, and the public was deliberately misinformed, for whatever reasons."

"I think the reasons are fairly obvious," blustered the spokeswoman for the atheist group. "The Roman Catholic Church has a history of underhanded tactics and spectacular dog-and-pony shows to cow people into believing in its fairy tales!"

"I can assure you," Father Finnerty said somberly, "the Church would never sanction such a spectacular hoax."

"Remember the Grand Inquisitor, padre?" baited the atheist. "'Miracle, mystery, and authority'?"

"Three cheers -- you know your Dostoevsky," Jessica said caustically. "I have to agree with Father Finnerty on this one. It seems implausible that the Catholic Church -- or any mainstream church, for that matter -- would dream up and then enact such an outrageous hoax."

"I think those anti-death penalty radicals are behind the whole thing!" Reverend Ingraham declared. "They've got motive, especially with more Americans than ever supporting capital punishment. They clearly felt they had to take extreme measures to turn the tide."

"Now, Reverend Ingraham, let's not get sidetracked back into that debate," Paul Duncan chided. "Let me pose a hypothetical to our two lawyers, whose job it is to be impartial and dispassionate. What if the coroner's report stands up to scrutiny? What if no doppelganger or long-lost twin comes forward and admits it was she, not Cordelia Davis, in that casket? What then?"

The split-screen on the monitor showed Jessica and the ex-federal prosecutor, a bearded, scholarly looking man, as they listened intently to Duncan's question.

The ex-prosecutor chuckled uneasily. "Animatronics?"

Jessica frowned. "I truly don't know, Paul. Not to sound like a hard-boiled cynic, but I'd have to think there was a rational explanation yet to be considered."

"Finally, a voice of reason!" gloated the atheist.

Duncan turned to Father Finnerty. "What about you, Father? I assume that you believe in miracles."

Even the theologian was rather circumspect. "Yes, I do, as I'm sure does Reverend Ingraham. I'm certain that even as we speak, the Vatican is dispatching a delegation to investigate this incident, just as the Church does when a man or woman is a candidate for sainthood. I will defer to the judgment of the Holy Father, and accept his decision."

"As if Rome doesn't have a huge self-interest in proclaiming this bogus resurrection a miracle," snorted the atheist.

"Actually," Jessica said, "there I'm going to disagree. We're not talking about Mother Teresa here. We're talking about a nun who was something of a thorn in the Church's side, who bucked authority on abortion and other issues of sexuality, including gay rights."

"That's exactly why I say it's the radical groups who staged this whole brouhaha!" insisted Reverend Ingraham.

On and on they opined into the night, suspending their punditry for "special reports" from investigative journalists in the field. The New Orleans Parish Coroner held a brief press conference, in which he declared that while certain forensic data had not yet been fully processed by his laboratory, his office stood by its preliminary findings. Cordelia Marie Davis, a black female aged forty-six, had died almost instantaneously from massive trauma to the left cardiac ventricle caused by a .44 caliber bullet fired at close-range. He absolutely refused to take any questions from reporters.

Just before seven, New Orleans time, the archdiocese released a statement: "Sister Cordelia is resting in seclusion within the Cathedral rectory. While the Archdiocese appreciates the understandable interest in Sister, we humbly request that the media and other interested parties allow all of those within the rectory a day or two of peace and privacy in which to contemplate prayerfully this momentous event." Of course, all the press release served to accomplish was an even greater swelling of the horde outside the iron gates of ordinarily serene St. Anthony's Garden, a pastoral plot of shade-trees and Catholic statuary and impeccable lawn that extended from the rectory to Royal Street. By eight, police in riot-gear showed up to clear the street, with only a handful of select reporters and cameramen allowed to maintain the vigil.

Not long thereafter, the Vice-President held his own brief press conference at New Orleans International Airport. Yes, he had spoken to the President, and they were in full accord that Americans, even while rejoicing at the possibility of a genuine miracle, needed to keep open minds until a full inquiry into the matter had been completed.

Though CNN's live coverage was round-the-clock, by ten Jessica was bleary and near-incoherent with fatigue. She caught a cab back to the Monteleone, where the doorman greeted her with a dazzling, beatific smile. "It's a great day, ain't it, Ma'am! A great day to be alive!"

She mumbled something pleasant and noncommittal.

As she passed the Carousel Bar, she noted wearily that tonight it was teeming with patrons, some arguing, some with voices and no doubt glasses raised in elation. Was Alex Trujillo among them, and if so, on which side would he be? She was too exhausted to care, for all that she now felt a twinge of guilt for the way she'd snapped at him this afternoon outside the Cathedral. She could only hope that he would understand someday that shock and confusion, not churlish ingratitude, lay behind her rudeness.

What a relief finally to walk into her room and shut the door on the world. She kicked off the cheap pumps she'd bought at Saks. Her feet were killing her; her toes were cramped and her heels blistered. From here on in, it was Bally's or nothing.

The message button on her phone glowed cherry-red. As much as she longed to ignore it -- easily two dozen acquaintances knew she was in New Orleans covering the funeral-that-wasn't -- she couldn't risk the thought that Gregg or Vicky had called to tell her something was wrong with Jordan. Though she was too tired to be hungry, she made herself order a salad, bowl of gumbo, and half-liter of chardonnay before retrieving her voice-mail.

"You have . . . eight messages!" the automated, impersonal voice informed her. She groaned.

Just as she suspected, the first five were from excited friends in D.C., eager to hear her first-hand account; the sixth was from her brother Steve in San Francisco, calling for the same reason. The seventh, surprisingly enough, was from an editor of a national magazine. Would she be willing to write an article for them? She jotted down the number on Monteleone stationary, vowing to get back to the magazine on Monday.

The last message was from Alex Trujillo. "Look, Jessica, I just wanted to say I hope you're doing OK." A pause. "I'm sure as hell not. Would you leave a message for me telling me how you are? I'm in 327."

She glanced at her watch. It was quarter to eleven, and he was a night-owl. It wasn't that she was avoiding him, really; she was just so tired, so bone-fucking-tired. Warily she punched in his room number.

"Yeah," he answered on the first ring, sounding much more tense and alert than he had on the voice-mail message.

"Hi, it's Jessica."

"You sound half-dead."

"I feel like it, too." Then the image of Sister Cordelia calmly sitting up in her casket flashed into her brain. "No -- let's not talk about anybody being half-dead. I'm just really, really tired."

"You ought to consider print journalism. At least you can stress out in the privacy of your own room with your laptop and fax machine and the libation of your choice."

"I don't think I'd trust myself to put my thoughts into writing at this point."

He chuckled grimly. "Go to bed, Jessica. If you feel like talking in a couple weeks, give me a call." He seemed concerned, but a little preoccupied; plainly he was still at work.

"Thanks, Alex -- for everything. Good night."

After she hung up, it occurred to her she didn't have his phone number in L.A. Oh well, she supposed she could always track him down at the *Times* if she wanted to. And who knew if she'd even want to? After this surreal Sister Cordelia fiasco blew over, wouldn't she be inclined to try to forget the entire episode? All of it: from the guy throwing up as he staggered out of the girlie joint, to her own foolish emotionality in church even before the pallbearers entered; the hours upon hours of nervous intellectual gymnastics on live TV, broadcast inter-nationally, as if any damn one of the pundits and experts and "legal analysts" had a fucking clue as to what, exactly, had happened inside the Cathedral today.

One thing was certain: she would never forget that moment, at once horrific and thrilling, when the waxen corpse of Sister Cordelia Marie Davis stirred to life. Sister's clear contralto echoed in her ears: "The Lord raised Lazarus from the dead."

Jessica was trembling violently, her heart banging in her chest. She fumbled with the minibar key, snatched out a miniature Stoly and a can of club soda. She ended up downing the vodka without benefit of soda.

But her panic refused to subside. Suddenly she remembered the cigarettes she'd bought that morning at Walgreen. So what if she was in a non-smoking room? Let them charge CNN twice the fee, or even toss her out into the street. She was going to smoke.

The soapdish from the bathroom made for a passable ashtray. When room-service arrived, she tossed the butt in the toilet.

Though she hadn't eaten all day, she could barely touch the food. She spooned up a couple of shrimp from the gumbo, but her appetite had abandoned her. Even the sight of food sickened her. She placed the carafe of wine on the bedstand, then removed the tray from the bed to the bureau.

A glass of wine and another cigarette failed to soothe her. The dark screen of the television set seemed to taunt her. "You sonofabitch!" she screamed, hurling the remote at the TV. It bounced off the console harmlessly.

Her outburst frightened her.

Frightened her enough to take up the phone and press "327."

"I'm really . . . scared. I don't want to be alone," she said, clutching the receiver.

"I'm just finishing up. I'll be there in ten minutes, fifteen, tops. Want me to bring anything?"

She laughed weakly. "Well, I'm in the process of drinking myself silly. My minibar is your minibar -- *quid pro quo* for last night."

"Sounds more like a borderline racist play on *mi casa, su casa*," he teased. She could hear his fingers clicking away on the keyboard of his laptop computer.

"Don't give me shit, OK?"

"OK," he said gently. "Give me ten minutes."

She finally got out of her Calvin Klein sheath and nylons, replacing them with leggings and a pullover. She tied her hair back in a loose ponytail. And she covered the mostly uneaten plates of food with their silver lids.

It was closer to twenty minutes later when Alex arrived, bearing a Walgreen's sack. He took out a six-pack of Dixie beer. "This stuff is really crap. But somehow, whenever I'm here, I can't resist."

He looked tired, too, his dark eyes slightly sunken, a vein in his brow visible and throbbing.

"Thanks for coming, Alex."

"Hey," he said, opening a beer. ""Ten, twenty years from now, when people ask each other just where they were when Sister Cordelia rolled away the fucking stone . . . "

He was as anguished as she.

Her heart was in her throat. "What -- what did you write?"

"My job was easier than yours. Just the facts, ma'am." He took a long swig of beer.

"But what are the facts? I mean, yeah, she climbed out of the coffin. She spoke. She disappeared into the sacristy." She passed a tremulous hand over her hair. "That tells us nothing."

His eyes narrowed. "You know what pisses me off? It's how fucking nervous everybody is over the possibility it might really be true. It's a hoax, it's a conspiracy, the Catholics are behind it, or the lefties. Trust me, by tomorrow some crackpot will be insisting it's a goddamn Communist plot! The tabs will be claiming Sister Cordelia is an alien!"

She was mildly taken aback by his vehemence. "What -- in your own heart -- do you believe?"

"Probably the same thing you do," he said, sinking into a chair across from where she perched, cross-legged, on the bed. "The attending physicians and coroner must have blown the call. It's happened before."

He looked profoundly sad.

"I keep wondering if she'd been embalmed. It was the one topic nobody seemed to want to touch on tonight," she said.

"AP is saying she was."

Jessica swallowed hard. "That's downright weird. If it's confirmed," she hastily amended.

"Jessica, none of this is the point. I'm pretty sure when the truth comes to light, there'll be a rational explanation to satisfy everyone. My question is, why the hell are the Powers-That-Be so fucking paranoid that people might believe -- however erroneously --

that a miracle took place? A miracle that might change some people's lives for the better?"

"Come on, Alex! Everybody's being cautious until the facts are in, and who can blame them?"

"'Everybody' spouting off on TV, that is," he retorted. "You were spirited away to CNN where a dozen so-called experts could pontificate from their ivory towers. I was talking to people on the streets, in the square, and to them it was a fucking miracle, and they fucking *believed*!"

She was starting to feel it had been a mistake to invite him up. She hadn't anticipated his anger. She thought of tonight's strident atheist, and her invocation of Dostoevsky.

Miracle, mystery, authority.

"People shouldn't be deliberately misled, even for their own good," she murmured.

"Fine! In that case, let's ban all religions, not to mention state lotteries and the Psychic Friends Network. And what about politicians, if we're talking false prophets?" He leaned over her, resting his fists on either side of her knees. His face was close enough for her to feel his breath. "What are they all so afraid of, Jessica?"

She was unnerved by his physical proximity, though there was nothing overtly sexual about his gesture. She squirmed away to replenish her wine. "I don't know what they're afraid of. Or maybe I do. A mass movement, even a messianic one."

"Exactly!"

A kind of wild elation fell over her, washing away the fear and confusion, as she grappled with his implications. "And what's wrong with having a messiah like Sister Cordelia?" she thought aloud excitedly. "Oh, my God, Alex, I've been so blind! You're right -- we've been asking all the wrong questions!"

Her thoughts were racing. Sister Cordelia, a living emblem of compassion, tolerance, non-violence, a force for good in a culture where bloodlust, bigotry, and blatant self-interest flourished. Sister Cordelia, offering a promise of eternal salvation in exchange for a renunciation of guns and violence and vengeance in the name of the Lord. Sister Cordelia, invested with a moral authority unprecedented since the time of Christ, only more so. For no one had caught the Resurrection on live TV.

Was it possible that Jordan really would grow up in a world better than his parents had? A world in which people treated each other with respect and kindness, emulating Sister Cordelia if only out of that incurably human trait of self-interest? Who but the most hardened sociopath could resist the promise of eternal life?

Whether or not it was a lie was strictly irrelevant.

Never in her life had she felt such a strong sense of clarity. "It could work," she breathed. She looked up at him and smiled tremulously. "It really could work."

He set down his beer on the dresser. "Come here," he coaxed.

She took a step forward, hesitated, but by then he had already swept her up in his arms. His kisses were smoky and hard. She would have melted into him, but he was too tall, and standing up, they didn't fit together right. She pulled him onto the bed and switched off the lamp, and then they were fine. Better than fine. She tore her clothes off, and unsnapped his Levis. She sucked on him like hungry baby at its mother's nipple.

Moaning, he undrew her hair from its ponytail. He pulled her up to kiss her, eased her onto her back to stroke her breasts, her vulva. When he entered her, she cried out, afraid she was going to come right away. But she didn't; they stole time from time, rocking together in shared madness until they were spent, and the digital clock on the nightstand showed two-twenty-two a.m.

Her hair spilled across his heaving chest. She felt at peace. Not guilty, as she imagined she would. All her life she'd struggled to be free of Catholic guilt. Maybe she'd achieved liberty at last.

Thanks, ironically enough, to Sister Cordelia.

At length he spoke. "You're leaving tomorrow?" he said, caressing her hair.

"I have to. My baby."

He kissed her face tenderly. "I don't want this to end here, Jessica. For lots of reasons."

Her finger traced his jawline. "Maybe we can have lots of lurid e-mail sex."

His smile was fleeting. "Look, there's something I'd better tell you."

Catholic guilt revived with a psychic thunderclap. *Oh my God, he's HIV-positive!* Married twelve years, she'd never even thought to insist he wear a condom. "What?" she said, shooting up, her heart racing.

"I'm married."

She'd almost have preferred he'd declared he had AIDS. "You *bastard*!" she spat, leaping out of bed. "You *creep*!" Every nasty epithet she'd had too much dignity to hurl at Gregg she flung his way. "You lying, cheating mother-fucker!"

"Hear me out, OK?"

"The hell I will! Trust me, muchacho, I've heard it all before -- you and your wife have 'grown apart'!" she mocked. "She doesn't understand you! You have different goals!" She was beside herself. "Look, I'm going into the bathroom to get dressed. When I come out, I expect you to be the hell out of here!"

In the bathroom -- whose door she pointedly locked -- she took a scalding hot shower as penance. She was too angry even to think.

She took her time brushing her teeth, blow-drying her hair.

Swathed in the thick white terry-cloth robe provided by the hotel, she emerged and flipped on an overhead light, as if to check the room for intruders.

He was gone, all right. But the rumpled blanket and sheets of the quaint four-poster bed were tangible reminders of her folly and his duplicity.

She couldn't stand another minute in this room, in this sinister city of deluded hopes and grotesquely misguided faith. She dragged out her garment bag and carry-on.

Surely if she caught a cab to the airport, even at this hour, some plane or another with a vacant seat would be Washington-bound.

Just after four a.m. Eastern, the panel discussions still ongoing on CNN, MSNBC, and ABC's extended version of "Nightline," were interrupted by respective network logos proclaiming in somber block letters "BREAKING NEWS." An unnamed source from the Baton Rouge Hall of Records had told the Associated Press that Cordelia Davis in fact had a twin,
Hattie, now living in West Virginia.

Moderators and panelists alike did little to contain their collective air of "I told you so." Several commentators, not the least of whom was Caroline Bruckner, gloatingly lay blame for the hoax upon the anti-death-penalty movement.

When an hour later, another bulletin broke in with a live feed from West Virginia, in which Hattie Davis, a corpulent white mother of four, told a CBS reporter she'd never even heard of Sister Cordelia "till that nonsense outside the gas chamber," anchors and pundits alike gulped and fell on their swords. It took only minutes to confirm the fact that while Cordelia and Hattie Davis had indeed both been born in Baton Rouge on January 6, 1953, they were no more twin sisters than Janet Reno and Ivana Trump.

Chapter 4

"Sometimes I dream . . . that he is me," she found herself singing absently to
Jordan. On the floor with him, working his pudgy little arms in playful circles as he
struggled to keep his balance, she was finally home. CNN had wanted her for its evening
"Impact" broadcast, but she'd pleaded the flu. Let them think that she, like Ken Gianelli,
had whooped it up too much in the Big Easy.

What did she care, as long as she was home with Jordy, and they were both
healthy and safe?

And she'd made a concerted effort not to turn on the TV, nor to check her faxes,
since setting foot in the townhouse a little after seven that morning. She'd dragged the
Sunday *Post* in from the doorstep, but had yet to strip it of its protective plastic.

In the last forty-eight hours, she'd just discovered something laughably banal.

There was no such thing as news. There was only spin.

Of course, that had been the conventional wisdom about politics since Watergate.
And really smart, really honest people knew in their hearts that the O.J. prosecutors had
not met the burden of "guilty beyond a reasonable doubt," even while the Geraldos and
Charles Grodins of the world flogged Middle America into a frenzy over imaginary flaws
in the greatest justice system in modern civilization. And then there was Kenneth Starr's
witch-hunt, worthy of Torquemada, designed to ferret out whether or not the President
had enjoyed a few inconsequential blow-jobs --

She forced herself to stop thinking. Jordan was attempting another bold, clumsy toddle. Laughing, she caught him just before his forehead collided with the soft nap of the Persian rug. She hugged him tightly, even while the inane, bouncy refrain jingled in her mind:

Like Mike . . . I wanna be like Mike.

The next morning she was back in the studio, providing legal commentary for CNN. Sister Cordelia had yet to appear from the rectory behind St. Louis Cathedral; no news had broken since the now-debunked report of a twin living in West Virginia; and both Washington and the Vatican were remaining evasive, if not outright silent. However, across the country and in parts of France, southern Italy, and Central America, ecstatic mobs were shaping into organized movements, bound by faith in Sister's principles. Non-violence, tolerance, equity between rich and poor.

New leaders were emerging: in California, in Boston, in Madison, Wisconsin; in Managua, La Paz, and San Salvador; in Calcutta, Beirut, and Belfast. They were mostly Catholic missionaries and human rights activists, united in a professed belief that Cordelia Davis had in fact risen from the dead, and that her resurrection was a mandate to the world to follow her message of peace, tolerance, and compassion for the poor and oppressed.

Not a single world leader, or government, or official spokesman, had issued a statement acknowledging -- or even suggesting -- that the resurrection might be authentic. All seemed to be following the lead of the United States, and the Vatican, for that matter: they would defer judgment until the "facts came out."

Such was the tenor of the morning panel in which Jessica participated.

"*I* say," thundered a right-wing mouthpiece for the Christian Family Values Institute, "that this Sister should willingly subject herself to a lie-detector test!"

Bev Wallace, a political conservative, was nonetheless nobody's fool. "You must be joking, Merle. Habitual liars and sociopaths *ace* polygraphs every day."

"What about O.J.?" grilled Laurie Dikstra, a "post-feminist" who had been booted out of NOW for her insistence that sexual harassment was a sour-grapes myth created by homely girls left dateless on Valentine's Day. "O.J. was guilty as all hell, and guess what, he flunked the polygraph!"

"Which proves," Bev smirked, "that polygraphs are unreliable. Defendants who know they're guilty fail them all the time. So do people who are innocent, but really nervous. Practiced liars sail right through them."

"Like Mark Fuhrman," Jessica contested hoarsely. She was having a hell of a time following the discussion.

Bev and Laurie and Richard Breem, a prosecutor from upstate New York, attacked her vociferously, but the moderator, Owen Shawn, cut them all off. "Hey, guys, isn't this old news?" he pretended to scold. "The question is, what should we in the media do when -- and if -- Sister Cordelia steps out to deliver her take on the Sermon on the Mount?"

Bev Wallace was, as always, unruffled. "Well, Owen, I think we need to hear what she has to say. We may be able to infer her agenda from the message she tries to get across."

Owen Shawn scowled and grimaced, as was his wont. "Jessica?"

She drew in a sharp breath. *Don't shoot the messenger*, she reminded herself. "Why are we all out to debunk her? Everything she preached and espoused in her . . . natural life was decent. I find this whole diatribe absurd -- why can't we accept this whole thing at face-value, and go on from there?"

On the video monitor in the lonely studio, she watched the moderator and other panelists regard her as if she were insane.

Owen Shawn mugged sympathetically. "It's getting to you, huh, Jessica?"

Her dignity ignited, she balked. "I'm no lunatic, Owen! You know it, and so do the people who watch this network! I'm just saying that we ought to keep our minds open, and suspend this obsession we have that there's some kind of ridiculous conspiracy -- "

Worldwide, the CNN signal fizzled, swiftly replaced by a static multicolor test pattern and a floating apology streaming in from left to right at the bottom of the screen: *"We are experiencing technical difficulties. Please stand by."*

The technical director in D.C. told Jessica she might as well go home. "We've got a mess on our hands," he apologized. "Somebody must have thrown the wrong switch somewhere."

She wasn't about to argue with him.

She caught a cab back to Georgetown, looking forward to a leisurely afternoon of reviewing her teaching notes and playing with Jordan.

She was stunned to find a dozen phone messages and half that many faxes awaiting her.

It was only after scanning the first three faxes that she grasped the popular perception that CNN had deliberately cut her off mid-sentence.

Suspiciously she turned on the TV, found CNN on the dial. Sure enough, Owen Shawn continued to moderate a vociferous panel of Bev Wallace, Richard Breem, Laurie Dikstra, and, evidently replacing Jessica herself, some retired appellate judge in Delaware.

She flicked to MSNBC. One of their anchors, blandly good-looking Lyle Thompson, was conducting a lively discussion among Caroline Bruckner, Father Finnerty, CNN's Ann Magee, and conservative lawyer Jack Cohn. Thompson was taking viewer calls, and a blurb at the bottom of the screen identified the speaker as Mercy in Andover, Massachusetts.

"Why are we giving this story so much attention?" Mercy cried. "The media is just playing into the hands of the people who staged the so-called resurrection in the first place!"

Caroline Bruckner twittered. "I agree with our caller, Lyle. This isn't about a miracle, it's about a specific political agenda!"

Father Finnerty spoke up. "Well, we don't exactly have the facts, yet. Let's see what happens when, and if, Sister Cordelia comes forth to face those who would question her."

"Oh, come on," Lyle Thompson said, rolling his eyes. "This has got to be seen as a case where there's no viable gray area. Either she's back from the dead, or she isn't." He tapped his ear-phone. "You still there, Mercy?"

"I am," she affirmed. "Has anyone considered the possibility of a mask? Look at how realistic the prosthetics in movies have gotten!"

Caroline Bruckner giggled contemptuously. "We don't even need to go that far. New Orleans politics is notoriously corrupt. Grease the right palms and lo and behold, you have a modern day Lazarus, an icon even the radical feminists can love. Black, pro-choice, pro-homosexual. How can anybody believe there isn't a left-wing agenda behind this? It's too perfect!"

"Bitch," Jessica cursed the screen. She channel-surfed nervously over the next half-hour, finding more pundits and panels, all effectively arguing over the same minutiae.

And not a single moderator, or reporter, or "special correspondent" seemed willing to grant, even hypothetically, as had Paul Duncan the night of the abortive funeral, the possibility that Sister Cordelia's "resurrection" had been anything but a hoax.

Impulsively she switched to the Christian Broadcasting Network.

A pious Reverend Norbert Patterson was gravely exhorting his brethren to beware of false prophets, citing the Bible, and urging the faithful to hold the course. Stop the baby-killing, stop the erosion of family values, support an America that was as strong morally as it was militarily.

"Brothers and sisters," he said, eyeballing the camera, "a lot of us have been lulled into complacency by the fall of the evil Communist empire. We've forgotten, perhaps, about the international bankers, and the secular humanists in our own midst, all of them dedicated to the establishment of the New World Order. Who more likely to have masterminded a phony resurrection -- "

Appalled, she turned the TV off. She'd never watched even a snippet of the so-called Christian network before tonight. Her intellectual commitment to the First Amendment fought with her visceral revulsion at the airing of such incendiary lies and propaganda. Damn the Founding Fathers! They had no more anticipated Reverend Norbert Patterson than they had Larry Flynt.

And the gleeful, ironic chorus from an old R.E.M song jangled through her mind: "*It's the end of the world as we know it . . .* "

Birthdaypartycheesecakejellybeanboom, you symbioticpatriotic --

The phone rang, but she ignored it. On the fourth jingle the machine picked up: her own emotionless voice, the one she used on TV, reciting the number reached and inviting the caller to leave a message.

The beep was long, since she had yet to play back the outstanding messages.

Then --

"Jessica, it's me, Alex. I know you're pissed, and I don't blame you. One of these years, maybe I can explain. But I just heard you got cut off on live TV." He sounded upset. "Baby, this is huge. I'm still in New Orleans at the Monteleone. Call me. Even if you hate my fucking guts, call me."

She glowered at the answering machine. "In your dreams, buddy," she muttered.

This whole Sister Cordelia madness was getting out of hand. Though Jessica was unnerved by the perhaps too tidy unanimity among media pundits, she no more believed that CNN had deliberately cut her off than she did that "the New World Order" had staged a resurrection.

She fished through her still-unpacked carry-on bag, found the number of the *Newsweek* editor who had contacted her in New Orleans. She dialed the New York number.

He told her that yes, they would love for her to write an essay on her first-hand observations of the bizarre event in St. Louis Cathedral. "What's your angle?"

"I'm still sorting that out."

"That could be an angle in and of itself. Now, here's the bad news, Jessica. We've got a short deadline. Is there any way you could fax us the piece by Friday?"

She'd never had a problem working under pressure, and assured him as much.

"Great. Now, of course, you know that should the course of the story change substantially -- or a World War break out in the Middle East -- we're under no obligation to run your essay or to compensate you."

"No problem. In that case, I'll pitch it to the *Enquirer*."

"Looking forward to reading the piece," he chuckled.

She had lunch with Jordan and Vicky, then sat down at her computer to begin drafting her article.

Basically, she wanted to elaborate on the point she'd tried to make this morning on CNN before a technical glitch cut her off mid-sentence. An idea that she grudgingly, privately credited Alex with inspiring. Her premise was simple: what if time passed, and no one were able to conclusively prove or disprove Cordelia Davis's resurrection? Weren't the American people above succumbing to yet another round of endless, paranoid conspiracy theories, especially when nothing but good could come of at least pretending to accept the reality of Cordelia Davis's miracle?

"OK, here we go," she muttered, writing a page and a half in about a minute. Out of habit she pulled down the "File" menu and clicked "Save." Over the years she'd simply heard too many horror stories about power surges and viruses suddenly effacing works-in-progress of infinite promise.

The so-called "dialog box" dropped down, requesting a name.

She frowned. For a few moments, absolutely nothing came to her.

She sighed, determined not to get stuck over such a minute point.

Impatiently, she typed in the word "FAITH."

Just after seven a.m. the next morning, the first real news since the "resurrection" broke. ABC scooped the other networks by at least half an hour, interrupting "Good Morning America" to report that Sister Cordelia had attended a dawn mass at St. Louis Cathedral. She had not spoken to the congregation, but had, according to eyewitnesses, participated fully in the rite, even taking Communion. There had been no cameras in the church, as the archdiocese had insisted on a strict ban since Saturday's circus. But a few canny reporters had been in attendance -- just in case -- and their intuition was richly rewarded.

"I saw her clearly," announced an excited ABC correspondent. "She was wearing a simple gray dress and a short veil. She looked -- well, completely normal, so far as I could tell!"

But within minutes, another eyewitness was questioning the ABC correspondent's report. "The woman I saw, I have to admit, bore only a passing resemblance to the pictures I've seen of Cordelia Davis," the man, identified simply as "a parishioner," told "Good Morning America." "I don't know, it was almost as if someone had tried to make up some little black lady to look like the Sister."

When asked to elaborate, the man fumbled. "It's hard to put into words. She just looked sort of . . . fake."

Jessica, as usual running late on a teaching morning, didn't learn of the report until she got to class. Knowing her students would be curious about her attendance of the "funeral," she began with what she hoped would be a preemptive strike. "I trust everybody here is serious enough about final exams and the Bar not to want to squander any of our precious minutes discussing matters tangential to substantive case issues," she said stiffly. "Now -- "

Bobby Carroll raised his hand.

She nodded to him.

"Just one question, Professor Anders, and then I swear I'll let it go."

She drew in a sharp breath. "OK."

"What do we make of the fact that no sooner does ABC report that Sister Cordelia attends Mass this morning, a whole battalion of naysayers crops up to say the woman looked nothing like her?"

Jessica concealed her startlement. "The networks are clearly bending over backwards -- and then some -- to appear balanced."

Another student, Jyotsna Sharma, spoke up. "I think there are a few serious First Amendment issues revolving around this case. I haven't found the news coverage to be balanced at all," she said in her measured, Indian-accented voice. "And Professor, do you believe there's any chance CNN 'conveniently' experienced technical problems the moment you started to make that very point?"

Jessica took a sip from her coffee mug. "No. I agree, there's been a rather startling -- how do I put it? -- *narrowness* in the range of discussion. But, come on, you guys! I refuse to engage in this whole conspiracy-theory debate. It's irrational and yes, it's paranoid. I don't even want to know what's being said on the Internet." Flustered, she rifled through her lecture notes.

"Can I make one last point?" Bobby Carroll requested.

"Go ahead. Underscore, 'last.'"

"Why won't the media present us with the facts, and then let us draw our own inferences?" Bobby posed. "They spin, and they spin, and then they spin some more, telling us how 'smart people' think, and since nobody wants to be thought dumb, we fall into line. But like you said, Professor Anders, the range of responses we can choose from is limited. They don't give us a 'none-of-the-above' option."

"Well, then," she replied briskly, "maybe this whole matter of Sister Cordelia will prompt a write-in movement for that option."

She, for one, certainly hoped so.

By two, she was back home, eager to resume work on her essay for *Newsweek*. Her students' skepticism impressed her as the inevitable consequence of the mindless, one-sided spin she was eager to indict.

But she also wanted to catch up with the latest on Sister's attendance at Mass that morning. In the study behind her computer, with Jordan rummaging around in his playpen two feet away, she clicked on CNN.

The network was running "Moneyline," and two thin-lipped economists were dryly discussing the Dow's moderate increase in trading.

She supposed CNN's resumption of regular programming might be a good sign.

She flipped to the more dependably frivolous MSNBC. Sure enough, the bland Lyle Thompson, in his distracting print tie and dopey cowlick, was bantering with a caller identified simply as "MICHIGAN."

"What I want to know," blustered Michigan, "is why this nun can't just be arrested? Isn't that the only way to get to the bottom of this nonsense?"

"Arrested for what?" bawled back some lawyer in San Diego. "Impersonating a corpse?"

Thompson snickered and made a crack about taking a broad interpretation of the writ of *habeas corpus*.

To Jessica's dismay, another petty officer in the Bimbo Brigade -- this one named Suzanne Sheridan -- appeared on the screen via a Manhattan remote. "I don't think we should belittle the caller's concern," she squeaked, beaming an incongruous girly grin. "People have legitimate questions about this nun that deserve to be answered. I mean, let's be real. She's wielding a lot of power by virtue of not explaining herself. People are probably donating money to the various causes she's espoused. I think there's a case to be made for fraud."

Cut to Lyle Thompson, shrugging. "What do you have to say about that, Martin Dale?"

Jessica did a double-take at the name. Martin Dale was a notorious screwball, a lawyer disbarred several years before for falsifying legal documents and a pattern of flagrantly frivolous suits. In the last year, Dale had resurfaced as a staple of right-wing talk radio, a born-again hate-monger who generally busied himself denouncing "big government" and trying to incite taxpayer revolt. "I don't think we should be sidetracked by the legal issues raised -- ha, ha, along with Sister Cordelia," Dale snickered in his thin, whiny voice.

"Bad joke," Lyle Thompson pretended to chide.

"But I'm not joking, Lyle," Dale grinned. "Maybe this nun did rise from the dead. That's not to say it was Jesus Christ who raised her. But only in a secular humanist society such as ours would we be rallying our forces like this, attempting to disprove the possibility of a message from either up there, or, as I happen to think, way down below."

Her blood ran cold. She saw exactly what they were doing.

They were trivializing the very notion of Sister Cordelia's legitimacy by designating a bona fide crackpot as her more-or-less defender.

Warily she left her desk, and pressed the "playback" button" on her answering machine, a task she'd been patently avoiding since yesterday's abortive turn on CNN.

There were easily a dozen messages. Again, friends and colleagues anxious to learn whether or not she'd been cut off; Steve, nagging her to call or at least e-mail him one of these years; Alex Trujillo, sounding urgent: "*Baby, this is huge. I'm still in New Orleans, at the Monteleone. Call me. Even if you hate my fucking guts, call me.*"

No message from CNN, scrambling to schedule her next appearance on one of their panels. Under ordinary circumstances, days might pass between invitations to contribute to "Burden of Proof" or "Larry King Live" or any other "legal issues" show.

But these weren't ordinary circumstances. She was their resident death penalty wonk; she'd been on the Sister Cordelia story from the beginning, and had been an eyewitness to the ostensible miracle in St. Louis Cathedral.

Martin Dale was rambling over the airwaves, but she had been politely silenced.

Or had she?

"Jordy, I'm going out of my mind," she declared, hoisting her son out of his playpen and embracing him tightly. How warm and soft he was; he smelled like talcum powder and baby. She loved him more than she thought possible; she felt her love for him in her fingertips that stroked his downy hair, in her grasp that supported his lumpy diapered bottom.

Jordy, help me to do what's right for both of us.

She rocked him in her arms for ten minutes, maybe fifteen.

She lay him down to sleep. Her heart swelled at the sight of his soft, placid little face, his contented frog-like posture, arms and legs splayed, atop the blankets in his playpen. He sucked drowsily on a pale yellow pacifier.

What if I do nothing, she argued with herself, pacing in the study. I'm not at leisure to play Joan of Arc; I'm thirty-six years old, I have a little baby to think about. An horrific thought crept into her consciousness. What if she took a stand on Sister Cordelia that would leave her open to charges of lunacy, the kind of lunacy she and so many members of the Bar quite rightly attributed to Martin Dale? Would Gregg sue for full custody of Jordan? And could she blame him for doing so, or blame the judge for deeming him the stabler parent?

She steadied her racing thoughts. There was no reason to believe that CNN was blackballing her; no doubt they'd call her tomorrow, or the next day. And even if CNN washed its hands of her, she still had her teaching, and her appellate work. Sooner or later, this Sister Cordelia story would dissipate. Likely the rumors and conspiracy theories would linger, as they had with O.J. and Diana and Flight 800, but they would be marginalized, shoved aside by newer, flashier, sexier *causes celebres*.

Yet as she lay down to sleep that night, struggling mightily to fight back images and remembered feelings that had everything to do with Alex and nothing with Sister Cordelia, her mind's eye conjured in the darkness of her bedroom the picture of a diminutive black woman prostrate against white satin, the woman rising slowly, swinging her legs over the side of the casket. Standing. Speaking.

The Lord raised Lazarus from the dead. In his infinite mercy, he has seen fit to raise me.

She saw again the confusion and anguish in the nun's expression.

Not my will, but Thine, be done.

Chapter 5

Ours is an age of skepticism.

Perhaps that's a good thing. We do not accept politicians' promises on face-
value. Very few of us grant credence to conspiracy theories that blame the United States
government for the Oklahoma City bombing. We are more charmed than convinced by
suggestions of a UFO crash-landing in Roswell.

Bitter experience has taught us, in fact, that blind credulity can be a dangerous
thing. We trusted our Chief Executive not to lie to us, then there was Watergate, Iran-
Contra, Monica Lewinsky. We trusted our police to protect and serve all of us, then there
was Rodney King, Albert Louima, and countless other less-publicized racially-motivated
brutalities. We trusted the integrity of the O.J. prosecutors, then there was Fuhrman.

We trusted the mainstream media to provide fair and balanced reporting, and
then there was Richard Jewell.

And now we have Sister Cordelia.

As one who witnessed first-hand the stunning incident inside St. Louis Cathedral
last Saturday, I am reminded of that adage, the one that goes, "Who do you believe, me
or your own lying eyes?" I know what I saw, and what everyone inside the cathedral
saw: a woman who appeared for all intents and purposes to be dead arise from her
casket and address the congregation. I am haunted by her image, by her words.

And, to be frank, I do not know what to believe.

None of us does.

As of today, no credible evidence has emerged to support either a hoax or a
genuine resurrection. We must be impartial in the absence of proof one way or another.
We must not rush to debunk Sister Cordelia and all she represents just because our
ingrained skepticism and the rationalist paradigm which has passed for "common sense"
since the Enlightenment urges us to disbelieve our own lying eyes.

In the absence of definitive proof to the contrary, we must entertain the possibility that what we collectively witnessed defies any rational explanation. Call it a miracle, or a paranormal event; quote Hamlet and remind all the learned experts and professional cynics hashing this out over hours and hours of TV talk that there are more things in heaven and earth that are dreamed of in your philosophy.

"O day and night, but this is wondrous strange!" Horatio exclaims at the antics of the ghost beneath the stage.

"And therefore as a stranger give it welcome," Hamlet rejoins.

What will we hardened skeptics do should it turn out that we have to welcome Sister Cordelia?

Or does our collective scorn at the very possibility already telegraph our answer?

Jessica was satisfied, more or less, with her essay. She tinkered with it an hour longer, adding and subtracting examples, but left the actual discussion of Sister Cordelia as it was. She half-expected *Newsweek* to edit out her more incendiary references to Rodney King and Mark Fuhrman; she herself had deleted an earlier draft's citation of wide-spread disbelief in the Warren Commission's report because it conceivably fell into both the "healthy skepticism" and "wacko conspiracy" camps.

Newsweek had requested the piece by Friday; she faxed it to New York Wednesday afternoon.

Relieved to have the essay out of her hair, she called her friend Grace Kerr, a partner in a Los Angeles-based firm's Washington office. "Want to grab a bite to eat tonight? I've been glued to the computer for most of the last forty-eight hours, and I've got a raging case of cabin fever."

They agreed to meet at eight at a little neighborhood Italian place in Georgetown within walking distance of Jessica's townhouse.

Grace was already seated at a table with a glass of Chianti before her when Jessica arrived. A tall, striking woman with a chic haircut and bright hazel eyes, she was an old friend from law school and Legal Aid. She had transferred from her firm's L.A. office four years before, when her literature professor husband accepted a tenured job at George Washington University. It was quite a step up from Cal State Long Beach and a four-four teaching load. Jessica knew Grace hated to leave California, but she'd been selfishly glad to have her in D.C.

"Chianti -- that looks good," Jessica said, removing her coat and sitting down. "How's tricks, kiddo? Mark and the girls doing OK?" Grace had two daughters, ages six and three.

"They're great. I'm the one who's going nuts. Today was a nightmare -- we had this important filing to do and our network crashed, so we couldn't pull up the documents." Grace made a comical "at my wit's end" face. "I'm so glad you called. How's Jordy?"

"Super, thanks for asking." Jessica caught the waiter's eye, pointed to Grace's glass then back to herself. In moments he was placing another Chianti on their table. "You ladies like a bottle?"

"Jessie, the man's a genius," Grace said, smiling.

"Well, you're drinking most of it then," Jessica replied. "I have to teach in the morning?"

"What are your classes this semester?"

"Con Law and Appellate Practice. Bring back happy memories of Boalt?"

"Oh, God, that prof we had for Con Law. What was his name, Weimeraner?"

"Weiner the weenie."

They both chuckled.

Grace glanced at her menu. "So do you want to talk about it or not?" she asked.

Jessica shrugged. "Why wouldn't I?"

"I don't know. I was afraid that maybe you were all talked-out," Grace said gently.

Jessica chewed her lower lip for a moment. "You know what? Maybe I am kind of OD'd on it." She leaned forward, lowering her voice. "Let me tell you instead what didn't make international headlines last weekend. I met a terrific guy who turned out to be a first-class asshole."

Grace's eyes sparkled in interest. "You're kidding. Details, details."

"I met him the night before the funeral, or whatever it was. He's a reporter for the L.A. *Times*. Smart. Latino. Drop-dead gorgeous."

It felt refreshingly normal to be sharing stupid girl-talk, as if her encounter with Alex had been the only momentous event of the last weekend.

"Drop-dead gorgeous -- that's an asshole, by definition," Grace said.

"I saw him again the next night. I'd been on the air forever, and I was tired and freaked out. I think I had a panic attack. I needed somebody."

"That's perfectly understandable, under the circum-stances. Why are you beating yourself up about it? Shit, Jessie, after what you went through with Gregg not too long ago, I think you're more than entitled to a meaningless romp in the hay with a hunk."

Jessica shook her head. "It wasn't until -- after -- that he told me he's married. Can you imagine how I felt, Grace?
It was like a cruel practical joke . . . after Gregg dumping me for little miss Coffee-Tea-or-Me!" Angry tears sprang to her eyes.

The waiter marched back to their table. "Would you care to start with an appetizer or antipasto, ladies?" he asked brightly.

"Not yet," Grace waved him away. She turned back to Jessica. "The deception was his, Jessie, not yours. You can't expect yourself to have been a mind-reader."

"It doesn't matter. I'm still in the position of that bimbo Gregg dumped me for. The sonofabitch even had the nerve to call me Monday. He left this message begging me to call him back."

"Well, did you?"

Jessica scowled. "Are you out of your mind?"

Grace reached across the table to pat Jessica's hand. "Jessica, I'm not quite sure how to put this without offending you. Promise you'll give me a swift kick if I cross over the line."

"When have I ever been able to shut you up?" she jested weakly. "Go ahead."

Grace looked her directly in the eyes. "Infidelity sucks. I know I'd be devastated if I ever found out Mark was screwing around. But marriages can be . . . complicated. Maybe you should at least hear the guy out."

"Yeah, I get it. He'll tell me that his poor wife's in a coma, or a mental institution, or even locked up in the fucking attic like in *Jane Eyre*. Of course, he's too noble and loyal to divorce her!" She rolled her eyes in contempt. "That's soap opera, and you damn well know it."

"OK, OK, I'll back off," Grace said with a groan. "You Catholics are so hung up about sex."

"This isn't a Catholic thing," she snapped. "It's a feminist thing, and yes, a personal thing." She tore open her menu.

"What harm would there be in hearing him try to explain himself?" Grace persisted anyway. "Let's face it, he didn't have to tell you he was married at all. And if he's calling you, it's obvious he didn't make the announcement to scare you off."

"Why do I get the distinct impression you don't think I'm getting laid enough?" Jessica said crossly, trusting her bluntness would counter Grace's allegation of Catholic guilt.

"Just tell me how he said it. Was it literally the first thing he declared after you guys did the big nasty?"

"Grace, he's an asshole, not a boor." She frowned, trying to recall. "I don't remember his exact words. Something to the effect of, 'I don't want this to end here, but there's something you ought to know first.'"

"See?" Grace said triumphantly.

"Give me a break. You know goddamn well what was about to follow. The old 'my wife doesn't understand me' song and dance."

"Well, maybe his wife *doesn't* understand him."

"Grace!"

Grace laughed. "Just don't let it get back to NOW I said that. I'll be booted out on my ass like that Dikstra bitch."

Jessica lay down her menu and forged a brittle smile. "Well, I've come to a decision."

"What? *Linguine alla vongole?*"

Jessica was disappointed. "How did you know?"

"Because, Jessie, despite the brittle, no-nonsense legal eagle you play on TV, anyone who knows you well knows you wear your neuroses on your sleeve."

Jessica bristled. "Shut up, and let's order."

It was past ten by the time they finished dinner and cappuccinos. Grace, who lived in Bethesda, Maryland, had her BMW, and she insisted on giving Jessica a ride home. A light snow was falling, and Grace claimed she saw no reason for Jessica to catch pneumonia on the four-block jaunt.

Jessica hugged her before climbing out of the car. "You're the best."

"Duh," Grace replied. "I dare you to call him back, Jess. Consider the gauntlet thrown."

"Go to hell."

During dinner, they'd actually chatted about matters other than Alex; Grace, bless her soul, had never pressed her about Sister Cordelia or what they did or did not believe about her. They talked about work and their various frustrations; Grace was particularly irked by a fellow partner in the firm who treated female colleagues like high-ranking personal assistants, even asking her, his co-counsel on a big wrongful-termination case, to call his wife when the jury came in with a huge verdict in their favor. For her part, Jessica, without delving too deeply into the Sister Cordelia matter, expressed doubts about the nature of her work as a TV pundit. "It's not journalism and it's not law. It's this awful hybrid that borrows the worst possible traits from both fields." And they talked about their kids and what remarkable talents they were exhibiting: Grace boasted that three-year-old Caitlin already knew half her ABCs, while Jessica countered that Jordan would surely be taking his first step any day now.

In short, it was one of the best evenings she'd enjoyed since Gregg dropped the bombshell.

She checked on Jordan, pleased to find him sleeping soundly in his crib. She then retreated to the study to review her notes for tomorrow's classes.

Switching on the light, the first thing she noticed was a fresh fax.

She snatched it up and scanned it.

It was from *Newsweek*.

"Regret to inform you your submission is not acceptable in its present form. The editorial board finds the structure unfocused, and all the Shakespeare at the end too esoteric. Perhaps understandably, you were too close to the event in question. Newsweek *wishes you the best, and we welcome any future submissions on other relevant legal issues."*

Jessica was outraged.

It wasn't that her writerly ego was wounded. This was no blind submission to the magazine's "My Turn" column; *Newsweek* had solicited her, not the other way around, clearly aware of her reputation as a legal scholar and television analyst. In Monday's conversation, the editor had said nothing to her about content, virtually promising publication just so long as no new information emerged between now and the magazine's deadline to pre-empt the premises or importance of her article.

But then perhaps, during the past two hours, news had emerged to discredit Sister Cordelia. Jessica surprised herself by hoping vehemently that it wasn't so. But determined to give the magazine the benefit of the doubt, she switched on the TV and found "Headline News."

They were reporting signs of unrest in Croatia.

MSNBC was rerunning a "Time and Again" on the life and times of Mother Teresa.

Exasperated, Jessica logged onto America Online. She activated a Yahoo search for "Sister Cordelia," which, of course, yielded thousands of documents. She clicked on the most recent, a Reuters entry titled "Sister Cordelia Returns to Convent."

She skimmed the story. As of five o'clock, central time, the Archdiocese of New Orleans had issued a statement claiming that Sister Cordelia had been taken, at her own request, to the Metairie convent where she had lived for the past twelve years. This had yet to be confirmed by either the Mother Superior or reporters camped outside the Convent of the Blessed Virgin. A spokesman for the Archdiocese refused to speculate on when, or if, Sister Cordelia would be making any public statements.

Jessica double-checked a slightly earlier AP report, found the information essentially the same.

In short, nothing had changed. The world was still suspended in radical uncertainty.

And now, the media seemed suddenly determined to make everyone forget all about it.

She turned the TV back on. ABC's "Primetime Live" was actually running a Sister Cordelia story. One of the nation's preeminent forensic scientists was expounding to a sympathetic Diane Sawyer his theory that a form of auto-hypnosis could account for the bizarre phenomenon in St. Louis Cathedral. "Here you have a grievously -- but not fatally -- injured individual, whose power of mind is so great that her body effectively shuts down in order for it to heal. The coroner quite naturally mistakes her as a DOA. Believe it or not, Miss Sawyer, there are dozens of documented cases in the literature."

"But Doctor," Diane said in her warm, just-this-side-of-throaty alto, "has it yet been established whether or not Cordelia Davis had been embalmed?"

"My understanding is that she was not," the scientist said flatly.

Sawyer didn't challenge him.

"How the fuck does anybody know that!" Jessica exploded.

She sat back down at her computer, and typed in another search topic: "Cordelia Embalm."

87 items found. She sampled about a dozen.

According to each story, the Archdiocese was refusing either to confirm or deny reports that the body of Cordelia Davis had been embalmed. One New Orleans mortuary was granting that it had "prepared" the body, but would not elaborate upon exactly what such preparation had entailed.

Jessica logged off in disgust. She had all the information she needed.

She located the piece of Monteleone stationary on which she'd jotted down the phone number of the *Newsweek* editor. Printed at the top of the paper were the hotel's local and 800 numbers.

The switchboard operator, with her melodious Southern accent, thanked her for her call and punched her in to Room 327.

"Alex Trujillo," he answered brusquely.

For a couple of seconds she couldn't speak. She just clutched the receiver to her face, hating herself.

"Hello?" he said.

For him, he sounded strangely patient. She would have expected him to slam the phone down.

"This is Jessica Anders," she finally managed. "Look, I don't want to get into any personal shit. Seriously, Alex."

"Then why call at all?"

He didn't sound quite like himself, or at least the self she'd perhaps foolishly believed she'd come to know over the course of an insane twenty-four hours. "I want to talk about what's going on," she fumbled, thrown by his impersonality. "I have reason to think I'm being, well, censored. At first, I thought the CNN thing was just a glitch. But now, I'm starting to doubt -- "

Or starting to believe.

"Look, Jessica, last weekend was crazy. We got drunk, and we said and did a lot of stupid things."

"Why the hell are you still in New Orleans?" she screamed. Really screamed. God forbid she'd wakened Jordan or Vicky.

He paused. "Why don't you call me back when you're feeling a little less strange? I really don't welcome calls from you when you're in this kind of mood. Christ, it's like I'm talking to a goddamn stranger."

Momentary puzzlement at his odd diction gave way to a stronger wave of anger and humiliation. "You bastard," she seethed. "Go fuck yourself -- you'll be doing both me and your wife a favor!"

She slammed down the telephone.

Overnight, a major explosion rocked Flanagan's mortuary on St. Charles Avenue in New Orleans. A three-alarm fire broke out, flames leaping into the black night, shooting sparks and embers.

The night was cold but humid; within an hour the fire was extinguished.

A dozen or so bodies being readied for burial were inadvertently, gratuitously cremated. The lavish, high-ceilinged parlor in which formal wakes were held was reduced to cinders. So was the office that housed files of now-charred documents, incinerated computers.

There was a lone casualty: Lester Beaumont, allegedly the mortician who had readied the body of Sister Cordelia for what was expected to be her final rest.

About the time that Flanagan's Mortuary blew, Renie O'Connor, a twenty-six year-old Stanford graduate student specializing in classics, was boarding a red-eye out of San Jose International Airport. Renie, in her jeans and oversized L.L. Bean sweater, looked to be a more-or-less typical doctoral candidate, more because of the battered satchel she carried, less because of her uncommon prettiness and the subtle touches she employed to augment it: brown mascara on her thick lashes, a perfect Borghese grape gloss on her lips.

Renie settled into her coach-class window seat. Even before the plane was aloft, she dragged out a stack of sure-to-be-appalling papers on the *Eumenides*.

She grimaced. Aeschylus was fucking impossible enough in Greek. Here were clueless freshman clod-hopping through the translation. She fished a pencil out of her purse.

When the plane was airborne and the co-pilot announced they were cruising at thirty-five-thousand feet, Renie, now assured the two seats to her left would remain vacant, shoved the student papers back into her satchel. The flight attendant pushed by with the beverage cart, and Renie asked for a vodka Collins and a club soda on the side.

Only when the peculiar airline ritual of drink service was concluded and the flight attendants were retired to the galley at the back of the plane did Renie take up her backpack again.

Sipping her cocktail, she reviewed the notes she'd taken during Alex Trujillo's frantic, five-minute phone conversation some three hours before.

Chapter 6

Her mind was made up. *No more Sister for me.*

It was Jessica's mantra as she showered, subjecting her slim naked body to the rigors of the relentless hot spray. Her fifteen minutes had elapsed prematurely, it appeared, but so be it. That was life. And sure, the mainstream media were obviously working overtime to kill Sister Cordelia just as effectively as the assassin outside the Louisiana death-house had attempted (*succeeded?*). As media figures, both Cordelia Davis and Jessica Anders had outlived their usefulness. In her heart, Jessica wished Sister the best.

But it was time to get on with her own life.

This morning, she refused to squander even five minutes of Con Law on the latest developments -- or lack thereof -- in the Cordelia Davis matter. Bobby Carroll shot her a look of frustration and betrayal, but she pretended not to notice.

On Thursdays, she habitually held two office hours between Con Law and Appeals. Bobby usually came during the first hour; she was advising him on a Law Review article treating of racial bias and the death penalty.

Yet she was sadly unsurprised when Bobby didn't show.

Maybe someday, he too would forgive her for not being Joan of Arc.

Joan. The only saint she never found off-putting and superhuman and hagiographic. (Ah-ah -- strike that "hagiographic" -- it was no doubt too "esoteric" for *Newsweek*.) She pictured the illustrations of Joan in the children's biographies she used to check out at the library. For some reason, what had bothered her most about Joan was her shearing off her hair. She'd crayoned in a long black mane flowing out from beneath Joan's helmet. Her mother had paid a hefty fine to the library when the "defacements" were discovered.

To this day she wore her own hair long, less as a concession to the fact she'd never be Joan of Arc than an odd testimonial to her desire for a disguise, a veil.

On a purely intellectual level, she knew she should cut off her hair, if only to mark a dramatic distinction between herself and the Bimbo Brigade.

Did those twittering, microskirted, mane-tossing GOParty girls keep their hair long and bleached and bouncy to ward off accusations from the very conservatives they represented that Opining Women had by definition to be sour, overall'd bulldykes?

Or, more likely, did the *de facto* members of the Brigade believe it themselves?

That was it; today, she'd make an appointment at the salon that always did such a fabulous job on Grace's hair. She'd OK anything between a "Murphy Brown" bob and Sinead O'Connor.

She was just about to call Grace at work to ask for the salon's name when a knock sounded on her office door. "Come in," Jessica said, setting down the phone. Likely it was Bobby after all.

A young woman of about twenty-six, with a long mane of naturally strawberry-blond hair, stepped inside. "Professor Anders?" she said uncertainly.

"Yes, I'm Jessica Anders. What can I do for you?" Jessica was a little wary; the girl didn't look like your typical Georgetown law student.

"I want some advice about maybe going to law school," the girl said, reaching into her purse and handing Jessica a folded paper. "These are my top ten choices."

Now slightly irritated, Jessica flipped open the paper.

"*Alex doesn't want to take any chances your office might be bugged,*" was written in a rounded, girlish hand. "*He knows all about your article and your being blackballed by the networks. Why don't you suggest we go have a cup of coffee at Starbucks?*"

Jessica's hands were clammy and trembling as she refolded the note. Was Alex out of his mind? More importantly, dared she take the chance that he wasn't? "You're going to need to place in the ninety-fifth percentile on the LSAT to have even a shot at getting into some of these schools," she said, affecting her no-bullshit TV manner. "Why don't we discuss it over a cup of coffee? What did you say your name was?"

"Renie O'Connor."

"What a coincidence. I was just thinking about Sinead." Jessica was throwing her purse over her shoulder.

"Yeah, people always confuse us," Renie joked.

Jessica grabbed her coat from the hook, and she and Renie made their way outside.

"Brrrrr, it's freezing," Renie shuddered, shoving her gloved hands into the pockets of her vintage velvet coat. "I could never live on the East Coast."

"Renie," Jessica said urgently, "what the hell is going on? Alex can't seriously believe I'm under surveillance!"

"I think he just doesn't want to take any chances. Oh, and he told me to give you a more specific message."

Jessica stiffened. Surely Alex hadn't been so crass as to confide anything intimate to his unlikely emissary. "What?"

Renie giggled. "I have it memorized. It's, 'You dumbshit, I was trying to tell you I knew about your article getting quashed.'"

At first Jessica was lost. Then it dawned on her. His peculiar diction and syntax last night; her call was not "welcome"; she was acting "like a stranger." "Christ, he does think I'm being bugged!"

"He also wasn't alone in his room."

Jessica didn't press for details on that.

Once inside Starbucks, they secured themselves steaming lattes and found a corner table. The cafe was packed, mostly with law students grabbing caffeine fixes between classes.

"Renie, how did Alex find out so quickly about the article? It had to have been within hours."

"He has a friend at *Newsweek*. Alex got the guy to fax him a copy."

Jessica grimaced. "I have to tell you, this all makes me rather uncomfortable. What's it to Alex if I'm being, as he claims, blackballed?" Deciding to test the waters, she added, "We barely know each other."

"He didn't give me all the details," Renie said. "I get the sense he's in staying in New Orleans supposedly to track Mother Cordelia -- "

"Sister Cordelia," Jessica corrected.

"Anyway, as far as the *Times* is concerned, he's following leads that are going to debunk the story once and for all."

"OK. Now, what's he really up to?"

"He thinks the real story is that reporters who don't tow the party line are basically being censored."

So his interest in Jessica's own situation was strictly journalistic. Good. "I'm assuming, then, he knows of cases other than mine where this is happening?"

"I guess. I'm only involved in this stuff as his friend. When he called me last night in Palo Alto and told me he needed a huge favor -- "

"Wait, hold on a second. You flew all the way out from California to tell me this?" Jessica said, stunned.

"Well, he paid for my plane ticket and everything."

Jessica fell silent for a few moments. It sounded as if Alex had become utterly swept up in this cloak-and-dagger business. And what was his relationship with this strange, charming young woman that he would ask her to fly from coast to coast at a minute's notice?

Renie had gotten up to buy a muffin. When she returned, Jessica had a question for her. "Tell me, Renie. How do you and Alex know each other?"

The girl answered with no apparent embarrassment. "We met a few years ago when we were both working on the No on 187 campaign. I had a gigantic crush on him, but he thought I was too young for him, so we just became friends." Then she did color slightly. "At least until he married that bitch Natalie."

"Renie, maybe you shouldn't be telling me this."

"No, it's OK. I can tell you're floored by the fact I flew all the way out here just because he asked me. I owed him big-time. You see, I went postal when he told me was going to marry Natalie. I said a lot of things I shouldn't have, but I was so pissed at him! I wasn't jealous, I swear I wasn't! I just knew he'd be making the biggest fucking mistake of his life, and I told him so."

Jessica felt mightily awkward. Even though Renie was offering the tale freely, listening to it still made Jessica feel she was prying into territory that was none of her business. "From what little I know of Alex, I can't imagine him responding well to anyone reading him the riot act," she said, hoping to steer Renie away from possible disclosure of the particulars of Alex's marriage.

"No kidding. He told me to mind my own damn business, and if I couldn't, our friendship was over. I told him fine, and to go screw himself." Renie toyed with the muffin from which she'd yet to take a single bite. "Until last night, I hadn't heard from him in over a year."

Jessica found herself sympathizing. "I've gotten into hot water myself over the years, shooting off my big mouth. Even when you know you're right, it's usually not worth it."

Renie managed a crooked smile. "He was a good friend, Professor Anders. Now do you see why I was glad to do anything to make things right between us again?"

"His request still strikes me as a bit extravagant, but if you're OK with it, then it's not my place to say." And then she realized she was likely sounding ungrateful. Alex, and Renie, too, had taken extreme measures to ensure she receive information he deemed it important she have in her possession. And it was clear he'd called on this young lady because he trusted her, and knew she was impetuous enough to jet across the continent to atone for her part in a thought-less squabble.

"Look, can I help you flag down a cab back to your hotel? I'd give you a ride but I'd better get back to office hours and my next class," Jessica offered.

"I don't have a hotel, exactly," Renie said. "I came here directly from the airport. But it's OK. I'll just hang out at the airport until the next plane back to San Jose."

"Don't be ridiculous," Jessica scolded, getting up and pulling on her coat. "You can't turn around and get right back on a plane." She insisted Renie go to her townhouse and have a nap. "I'll call Vicky -- she's my son's nanny -- and let her know you're on your way over. When I get home we'll have an early dinner, then I'll take you to the airport, if that's what you want."

Renie didn't put up much of an argument; she was obviously exhausted. Jessica saw her into a cab, then went back to her office to phone Vicky about the imminent arrival.

She forgot all about making an appointment to have her hair cut. Everything about Alex's message disturbed her, far more than she'd let on to Renie. It was one thing for *her* to suspect she was being blackballed, but quite another for Alex to be apparently so convinced he wouldn't even talk to her on the phone. Yet it all seemed too farfetched;

she was just an occasional legal analyst, wielding no particular influence over public opinion. If the mainstream media didn't like what she had to say, all they had to do was refuse to invite her to participate on panel shows and reject her essays for publication. What need had anyone to tap her phone lines?

Alex was paranoid; that was all there was to it. Maybe his journalistic zeal had gotten the better of his common sense, not unlike that reporter a few years back for the San Jose *Mercury-News* who claimed to have uncovered a massive CIA plot to introduce crack cocaine into South Central Los Angeles.

Every major news organization had refuted the story.

The only problem was that Jessica had always wondered if at least part of it wasn't true.

"Now who's sounding paranoid," she grumbled.

She forced herself to dwell on a less sinister matter: why Renie thought Alex's wife was such a bitch that the girl had risked a valued friendship to tell him so in no uncertain terms.

Jessica had to trust herself to be a big enough person not to press for further details.

Yet by the time she walked into her Appellate Practice class, that nagging unease over Alex's warning had returned, flitting about the edges of her consciousness. Because Appeals was an elective and not a core course like Con Law, she had about half the number of students and the atmosphere was generally less formal. Impulsively, Jessica decided to undertake an experiment, one that would prove to herself definitively that Alex was being hypervigilent.

"Before we look at today's reading assignment," she began, "let me just throw out a question to you guys. Is it me, or has the Sister Cordelia story virtually vanished into thin air?"

"There was something last night on 'Primetime,'" one student noted.

"No, I think Professor Anders is right," countered another student. "It's not like the whole issue of what really happened has been resolved. I think the networks have suddenly gone goosey."

"I wonder why," Jessica mused aloud. "Do they know something they aren't telling us?"

The students were paying avid attention. "If you ask me, the media's gagged itself because the government's so heavily invested in the death penalty," declared an abolitionist. "If people start to think, even in the back of their minds, that maybe the nun is the real thing, how can they not take the next step and question the morality of capital punishment?"

Jessica played devil's advocate. "On the other hand, the Karla Faye Tucker seemed to reopen the debate over the death penalty -- for all of two weeks, if that."

"But this is different, for obvious reasons," rejoined the same student. "Everybody I know is still talking about Sister Cordelia, and yet there's next to nothing on TV."

"Let me pose a hypothetical," Jessica said. "What if she really did rise from the dead with this incredible moral mandate? Not just to stop state-sanctioned murder, but to take greater responsibility for the poor, root out intolerance, end gun violence. In other words, everything she stood for in life. Who would have reason to be alarmed?"

She felt elated to finally say it in public. She may have been deprived of a wider forum, but she still had her classroom.

She resolved to call Bobby Carroll after class and apologize for being so timorous this morning.

She gave over half an hour to the lively debate before reluctantly reining the students in and redirecting their attention to the assigned reading.

Back at home, Vicky told her Renie was still asleep in the study. Jordan was peacefully napping, too. Jessica sat down at the kitchen table and started rifling through bills. To keep her company during this always-tedious task, she flipped on the TV in the adjacent den, mostly for background noise.

Maybe she'd spoken too soon in her Appellate Practice class.

CNN was airing a live panel discussion on Sister Cordelia.

"What I want to know is why she's hiding out," Suzanne Sheridan, seated in the Washington studio alongside Bev Wallace, Arthur Salm, a D.C. defense attorney whom Jessica actually knew fairly well through Gregg, and moderator Owen Shawn. All were perched atop barstool-like chairs, and Suzanne was wearing one of the shortest miniskirts ever to have graced a legitimate news program. "Doesn't that strike you as a little suspicious?"

"Now, Suzanne, you're not gonna try and push that animatronics theory, are you," joshed the mugging Owen Shawn.

Salm, a bearded, serious man of forty, spoke up. "I'm troubled by the passivity on all sides. Why are we all just sitting around waiting for something to happen?"

"What do you propose we do, Art?" smirked Bev. "Storm the Bastille?"

"The *Enquirer*'s reportedly offering a million dollars to anyone who can prove the whole thing wasn't a hoax," Shawn said.

Salm chuckled. "I think the *Enquirer*'s spending its money well."

Jessica surprised herself by feeling strangely left out of the discussion.

Renie, yawning, came into the kitchen. Jessica snapped off the TV. "Feeling human again?"

"Almost," Renie said. She spied the Braun on the counter. "Can I have a cup of coffee?"

"Help yourself. The cups are in that cupboard to your left."

"Your baby's adorable," Renie said as she located the milk in the refrigerator. "Vicky let me play with him for about an hour before putting us both down for naps."

Jessica was half-amused at how Renie had managed to make herself so at home. "Just so long as you didn't insist Vicky bring you your bunny and pacifier." She stacked the unpaid bills and set them aside. "Have a seat."

Renie brought her coffee over to the country-style pine table. "Do you like doing shows like that -- like the one you just turned off?"

"It's sort of fun. You get to perform mental gymnastics alongside some very smart people -- and some bona fide morons."

"Sounds like grad school."

"You must be at Stanford. What are you studying?"

"Classics. It's a total nightmare."

"Sounds pretty challenging."

Renie smiled wryly. "Alex used to tease me that the only reason I liked Latin was for all the obscene poetry."

Jessica's smile was fleeting. "I suppose that's as good a reason as any."

Renie struck her as something of a paradox, at once much older and younger than her age. When she talked to Jessica about her studies, it was clear the girl was smart as a whip, perhaps even prodigious. But she had an air of breezy frivolity about her as well that was downright teenage. She seemed to regard her impulsive trek to Washington as a grand adventure, and it was hard to tell exactly what, if anything, she thought about Alex's urgent message in particular or Sister Cordelia's "miracle" in general.

But Jessica couldn't help but like her all the same. When Jordan awakened from his nap, Renie took as much delight in playing with him as Jessica did. Renie did an uncanny impression of a meowing Siamese cat, which fascinated Jordan. Jordan, in turn, tried to imitate her, which caused Jessica and Renie to convulse with giggles. "Now you've gone and done it," Jessica gasped, clutching her sides as she sat cross-legged on the living room floor. "I'm getting us a cat."

"I've got two my roommate's looking after in Palo Alto," Renie boasted. "Edina and Patsy, after *AbFab*."

"I've wanted one for years, but my ex-husband was allergic, and I refuse to have outdoor cats. They have an average life-span of something like three years." She pulled Jordan into her lap and bounced him. "You want a kitty-cat, Jordy?"

"Jessica, you're way cool," Renie laughed. "I wish you and Alex would get together. You guys would make a great couple."

Jessica was momentarily tongue-tied. For one brief, suspicious moment she wondered if Alex coached the girl to make a case in his favor. But then she realized she herself had give Renie an opening, by referring to her "ex-husband." And how insufferably vain to think, even for a moment, that Alex was so smitten he'd employ a twenty-six year-old go-between to travel all the way from California to butter her up.

"I'm sorry," Renie said, almost plaintive in apology. "Me and my big mouth again."

Jessica decided to be candid -- to a point. "I don't know Alex well, Renie. But I like him, difficult, pigheaded S.O.B. though I suspect he is. But you said the magic words yourself. He's married. And I would feel somehow dishonorable if I allowed you to tell me anything about his marriage."

"OK, I won't. But you have it right about Alex being pigheaded and difficult. That's why he'll never admit what a disaster marrying Natalie was -- "

"Renie," Jessica warned.

"All right, all right. I'm starving. Where shall we go to dinner?"

They went to a nearby seafood place that specialized in world-class Maryland crab cakes. It was a favorite spot among Georgetown non-law students, and Jessica figured

Renie would enjoy the atmosphere. Radiohead, Beck, Sonic Youth, and Patti Smith blared above the clinking of silver and glasses and the clamor of light-hearted conversation. "I'm confused," Renie said, after she and Jessica had ordered beer and clam chowder for starters. "You said Georgetown students hang out here, but it's so far away from campus."

"No, it's actually the law school that's far away. The main campus is two blocks from here, and it's old and venerable and pseudo-Ivy League, not like that antiseptic mini-monstrosity over on Capital Hill."

Renie nodded. "Kind of like Loyola law school in L.A. It's downtown, but the real campus is on the Westside. My best friend Stephanie goes there."

"To law school?"

"Yeah. We both majored in Comp Lit at UC Irvine, and she, unlike me, decided to prepare herself for the prospect of actual employment." Renie took a swig from her Newcastle. "I don't know -- every once in a while, I think about law school. I think I could probably do the work, because I ace theory and argument. And abject poverty is getting stale fast."

Jessica chuckled. "Oh, what's that line from Marlowe's *Hero and Leander*! I used to know it by heart."

"Don't tell me you were a lit major, too!"

"I double-majored in philosophy and English at UCLA. Wait -- I think I have it." She paused, running over the couplet in her mind before reciting: "'And to this day is every scholar poor; Gross gold from them runs headlong to the boor.'"

Renie applauded. "I love it! Make sure you write it down for me. I want to tack it up on my office wall."

"I'm not sure I can remember it a second time," Jessica admitted, shaking her head. "It's been ages since I thought of that."

"Excuse me -- are you Jessica Anders?" broke in a husky male voice.

Both Jessica and Renie looked up, startled. A goateed young man with a shaven head, dressed in jeans and a Rage Against the Machine T-shirt, hovered above them. Silver cross earrings dangled from each of his lobes.

Jessica straightened. "Yes?"

"Sorry to bother you. I'm Eric Muller. I write for the Georgetown alternative newspaper." Uninvited, he pulled up a chair. "Would you possibly be willing to do an interview with us on Sister Cordelia? You seem to be one of the few people willing to stick up for her."

Jessica, caught off-guard, was evasive. "I'm really busy. Give me your number, and I'll call you next week, OK?"

Smoothly he whipped out a notepad, scribbled a phone number. "Sorry to have bothered you," he repeated. "But a whole bunch of us think you're just great. If you could spare five, ten minutes over the phone, even, we'd be super grateful."

Jessica accepted the paper, mindlessly tucked it into her purse. Eric Muller apologized for a third time, before leaving them in peace to join a group of friends at the bar.

Renie's eyes followed him there, made sure he was safely ensconced among brewskis and buddies before turning back to Jessica. "He gave me the creeps."

Me too, Jessica thought. But she tried shrugging it off to Renie. "No big deal. He just looked a little weird, that's all."

"He didn't look weird -- he looked straight out of central casting," Renie corrected. "The only things missing were the obligatory tattoo and the nose ring."

"Stop," Jessica ordered sternly. "Between you and Alex, you'll have me certifiably paranoid. Jesus Christ! You people have watched too many episodes of *The X Files*!"

"Greatest show ever," Renie said. "Don't you like it?"

"That's beside the point. You might as well tell me *your* theory of what happened with Sister Cordelia," Jessica challenged.

"You know what? I don't have one." Renie sounded almost sad about it. "It sounds so chickenshit, but it's true. I'm an atheist, but it pisses me off to listen to all these self-righteous jerks expounding on both sides. And now that the mortuary's been blown to smithereens --"

"What? Back up, Renie!"

Renie gasped. "Oh, I'm so sorry, I forgot to tell you! I called Alex from the airport this morning, and he told me all about it!"

Loath as Jessica was to give in to paranoia, she nonetheless motioned for Renie to lower her voice.

Renie complied. "He said the major news organizations were sitting on it, but that it would break sooner or later. Supposedly, a natural gas explosion totaled the mortuary that handled the body. Blew away the mortician in the process."

Jessica's blood turned icy. For the first time since the "resurrection," she was truly scared. Scared not just for the country, or for the fate of truth.

She was absolutely terrified for Jordy and herself.

For one side -- either the skeptics or the true believers -- was so determined the truth about Sister's resurrection never be established they were willing not only to destroy possible evidence, but to commit murder.

The room seemed to be closing in on her. The music -- R.E.M.'s haunting "Drive" -- bore into her brain.

What if I ride, what if you walk, what if you rock around the clock, Baby . . .

"Renie," she said hoarsely, "I hope you understand, but I've got to get home to Jordy." She fumbled in her purse for two twenties; that would more than cover the chowders and beer.

"Of course I do, Jessica. But Alex thinks the death of the mortician was an accident --"

"I'm fucking tired of hearing what Alex thinks! I just want to be with my baby!"

Renie put up no argument.

They made a point of appearing to exit unobtrusively. Renie flirted with a few of the collegians at the bar as they passed, trading obscenities with a drunken frat boy who asked her if she was a "real" redhead.

Once outside in the cold, however, Renie turned grim. "Sometimes I fantasize about being Susan Sarandon in *Thelma and Louise*. Why do men suck so much?"

Jessica had barely heard her. "Hurry, we have to hurry home. Renie, I don't think I can take you to National tonight. I'll pay for the cab. But I need to be with Jordy."

"My return ticket's open-ended, but I'll leave if you want. I personally would feel better staying with you the night," Renie offered tentatively. "But if you'd rather --"

"No, that's fine. I could use the company. Let's just hurry!"

If speed-walking were an Olympic event, they would have taken the gold.

At home, Jordan was fine, and Vicky was watching "Must-See TV" in the den. Jessica almost wept with relief. At once, she felt like a fool. Alex's little friend Renie had to think her a certified Woman on the Verge of a Nervous Breakdown.

And if so, perhaps she wasn't far off the truth.

"What do you say I whip us up some Eggs Benedict -- I'm a master at hollandaise -- and we'll light a fire in the living room and knock off a bottle or two of wine?" she suggested sheepishly.

"That sounds awesome. Can I put some music on, or will it disturb Jordy?"

Now was Vicky's turn to laugh. "Are you kidding? Jordy's survived his mom's forty-minute workouts on her treadmill to Social Distortion!"

"Social D -- I *love* them!" Renie squealed.

Jessica was starting to relax. "Let's go easy on the kid's ears tonight. Any objections to Billie Holiday?"

She didn't have any bacon or ham for the Eggs Benedict, but thick slices of tomato substituted nicely. They ate in the living room, keeping Lady Day low on the CD player so as not to disturb Vicky's enjoyment of TV in the adjacent den.

After a couple of glasses of wine, Jessica was starting to relax -- at least enough to broach the subject of the explosion at the mortuary. "Why does Alex believe the mortician's death wasn't intentional?" She poked at the crackling fire in the brick hearth with an andiron.

"I asked him if he was in any danger, and he said no way. The undertaker wasn't supposed to be there."

Jessica's brows drew together. She really wished she could talk to him, find out what he really thought. But so long as he insisted on assuming the worst -- that her phone might be tapped -- her only recourse was to send messages to him via Renie. And Jessica was reluctant to do so, not because she didn't trust the girl, but because she felt Alex had almost exploited his erstwhile young friend by embroiling her in this unpleasant business to begin with.

"Do you think we'll ever know the truth?" Renie asked, refilling her goblet.

"Oh, I suppose a version of the truth will eventually emerge," Jessica said, pensive again. "Some middle-ground explanation that everybody can live with. But what that might be is anyone's guess."

"Alex says he's going to stay in New Orleans until he's gotten the whole story."

"He'd better watch it. If the L.A. *Times* is anything like CNN, he's likely to find himself out of a job."

Renie gazed into the fire, her eyes narrowing slightly. "I wonder if he isn't also putting off going back to L.A. for as long as he possibly can."

Exasperated, Jessica raised her hands in a gesture of surrender. "You're just not going to let me be noble about this, are you. All right, spit it out. What's wrong with his damn marriage?"

Renie looked at once guilty and pleased that the bait had finally been taken. "Natalie Rivard -- how do I describe her? She's a clinging and manipulative bitch. I can't put it more delicately than that."

Jessica shrugged noncommittally.

"She and Alex dated for about a year, and it was always Natalie who was begging him to commit. When he finally does tell her he loves her, she dumps him in a flash. That was right around the time I met him."

"Obviously they patched things up. If he doesn't hold it against her, why should you?"

Renie knotted her long hair into a ponytail. "It gets worse. Two years ago she starts calling him out of the blue, whining that her new boyfriend isn't treating her well. She even hints that the guy's beating her. I don't know if you noticed, but Alex has that Latin machismo thing."

"I had occasion to notice, yes," Jessica said ironically.

"One night Natalie calls and tells him she's taken half a bottle of Valium. He races over there, rushes her to the hospital. Next thing you know, they're living together, and it's starting all over again." Renie made no effort to conceal her disgust. "She's pressuring him to get married, isolating him from all of his friends except the ones who treat her like this fragile baby bird to be coddled and indulged. Out of nowhere she announces she's a manic-depressive, but I never bought it. I think she's just a spoiled little drama queen."

Now Jessica was refilling her glass. The story held a kind of lurid fascination, despite Renie's obvious prejudice against Natalie. "I take it you told him as much, and that's what caused the big-falling out."

Renie nodded. "I really didn't think we'd ever talk again. But every once in a while, his younger sister Lily would call me. She could never stand Natalie either."

"Now, there, maybe I have a little sympathy for Natalie. I never felt my in-laws much liked me. They thought I was too serious, too ambitious."

"Trust me, nobody ever thought that about Natalie. As soon as she and Alex married, she quit her job as PR director for the Pasadena Playhouse. Claimed burn-out. Said she needed time off to try to write short-stories."

"Ugh -- an *artiste*. My brother Steve is addicted to the same type." Jessica got up to replace Billie Holiday with Cassandra Wilson.

But Renie wasn't quite done. "About six weeks ago, Lily called me from L.A. She was more pissed than I've ever heard her. Alex caught Natalie screwing this buffed-out surfer dude who lived across the street from them. Alex was about to beat the shit out of the guy when Natalie started screaming hysterically and charged headlong through a sliding glass door. She wasn't hurt that bad, but she was so out of control the paramedics had to take her off in restraints." Renie's expression was bitter but not gloating.

Jessica shuddered. "That's . . . horrible. Horrible."

"They kept her in the hospital just overnight. She swore to Alex, according to Lily, she hadn't known what she was doing, it was a supposed manic episode."

Jessica gave up trying to be objective. "No it wasn't," she said, her voice heavy. "She was bored, and wanted to get his hackles up."

"Exactly!" Renie said triumphantly. "He didn't come home unexpectedly. It was his usual time. She wanted him to find her with the guy." She paused to catch her breath. "How did you know?"

Jessica sat back down wearily. "Because I've known women like this. Charming and narcissistic, with incredibly low thresholds for boredom. Men, too, now that I think of it. The ones who like the chase until they've snared the prize."

"I don't know why he didn't throw her out on her sorry ass," Renie said. "I can't believe he buys this 'manic' bullshit. And he's sure as hell not the forgiving type."

Jessica felt a little sick at heart. "Maybe it's out of sheer stubbornness. You and his sister probably aren't the only ones who've worn your disapproval on your sleeves."

Renie considered it. "Could be. But I think she's somehow convinced him that she needs him. According to Lily, Natalie's been wearing a size 4 hairshirt and prostrating herself at his feet ever since. Still, it's got to be a good sign he's not rushing to get back home." She stifled a yawn. "Sorry! The wine's going to my head."

"No apologies necessary. You've had a long twenty-four hours. Why don't you go up to bed? Use my room -- I'll sleep on the couch in the study."

Renie balked. "No way am I throwing you out of your own bed."

"No, I prefer it. I need to do a little work on the computer, and it might take me a couple of hours."

Reluctantly, Renie accepted the invitation.

To Jessica's mild surprise, Renie gave her a brief, spontaneous little hug before starting upstairs. "Thanks for everything. You've been great."

Jessica waited for Renie to ascend the stairs before sinking to her knees by the hearth, resting her forehead on one hand.

Quid pro quo. His ego wounded by his wife's infidelity, he'd merely been reciprocating in kind. She'd been right all along; Renie's story offered just a new spin on the time-honored *my wife doesn't understand me* routine.

Grace's irreverent rejoinder popped into her mind: *"Maybe she doesn't understand him."*

Well, at least her own conscience was more or less absolved. Better to be used than to think she'd unwittingly played Miss Coffee-Tea-or-Me to Mrs. Trujillo's naively faithful Wifey.

"Christ," she muttered, downing the last of her wine. What a day; what a goddamn week. Would her life ever return to sanity?

"'And then she opened her eyes, and realized it was all a dream,'" she mocked herself.

She squeezed her eyes shut, but when she reopened them, she was still sitting alone before the dying fire hating herself for wishing Alex Trujillo were there next to her.

Chapter 7

The next morning, Jessica drove Renie out to National Airport, and after promising to stay in touch, dropped her off at the American terminal. Although Jessica generally preferred listening to music while she drove, the tapedeck in her Land Rover was on the blink for the umpteenth time, currently threatening to chew up a favorite old Echo and the Bunnymen cassette, one she'd been listening to since law school. As she negotiated morning rush-hour back to Georgetown, she fiddled with the radio until she found a news show.

Two minutes into the news, the announcer reported that an obscure terrorist group calling itself "Christians For Truth" was claiming credit for the bombing that had destroyed Flanagan's Mortuary early yesterday, killing the proprietor. "It has still yet to be confirmed that Flanagan's was the mortuary that handled the ostensible burial preparations for Sister Cordelia Davis. The FBI has reportedly received hundreds of tips about the Christians for Truth, but are not releasing any details."

But hadn't Alex had told Renie the blast was going to be attributed to a natural gas explosion? Not that it mattered one way or another, she supposed. Regardless of the purported cause, the effect stayed the same, rendering it all but impossible to ascertain whether Sister Cordelia had been embalmed. Even the name of the so-called terrorist group was ambiguous. "Christians for Truth" -- but for *which* truth? Whose truth?

She vowed to fight the temptation to switch on the TV as soon as she got home. Why bother? She could guess already who the panelists would be, and what they would be saying. She'd watch and listen, feeling frustrated and angered by her deliberate exclusion from the debate, fueling her paranoia until it reached epic proportions and she ended up ranting on streetcorners and foisting hand-printed flyers upon unnerved passersby.

The blinking red button on her answering machine informed her she had two messages. The first was from Bobby Carroll, pleasantly requesting a meeting at her convenience to discuss his Law Review article. Jessica bit back a smile. Maybe Bobby had heard of her mini-diatribe in Appeals yesterday and decided she wasn't such a wimp after all.

The second was from the assistant to the Dean of Faculty. "Dean Mitchell would like to discuss a matter with you at your earliest possible convenience," she said in a chipper, it's-nothing-to-worry-about voice. "Please call me to set up an appointment."

Jessica decided to call the Dean first. If she could see him today, she'd then try to set up a time with Bobby when she would already be on campus.

Sally, the Dean's assistant, asked her if she could come in at two.

"No problem," Jessica said. "What's this about?"

"Oh, I'm not sure, but I imagine it has to do with next fall's schedule. Frank Antonio's going on leave, and Dean Mitchell's been knocking himself out trying to get someone to cover his Jurisprudence class."

Bobby was not in, so Jessica left him a message telling him she'd be in her office from three to four that afternoon, and inviting him to stop by if he was free.

It was only eleven; that gave her plenty of time to give Jordy his lunch, change out of her jeans and sweatshirt into a DKNY pantsuit, and praise herself for not turning on the TV.

Not that the news had changed. As she drove downtown to Capital Hill, she heard the same report about the New Orleans bombing, with no new details.

She made up her mind to replace the cassette deck this weekend. Maybe even splurge for a CD player. How far she'd come from her days at the ACLU. Upon Mama's death she and Steve had inherited a rather handsome trust-fund set up by their father, a San Francisco neurosurgeon who had himself succumbed to a brain tumor when they were still little kids. Jessica, who'd been eight, barely remembered him. According to Mama, Dad had been a workaholic, rarely even taking time to join his wife and two children for family vacations or weekend trips to the zoo or Golden Gate Park. Even after his death, Mama had lived rather modestly, keeping the pretty wood-and-glass house in the Oakland hills, making sure Steve and Jessica never lacked for clothes and school field trips and college, but seldom indulging in luxuries save for an occasional weekend jaunt to Las Vegas with her divorced sister Nelda. It wasn't that Mama had been a martyr; rather, from the time of her husband's death, and perhaps even before then, she seemed perfectly content to live for, and through, her children and their accomplish-ments in which she took such unbridled pride. Steve must have inherited his taste for fancy sports cars and Jessica hers for designer labels from their father, for Mama tooled around for years, to their consternation, in the same old Buick she'd had when Dad died. and didn't think twice about buying her clothes from J.C. Penney's.

Thus, it was to their great surprise that Jessica and Steve discovered, after Mama's death, she'd left them an estate, not even counting the house, worth nearly four million dollars.

Why the hell hadn't Mama spent at least part of it on finding herself a better doctor than the quack who'd misdiagnosed her congestive heart failure as the symptoms of late-onset menopause?

Gregg had urged them to pursue a malpractice lawsuit, but she and Steve were too angry, too shell-shocked. And she knew, had known even then, that litigation would mean an ongoing nightmare of stress and a ruthless invasion of personal privacy. She'd written an impassioned letter of complaint to California's Board of Medical Quality Assurance, but never received a response.

But it was Mama's ridiculous frugality that spared her the dire economic fate of most women whose marriages ended, enabling her to keep up the mortgage on the townhouse and continue to shop for herself and Jordan wherever she chose. Mama's frugality allowed her to pay her own way through the L.L.M program at Yale rather than depending on Gregg's largesse, for all that he had offered to pick up the cost of her tuition. And today, thanks to Mama, she was able to entertain the thought of distracting herself from her current worries by the possibility of a new, expensive sound-system for the Land Rover.

When she reached the Dean's office at five of two, Sally, uncharacteristically formal, told her, "Go right in, Professor Anders. Dean Mitchell's ready for you."

It was only then that Jessica began to suspect this meeting didn't have a damn thing to do with finding a replacement to pick up Frank Antonio's teaching-load next year.

Dean Benjamin G. Mitchell, a mild gray man who favored sweater-vests and sportcoats over suits, shook her hand, but his grip was weak, his smile wan. "Have a seat, Jessica. Can I have Sally bring you a cup of coffee?"

"No thank you." She sat down stiffly in the chair opposite his desk.

"Are you sure? It's actually halfway drinkable today."

His joshing seemed patently forced.

Again, she politely refused.

The dean eased himself into the chair behind his desk. He folded his hands in front of him. "Jessica, I hope you'll forgive my perhaps overstepping myself. But I know these past few months have not been easy on you."

She grimaced, thinking, *Fucking sexist busybodies*. She'd made no attempts either to hide or to discuss her separation from Gregg with fellow faculty; she'd simply ceased wearing a wedding ring. But in the Washington legal community gossip traveled especially fast, and God knew it was a way of life on Capital Hill, whether you were a lawyer or not. "Let me assure you, Dean Mitchell -- I'm fine."

But it was as if he hadn't heard her. "It may well be you came back from maternity leave too soon, for your own good, and for the good of your students." He unfolded his hands, placing them flat on the desk-top. "In short, Jessica, I want to cut you as much slack as I am legally and ethically able to."

"Legally and ethically?" she repeated, her voice rising. "Dean Mitchell, I have to tell you I don't know what the hell you're talking about! Are you alleging I've done something -- anything -- improper or unprofessional?"

Mitchell regarded her with a sad little smile. "I might as well give it to you straight. Two of your students have complained this semester that you came into class disorganized and disoriented. They both insist you had liquor on your breath."

She was outraged. "That's complete, utter bullshit! Who are these supposed students?"

"There's more, I'm afraid. A week ago, before you left for New Orleans, a third student reported that you offered her cocaine during your office hours. That you told her your nerves were shot because of Sister Cordelia's death, and you needed a lift."

"Who the hell are these students?" she demanded. "These are absolute, bald-faced lies, and I defy anyone to repeat them to my face!"

"They've requested confidentiality. But I did verify that all three are currently enrolled in your classes."

"Fine -- that still doesn't explain why you're taking their word over mine! Ask any of my other students if they've ever smelled booze on me or seen me use drugs. Jesus Christ, Ben, I haven't even smoked pot in ten years!"

The dean continued to regard her with a kind of pitiful resignation. "Jessica, a small vial of what appears to be powder cocaine was found in your office desk. By law, we should have reported you to the police. But because of the high regard in which I personally hold you, as a lawyer, scholar, and teacher, I went out on a limb for you. We all agreed that as long as you tender your resignation, effective immediately, we'll keep this thing under wraps."

Jessica fought with all her might to maintain composure. "Ben, this is a witch-hunt. From the moment I refused to tow the party line on Sister Cordelia, certain forces -- I don't know who -- have been working overtime to discredit me. Think about it, Ben! Has there ever been a whisper, even an inkling of one, about my competence or professionalism before this week?"

"My understanding is that CNN also found your work erratic." He affected a paternal tone. "I'm not judging you, Jessica. I can't imagine the shock of seeing such a grotesque spectacle inside that church, especially after all you've gone through -- having a baby, and your husband --"

"And so the consensus is now that it sent me over the deep end!" she spat. "Well, I've studied the faculty by-laws, Dean Mitchell, and I'm just as entitled to due process as any defendant. You'll be hearing from my lawyers, trust me!"

"Jessica," he pleaded, "this would be no cut-and-dry wrongful-termination suit. It could damage your career permanently. There's the matter of the cocaine --"

"Illegal search and seizure, and you goddamn know it." She shot out of her chair, stalking for the door.

"Do yourself a favor," he urged not unkindly, rising as well. "Agree to resign, then take a real sabbatical. Maybe check yourself into a clinic, Jessie. There'll be no ugliness, no paper trail."

To her horror, he actually sounded sincere.

"Dean Mitchell," she said icily, "I hereby compel you to go fuck yourself forthwith."

Shock and anger so numbed her that she was actually able to drive home with nothing more than *I can't believe this! I can't fucking believe this!* drumming in her head. Crazily, she felt like Mia Farrow in *Rosemary's Baby,* trying to convince nice young Dr. Hill (played by a yet-to-blossom-into-full-loathsomeness Charles Grodin) that she was perfectly sane, thank you, but everyone really was out to get her.

And nobody had believed her.

But the moment she walked into the townhouse she became hysterical. She broke into sobs that wouldn't quit, banging her fists against the door even as she bolted it shut and activated the alarm. Vicky, upstairs about to give Jordan his bath, came racing down, clutching the diapered baby in her arms. "Jesus Christ, Jessica! What's wrong?"

Weeping, Jessica took Jordan and cradled him closely. A hideous thought occurred to her. If the Powers-That-Be were so deadset on silencing her that they'd lean on CNN and *Newsweek* to blackball her, bribe students to lie about her, and plant cocaine in her office, what vulnerability had she left but her infant son?

How could she persuade them that she'd never breathe another word about Sister, so long as they left Jordan alone?

In the old days, she could have waved a white flag to signal her surrender. But now, with the enemy at once everywhere and anonymous, she didn't know where to turn in supplication.

As her hysterics subsided, she returned Jordan to Vicky. "I've just had a bad day at work," she forced herself to say. "Go give Jordy his bath."

"Of course," Vicky said, though her eyes were wide with a mixture of bewilderment and compassion.

"One last thing, Vicky. Until I tell you otherwise, I don't want you answering the door or taking Jordan outside in his stroller. Under any circumstances -- not even if it's Gregg. Is that clear?"

"Jessica -- "

"I can't explain now. Promise me."

"You have my word," Vicky assured her, for all that she was visibly frightened.

"Thank you." Jessica planted a quick kiss on the baby's downy head, then waved them both upstairs.

She needed quiet time alone to think.

She knew what she had to do; it was the *how* that needed working on.

She had to fall on her sword publicly, discrediting herself as an authority on Sister Cordelia without compromising herself ethically or professionally.

A damn good thing she hadn't cut her hair. She couldn't be Joan of Arc: Joan hadn't been a mother.

She had an idea. She called her brother Steve at the San Francisco *Chronicle*.

"About time you got back to me," he said, pretending offense. "I was starting to worry you'd put on a purple shroud-in-reverse to follow Sister Cordelia's Cult of Eternal Life."

Mindful more than ever that her phone might be tapped, she forced a laugh. "Yeah, we could call our comet Hail- Mary instead of Hale-Bopp."

"Bad Catholic joke, Jess. What goes?"

"Look, how would I reach Debby King -- you know, that gossip columnist for the New York *Daily News*?"

"She's syndicated -- don't they list her Website in the *Post*?"

"She has a Website?"

"Jesus, where've you been?"

"To New Orleans, or, if you prefer, to hell and back. Someday I'll tell you about it."

He paused. "Are you OK? How's Jordan?"

"We're both just peachy. Really, Steve. I'm thinking of taking a sabbatical. Maybe we'll come out to the City and annoy you for a few months."

"That'd be great. Except I'm going to New York for the Grammys next month, and then Kris and I may spend a week or two in Italy."

"Don't worry, I have no intention of cramping your style. So I just locate Debby King's Website on the net?"

"Wait a sec."

He put her on hold, and a Muzak version of Radiohead's "Karma Police," of all things, came on.

Steve was back in half a minute. "Here's her phone number. Got a pen?"

She jotted down the ten numbers furiously.

"Care to tell me what this is about?" he prodded.

"Nothing big. Let's talk soon, OK?"

"We're going skiing in Tahoe this weekend, but I'll ring you when I get back. And Jess?"

"Look, Steve, I have to go -- "

"Take care of yourself. I've been worried about you."

"Debby King's office," chirped a receptionist.

"This is Jessica Anders -- I'm a legal consultant for CNN --"

"I'll put you through right away, Ms. Anders."

Far from a celebrity, Jessica was surprised by the red-carpet treatment. But then again, she wasn't. Nothing could surprise her anymore.

And if her line was tapped, the eavesdroppers were about to get an earful.

"Hi, Jessica, this is Deb King," came a brisk, unmistakably New York voice. "Is it true CNN's booted your butt off the air?"

"That's why I called -- to set the record straight. I requested a leave from CNN, as I have from my teaching duties at Georgetown, for personal reasons."

"Really!" Deb King sounded openly skeptical. "Have you checked out the Internet chat rooms lately? The consensus seems to be that you, dear, are being blackballed."

"That's bullshit. I have a baby, and I'd like to spend more time with him. I can't believe this has become even a minor *cause celebre*."

"Ooookay," King said, obviously humoring her. "Just tell me this, Jessica, off the record or on, whichever you prefer. Who, in your own mind, is Sister Cordelia Davis?"

Jessica didn't hesitate a moment. "Sister Cordelia," she said emphatically, "is a fraud. And yes, you can quote me on that."

Chapter 8

His editor was cutting him some slack, "enough slack to hang yourself," as Crowell put it, only half-joking. The top brass at the *Times* was willing to support him, but within limits, Crowell warned. They were sufficiently impressed with his dispassionate reports on the zealots now camped outside Sister's Metairie convent, holding lit candles and patiently awaiting an appearance that had yet to manifest. Management was even more delighted by Alex's scoop on the explosion at Flanagan's Mortuary; the fucks were actually whispering among themselves about another Pulitzer, according to Crowell. And yes, they were most anxious to print anything he was able to learn and confirm about this obscure terrorist group, the Christians for Truth. The problem was less editorial than economic; Alex had been in New Orleans for over a week, on an expense-account. He was starting to feel not-so-subtle pressure either to conclude his investigation in the next day or so, or at the very least, move to a cheaper hotel.

On the Saturday that marked the first-week anniversary of the resurrection, Alex checked out of the Monteleone and into the humbler Richelieu, a quaint, smaller hotel in the southeastern corner of the Quarter less than a block from the Old Ursulines convent where Cordelia Davis had lain until the afternoon of the funeral. A week later, fresh flowers still marked the path of her cortege from Ursulines to the Cathedral. The city was flooded with pilgrims who arrived daily, mostly from Mexico, the Caribbean, Central America, and Southern Europe. Despite no official sanction from the Vatican, groups of the devoted in threes and fours retraced the route of the procession as solemnly as if following the Stations of the Cross.

Alex was glad to see them. Interviews with them could justify at least another week's stay in New Orleans, especially given an avid Hispanic readership back home.

Not to his great surprise, many of the pilgrims had never heard of Sister Cordelia before her resurrection, had not even owned televisions or radios through which they learned of the miracle. The news had traveled via word of mouth, reaching remote villages in Mexico, Guatemala, El Salvador, and the only thing that amazed Alex was the relative accuracy of the tale the peasants repeated to him. He suspected the Jesuit missionaries, most of them committed liberation theologians, were chiefly responsible for disseminating the information so objectively. After all, the Jesuits had no need to put a spin on the story: one of their own, a radical Catholic social activist, had appeared to rise from the dead.

Those were just the facts, ma'am.

And those were the facts he stuck with, choosing every word, every fucking letter, he typed on the keyboard of his laptop with utmost precision. He no longer modemed off so much as an e-mail without proofing it half a dozen times to ensure no word or phrase betrayed even a hint of editorial bias. And as a result, the *Times* continued to publish his stories, even if they'd begun to bump him from A1 to A3. Crowell said that readership in the Latino community was up fourteen percent since the resurrection and holding steady. Alex knew management was not going to fuck with a good thing, despite their bitching about the cost of putting him up in a four-star hotel.

Had he been any less committed to seeing this bizarre story though to the end, whatever it might be, he would have gladly stuck the *Times* with the cost of Renie O'Connor's round-trip plane ticket from San Jose to Washington. Instead, he'd applied a chunk of his personal frequent-flier miles. Once his old Stanford pal Geoff Cade, now a reporter for *Newsweek,* told him about Jessica's essay getting quashed, Alex hadn't thought twice about contacting Renie and asking her to deliver a message. Jessica's panicked call to him that same night had scared the shit out of him. It was a call he couldn't respond to, because his hotel room was full of hard-bitten, whiskey-guzzling print journalists who believed to a man that fucking Disney had engineered the nun's apparent revival as a publicity stunt to plug a forthcoming, animated version of *The Sound of Music*.

And he'd paid for the favor dearly, not just in terms of frequent-flier miles. Renie had shown uncharacteristic restraint, not bringing up Natalie even once. But she'd gushed a good half-hour about Jessica's virtues, about how cool and funny and pretty and elegant -- Renie made a point of emphasizing *elegant* -- she'd found Jessica. But when Alex pressed her for details, Renie responded somberly.

"She's really scared, Alex. I don't think it was such a great idea telling her she might be bugged. It made her super-paranoid."

Alex disliked the implied reproach. "Maybe she ought to be paranoid. I gave her the worst fucking advice I've ever given anybody." He'd encouraged her to promote the notion that the resurrection was authentic; twelve hours later, he'd learned better, but she'd already jetted back to D.C. in a huff, too late for him to warn her to keep her mouth shut.

He'd hinted to Renie that it was common knowledge, conventional wisdom, that Jessica Anders had been given the big heave-ho by CNN. What he hadn't shared was that Jessica was now rumored to be emotionally unstable, shattered by the surreal "mock"-resurrection inside St. Louis Cathedral. The contingent of national reporters lingering in New Orleans in hopes of documenting the smallest sign of Sister's reemergence fought boredom with gossip, a good deal of which centered on Jessica. She was a lipstick-feminist and ivory tower intellectual insufficiently tough to do real journalism. She'd been a flake since her husband dumped her for a younger woman. Her rejected

Newsweek essay had been an incoherent diatribe advocating a millennial Cult of the Virgin consecrated in the name of Cordelia Davis.

The woman had quite obviously suffered a nervous breakdown.

He'd deliberately not spoken a word in her defense. But he listened, and filed away certain comments for future reference.

Not a day had passed since she fled New Orleans that he didn't think of her. She'd made ferociously clear the fact she wanted nothing more to do with him.

He could accept that.

What he couldn't accept was that she was under attack. Whether she liked it or not, he was going to do his damndest to look out for her.

He spent most of the afternoon chatting in Spanish with an extended family of eighteen Salvadorans -- various grandparents, in-laws, nieces and nephews. Tattery excited toddlers sucked on candies and begged their parents for rides on the mule-drawn wagons that, for forty bucks, trundled tourists along on half-hour tours of the "historic French Quarter." The children yanked on parents' hands and hems, captivated by the carnival that was Jackson Square. But the adults spoke with quiet passion and dignity of their pilgrimage. They came to see, and, if possible, to touch, Sister Cordelia.

It seemed to matter little that Cordelia Davis had not been spotted since the afternoon of the funeral.

They were certain she would appear to them. God had sent Sister back to the world for a purpose, insisted a toothless old woman in a black lace *mantilla.* Her dark eyes, sunken into folds of leathered skin, shone fiercely.

Alex took several pages of notes, and then went back to his hotel room to compose the story. He grabbed a beer out of the miniature refrigerator the hotel provided in lieu of a minibar, then snapped open his laptop.

The phone rang. "Yeah," he said, cradling the receiver under his chin as he typed.

"It's me. I miss you."

Her voice was at once plaintive and faintly accusatory.

He said nothing, and just kept writing.

"What if I catch a plane tonight and join you in New Orleans?"

"Not a good idea. I'll be back when I'm back."

By now she was crying. "Why won't you forgive me? It wasn't my fault . . . I'm back on my meds, I was an idiot to stop taking them in the first place." Her "meds" were Prozac and Trazadone, two drugs she'd been on and off dozens of times over the years he'd known her.

"This isn't about whether or not I forgive you, It's about work, and I have a hell of a lot to do."

"I love you, Alex! I don't know how much longer I can stand being without you," she sobbed.

"I'll call you later."

He hung up the phone, then punched the operator. "Hold my calls for the rest of the day, OK?"

The story took under two hours to write. After proofing the article, Alex sent it via modem to the *Times*. Then, as had become his habit almost from the day his plane landed in New Orleans, he wandered up to Bourbon Street in search of drink and mindless distraction.

He ended up at Lafitte's Blacksmith Shop, one of a handful of French Quarter haunts grown popular with visiting journalists. It was a few blocks east of the more raucous, touristy heart of Bourbon, and less stuffy and formal than hotel cocktail lounges. Alex sat down at the bar, lit a cigarette, and ordered a gin and tonic.

"Hey, *hombre, como esta*?" Walt Haberman, a stringer for the Associated Press, clapped him on the shoulder and boosted himself up on the adjacent barstool. Walt was a former L.A. *Times* copy editor who'd left five years before when the opportunity arose to cover news, not just compose headlines. He was a fidgety little guy, chubby and balding, a decent and honorable journalist.

Alex had always liked him. "What's going on?"

"Not damn much," Walt groused. "Spent the third day in a row camped out in Metairie. Shit, you'd think that even a nun would be getting cabin-fever by now."

"What, you expect her to show up at Tipitina's?"

Walt chuckled. "Wanna hear the weirdest rumor currently circulating out there among the true believers? They think she's the reincarnation of Marie Laveau, the nineteenth century voodoo queen. Laveau's supposed to have given thousands of dollars to the Church."

"Yeah? That's not bad. Better than some of the conspiracy theories you hear on CNN and the Big Three."

"Speaking of CNN, you get wind of the latest on Anders, that feminist lawyer they booted? She's come out and practically retracted everything. Told Deb King she has no doubt Sister's a phony. It's all over the wires."

Alex was careful to show no particular reaction. "No kidding."

"She's either resorted to flagrant brown-nosing to get her face back on the tube, or gone completely bonkers," Walt concluded, shaking his head. "Damn shame. I always thought she was one of the smarter ones on the talking-heads circuit. A real looker, too."

"She probably just wants to wash her hands of this entire fiasco, and who could fucking blame her?" Alex downed the remainder of his drink. "Gotta run. Conference call with my editors in half an hour."

Striding at a brisk clip back toward Le Richelieu, he was oblivious to the whooping, boozy tourists and occasional, somber pilgrims sharing the night in the Quarter. He kept hearing Renie's voice in his head: "*She's really scared, Alex.*" She had to be; Jessica was not only principled but smart, as Walt had noted. Why would she expose herself to public ridicule if not out of abject fucking terror?

Nor did it seem likely that the story was planted. Deb King, for all that she was first and foremost a gossip columnist, was well-known in journalistic circles for her integrity and her double- and triple-checking of sources. A few years back, when several major news organizations were heedlessly proclaiming that they had at long last uncovered the identity of Deep Throat of Watergate infamy, it was Debby King who traced the "source" to a fraternity of computer nerds at MIT.

He packed an overnight bag and his laptop, but left the rest of his belongings in his room. From the noisy airport, he called Renie in Palo Alto. "Do you know anything about Jessica issuing some kind of retraction about her reporting?" he asked.

"No -- what would she have to retract, anyway? All she's ever said is that she has no idea what happened. Shit, Alex, are you calling from a bowling alley or something?"

He thought that the fewer people who knew about his impromptu travel plans the better. "Wish to hell I were. No, I'm at this cheesy no-host media party at the Marriott. Six-fifty for a fucking well drink."

She giggled. "That, amigo, is why God invented beer. That is, if there was a God."

"Talk to you later, Rain." It was his pet name for her, one he'd virtually forgotten until just now.

"You'd better," she replied happily.

Since her conversation with Deb King, Jessica had for all intents and purposes cocooned herself and Jordy against the world. She turned the ringer off the phones and let the machine record messages she had no intention of retrieving. She'd barely slept in the thirty-six hours or so that had passed since her meeting with Dean Mitchell, but she stayed in her worn flannel pajamas, yesterday's mascara smudged around her eyes, her hair haphazardly gathered up by a scrunchy. Vicky, concerned, fixed her a tuna sandwich and a bowl of soup, but Jessica could barely touch it. She spent most of her time in the rocking chair in Jordan's room, holding him until he grew either antsy or sleepy, loving him and positively despising herself.

It wasn't that she regretted "confessing" to Deb King. Recanting seemed a relatively small price to pay for her son's safety and a peaceful if unsought early retirement. In six months, a year, at most, she'd test the waters, send out resumes to a handful of low-profile law schools in California. Unquestionably, in California. She missed her mother more than she had since the immediate aftermath of her death. Mama would not be waiting for her in California, but all the same, Jessica wanted to go home.

For the second consecutive night, the most tortuous hours began the moment she put Jordan down in his crib and Vicky discreetly retired to her room. In the semi-darkness of the den, Jessica curled up in a fetal position on the sofa, trying unsuccessfully to concentrate on a frothy screwball comedy airing on Turner Classic Movies. She nursed a glass of chardonnay, but couldn't savor it; the wine was a tangible reminder of the vicious accusations with which Dean Mitchell had confronted her in such patronizing fashion. What had she done that was so wrong, that had been perceived as so dangerous, that they -- whoever the hell "they" were -- swiftly resorted to Gestapo-like tactics to bully her into submission? This was a country where the First Amendment guaranteed the right of every racist militia-man and hate-mongering Bible-thumper to advocate stockpiling explosives, bombing abortion clinics, and shipping blacks back to Africa; where Nazis could proudly parade through Jewish communities, and smut peddlers could publish the most hateful, degrading photographs of naked women bound and spread-eagled and defecated upon; where lunatics on the Internet could propound labyrinthine, paranoid theories about bar-codes and black helicopters and the "Zionist Occupied Government."

In this, the land of the free and home of the brave, she was being forcibly silenced for merely daring to suggest that maybe, just maybe, an authentic miracle had taken place. A miracle in which she didn't even believe.

Suddenly, it all struck her as ridiculously absurd. She burst into jagged laughter. She kept thinking of an elaborately choreographed scene from an old Mel Brooks movie, "The History of the World, Part 1," where a chorus-line of enrobed Torquemadas danced and sang "*The In-qui-siiiiii-tion!*"

"So silly. So silly," she whispered to herself, cuddling an oversize cushion.

And then the doorbell rang.

Panic jolted her into alertness. She shut off the TV, and huddled, still as ice, in the darkness.

The bell rang a second time.

What should she do? If she continued to ignore the bell, the Men in Black might break down the door, burst in and seize upon Jordan, as a means of assuring her cooperation. On the other hand, if she answered, and they abducted her then and there, what motive would remain for harming her son?

She leaped to her feet.

She'd been a goddamn coward yesterday, capitulating to them in declaring herself as well as Cordelia Davis a fraud.

Her fledgling career as coward made her hate herself.   Jessica squared her shoulders and went to answer the door.

She peered through the peephole, and her heart flew to her throat. Her fingers fumbled with the burglar alarm, the chain, the dead-bolt.

Icy wind rushed in, but she didn't feel it as he swept her into his arms and held her tight.

Chapter 9

Only after breaking the embrace and locking the door behind him did she feel awkward, suddenly self-conscious. She wished her bathrobe was handy. "You're crazy -- what are you doing here?"

"I need to hear from you face to face what the hell's going on."

Here in the bright light of the foyer, he looked tired, haggard. Seven days had seemed to age him that many years.

She wondered if he was thinking the same thing about her.

She led him into the living room. But neither of them sat down. "I'm not going to tell you anything. I want out, Alex. Absolutely, one-hundred-percent out."

"You know that anything you tell me will be confidential." He shook a cigarette out of a softpack. "You mind . . . ?"

Ordinarily she would have, but the very sight of the Marlboros sparked a Pavlovian reaction in her. "Not if you let me bum one." She reached into a squat "bombe" chest and found an ashtray.

After taking a long drag, she felt somehow more confident. "Look, Alex, I'm sure you know what's happening to me, and maybe you even have some ideas as to the who and why. But I don't want to hear it. This is your crusade, not mine anymore."

"Jessica, you don't have to give up the fight. You've just gotta be careful about how you wage it."

"Like you?" she challenged quietly, pouring them each a cognac from a lead-crystal decanter. "Aren't you taking a huge risk flying out here? For all I know, the sons of bitches have me under surveillance."

"I don't think so," he said, accepting the cognac. "You've done exactly what they wanted. Shit, Jessica, you could call a press conference tomorrow and retract your retraction. You could proclaim to the whole goddamn world how your life has been practically ruined just for suggesting Sister might be for real. And you know what? Nobody'd believe you." He didn't bother disguising his anger. "They foisted on you Apollo's gift to Cassandra, and you fucking accepted it."

Jessica bristled. "I'm sure Renie would be proud of your grasp of Greek mythology!" Poor Cassandra, blessed with the gift of prophecy, doomed never to be believed. She didn't appreciate the analogy.

"What I'm saying is that you're safe. Completely ineffectual, but safe."

"Get off your goddamn high-horse!" she snapped. "Who are you to show up at my doorstep in the middle of the night to lecture me about my integrity?"

He brushed back an unruly strand of black hair from his face. "Look, I didn't mean to put you on the defensive."

"Like hell!"

"C'mon, Jessica. Don't you want to know who's behind this bullshit? Don't you think that everybody's entitled to know what's going on?"

She sank into an oversized, boxy chair, tucking her feet underneath her. "They essentially got me fired from Georgetown, Alex. Somebody even went so far as to plant cocaine in my office. Don't you get it? I'm outgunned, you're outgunned, we're all fucking outgunned. Whether it's the FBI or CIA or Interpol, it ultimately doesn't matter. They hold all the cards, and I'm not going to risk my child's well-being to take up arms in a losing battle."

Her own flat, dispassionate voice sounded almost strange to her ears.

Alex's expression tautened; a tic worked in his clenched jaw. "This is an outrage. I wish to God you'd let me tell your story."

"Don't you dare," she hissed. "Do you want me to lose my son?"

"Christ, they chose their target well!"

She hugged a pillow. "Why don't you try it yourself, Alex, and see how far you get? What do you think might happen to you if you started writing stories about the possibility Sister's anything other than a sham? Your editors would start rejecting your pieces, and if you persisted, they'd invent a reasonable cause to fire you." Her lips curled bitterly. "Where would you go from there? Wouldn't you begin to wonder about your personal safety -- about the well-being of your friends, your family -- your wife?"

He scowled, lit up a fresh cigarette.

Jessica eyed him coldly. "Or maybe there's more you neglected to tell me. Maybe you have children, too."

"Look," he said, pacing, "you never gave me a chance to explain myself. I don't have kids, and as far as I'm concerned, my marriage is over."

Now she was sorry she'd raised the topic. "Stop -- stop. I really don't want to get into this. What I'm saying is that even if you were to uncover the cover-up, and even if I were fool enough to help you, do you honestly think you'd find a single medium to air it? You'd end up just another wacko on the Internet with a Website and e-mail address." She sighed unhappily. "Cassandra again."

He finally sat down on the couch opposite her, leaning forward tensely. "I don't think so, Jessica. There's a popular movement afoot in New Orleans that nobody's really covering. I've been following it, but only from the most apolitical, human-fucking-interest angle. Every day, more people are showing up in the city, not as tourists but as pilgrims. Right now, they're mostly from Central America. But I have a feeling that's gonna change soon."

This was startling news. She'd seen no such reports in the *Post* or on the evening news. "But what does that change? Think how easily these people could be trivialized as poor, illiterate peasants who can see the image of the Virgin Mary in a loaf of day-old bread!"

"True -- except probably a hundred million people saw that same loaf of bread on live TV."

At once she sat up with a jolt. "Something just occurred to me," she said nervously. "I can't recall seeing a single replay of the video from the Cathedral. Until the last couple of days, I've watched TV almost constantly." She wracked her brains. "Sometimes they show the funeral cortege, or the protest outside the Louisiana death house when she was shot. But they never show her in the church, climbing out of the coffin and speaking."

"Shit," Alex said, impressed. "I've barely had the TV on. I'll follow up on that."

"How could I not have noticed before!" Jessica said, still reeling from the revelation. "I mean, think of all of the media images burned into our brains, from Jack Ruby shooting Oswald to the Bronco chase and Diana's wrecked Mercedes. They were aired over and over on TV until you couldn't escape them if you wanted to!"

"Aren't you a little young to remember Ruby?" he jested darkly.

She ignored him. "This is sinister, Alex. This is so sinister. Why are they so frightened by her?"

"I think we both know the reasons for that. I think what's really gotten them running scared is the absence of a single, plausible explanation. When TWA 800 blew up mid-air and popular opinion started leaning toward the missile theory, there was the FBI and CIA presenting their pretty computer graphics and a single, credible alternative theory. True or not, it calmed people down."

She nodded, leaning forward to swipe another cigarette from his pack on the glass-top coffee table. "Same thing with the CIA-Contra drug story. They held public hearings that really didn't resolve much of anything, but it was as if the ritual of just *seeming* to look into the charges made the story go away." It was as if her mind, numbed by the events of the past few days, had been jump-started. She felt alive again.

She leaped to her feet to freshen their drinks. "What you're talking about is really analogous to a prosecutor preparing to go to trial," she said as she replaced the crystal top on the decanter. "It's not enough just to have a series of facts, however damning. You have to put forward a theory of the case, a unified story that will tie all the pieces of evidence together for the jury. And that's precisely what Cordelia's naysayers lack -- some blame the anti-death penalty movement, some the Vatican, some the incompetence of the New Orleans coroner --"

"No shit. I heard the other day that Disney was behind it all."

She laughed. "It's finally making such sense! I couldn't understand why they were so anxious about me, when all I did was try to point out that none of us yet understands what happened."

He smiled back. "And now you realize why that's the most dangerous thought of all." He set down his drink. "You checked out the chat rooms lately?"

She made a face. "Not for years. I can't stand them -- all they do is provide sexually frustrated teenage boys a forum for venting their rage against women and gays. One time Gregg and I were bored and logged onto the NBA chat, and these idiots were accusing this player or that one of being a quote, unquote fag."

"Where's your computer?"

"Upstairs in my study."

"Come on, I want to show you something."

Though mildly skeptical, she grabbed her drink and the ashtray, and they tiptoed up to the study. Though Jessica closed the door, she warned him that they should keep their voices low. "Jordan's bedroom is just across the hall."

He nodded.

He sat down at her computer table, while she yanked another chair to his left. He logged on to America Online, using his own account and screen name. Which, she happened to notice, was "CHE 1999." "Now you show your true colors, you commie," she teased.

He chuckled. "That's me -- '*socialisma o la muerta.*'"

To her astonishment, there were at least a dozen Sister Cordelia Websites, about half devoted to the nun and committed to the reality of her resurrection, the others promoting conspiracy theories about the hoax from the various perspective of atheists, Evangelical Christians, right-wing survivalists, and cyber-nerds. "These sites tend to attract the extremists on both sides," Alex explained. "I want you to see what's going on in the public rooms."

His fingers darting over the keyboard, he finally double clicked on "From the Left." The box on the right of the screen informed them that twenty-one people currently "occupied" the room, most with cryptic, occasionally colorful monikers.

"Just watch," he said.

She leaned closer to scrutinize the live text appearing on the monitor.

"*BYTEME14: Tracy! That you? It's been ages!*

DEMOGRL: It's moi. Been dying -- work sucks and so do I. :)

BYTEME14: LOL.

GOPROCKS: I bet you do. Or do feminists still believe in giving head?

DEMOGRL: GOP, spare us your ignorance. You're probably into autoeroticism -- the only way you'll get any.

BYTEME14: LOL, Tracy."

Jessica gave Alex a wry look. "I'm supposed to find this somehow enlightening?"

"Patience, mi amiga. Sometimes, their asses need a little kicking." He furiously typed a message into the long rectangular box at the bottom of the screen, punctuating it with an "ENTER."

"Che 1999" had officially joined the chat.

"*CHE1999: I hear Disney raised Sr. C. as PR for its next cartoon.*

DEMOGRL: What a bunch of crap. Where did you hear it, Che?

MIKE477: This is such a fucking conspiracy it's not even funny.

BYTEME14: Conspiracy on whose part Mike?

GOTHBABE99: Duh -- it's so obvious she's resurrected, and the media's trying to kill her again

CYBERSUX8: She's alive like my dick is

BYTEME14: Got problems with your virility, Cyber?

GOTHBABE99: Sr. Cordelia lives!

NOTPC333: It's a left-wing conspiracy. God wouldn't raise

DRAGON909: She does live. And the assholes on TV can't stand it

NOTPC333: a commie black bitch who stands up for murderers and babykillers!

CYBERSUX8: Obviously ZOG's behind it. A last-ditch assault on personal freedoms

NOTPC333: Last bitch attempt

CYBERSUX8: LOL, NOTP!

FIRE24: Personally, I believe in her. And I'm an agnostic.

DRAGON909: Me too Fire. And don't you find it weird the mortuary was blown up?

NOTPC333: The tree-huggers torched it so nothing could be proved.

FIRE24: Or disproved. And what about that CNN chick who was squashed like a bug?"

Jessica chilled. "I think I've seen enough."

Alex shook his head. "No -- just keep watching."

"SUECIDE2: She was friggin great. And now they're painting her like a crazed femin

DRAGON909: Right on, Sue. And she was inside the church, she saw everyth

SUECIDE2 : ist when all she said was that nobody knows!

DRAGON909: ing

NOTPC333: Bulldyke feminist probably wants to do the nun

MIKE477: FREE JESSICA ANDERS!

NOTPC333: The crazy bitch said Sissy was a fake, remember?

DEMOGRL: Like that wasn't coerced! Jessica rocks, Mike!

FIRE24: Jessica's the first victim of the new McCarthyism

SUECIDE2: No shit, Fire. Welcome to the Occupation."

Seeing how upset she was growing, Alex exited the chat room. The scroll of rapid-fire dialogue on the screen was replaced by a cheery generic AOL menu. "I know that must have been tough," he said. "But you see my point."

"It's just too strange," she murmured. "What does it mean?"

"It means this thing is too big to be quashed simply by shooting the messenger -- in this case, you -- or by supposed editorial decisions not to air the video from the funeral Mass. It's all over the Net, Jessica."

Jessica studied her hands, thinking. "No single, coherent theory. That's why they can't kill this." She looked up at him. "You know what, Alex? I believe I am safe. Thanks for showing me that. It's got me thinking -- they don't dare hurt me any more than they have. Those people, whoever they are -- Dragon and Suecide and Fire, all of them -- they'll recognize it can't all be coincidence."

"That's right," he said gently, taking her hand in his but barely squeezing it. "See, Jessica, they're flying blind too. This whole situation is so damned unprecedented, and you were an easy target, except their overkill tactics with you got a lot of people thinking, as you just saw for yourself."

Intellectually she wanted to yank her hand free, but emotionally, she couldn't bring herself to stir. "Who, deep-down, do you think is behind this?"

"CIA, FBI, multinational corporations," he said as casually as if reciting his Social Security number.

"You're joking."

"Nah, not really. I don't think it has a damn thing to do with ideology or theology, Jessica. I think it has everything to do with money."

"'It's the economy, stupid'?"

"Something like that. Render unto Caesar -- "

"*YOU HAVE MAIL*!" announced a bright electronic voice from the computer.

They both jumped, as if Oz the Great and Terrible had announced he'd been eavesdropping on them.

"Oh my God," Jessica gasped. "What -- "

"It's OK," he said, though he too had gone ashen. "I'm still logged on to my personal account."

Now Jessica flushed. "Look, I'm going to go back downstairs." She clambered to her feet.

"It's probably Renie," he said. "Either that or one of our friends from the chat room."

"You can tell me all about it." She snatched up her cognac and left him alone in the study.

Jessica had her own ideas as to the identity of his correspondent. But for the moment, their complicated personal situation was more than she could deal with. She took the opportunity to race to her bedroom, brush her teeth and comb her hair. Changing out of her pajamas into a silk nightgown would appear too obvious, but a spray of perfume -- Givenchy's Ysatis -- and her black velvet Donna Karan Couture robe over her flannels certainly could do no harm.

She slipped back downstairs, and plunked a fresh pine log into the fireplace. Spitefully crumpling the morning *Post* for kindling, she struck a long match and touched its flame tip to the newspaper.

God forgive her, but she was head-over-heels crazy about a married man.

And she feared she would be even had Renie O'Connor not conveniently spilled to her a veritable litany of personal indictments against Natalie Rivard Trujillo.

She refilled her cognac and leaned back against the couch, toasting her bare feet against the hearth.

She heard Alex's steps on the staircase, and she spun around.

Her smile froze, half-formed, on her lips.

Where before he'd been ashen, now he was a dull gray. His eyes seemed dark, hollow sockets in his skull. "I gotta go."

Jessica jumped up. "Oh, God, what is it?"

He was moving woodenly toward the door. "The e-mail was from my sister. My wife has killed herself." He spoke unemotionally, automatically, the depressive counterpart to the manic mechanical voice that had proclaimed, ten minutes before, "*YOU HAVE MAIL!*"

"Alex, I'm sorry, I'm so sorry! Could they have followed you here, and killed her as some kind of warning -- "

He seized her by the shoulders; for a moment she thought he was going to shake her, and she was afraid. His eyes were no longer dead; they were violent, and she would have cringed had she not glimpsed a flicker of anguish and self-recrimination that might have been her own reflection.

He bowed his head and kissed her, and his kiss was violent, too. Violent and despairing, and it told her everything. Natalie's death had nothing to do with the CIA or Sister Cordelia or multinational corporations.

Jessica felt his heart pounding against hers, and she knew that he blamed himself, and that maybe he had good cause. She clung to him all the tighter.

Finally he unwound her arms from around his neck, tender and reluctant. "I'd better go."

"I know this sounds crazy, but is there anything I can do?" Her hand lingered on his face, her thumb tracing his cheekbone.

He grasped her fingers and kissed them briefly. "Keep fighting the good fight, Jessica. Even if you have to do it on the sly."

She longed to tell him that he had proven himself to be her courage and her conscience, but it seemed somehow inap-propriate. So instead, she gave him a quick hug, and sent him off into the night.

It was the hardest decision she'd ever made in her life, no less difficult for the moral imperative behind it.

She asked Gregg if he would take Jordy for a couple of weeks while she returned to New Orleans.

They sat in the kitchen over steaming cups of coffee, just as they had so many mornings over the years. Gregg, still boyish at forty, his sandy brown hair only tinged by a random glint of silver, listened soberly as she told him everything. He had, of course, already heard the rumors about CNN blackballing her, but he was patently horrified by her coerced resignation from Georgetown. "Jesus Christ, Jessie, you've got to fight this! Let me set up a meeting with one of the firm's employment law specialists. Nancy Meyer's real good -- you two will hit it off."

"No," she said flatly. "At least, not right now. Yes, I know the statute's short, but I don't want to deal with the publicity."

"But if you leave things as they are, your reputation's going to be tarnished. You know how the grapevine is."

Jordan, in his high-chair, gurgled. Gregg leaned over to chuck the baby under his chin. "That's my kid," he smiled. "That's my boy."

Jessica watched him. He may have turned out to be a lousy husband, but he was a damn good father.

Gregg turned back to her. "Won't you at least meet with Nancy?"

"Gregg, I can't. It's important that whoever is behind this believes I'm no longer a threat. Why do you think I called Debby King?"

"OK, OK. Consider me duly backed off. But I still don't understand exactly what you hope to accomplish by returning to the scene of the crime. Don't you think that will attract unwanted attention to yourself?"

"It may, but I think the media's predominant view of me is that I'm a little nutso. I'm going to make sure that works in my favor."

"To what end, though, Jessie?"

"I want to find out for myself what the truth is. Not to broadcast it, or even to clear my own name. For my personal peace of mind, Gregg, I've got to know." She searched his eyes. "Can you possibly understand that?"

A hint of wistfulness flickered in his expression. "I suppose I can." He paused, took a sip of coffee. "Yep, I suppose I can."

She knew what he was thinking. "Don't beat yourself up. It's not like you're general counsel for the GOP -- or like I'm still putting in eighteen-hour days at the ACLU."

"Funny how things change, though." He stood. "I'll come back tonight for Jordan and Vicky, if that's all right with you."

She booked a ten p.m. flight; that gave her about four hours to effect her transformation from the time Gregg picked up Jordy and when she had to leave for the airport. If the good old boys -- and girls -- wanted to think she'd lost her mind, she would do her best to appear to confirm their suspicions.

The magenta dye made a huge mess in the bathroom, but it took well to her softly highlighted ash-blonde hair. She jumped back at the sight of herself in the mirror. The fuchsia was a color she was sure appeared nowhere in nature; for five minutes she intensely regretted her impulsive act, and wondered where she could secure a decent wig at this time of the evening.

But then she reminded herself she was adopting this costume not as a fashion statement, but for purposes of utmost gravity. She peered back into the mirror and laughed. "You do look like you've lost your marbles, lady!"

She blew dry her newly roseate mane, then carefully applied the makeup she'd purchased at the same bohemian cosmetics boutique where she'd bought the dye. With a slender brush she applied violet eyeshadow in huge raccoon rings around her eyes. She hadn't been able to bring herself to buy black lipstick, but the wine-red was still more flamboyant than any color she'd worn since Steve's Halloween party nine years ago, when she'd come as a vampire.

Her sleek, elegant Calvin Klein and Donna Karan suits would remain hanging in her closet. She packed jeans, sweaters, leggings, and tee-shirts. One dress -- a gypsyish black velvet Betsey Johnson that Grace had talked her into buying two years before. Jessica had never worn it because she was afraid it made her look like Stevie Nicks, circa 1975. It was the kind of dress in which the Jessica Anders she played on TV wouldn't have been caught dead.

Well, for all intents and purposes, that Jessica Anders *was* dead. All that this flame-haired phoenix shared with her was a name. And maybe not even that.

Maybe she'd take to calling herself Cassandra.

Chapter 10

It was nearly one by the time she checked into the Royal Orleans Hotel on St. Louis Street. Despite Jessica's wild hair and black sunglasses, the reservationist was chipper and polite. In this town of Mardi Gras and Anne Rice publicity stunts, Jessica guessed her "costume" was pretty tame stuff.

As she crossed the lobby to the elevator, she actually passed a CNN stringer she knew fairly well. He didn't look twice at her. In her third floor room, with its iron grillwork balcony overlooking St. Louis, Jessica tossed off her dark glasses and dialed Renie in Palo Alto, where it would only be ten.

"Renie, this is Jessica. How's Alex?"

"Oh, God," Renie half-sobbed. "You heard?"

"Yeah. Have you talked to him?"

"No," Renie said, "but I've talked twice to Lily. Jessica, it's terrible. Lily says he's torturing himself with guilt. Damn that little bitch! She did it to punish him!" Renie was now crying openly.

"Maybe. Are you going to the funeral?"

"Lily doesn't think there's even going to be a funeral. Natalie was one of those smarmy atheist poseurs who claimed she wanted her ashes scattered at sea, and then a big party held in her memory. The bitch!"

"I wish there were something I could do for him. Maybe you should fly down there anyway, Renie. I'm sure he needs the support of his good friends at a time like this."

"I'm going to talk to Lily about it tomorrow. Do you have Alex's home number, just in case you want to call him?"

"I doubt I'll be calling him, at least not for a few days. But give me his number anyway."

Renie recited the number, and Jessica scribbled it down. "Thanks, Renie. I'll stay in touch."

"Jessica?" Renie said timidly.

"Uh-huh?"

"You and Alex are in love, aren't you."

Jessica said nothing.

"I hope so. I hope you are," Renie said softly.

"I'll talk to you soon, kiddo. You're a good friend to Alex."

She grabbed her leather swing-coat and dark glasses, and left her room.

But this time she didn't head for Bourbon Street. Rather, she set off in the opposite direction. A two block stroll took her to Jackson Square. St. Louis Cathedral looked all the more imposing and luminous against the dark sky; its Gothic spires seemed to shoot directly up into the night. A lump formed in Jessica's throat as she stared at the cathedral in all its starkness and grandeur.

Then she saw them, the people Alex had referred to as "pilgrims." Several groups of them, gathered in loose semicircles in the square, on their knees, praying. Some seemed to be saying the Rosary. Meanwhile, the usual packs of giddy, drunken tourists trampled through the square, most ignoring the devotees, a few jeering obscenities.

Oh, if it were only true . . .

For half an hour, she just stood there, watching them pray, moved by and envious of their faith. Lulled by the cadences of their murmured Spanish, she barely noticed when it started to rain.

Then the old Jessica Anders revived with a start. Shit, she'd better get back to the hotel before magenta hair dye dripped all over her nine-hundred-dollar leather coat.

She requested a wake-up call for six a.m., but it turned out she was wide-awake well before the phone rang. She'd actually slept better than usual, but at five-thirty her eyes had snapped open and she knew there was no point in tossing and turning for the next thirty minutes.

Due to the early hour, her room-service coffee arrived promptly. She glanced at the copies of the *Times-Picayune* and *USA Today* the porter had brought in along with her tray. For the local paper, at any rate, Sister Cordelia still merited front-page coverage, though not the lead headline. One brief story simply stated that the nun was still believed to be in seclusion within the Convent of the Blessed Virgin in Metairie. Another, longer story detailed the recent influx of believers from Latin America. The angle of the story was distasteful, the reporter emphasizing the complaints of local merchants and bar owners about "loitering," which they claimed was hurting business. Dozens of grievances had been filed with the police and city managers about rampant urination and defecation in alleys and gutters. "And here, we're not even into Mardi Gras season yet," one pub-keeper griped.

When, presumably, it was quite all right for locals and visitors alike to piss and shit in public to their heart's content.

USA Today didn't carry a single item with a New Orleans dateline.

Outside, it was raining steadily. Jessica dressed warmly, tights under her jeans, a cotton turtleneck beneath her black cashmere pullover. Back on went the white pressed powder, the violet raccoon shadow, the vixenish lipstick. The dark glasses. Umbrella tucked under one arm, she stepped outside the Greek Revival hotel and asked a doorman to wave over a cab.

The driver was a pudgy towhead who smoked openly. "Where to, Miss?"

"The Convent of the Blessed Virgin, in Metairie."

"Okie-dokie." He pulled away from the curb.

Through her dark glasses, she saw him eyeing her curiously in the rear-view mirror.

"Betcha you're a writer for one of them rock magazines," he guessed.

She'd never been mistaken for that before. "No, I'm just curious, that's all."

"You'll be in good company then," he replied cheerfully, plainly not believing her. "Though maybe on a day like this, folks'll keep away." He maneuvered the cab onto the congested I-10. A few minutes later, he asked, "Ya'll from California?"

Jessica bit back a smile; the damn hair color had apparently altered the very way she was perceived by the world. Yesterday a serious, no-bullshit legal scholar; today, a rock'n'roll scribe from La La Land. "I'm from San Francisco," she said, which was technically the truth.

"Frisco. That used to be a great damn city till the fags took it over." He lit up a fresh cigarette. "Now, don't get me wrong. I'm not tryin' to pass judgment against anybody's 'lifestyle.' I just don't want to see it right under my nose, on every friggin' streetcorner. Does that make me a bigot?"

"Yes, as a matter of fact, it does."

He wheezed with laughter. "'Course, you're used to it, bein' from there and all! You sure shoot from the hip, I'll give you that, Miss!"

By the time the cab reached Metairie, the rain was driving down so hard the windshield wipers could barely keep up. The cabbie stopped. Through the rain-spattered window, Jessica could make out a crowd of perhaps three hundred people milling about, and, just beyond them, a gated two-story white stucco building topped by a cross.

"Y'all want me to swing back by in an hour?" the cabbie offered as Jessica paid her fare. "Taxis can be hard to come by on a day like this."

"Thanks, but I don't know how long I'll be."

She pushed out of the cab, opening her umbrella. If this were a small crowd, she had to wonder what the turn-out was like on a sunny day. Why the hell weren't the news media covering this?

Here, the assembly was more heterogeneous than in Jackson Square. Black and white faces mingled among the brown; prayers were accompanied by quiet hymns. Jessica spotted more than a dozen members of the Catholic clergy, priests in their collars, nuns in their simple head-dresses. There was also an identifiable faction of nonideological curiosity seekers, mostly in their twenties, laughing and sharing binoculars and Thermoses of coffee.

And most maddening of all, there were the media people, press passes dangling from lapels of London Fog and Burberry's raincoats. Two cameramen, one from CNN, the other from ABC, trained their huge lenses through the iron gates of the austere convent.

They knew what was going on, and were simply choosing not to report it. Sure, they'd excuse themselves by insisting that without an appearance by Cordelia Davis, they had nothing to report. But what about all these people gathered here, and in Jackson Square, and on the Internet, who wanted so desperately to believe in the miracle? Why wasn't their story being told?

Jessica managed to slough her way through the mud, and reach the gate. She wrapped one gloved hand around a wrought iron bar, the other clutching her umbrella. The lace curtains of the convent were drawn, but behind them was light, the flitting of occasional movement within. The sisters were going about their business.

Presently the front door opened. Jessica gasped, but no one else holding vigil seemed especially surprised. A plump, pigeon-like nun in a yellow slicker waddled out, carrying a tray of what looked to be wedges of fresh skillet cornbread covered with a sheet of cellophane. Grinning, Sister bade everyone "Bonjour," yanked open the gate, and handed the tray to a young, earnest-looking priest. He helped himself to a slice, then passed the tray on.

Jessica, fascinated, realized that this repast had become a ritual. She half-expected the cornbread to keep multiplying. But within minutes the tray was empty.

Here came the pigeon-like Sister again, with reinforcements.

Jessica observed several of the journalists eagerly gobbling down the skillet-bread, and she glowered at them through her dark glasses.

She took none for herself. It was clear to her that many, if not most of the people here had been camped out for days. She, a neophyte with fake hair and little faith, was but a cab-ride away from a rich Creole lunch of oysters Rockefeller and bouillabaisse, if she so chose.

The skillet-bread smelled superb, nonetheless, cutting through the heavy scent of rain and Spanish moss.

When the door opened a third time, no one paid any particular heed, not the faithful nor the curious, not the journalists nor Jessica herself. It was only when the slight black nun was halfway to the gate that they all realized, at once, she was not Sister Mary Pigeon bearing a fresh tray of cornbread.

It was Cordelia Davis, walking slowly, naturally, toward them, her large eyes worried and fixed upon a figure concealed to most of the shocked onlookers by an umbrella.

Had the crowd, the world, gone silent? Jessica thought, her heart banging as the nun's huge liquid eyes met hers. And then Sister Cordelia was inches away from her, and her warm, bare hand wrapped around Jessica's gloved one gripping the iron bar. "I know what you've been going through," Sister Cordelia said softly, in that low, almost musical contralto that Jessica had grown to love. "Be strong, and have faith. You'll be fine."

Jessica, tears streaming down from her dark glasses,
clutched Sister's hand. "I need to know --"

"You'll know."

Three hundred stunned witnesses seemed to recover simultaneously. They pushed
and shoved toward the locked gate, shouting, wailing, a few waving microphones, as
Sister Cordelia released Jessica's hand and headed back toward the convent, her spine
straight, her pace brisk and dignified.

A young woman shrieked as she was knocked in the head by a video camera.
Serpentine hands reached through the iron grillwork fence, grasping after Cordelia Davis
even as she disappeared into the convent and the heavy door shut. Jessica's umbrella was
crushed against the gate, and she was glad for her stupid sunglasses, as an exposed spoke
narrowly missed gashing her left temple. Someone was yanking her elbow, dragging her
away from the gate. Jessica fought until her fingers lost their grip on the curved bone of
black iron.

"What happened? What did Sister Cordelia say to you?"
Ann Magee of CNN demanded excitedly.

The minicam bore in on her. Jessica recognized the familiar "on" light. They
were being carried live.

Jessica removed her sunglasses and looked directly into the camera. Ann
blenched, recognizing her despite her bizarre hair and makeup.

But it was too late; the camera was running, and the live-feed was airing nation-
wide.

In a clear, composed voice, Jessica replied. "She said I was right, and you guys
were wrong."

Be strong, and have faith. She forced her way through the swarming mob,
ignoring the microphones pushed toward her face, the shouts of "Jessica! Just one more

question!" that chased after her. She kept her eyes straight ahead of her, dully regretting she hadn't taken up the homophobic cabbie on his offer to swing back by in an hour.

A chunky, balding man in his late thirties, press-pass pinned to his oversized down jacket, dodged in front of her. Jessica drew back, startled, but the man barked at the media throng, "Hey, you guys, cut her some goddamn slack! She said she doesn't have anything else to say!"

Jessica stared at him dumbly. Surely this blustery, agitated little man was, despite his press-credentials, a CIA operative, ready to sweep her off for a "debriefing." For even as he was lambasting the horde of reporters he was waving frantically for a cab.

Miraculously, a bright yellow taxi slid over. The man shoved her inside. To her surprise, he slammed the door shut without joining her.

She'd caught a glimpse of his name on his press-pass before the cab zoomed off.

Haberman, Walter, Associated Press.

She promised the cabbie, this time a Caribbean black man, a hundred dollars if he could contrive to lose the motorcade pursuing them along the 10 East. It was a wild ride indeed, as he cut onto Orleans Avenue and ripped down Lakeshore Drive, tires screeching, the rain pounding furiously.

Somewhere near the Southern Yacht Club, along the silvery waters of massive Lake Pontchartrain and the bleak, flat horizon, she realized they were no longer being pursued.

Jessica counted out five twenties, plus the regular fare. "Now, if you'll drop me off at one of these little seafood restaurants, I'll be just fine." She was well aware that even though they'd temporarily ditched the reporters, someone would have surely taken down the cab number and license plate.

He was clearly thinking the same thing. "Tell ya what, lady. I go get Mista Broussard from the club. He big rich man -- he let you use his limo."

"I don't know," she fumbled.

He twisted around and winked at her. "This 'bout Sister, lady. She talk to you -- I wanna keep you OK."

She studied his face, decided to trust her intuition. "All right."

Ten minutes later, she was comfortably ensconced inside a stretch limo speeding toward downtown New Orleans.

Clearly, no one had yet learned where she was staying, for Royal Orleans' marble lobby was all but deserted. Jessica asked the receptionist to have the switchboard operator hold all calls save any from Gregg Monahan.

Safe in her room, she exhaled deeply and allowed herself to feel the exhilaration she'd held in check until she could regain her privacy. Now she could give in to an inexplicable wild joy headier than champagne. The memory of a scared little woman curled up fetal-style in the dark, afraid of her own heartbeat, dissipated like a bad dream.

She talked to me. She touched me.

And if the FBI charged through her door this very moment and dragged her off kicking and screaming to the same Federal loony bin that had housed John Hinkley and Ezra Pound, they still couldn't rewind the videotape that showed Sister Cordelia talking to her, or Jessica's triumphant interpretation of her message.

That was why she knew they weren't going to bother breaking down the door.

She could imagine what the pundits were opining, in all their sonorous mock-authority. Jessica, a disgruntled ex-employee, was in cahoots with Sister Cordelia; obviously the two had set up today's "surprise" encounter. A few eyewitnesses would be interviewed, and they would express doubts as to whether the black nun had actually been Cordelia Davis. After all, it was so crowded, and the rain hampered visibility. And, of course, all black people looked alike. No one would say it, but it would be implied, which was somehow worse. Owen Shawn would mug and encourage his panelists to shout over one another. And ultimately, they would all conclude that Sister's brief emergence from the convent meant absolutely nothing, and that Jessica Anders had gone from respected legal analyst to flake and publicity whore in the mere span of ten days.

But more people previously suspended in uncertainty would be swayed, if not to believe, then to hope it were true. More and more people would flock to New Orleans and join Internet chats, and sooner or later, the media would have to stop pretending that the resurrection -- whatever it ultimately turned out to be -- had simply never taken place.

She was too thrilled to ponder a more recent mystery: what Cordelia Davis had meant when she'd said, "I know what you've been going through."

Strange -- she wasn't the least tempted to turn on the television.

Instead, she drew the curtains, stripped down to her camisole and bikini underwear, and crawled back into bed.

For five, ten minutes, her mind continued to race, replaying her brief exchange with Sister, the crush of people against the wrought-iron gate, her defiant response to CNN's Ann Magee, her mad escape, facilitated by the rumpled reporter who reminded her of George on "Seinfeld." But then, it was as if nearly three weeks of four-hours-a-night sleep caught up with her. She drifted off.

She dreamed it was her wedding day, her wedding day to Gregg. She was in a long, lacy white dress with a chiffon veil and huge train, and she felt ridiculous. Why had she let Grace talk her into this gown? It was more appropriate to a twenty-year old June bride, not a thirty-six year old divorcee. And why was Gregg insisting they marry in a church, when she was an agnostic and he an atheist?

And, a part of her subconscious nudged, weren't she and Gregg already married?

She was walking down the aisle of St. Louis Cathedral, clutching a bouquet of pink roses. Because her father was dead, she walked alone. All of a sudden she realized she was wearing her Nikes instead of white satin pumps, and she could only hope her long skirt concealed her scuffed running shoes.

Gregg, handsome in his tux, awaited at the altar. His best man was Owen Shawn, who was mugging and rolling his eyes. Stranger still, the usher was the President, and Jessica thought Gregg had committed a grave *faux pas* by asking Owen Shawn, and not the Chief Executive, to be his best man.

Jessica and Gregg knelt down before the altar. But the priest was nowhere in sight. Sister Cordelia, looking worried, emerged from the sacristy. "He's caught in traffic. You'd better think about rescheduling."

Jessica woke up, at first disoriented. Where was she? What time was it? She switched on the nightstand lamp. My God, it was one in the afternoon; she'd slept over three hours.

She threw on the silk kimono-robe she liked to travel with. The message light on the phone was illuminated. Jessica grimaced. It could only mean the media had tracked her down. Damn, why hadn't she the foresight to register under an assumed name? She wasn't even a real journalist, and *she* knew how easy it must have been to find her. All anyone would have to do was grab a phone book and start calling hotels. She'd made the task all the simpler by staying at one of the Quarter's most visible instead of a discreet bed and breakfast.

Ignoring the message button, she called the switchboard directly. "How many messages do I have?" she asked, holding her breath.

"Over thirty, I'm afraid, Miss Anders. The voice-mail tape ran out and we had to start taking them by hand."

"Damn. I suppose the lobby is crawling with reporters."

"Actually, Miss Anders, last I checked, at least half of them had left. Looked to me like the ones hanging around were pretty much local folks."

Jessica frowned. "OK. Thanks. No calls from a Gregg Monahan?"

"No, ma'am. Do you still want his calls put through?"

"Absolutely. Now, could you do me a great favor and transfer me to Room-Service?"

"Have a nice day, Miss Anders."

She ordered coffee and a turkey sandwich, then reluctantly turned on the television.

ABC news, their "special bulletin" banner at the bottom of the screen, was covering a live press conference with the head of the FBI. "We are in contact with the terrorists aboard Delta Flight 79," the FBI chief was saying grimly. "We continue to negotiate for the safe release of the three-hundred-and-ten passengers and the eight-man crew."

""Have you verified their claim that they do in fact possess plastic explosives?" a reporter asked.

Jessica switched to CNN, which was covering the same press conference. Their bulletin read "Breaking News: Hostage Crisis at JFK." A split screen showed a live shot of a Delta 747 on the runway in New York.

Not even she had grown so paranoid to think this crisis had been staged to deflect attention away from the Sister Cordelia story. Surely not even Alex could believe the Powers That Be, as he liked to call them, would go so far as to jeopardize the lives of over three hundred people. That is, if Alex was in the state of mind to still give a damn.

The FBI press conference ended, and the CNN anchor recapped the events as they currently stood. About an hour before, two men in their early thirties, both apparently of Middle Eastern origin, managed to smuggle a semi-automatic handgun aboard a flight bound for London. The huge plane had just begun taxiing when one of the men drew the weapon from of his carry-on bag. They were threatening to blow up the plane unless a number of Palestinian detainees were freed from an Israeli prison.

Jessica herself was enrapt. Those poor people on the airplane; how terrified they must be. She couldn't even bring herself to channel-surf to check if any of the local stations were carrying the Sister Cordelia story.

The precarious hostage situation at JFK was plainly the reason the national media cleared out of the Royal Orleans.

All the same, when a knock sounded on her door, she peered through the peephole to make sure it was only room service.

She accepted the tray, signed off on the tab, then set the covered silver dish and coffee pot on the night-table, planning to eat while she watched TV. The 747 looked eerily abandoned on the tarmac. Much of JFK had been shut down, producing a nightmare for travelers across the country, as flights were re-routed, delayed, and cancelled from coast to coast.

Eyes still glued to the screen, Jessica removed the lid from the plate and picked up a half of her sandwich. Something fluttered to the floor.

Jessica set the sandwich back on the plate and looked down. A folded paper lay by her bare foot.

Uneasily, she picked it up.

"Ms. Anders, I'm the guy who got you into the cab in Metairie this morning. I'm also a friend of Alex Trujillo, who's going nuts trying to get in touch with you. He wants you to call him in L.A. ASAP. If you're pissed about my investigative techniques, please take it out on me and not the bellboy who let me stash this note on your tray. Best, Walt Haberman, Associated Press."

Jessica could not imagine what Haberman hoped to gain by lying to her. She hastily dialed the number Renie had given her last night.

"Hello?" answered a woman's somber voice.

"May I please speak with Alex? This is Jessica Anders."

"I'll get him right away." Jessica heard the woman calling his name urgently.

"Jessica!" He sounded both relieved and worried.

"Your friend Walt Haberman managed to get a note to me." She paused. "How are you?"

"Forget how I am. Jessica, baby, are you out of your fucking mind?"

"Apparently, if you listen to the media."

"What you did today was either the bravest or the stupidest thing I've ever seen. Did you notice the expression on that reporter's face after you said what you did?"

"It seems like a blur. How much coverage did it get, and what the hell were you doing up that early in the morning to have seen it?"

"CNN gave about an hour to it before returning to regular programming. I'm sure you can guess what they were saying." He left the second part of her question unanswered.

"Right. They got a lot of mileage out of the purple hair."

"Mileage you handed them on a fucking silver platter, chica," he said sternly.

"Don't you see, as long as they think I'm a kook, I'm OK?"

"Maybe. I'm bothered by the timing of this hostage thing in New York."

"Alex, we can't go on endlessly thinking every national or world crisis is somehow connected to Sister! The world can be a pretty horrible place all on its own."

He was quiet for a second or two. "When are you going back to D.C.?"

"I'm not . . . sure."

"I'll be back in a couple of days. Try to lay low until I get there. You can trust Walt. He's a bulldog, but a decent guy."

"Alex, do you think that's such a hot idea? You should take more time -- "

"Don't go there, Jessica," he warned.

"All right, I won't," she said gently. But she silently hoped that his family would talk him out of returning to work while the shock, and, surely, the grief were still so raw.

"Jessica."

"Yes?"

"What did she really say to you?"

"It was strange, Alex. She came right over to me and she clasped my hand. She said, 'I know what you've been going through. Be strong, and have faith.'" Her voice trembled as she repeated the words aloud for the first time.

"Oh God," he said jaggedly.

Afraid he was crying, she struggled mightily not to follow suit. "Hey, listen. I'm going to tell you something that will probably convince you I really have gone crazy."

"What?" he said, his voice strained.

"Don't breathe it to a soul. But for the first time, I'm starting to think maybe she is for real."

She hung up soon after, ate her lunch and watched hypnotically the images on the screen: the airliner under siege; the latest FBI debriefing; the Attorney General expressing quiet outrage and vowing to end the crisis through negotiation, not violence. CNN had learned more about the two terrorists: each held Egyptian passports, and one had apparent links to Hezbollah.

It was with great reluctance that she muted the sound and pressed the message button on the phone.

The first several were from legitimate news organizations: CNN, MSNBC, Reuters, the Associated Press, the last represented, she noted by Walt Haberman. These were followed by a couple of interview requests from local TV stations, the *Times-Picayune*. But then came the money offers from tabloid TV shows, the *Enquirer*, the *Globe*. Two rather unnerving obscene messages, one calling her a "stupid lying cunt," the other a servant of the Antichrist. Another message from Walt Haberman, informing her that Alex had contacted him and was worried. Haberman added that he was staying at the Royal, as well, begging her to call him or get in touch with Alex in Los Angeles. Three frantic calls from Alex.

She decided she'd better let Haberman know she'd gotten his message, at least the last, unorthodox one nestled between the two halves of her turkey-on-rye. She had the operator ring his room.

"Yeah, this is Walt Haberman."

"Walt, this is Jessica Anders. I appreciated the garnish on my sandwich."

"Whew! Believe me, I hated to invade your privacy like that. But Alex was driving me nuts. You call him?"

"I just got off the phone with him a little while ago. You did the right thing, Walt. I wanted to thank you, and thank you also for getting between me and that mob this morning."

"Man, you gave half the reporters in town a hell of a runaround. Who was that cabbie -- last year's Daytona 500 champ?"

She chuckled. "Trust me, I've had more harrowing rides to and from the airport."

"You've got guts, Jessica. Coming back like you did and getting Sister to talk to you."

"I didn't get her to talk to me. That's all I'm going to say on that matter, and you may, if you like, quote me."

"I guess you aren't interested in doing an interview? Sorry, but I've got to ask."

"I'm not playing coy, Walt. I just don't see the point. The media has portrayed me as someone who's off her rocker. If I try to present my side of the story, I'll come off sounding paranoid, and your credibility will be damaged if you appear to take me seriously."

"I'm not so sure anymore. What happened this morning has got a lot of us -- OK, a few of us -- thinking. Look, can we get together and discuss this in person?"

"I guess I owe it to you to hear you out, but no promises. You're in 421? I'll be up in half an hour."

Walt Haberman ushered her in distractedly. "Something's happening at JFK," he said, gesturing toward the TV.

Onscreen, a paramedic van was rolling up to the Delta 747. CNN's on-site reporter was providing a breathless narrative. "I'm not sure what's going to happen, Bernie. We have unconfirmed word that a passenger has taken ill. But how they're going to transport him or her to the emergency medical technician's van is anybody's guess."

"Shit," Walt muttered.

Now a firetruck was cruising up to the jet. "Jesus Christ, are they going to hurl the poor soul out the door like a sack of potatoes?" Jessica said, incredulous.

"If this weren't so dangerous it'd almost be funny," Walt agreed, as they watched a crew of firefighters hurrying to unfurl a large net.

Sure enough, the plane's door opened, and what appeared to be an elderly woman is a jogging suit was shoved out. Both the CNN reporter and anchor gasped audibly as the woman bounced down onto the safety net. "I see her moving, Bernie. Looks like she's OK," the reporter said.

"Can we turn this off for a while?" Jessica said, stomach churning. She fought a sudden impulse to dash from the room, out of the hotel, and hop a plane back to Washington and her Jordy. Only the knowledge that she'd have a damn hard time booking a flight, given the mess at JFK, kept her in place.

Walt snapped a button on the remote, and the screen went black. "You want some coffee?"

"No, I'm fine."

She sat down in an armchair, he on the bed. His room, unlike hers, had a view of the hotel's interior courtyard, but the brick patio and bubbling fountain were washed gray with rain. She wondered if New Orleans would ever feel the same.

Walt seemed awkward. "You sure I can't order you some coffee?"

He was obviously nervous around her, but why? Did he believe she was the lunatic, the loose cannon, the media were depicting?

She asked him outright.

"No, no," he said, and his surprise struck her as sincere. "It's just that you're so calm and ethereal. I'd be a nervous wreck if I was you."

"Calm and ethereal? Jesus, I have to dye my hair more often. First the redneck cabdriver who took me out to Metairie mistakes me for a stringer for *Spin* magazine. Now I'm 'ethereal.'"

Her open irony seemed to break the ice. "Let me tell you why I think an interview with you -- right now -- would have particular impact," he said, relaxing and getting down to business. "It's no secret, at least among us stragglers who've stuck around in New Orleans, that the major networks muzzled you. They don't like this Cordelia Davis story. The nun won't play the game -- she refuses to hold a press conference or turn water into wine. Until today, it was like, she rose from the dead, and that was that."

Jessica thought he was oversimplifying, but nodded and said nothing.

"In short, the story's static," he went on. "Alex has done a better job than anybody keeping it alive, because he has both an angle and an audience. The rest of us are left pretty much tracking Elvis sightings."

"Why has no one looked more closely into the bombing of the mortuary?" she said. "It hasn't received anywhere near the attention that Olympic Park did in '96, or the Birmingham abortion clinic in '98. A man was killed, and potentially important evidence destroyed."

"I can't answer that," he admitted. "It is kind of weird how quickly that trail turned cold."

"That's why there's no point in my giving you, or anyone, an interview. It's not as if I even know anything, Walt! All I ever did was act like a good lawyer, and presume Sister innocent until proven guilty. And look what's happened to me."

"But you came back," he said steadily. "You wouldn't let the fuckers keep you down, and so you came back. And she knew you did. She walked right up to you -- I saw it with my own two eyes. And she touched you, and she talked to you."

Jessica longed for a cigarette. "You don't smoke by any chance, do you?"

"Sorry," he said, reaching for the phone. "I'll have a pack sent up --"

"No, don't. I used to smoke two packs a day. It wasn't until I came here, to cover the funeral, I started up again."

She thought she was being discreet, but evidently not discreet enough. For Walt shrugged clumsily. "Alex's evil influence, I gather?"

She made a quick recovery. "Don't you see, Walt, what would happen were I to spill my guts to you? Some media flunkey, under the guise of investigative journalism, would uncover the fact that you're Alex's friend, and Alex and I are -- not involved, exactly -- but have a somewhat complicated relationship." Dying for a smoke, she knotted and unknotted her fingers.

"I heard about Alex's wife," Walt said. "Horrible."

"Yes, it was, and is, horrible. Can't you envision what they'd make of it? Let me be perfectly frank. I inherited a hell of a lot of money when my mother died at the obscene age of fifty-three. I can literally afford to be called a crackpot. Can you? Can Alex?"

Walt Haberman looked miserable. He had no answer for her.

"Good," she encouraged coldly.

"It's not," he said. "If Big Brother's out there, he should be exposed as the sonofabitch putz he is."

"Listen to me, Walt. He will be. People are smarter than the spin that's force-fed to them. They'll come, and she'll receive them. And then you'll have a real story to write."

She got up, patted him on the arm, then left him to his bewilderment.

Chapter 11

The hostage situation at JFK Airport continued into the night. Heeding Alex's advice, Jessica maintained a low profile. Shortly after leaving Walt Haberman's room she called Gregg to check on Jordan. He irritably informed her that he'd been besieged by reporters who'd gotten hold of his unlisted home number. "What are you doing, Jessica?" he demanded. "Do you even know anymore?"

She refused to justify herself to him. "I'm doing what I have to do." She insisted he bring the baby to the telephone, and she crooned for half a minute into his ear, hoping he recognized her voice.

She ordered a shrimp salad for dinner and watched the 747, now bathed by floodlights, until her eyelids grew heavy and she fell asleep with the TV still on.

This time she slept long and dreamlessly. She awakened to find the airliner still under siege, and journalists nervously speculating on the possibility of an Entebbe-like raid. The President was scheduled to address the nation at ten a.m. Eastern-time.

A mere hour from now.

That left her just enough time to shower, dress, and pin her now ridiculously identifiable hair into a hasty chignon. She draped a silk scarf over her head, and slipped downstairs to catch a cab back out to the convent in Metairie.

She couldn't imagine that more than a handful of local news minicams were still keeping watch outside the convent. The eyes of the country, guided by the media, were glued to the image of a lonely 747 on a Long Island runway. The Big Three and CNN finally had a legitimate excuse for ignoring the miracle in Louisiana, and Jessica was damned if she wasn't going to take advantage of it.

This morning, her cabbie was a morose-looking Iranian who kept volume on the radio high as he listened to the latest developments out of New York.

Her instincts served her well. Despite a mild drizzle, the crowd outside the convent had swelled to nearly a thousand people, many no doubt drawn by Sister's unexpected appearance in the garden the day before. But, so far as she could tell, no network cameras or crews were in sight, and the minicams bore the numbers and call letters of local affiliates.

Jessica lost herself easily in the throng. In her head-scarf and dark glasses, no one seemed to recognize her from yesterday.

A group of college kids in Tulane sweatshirts were sharing smoothies and blasting R.E.M.'s *Document* from a boom-box. *"Who bought the myth? Buy a jingo, buy America!"* jeered Michael Stipe. Jessica paused, remembering the song: "Exhuming McCarthy."

Many of the raggedy families from Jackson Square had joined the congregation. Wizened walnut faces and fidgety dark-eyed babies. Elderly *duennas* veiled in black, murmuring and blessing themselves. They milled about, clutching their candles and rosaries, as R.E.M.'s apocalyptic anthem, "It's the End of the World As We Know It (And I Feel Fine)" blared.

As the final, harmonic chorus sounded, it occurred to her again how flat the horizon was beyond the convent, a bleak crayon crease along Lake Pontchartrain --

"This one goes out to the one I love . . . "

She shoved past bodies toward the wrought-iron gate. She clung to the bars like a prisoner, but this morning, not even Sister Mary Pigeon seemed inclined to put in an appearance. Everything that yesterday seemed surreal and magical was by today's grim light muddy and material.

"Fire!" Michael Stipe wailed.

At length a nun came out, neither Sister Cordelia nor the cheerful plump dispenser of skillet bread. This woman was gaunt and bespectacled, perhaps sixty. "Please," she implored, having to virtually shout above the boom-box.

"Turn that thing off!" several in the crowd yelled.

Relative silence befell the assembly.

"All of our sisters are praying for the safe resolution of the situation in New York," the sister said. "I beg you to do the same, and afford us a little quiet and privacy in which to petition Our Lord for His mercy." Then she turned and went back into the convent.

Soon, many people began to shamble away, as if duly shamed by Sister's reproach. Catholics, Jessica guessed wryly, ones who likely remembered some Sister Mary Pius's first guilt-inducing reproach from kindergarten. Even she herself was feeling sheepish, selfish for coming again to Metairie in hopes of Sister Cordelia's singling her out a second time.

With great reluctance she released her grip on the fence. The Tulane students with the boom-box offered her a ride back to New Orleans in their Dodge van, and she accepted, given the scarcity of roving cabs today in Metairie.

"If Sister Cordelia puts in an appearance after all, I'm gonna kick myself," groaned the driver, a pony-tailed fellow with a Georgia accent.

"I'm sure she won't," said another student, a serious young woman wearing braces on her teeth. She swung around to address Jessica. "Your first time out to the convent?"

"Yes."

"Mine, too, though Rick and Cheryl have been before." She nodded toward the tall black girl sitting across from Jessica. "Cheryl was lucky enough to have been there yesterday."

Cheryl nodded. "It was definitely her -- Sister Cordelia. I had a great view, maybe ten feet down from the fence where she spoke to that crazy lady from CNN. I got so mad when all these people told reporters they couldn't be sure it was really Sister."

"Duh," mocked the young man driving. "Are you only *now* noticing that the media's been picking and choosing who they put on TV or quote in the paper?"

Jessica said very little; mostly she just listened and nodded. But their discussion heartened her. Even if they thought Jessica Anders crazy, all seemed healthily skeptical about the media's take on Sister Cordelia.

The morning hadn't turned out to be a complete disappointment after all.

She had them drop her off near the corner of Canal and Royal Streets. It was only a few blocks to her hotel, and she couldn't take the chance a media ambush might await her outside the Royal Orleans.

She ran into Walt Haberman in the lobby. "What's the latest out of New York?" she asked

"Still going on. The President said they're negotiating to get the Red Cross in to make sure the people on board are OK, and have enough supplies."

"You off to Metairie?"

"Don't tell me -- you just got back, and Sister delivered a revised version of the Sermon on the Mount. There goes my job."

"Your paycheck's safe, I think. Another nun -- she may have been the Mother Superior -- told everyone to let them alone. The sisters are praying for the hostages."

His eyebrows shot up. "And people actually left?"

"About a third, I'd say. The crowd's still pretty huge."

"Then I'm on my way." He buttoned his raincoat. "You free for dinner tonight?"

"Sure. As long as it's some place reasonably private." Then she colored, afraid she'd given him the wrong impression.

To her relief, he laughed. "I get it -- you're using me to make Alex jealous," he teased.

She started to remind him again that she and Alex were not involved, but chose not to. Walt was likely to wind up believing she really was making overtures to him!

But the thought of spending the rest of the day holed up in front of the television made her mildly queasy. She stopped at the gift-shop and purchased a pack of Merits. Once in her room, she left the TV off.

She ached for Jordan. What was keeping her from going home, plane delays or not? What was she really hoping to accomplish by remaining? She'd seen Sister Cordelia; she'd touched her and knew her to be real. She'd thumbed her nose at CNN and *Newsweek* and Georgetown, fittingly, on live TV. She'd done a decent job of fomenting faith in the nun; how many others were there like Cheryl, who'd also borne witness to Sister Cordelia's emergence from the convent and were telling everyone they knew exactly what they had seen?

But Jessica had done more than see Cordelia Davis. She had touched her, been spoken to by her. "*I know what you've been going through.*" Sister had to have singled her out for a reason, and Jessica could not bring herself to leave New Orleans until she understood why.

Mindlessly she unfolded the *USA Today* she hadn't taken time to scan earlier. All of the front-page stories related to various aspects of the terrorist siege of Delta Flight 79. Nothing she hadn't already learned last night from CNN. Her brother Steve was always bemoaning the pernicious effects, first of CNN, then of the Internet, on newspaper readership. Print journalists just couldn't keep up with twenty-four-hour cable stations or instant news on the Web. What do you care? she used to tease; you're a damn entertainment writer.

But on page 6 of the paper she spotted a brief wire account of Sister Cordelia's unexpected appearance in the yard of the Convent of the Blessed Virgin. Of course, the

African-American nun only "reportedly bore a strong resemblance to Cordelia Marie Davis." Two eyewitnesses were quoted as disputing whether the sister particularly looked like the late Cordelia Davis. "The nun appeared to exchange brief words with a woman outside the gate, later identified as Jessica Anders, a former legal correspondent with CNN. (For a related story, see A12)."

Jessica hastily flipped to page 12.

A headline leaped out at her. *"Who Is Jessica Anders?"*

The byline read, *"From the Washington Post."*

And a color picture showed her, with her wild hair and raccoon eye makeup, talking to CNN's Ann Magee outside the convent.

She was oddly calm as she scanned the story.

"From virtually the moment Sister Cordelia Marie Davis was apparently shot to death while protesting a Louisiana execution, Jessica Elaine Anders, 36, has been poised at ground-zero of the bizarre story. The former CNN legal analyst and Georgetown law professor was providing live on-air commentary when the murder took place. Anders was inside St. Louis Cathedral, on assignment for CNN, when Davis's 'resurrection' occurred. As recently as last Friday, Anders told syndicated columnist Debby King that she has resigned from both the cable news giant and her teaching post at Georgetown Law School for 'personal reasons,' stating emphatically she believes the so-called resurrection to be a fraud.

"Yet yesterday, it was Anders, her trademark blond hair dyed tomato red, whom Sister Cordelia Davis approached in her first public appearance since the abortive funeral. When asked by CNN's Ann Magee what the nun had said to her, an evidently hysterical Anders replied, 'She said that I'm right and you guys are wrong.' Anders managed to evade other reporters' questions and could not be reached at her New Orleans hotel.

"The recent, erratic behavior of a respected appellate expert and death-penalty foe cannot help but bring to mind for many another famous Jessica: Jessica Savitch, the late NBC anchor whose on-air breakdown, later linked to alcohol and drug abuse, effectively ended a promising career in broadcast journalism. Former colleagues at Georgetown, who have requested anonymity, hint that Anders had grown increasingly high-strung and unpredictable since filing for divorce late last year from husband Gregory H. Monahan, a partner in the prestigious Washington law firm of Montrose, Wayne, Davidson and Dubois. (The couple has a six-month old son.) 'Jessica was always the epitome of the Type-A, control freak personality,' says one former colleague. 'When she and [Monahan] split, she did her best to carry on as if it were business as usual. But a lot of us noticed little cracks around the edges.' CNN offered no official comment, but a Washington-based technical director for the news organization, Brent Fallows, disclosed last week to the Post that Anders seemed unusually distraught after the apparent assassination of Cordelia Davis, adding that he was surprised she was able to continue offering live commentary on the event.

"Fellow legal pundit Caroline Bruckner, who has shared dozens of televised panels with Anders, released the following statement: 'I regard what's happened to Jessica as a genuine tragedy. While we disagreed on many points of law, I always respected her as a scholar and lawyer. I'm just praying she gets the help she so clearly needs.'

"Jessica Anders was born in San Francisco, California, the second child of a neurologist and homemaker. (Both parents are deceased.) She received law degrees from the University of California at Berkeley's Boalt Hall and from Yale University. She worked as a deputy District Attorney in San Francisco, specializing in the prosecution of hate crimes, and at the American Civil Liberties Union, co-authoring several death-penalty appeals, before moving with her husband to the east coast. In an article arguing *against the constitutionality of the death penalty published in last year's* Stanford Law Review, *Anders described herself as a 'non-practicing Roman Catholic.'"*

Jessica had the eeriest sensation she was reading her own obituary.

Nothing she had read surprised her. Nor would she give the *Post* the satisfaction of outrage. Yes, they had effectively libeled her, implying not only that she was emotionally unbalanced and possibly a drug addict, but that she had a neurotic quasi-religious motive for insinuating herself into the Sister Cordelia affair. But how dare Steve, or Alex Trujillo, for that matter, argue for the loftier ethical standards of the print media as opposed to broadcast journalism?

Then she had a horrible thought. What if Gregg, however supportive he seemed about her need to return to New Orleans, started believing this bullshit? What if he sued her for permanent custody of Jordy?

She called him at work. "Gregory Monahan's office," answered his secretary.

"Denise, this is Jessica. Is Gregg in?"

"I'll put you right through, Jess." Denise's voice was pleasant, markedly nonjudgmental.

"Hi, how are you doing?" Gregg said urgently.

"You see the crap the *Post* published about me?"

He sighed. "Yeah. Oh, Jessie, have we ever got a lawsuit once this thing finally blows over."

Her eyes welled. Suddenly his loyalty counted a hell of a lot more than his marital fidelity. "Thanks for believing in me."

"I'm just sorry I didn't take any of those bastards' calls yesterday. After I saw that piece of crap in today's paper, I issued a statement, and if they don't publish it, then I'm the one who's filing suit." Papers rustled. "Want to hear it?"

"I would absolutely *love* to hear it."

"OK. 'I was married to Jessica Anders for twelve years, and I feel I know her as well as anyone in the world. Despite the dissolution of our marriage, which was amicable, I regard Jessica to be a lawyer and human being of unassailable-able integrity and deep principle. She also is a loving and conscientious mother. She is unequivocally not an abuser of alcohol or drugs. I am in frequent contact with her, and I can personally attest to her emotional stability. I resent the invasion of her privacy, and by extension, that of our son and myself. I am shocked and dismayed that the Washington *Post* would print such scurrilous allegations about Jessica, and am considering taking legal action.'"

She smiled weakly. "Better be careful, or they'll be calling you a loony next. You're a good Joe, you know that?"

"I hope you don't mind my little white lie."

"Which one -- that you found me to be emotionally stable?" she jested.

"That our separation was amicable," he replied carefully.

"I don't think it's a lie -- even a white one -- anymore."

"I'm sorry for what happened to us, Jessie. Can you ever believe me?"

She lit a cigarette. "Marriages are complicated. Grace tried to tell me as much a week or so ago, and I'm finally understanding what she meant. I want us to be friends, Gregg. For Jordy, but also for us."

"Will you let me file the mother of all libel suits when you get back?"

"I'll think about it. Kiss our baby for me, OK?"

"I will." He paused, then added, "Good luck on your search for clarity, Jessie. I have a feeling you just might find it."

Clarity. Gregg was right; that was precisely what her strange quest was all about. Not just clarity as to what exactly Sister's resurrection meant, for her and for the world. But clarity about herself, about discovering what she did and didn't believe. About which beliefs were worth fighting for, and which were best kept to herself.

Kierkegaard, she recalled from college, wrote that at a certain point one needed to take a leap of faith, ignoring the complacent rituals of what he contemptuously termed "Christendom." She still remembered a phrase that had struck her as an appropriate battle-cry even for an agnostic: "Purity of heart is to will one thing." But this gray afternoon, her youthful infatuation with Kierkegaard seemed sophomoric and jejune, the very notion of the "leap of faith" quaintly Protestant.

She thought of a conversation she'd had with her mother, maybe two years before her death. Mama, though only a Christmas-and-Easter-Catholic herself, had been a great admirer of Augustine and Aquinas. Jessica recalled scoffing at any notion of intellectually rationalizing the existence of a God. "Even if you believe, the very idea is irrational-al. I personally would love to believe that there's a God, and a divine order to the world. But how can any person of intelligence not doubt?"

"You feel that way because you've had your head filled with Marxist propaganda at UCLA and Berkeley," her mother rejoined in her maddeningly matter-of-fact way. Mama could make the most preposterous utterances with an air of such common sense that it wasn't until later you realized she was talking like a crackpot.

"Give it up, Mom. The Cold War's over."

Mama picked up her worn copy of St. Augustine's *Confessions*. "You know, Jessica, this may sound strange to you. But I've always had a harder time believing *emotionally* than intellectually. That's why I could never be anything other than a Catholic."

Jessica, as was her habit, dismissed Mama's reasoning as fey and illogical. Mama might as well have held a doctorate in "fey and illogical."

But now, as she relived the conversation, she finally understood. Her mother had been alluding to the Roman Catholic doctrine of "justification by works," not by faith alone, which was Luther and Calvin's innovation. And Alex's impassioned speech in her room at the Monteleone, the night after the resurrection, sprang to mind as well. So what if a miracle had probably not taken place, he'd argued; consider the tangible good that could be done by fostering belief.

Simply believing -- or not believing -- wasn't enough.

And that was why she'd come to New Orleans, and why she still lingered.

Now was time to walk the walk.

The hostage crisis aboard Delta Flight 79 came to a peaceful resolution just after seven p.m., Eastern Time. Federal agents boarded the 747, freeing the captives, and apprehending the two suspects. No explosives, plastic or otherwise, were found on either man's person. Jessica was holding fast in her determination to avoid television, but Walt Haberman told her about it when he showed up at her door to take her to dinner.

They went to the nearby Napoleon House, a bar and cafe in a Chartres Street building supposedly offered to the exiled Emperor in 1821. Although the Napoleon House was crowded, it was dark. Seated in a corner of the heated outdoor patio, Jessica felt confident enough of her anonymity to remove her scarf. "Anything happen out in Metairie this afternoon?" she asked Walt, after they ordered cocktails.

He shook his head. "Mostly people praying -- about five hundred of 'em. It's clear that the only reason she came out yesterday was you."

She lit a smoke, exhaled restlessly. "If you're expecting me to say something enlightening, you'll have a long wait, Walt. I don't understand it myself."

"Hey, maybe there's no big mystery. Maybe she's a fan of CNN. Hadn't missed an episode of 'Crossfire' or 'Money-line' until some redneck jerk shot her."

The waiter set a chardonnay before her, a Beck's in front of Walt. Jessica traced the frosty rim of her wine glass. "I know you're being facetious, but there could be a grain of truth in what you're saying. Not that she knew me from TV, necessarily, but I've been professionally involved in fighting the death penalty for ten years."

"You'd never met her, though, right?"

"No. But someone inside the convent could have pointed me out to her."

"OK. You're a lawyer -- let me give you a hypothetical. What would you do if you got word that Sister Cordelia was willing to let you interview her?"

She sipped her wine. "I'd have to refer her to a journalist who didn't carry the excess baggage I do. Not that I wouldn't love to talk to her."

"As a lawyer cross-examining a witness?"

"What else?" She picked up her menu. "Jambalaya sounds good."

But Walt was like a dog with a bone. "Look, Jessica, I gave you my word yesterday anything you say to me is off the record. And Alex would kick my sorry butt from here to Halifax if I dirty-dealt you."

"My God," she said, half-amused, half-aghast. "What exactly did Alex say to you yesterday?"

"Just that he's crazy about you, and worried about some of our colleagues in the Fourth Estate tying you to the stake and burning you alive."

"Was that his metaphor or yours?"

"His, and I'm not entirely sure he meant it as a metaphor."

She glanced away for a moment. "I just hate what he must be going through."

"Yeah. I can't imagine."

"Catholicism is, at its worst, such a religion of guilt," she said, melancholy.

"Hey, I'm Jewish. You Catholics got nothing on us in the guilt department."

"I suppose that's true. But from baptism on, it seems, the Church drums into your head this notion that pleasure must be paid. You end up carrying around with you a kind of chronic mistrust of even the possibility of joy."

"Jeez! That's really . . . depressing."

"I'm sorry," she apologized. "Let's lighten up, shall we? Do you like basketball?"

Walt was meeting up with a few fellow reporters at the Absinthe Bar after dinner, and urged Jessica to join him. "They're good folks, real pros. No one will give you a hard time." But she declined anyway, pleading, with some honesty, fatigue.

She returned to the Royal Orleans, stopping again at the gift shop for a fashion magazine she could browse in bed. She was striding toward the elevator, the current *Vogue* tucked under her arm when she heard him call her name from a few feet away. Incredulous, she spun around, positive her ears were playing tricks on her.

They were not. Alex Trujillo was hastening toward her across the lobby.

Chapter 12

He looked bad. His eyes were dull and sunken deeply in their sockets, his olive skin stretched too tautly over his cheekbones. She longed to tell him she wished he hadn't come, but she couldn't get the words out.

Once in her room, he said little. She poured him a gin-and-tonic from the minibar. Only then did she finally say, "You should have stayed put, muchacho."

He downed his drink in a couple of gulps. "What for? The patient's already dead."

"I know this sounds like such a cliché. But you shouldn't blame yourself."

He helped himself to another miniature bottle of gin. "Why the hell not? I made it clear I didn't want her around, and she decided to oblige."

Jessica masked her concern as he quickly polished off the second gin, no tonic. "Look, I know it's none of my business. But Renie told me your wife was something of an accident waiting to happen."

"Yeah. To paraphrase you, Renie was right and I was wrong. And it's all bullshit. OK, I was a fucking jerk to marry Natalie. But that doesn't make her any less dead, or it any less my fault."

Jessica pursed her lips. "All right. Now tell me this -- would you feel as guilty if you and I hadn't slept together?"

He scowled. "Natalie had no idea. Maybe I should have told her. Maybe she would have been pissed off enough to want to live." Distractedly, he picked up the phone and pressed room-service. "Yeah. Send up a bottle of Bombay Sapphire."

Jessica could no longer hold her tongue. "Look, if you flew all the way out here to drink yourself into a stupor, you're going to have to expect me to speak my piece. You need to talk to somebody --"

"Don't you think that's all I've been hearing? From my mother and sister. My friends Nick and Leah. I don't do psycho-babble."

"What, you're too macho for it?" she baited. "Too much of an *hombre*? I'm not going to play therapist for you, Alex, just because you're too pigheaded to seek the real thing. In case you haven't noticed, I have a few issues of my own to deal with right now."

He sat down next to her on the bed, suddenly less agitated. He took her hand. "I didn't come here because I want you to play therapist. I came because of your courage, Jess. Mine seems to be in short supply lately."

"I'm not courageous," she said, stroking his shaggy hair. Soon it would be long enough to pull back in a ponytail, she mused absently.

"How can you say that? What you did yesterday --"

"No. That was Sister's doing, not mine. When you turned up at my door last Friday night to read me the riot act, when you told me about the pilgrims and showed me the chat room -- that's what gave me the courage to come back to New Orleans and see this thing through."

He kissed her briefly. "And now it's time for me to take my own goddamn advice. It's not therapy I need, Jessica. I need to get back to following this story. And I need you."

They lay back on the bed and just held each other for several minutes, not talking. But the stillness was shattered by the arrival of the gin, which Alex paid for in cash.

Resigned, Jessica got up and grabbed the ice bucket. "There's more tonic in the minibar," she said. "I'm going to get some ice."

I won't lecture him, she vowed as she padded down the hall to the ice machine. *He's just self-medicating.* Damn his overweening machismo! A good therapist would prescribe Xanax, more efficient at calming anxiety and far less likely to leave in its wake increased depression and a nasty hangover. She knew from first-hand experience.

When she returned, she found him poring over the *USA Today* she'd left folded on the bureau, his brow creased, his expression black. "What is this shit? It's fucking McCarthyism, that's what it is!"

"Look, I'm refusing to let it get to me," she tried to calm him. "Anyone who knows me will see it for exactly what it is. As for the rest of the world, screw 'em." She dropped a few ice cubes into a glass, poured in an inch of gin and half a can of Diet 7Up.

Alex tossed aside the paper in disgust and took up his own drink. Straight gin. "That's not the point. You can be fine with it if you want, but don't you think there are a few larger issues at play? If they can do this to you, they can do it to anyone!"

"Didn't we have this argument a few nights ago?"

"Yeah, and I thought you'd come to your senses."

"I have," she insisted. "You're sounding just like my ex-husband. All he can think to do is sue, sue, sue. I don't want this to be about me, Alex! Don't you get it? These *ad hominem* attacks are just more diversionary tactics. When the truth comes out about Sister Cordelia, I'll be vindicated!"

He relented a little. "So you meant what you said yesterday on the phone. About starting to believe."

"It's practically all I've been able to think about. I had dinner with Walt tonight, and he kept pressing me, asking why I thought she came up to me. And you're the only one to whom I've repeated exactly what she said." She shrugged. "Sure you can explain it away. That's basically what I did to Walt. But I've concluded that the only truly rational, plausible explanation is that she's risen from the dead. She didn't know me from CNN, or from my work against the death penalty. Whatever miraculous force brought her back to life also led her to me." A fresh surge of joy trembled in her veins as she spoke the words.

Alex regarded her moodily. "I'd give my right arm if it were true."

"Save your right arm. I've grown pretty fond of it, along with the rest of you." She slipped her hands around his waist.

"I feel like I've known you forever," he murmured, touching her face, her hair.

"Me too. I keep arguing to myself that I can't possibly be in love with someone I've only seen, what, three times? Four?"

"So you've been counting." A hint of the old cockiness returned to his voice. "Who won the argument?"

"You did." She drew in a sharp breath. "I know you feel so awful, so horribly responsible for not saving Natalie's life. But you gave mine back to me! If you hadn't come to me last Saturday, I'd still be cowering in a dark room, afraid of my own shadow, afraid to speak what's right and true. I must sound selfish for putting it this way, but you need to know how much I owe you. And yes, how much I love you."

He winced, as if her words caused him physical pain. "Can you imagine how I've been beating myself up for wanting to be with you, even while I was flying back to LA with my wife's blood on my fucking hands? And I hated her for somehow intuiting, three thousand goddamn miles away, that it was finally over, that I'd found someone worth bowing out of that sick soap opera we'd been from the very beginning."

His torment was palpable. She rested her cheek against his chest, and his heart banged rapid-fire beneath his denim shirt. "Don't do this to yourself. Please," she whispered.

He raised her face toward his. "I do love you, Jessica, and I pity you if you really do love me. The last thing you need in your life is the kind of shit I'm trying to deal with."

"This has nothing to do with heroic self-sacrifice," she smiled. "Two weeks ago, I wouldn't have recognized myself today."

He tugged on a strand of her bright cranberry hair. "Literally."

"And figuratively. I was so complacent, Alex! I was as smug and self-righteous as every big-haired bimbo I'd out-debated on TV. Except for my son, everything in my life was window-dressing. I could pontificate on TV or to my students, and ease my social conscience from the safety of my ivory tower cocoon. I could be holier-than-thou about the failure of my marriage, because it was so obvious that it was Gregg's fault, not mine. When I first came to New Orleans for the funeral, my most pressing concern was that I'd forgotten to pack a pair of three-hundred-dollar Italian pumps to coordinate with my Calvin Klein suit!"

"'You must lose your life to find it.' Christ, you *have* gone religious on me, haven't you." A morose stab at humor on his part.

"Only in the best sense of the word, I hope. I don't believe Sister's resurrection validates any particular doctrine, Catholic or even Christian. I don't know what it means, but I'm sure we're going to find out."

His gloom was faltering in the face of her passion. She could see it. She stretched on tiptoes to kiss him. This time a deep, languorous kiss, their tongues entwined and hungry.

This time, they made love with the lights on.

And this time, their coupling was followed by no unwelcome revelations.

Only then did Jessica shut off the bedside lamp.

Her arms and legs wrapped around him, she nuzzled his stubbled chin. "I'm so glad you're here," she breathed.

He caressed her nipple. She moaned, pressing her body even closer into his. Between her thighs, she felt him growing hard again.

Weak sunlight was streaming into the room by the time they fell back against the pillows. "Oh God," Jessica panted. "I might actually sleep eight hours today."

"Sleep, *querida*," he coaxed, kissing her temple. "I'm gonna ask for an eight o'clock wake-up call."

"Why?" she mumbled, curling up against him. Her eyelids were impossibly heavy.

"'Cause I'm going to Metairie today."

She scarcely heard him, but her lips formed a soundless "wake me, too" against his shoulder before she succumbed to sweet oblivion.

Walt Haberman was all but apoplectic when he happened upon Alex, with Jessica, in the lobby. "You guys better watch out, or I'm gonna write the Sister Cordelia version of *Primary Colors*, starring you two, when this thing's finally over," he said, pumping Alex's hand, and adding, *sotto voce*, "I'm so damn sorry."

"Thanks," Alex replied tersely.

The three shared a cab out to Metairie. Where the past few days had been rainy and dank, this morning was bracingly clear and breezy. The sky was a deep crayon blue, and cloudless. "The true believers are bound to be out in droves," Walt remarked.

He was right. The convent, and its humble front yard and garden, were virtually indiscernible. Easily a thousand people spilled onto the street, obstructing traffic. Police with bullhorns were advising the assembly to remain orderly, under penalty of arrest.

"Has something happened?" Jessica wondered aloud.

"Sure," Walt said, as Alex scrawled furiously into his notepad. "Remember what you told me yesterday? How the Mother Superior announced all the sisters were praying for the hostages? Looks like these people took the lady at her word."

Alex's smile was brittle, ironic. "Serves the motherfuckers right. Their little 'diversionary tactic' blew up in their fucking faces."

Jessica was still uncomfortable with his conviction that the hostage crisis had been engineered. "Watch your language, amigo. We're in spitting distance of a crucifix."

"Be right back," he said. He pushed his way toward a group of raggedy Latinos listening intently to a swarthy, somber priest.

Walt shifted awkwardly. "He OK?"

"Far from it," Jessica conceded. "He's such a stubborn sonofabitch. He won't allow himself any time to heal."

The wind had blown her silk scarf from her head, but neither she nor Walt noticed. They snaked through the throng as best they could, hoping to get closer to the gated yard.

Today, many of the acolytes were bearing hand-lettered signs. "PRAY FOR PEACE!" "SPEAK TO US, SISTER!" "PRAISE BE TO GOD AND SR. CORDELIA FOR FLIGHT 79!"

Walt turned to Jessica, incredulous. "I gotta tell you, this is the strangest football pep rally I've ever been to."

But the gathering was not immune to darker under-currents. A sweet-faced woman in braids was passing out pamphlets a few feet away. Walt managed to get his hands on one. His face crinkled in disgust. "Take a look at this."

Jessica took it from him. "*And I saw three unclean spirits like frogs come out of the mouth of the dragon, and out of the mouth of the beast, and out of the mouth of the false prophet.*

"*For they are the spirits of devils, working miracles, which go forth unto the kings of the earth and of the whole world. to gather them to the battle of that great day of God Almighty. Revelations 16: 13, 14.*"

On the opposite page was a grisly photograph of an aborted fetus, underscored by a quote from Sister Cordelia: "*I believe in my heart abortion is a matter best left to personal conscience.*"

Jessica flipped through the rest of the flyer. Predictably, it also included vicious diatribes against homosexuals, secular humanists, and "the Jewish bankers." Jessica felt sullied even holding the thing, and she dropped it to the ground as if it had caught on fire. "Nasty stuff," she muttered.

"I saw some people with a dog. You think we can induce Fido to come over and take a crap on it?"

"I think it's a splendid idea --"

"Hey!" someone shouted nearby. "It's her! It's Jessica!"

She touched her head, realized immediately the scarf had blown off. Dozens of excited pilgrims pushed toward her even as Walt was fighting to draw her away. Jessica raised her hand against the throng. "I'm here for the same reason you are!" she tried.

But her voice was drowned out by a cacophony of eager questions.

"What did Sister say to you?"

"What did it feel like when she touched you?"

"Why did she choose you, Jessica?"

One of the local minicam crews, alerted to the sudden swarming twenty feet from the convent gate, was now shoving over as well. The police, fearing trouble had erupted, left their posts around recently erected barricades.

No one saw the battered Ford pick-up roll up slowly to the curb.

The driver lowered his window and proceeded to spray automatic gunfire into the crowd.

At first, Jessica thought someone was setting off firecrackers, but when people started screaming and running frantically in all directions, she realized what was happening. "Keep down! Keep down!" Walt barked. Arms locked, they managed to crawl to the gate, where others huddled in terror and prayed they were safe.

"Alex -- what if Alex is shot! He was near the curb -- " Jessica was screaming, but hers was just one of hundreds of voices shrieking in terror.

Then all at once, the report of gunfire ceased. Above the wailing of approaching sirens, someone, presumably a policeman, shouted into a bullhorn. "Everyone please stay where you are. Your movement will gravely hamper the rescue efforts of the emergency medical team. The suspect has been apprehended. Repeat, the suspect has been apprehended."

"Alex!" Jessica screamed.

Walt patted her shoulder comfortingly. "I'm sure he's OK."

But she knew he couldn't be sure, no more than she.

Three nuns, none of them Sister Cordelia, stood on the porch, looking anxiously into the crowd. Soon a news helicopter whirred overhead, and Jessica had to cover her ears. How long would they have to stay huddled and still? How many had been injured or killed, and, God forbid, was Alex among them?

Ten, fifteen minutes of frozen uncertainty elapsed before the cop on the bullhorn commanded the crowd to disperse in a peaceful and orderly fashion.

Jessica desperately scanned the shell-shocked throng for any sign of him. Many people were holding onto each other and sobbing. "Alex!" she cried out imperatively. "Alex!"

And then someone grabbed her from behind. She almost wept with relief. She'd know those strong arms anywhere. "I couldn't find you," he whispered into her hair. "Thank God you're OK."

"What the hell happened?" Walt, face drained of color, demanded.

Alex, still clasping Jessica's shoulders, lit a cigarette with a shaking hand. "This sniper in an old Ford truck pulled up and just opened fire. He must have hit a dozen people before the cops blew him away."

Jessica's hand flew to her throat. "How many people were killed? Do you know?"

He was grim. "Three outright. Of the rest, I'd say half looked pretty bad."

Jessica shut her eyes and silently blessed herself, a half-forgotten reflex suddenly returned to her.

"Just my luck," Walt was joking nervously. "While I'm crouching like a cornered rabbit in a warren, you're on the front-lines, probably earning yourself another friggin' Pulitzer."

Her eyes snapped open. "You won a Pulitzer?"

But he was addressing Walt. "You did something a hell of a lot more important, man. You made sure Jess was safe."

"And vice-versa," Walt replied.

"You won a Pulitzer?" she persisted, parrot-like.

She didn't realize she was shivering violently.

Alex and Walt exchanged glances. "We gotta get her to a doctor," Alex said.

"Absolutely not!" she protested. "I'm fine, and you guys have work to do!"

The pigeon-like nun, distributing plastic cups of coffee to the journalists, police, and paramedics still lingering at the scene, overheard. "Is the young lady not feeling well?" she chirped. "We've sent for a doctor for Sister Arlene -- she's experiencing some chest pains. Would the young lady like to wait for him inside?"

Alex and Walt, each struggling to conceal utter amazement, looked at Jessica. "I think it's a good idea, baby," Alex said levelly.

"All right. Yes, that would be nice." Still too shocked by the sniper attack to fully appreciate the magnitude of the invitation, Jessica accepted the nun's helpful arm and, on wobbly feet, let the woman guide her through the open gate, and into the convent.

Alex and Walt stared after them. "It's almost scary," Walt said, slowly shaking his head.

"You gonna report it?"

"No."

Alex clapped Walt gratefully on the shoulder. "Gracias, amigo. I owe you one."

They set off for the improvised media headquarters across the street, where a battalion of cops, TV remote crews and satellite vans were mobilized.

The nice, pigeon-like nun, who introduced herself as Sister Beryl, took Jessica to a small, austere sitting room toward the back of the convent. The room was comfortably dark, with a couple of worn settees and a *prie-dieu* beneath a portrait of the Assumption of Mary. Sister Beryl brought her a cup of coffee, and tucked a patchwork quilt around her knees. "You just stay here and warm up, my dear. I'll check on you in a few minutes."

Jessica clutched the coffee mug, trying to warm her clammy hands. Her teeth still chattered. She couldn't tear her eyes away from the portrait. That beatific face, the gracefully upswept arms, the powder blue and soft white of her flowing robes. *Pray for us now, and at the hour of our death.*

The sitting room door opened, and Sister Cordelia came in.

Jessica was strangely unsurprised.

Sister Cordelia pulled up a cane-backed chair and sat down right across from her. Leaning forward, she took Jessica's hands in her own warm ones. "Jessica, listen to me," she said gently, her large eyes somber and entreating. "It's time for me to come forward. Are you ready?"

Jessica nodded mutely, clinging to Sister's hands.

"I don't know what the future will hold," Cordelia went on steadily. "I've been praying these weeks for guidance. I never expected it to come in the form of more bloodshed."

"Sister, it's on my conscience." Jessica swallowed hard. "If I hadn't come back to New Orleans . . . "

"That's not true. You came because you had to."

She spoke with such quiet authority Jessica had no choice but to accept her words. "What are you going to do?"

"I've never been cut out for the cloistered life. I'm going to get back to God's work as I've always understood it to be."

"Can I help?" Jessica whispered.

Sister Cordelia lightly touched her cheek. "My daughter, you already have."

The convent and three square blocks surrounding it were completely cordoned off from public access by the time Jessica slipped, unnoticed, through the convent gate. Her shattered nerves becalmed, she walked slowly to the media enclave across the street. "Figures *she*'d have to show up," she heard someone snicker. The big guns from the major networks were back, but their representatives, even those who knew her, uniformly ignored her.

Alex and Walt were just stepping away from a police debriefing. Alex was talking into a cell phone when he spotted her. "Get right back to you," he said, and quickly folded up the phone.

He embraced her tightly. "You feeling better?"

"Lots. Not even cold anymore."

"Yeah, I can tell. Look, I have about another hour's work here, then we can go back to the Quarter."

A uniformed cop approached them. "Sorry, Miss, but I've been informed you have no press credential. You're going to have to leave," he drawled.

Alex's eyes flashed. "She's with me," he snapped. "Less than an hour ago she was in shock -- she's not going anywhere!"

"Sorry, but the sergeant says press only."

Alex appeared on the verge of losing his temper, but Jessica intervened. "He's right, Alex. I'll be OK. Call me when you're finished."

The cop, pleased she hadn't made a scene (especially when he knew damn well who she was), made a kind of peace offering. "Tell you what, Miss. I'll even have a squad take you back to your hotel. Cabs can't get anywhere near here."

"Thanks, that's kind of you." She kissed a still-steaming Alex goodbye. "I'm fine," she reiterated.

She supposed she should resent whoever had "tattled" on her to the cops; likely someone from CNN, who knew she'd been basically stripped of her credentials. But she just couldn't get herself worked up over it. And the last thing she wanted was to distract Alex from doing the job he plainly loved. It was his lifeblood. The shadowy, tortured soul who'd shown up at the Royal Orleans last night had been revitalized in the last harrowing hour or so. Even the haunted look in his eyes was all but vanished, replaced by the steely intensity that had drawn her to him in the first place.

The patrolman drafted to escort her back to the city wasn't exactly loquacious, but Jessica managed to glean a few facts about the bloody rampage. The sniper had a record as long as the Mississippi, and had been a member in good standing of Aryan Nations. He'd been released from prison only a month before, where he'd served time for his part in the torching of a predominantly black church in Alabama.

The body-count was currently up to seven. The cop didn't know how many of the survivors were in critical condition.

Once back at the Royal Orleans, Jessica headed straight for the Rib Room bar. It was not so much that she wanted a drink than that she wasn't yet willing to be alone with her own thoughts.

And in the elegant bar, she was far from alone. Even on a typical day, it was far from unusual to find a heartily drinking lunchtime clientele in any French Quarter bar. But today, the attractive, upscale Rib Room was packed, with ordinarily insouciant Orleaneans frazzled and compulsively downing cocktails. Jessica took a seat at the bar, and while several patrons clearly recognized her, none seemed inclined to invade her privacy. Maybe they noticed that she was as shaken up as they were.

Or maybe they realized that this story had today gotten much, much bigger than a madwoman with fake red hair.

The bartender placed a glass of chardonnay and a club soda before her, leaned over to light her cigarette. "Sure you don't want a little vodka with that soda?"

"I'm not sure, but I'd better not."

She ended up making nervous chatter with a New Orleans businessman type who either didn't know or didn't care who she was. "This all's gone way too far," he remarked, nursing a martini. "Those poor folks out in Metairie were all sitting ducks for any gun-toting maniac. Why didn't the police go in earlier? Either make them leave, or provide better security?"

"Good point," she agreed.

"What's the damn world coming to," he complained. "If I were a God-fearing man -- and I'm not saying I'm not -- I'd half-think Armageddon was upon us."

She cringed, remembering that hateful pamphlet with its copious citations from the Book of Revelations. And she thought of those great kids from Tulane yesterday, with their boom-box blasting "It's the End of the World As We Know It." What if one of them had been among the slaughtered?

She took a hasty gulp of wine. "It's a scary world, that's for certain."

"Yes ma'am, and growing scarier by the day, it seems."

"There you are!" broke in Walt Haberman, striding up to her. Walt looked only slightly less rattled than he had in the immediate aftermath of the sniper attack.

The businessman politely excused himself, freeing up the barstool next to Jessica's.

Walt signaled for a beer. Then, lowering his voice, he asked Jessica, "So what happened? Did you see her?"

"I can't talk about it just yet. OK?"

Walt nodded. "Alex went back to the Richelieu to file his story. Needless to say, he's got more to write. He saw everything, Jessica. He's damn lucky he didn't end up -- " He stopped himself as she turned ghostly white. "Anyway, he said to tell you he'll be here as soon as he can."

"What did he win a Pulitzer for?"

"I can't believe he turned shrinking violet and didn't tell you. It was a couple years back, 1997, I think. He covered that popular uprising in Chiapas, Mexico. Damn near got himself shot then, too." Then he winced. "Jeez, what's wrong with me? Sorry."

"Don't apologize. We're all nervous wrecks. We'd be crazy not to be after today." She rubbed her hands together; they were growing chilly again. "Do you know anything about the victims?"

"Their identities haven't been released yet." He took a chug from his beer. "Maybe the old copy desk isn't so bad after all."

"You ever been married, Walt?"

"Once. My college sweetheart from SC. It just didn't work out. Why do you ask?"

"I don't know. I used to think being married was nice." She was feeling a little woozy again. The wine had not been a good idea.

Walt hopped down from his stool. "Look, let me help you upstairs."

"I can make it. Really." She fumbled in her Coach bag for a few bills, and wound up spilling the entire contents of her purse onto the carpet. Her wallet, a lipstick, random change, her credit-card-like room key. A Chanel compact and a small hairbrush. A clear plastic accordion holding a dozen little pictures of Jordy.

Walt scrambled on the floor to retrieve the articles, while all she could do was dumbly hold her purse open as he dropped the items in one by one.

After that, no amount of protest on her part could keep him from escorting her to her room.

"You're never going to believe this," she said weakly, "but once upon a time, I was a certifiably competent human being." She pushed open the door.

"Yeah, but who was doing the certifying?" he cracked. "Forget it. I always thought competency was an overrated virtue."

She found a Xanax in a pillbox tucked into an inner pocket of her carry-on. She chased it down with lukewarm tap-water. In twenty minutes, she was out.

Chapter 13

"Oh my God," she said, stifling a yawn as she let him in. "What time is it?"

"About quarter after three."

"I took a pill," she admitted, tightening the sash on her kimono. "Do you want some coffee?"

"Sure, why not." He took a seat on the rumpled bed while she ordered coffee from room service. The moment she set down the receiver, he drew her into his lap. "How are you, really?"

"Groggy."

"You're being evasive, *chiquita*."

She replied by way of a feeble jest. "I am most certainly *not* a banana."

He didn't smile. "You're ice-cold again."

"Come on, Mr. Pulitzer Prize. You know damn well sleep lowers the body temperature." She eased out of his arms, and took a hasty brush to her hair.

"OK. You don't have to talk about what happened until you want to."

She adjusted the thermostat upward five degrees. "What's the latest on the massacre?"

"Come here, get under the covers."

She first lit a cigarette, then crawled back into bed, propping a pillow against the headboard. She rubbed his back along the spine. Warm. "Tell me what you've learned. I've sworn off TV, you know."

"Eight people dead. Three on the critical list, and one of them is on life support." He borrowed the cigarette from her and took a drag. "Another eight in conditions ranging from fair to serious. A seven-year-old kid from Guatemala lost a hand." He returned the smoldering Merit to her.

"Do you think the Powers That Be were --"

"Not this time. This is their worst nightmare. The last thing they could have wanted was some Aryan racist puke to pull a stunt like this and draw the whole world's eyes back to Louisiana and Cordelia Davis. Damn! This whole fucking bloodbath could have been avoided!"

"How?" she said in a small voice.

"How? Easy. If the goddamn city authorities and cops hadn't kowtowed to external pressure to make this thing just go away, there would have been adequate security around the convent!"

She exhaled deeply. "Yeah, some man down in the bar was saying pretty much the same thing."

He cast her an exaggerated sideways look. "You chatting up strange men in bars again?"

"What can I say? I'm incorrigible." She pulled him down and kissed him languidly. "I'll tell you everything -- just make love to me first, OK?"

His tongue lapped at her ear. "What about the coffee guy?"

"Oh shit. Put the Do-Not-Disturb sign on the door, and he'll probably just leave it."

But at that moment, a knock sounded. "Room service!"

Jessica groaned. "Wouldn't you know this would be the one time they're prompt!"

Alex got up to accept the tray, paying again in cash.

"I wish you wouldn't keep picking up the tab," she sighed, as she poured coffee and a couple of drops of milk into a cup. "It's not just a feminist issue. I might as well tell you now -- I'm fairly well off."

"And you withheld this information 'cause you thought my outsized *machismo* couldn't deal with it?" he countered.

"Sorry, I just have to put it on the table. Some men are funny about it." But apology or not, she'd certainly spoiled the moment, and she wanted to kick herself.

"Was your old man?" he asked curtly.

"No, but we were already married when I came into my inheritance. Look, forget I brought it up. You have to remember I haven't even dated in more than twelve years. For all I know the etiquette's changed, and it's *pro forma* for the guy to pay for everything again."

An angry retort seemed on the tip of his tongue, but then he relaxed, and smiled. "Praise be to Lord Jesus. The woman's starting to sound like herself."

"I see. And according to you, what does 'myself' sound like? That know-it-all lipstick feminist in Donna Karan who used to spout off on CNN?" But she was smiling back.

Friends again.

But she saw that she still had a ways to go before restoring the erotic charge between them that the "coffee guy" and her own crass reference to her finances had shattered.

How could she explain to him how much she needed him right now? Not just his love, and friendship, and support. She needed his body, needed to feel him inside her. She needed to be filled with his warm seed, the literal testament to how truly alive they both were on a day when so many innocents had been slaughtered.

She set her cup on the nightstand and lowered the pillow, turning her face away from his.

"What's wrong, baby? You want to go back to sleep?"

He adjusted the blankets around her.

"I'm so damn stupid," she said, through clenched teeth. Not looking at him.

"Since when?" he rejoined lightly.

She tore around with a kind of violence. "I want you to make love to me so bad . . . it's shameful, I know, but it's all I can think about!" She was half-sobbing.

"Sshh, sshh. It's nothing to be ashamed of."

"But all those poor people who were gunned down so stupidly --"

He rocked her against his chest. "I know. I know."

He bent his head to kiss her tenderly, but she wouldn't settle for tender. She wanted him to engulf her, and she kissed him so hard their lips bled. They rocked together frenetically. She moaned as he thrust deeper and deeper, shrieking in mad joy when he at last spilled into her.

Life.

True to her word, she told him everything that had transpired within the convent. How Sister Cordelia had come to her again, and what she'd said, clasping her hands and gazing deep into her eyes. How Sister had addressed her as "my daughter."

Alex did little to hide how troubled he was by her account. Sitting up in bed, he grabbed his cigarettes. "Didn't you ask her anything?"

"Like what?" She was still savoring the afterglow of his embrace, the warm stickiness between her thighs.

"Like, how she knows you. Why she's singled you out." He impatiently struck a match and raised its flame to the tip of his Marlboro.

"Don't you see? I couldn't."

"Why the hell not?"

"Because," she said pensively, "I have faith."

He grimaced, said nothing.

"It's your job to be skeptical -- you're a reporter," she granted, for all that his skepticism wounded her profoundly.

"I didn't come back to New Orleans as a journalist, Alex. I came back because I needed to know the truth."

"And now you feel you do. No questions asked."

"I told you myself I'd made up my mind about her. To grill her like opposing counsel on cross would have seemed -- despicable."

"Like Doubting Thomas?"

"Why do you mock me when you know how serious I am?"

"I don't know. Maybe because it's just so crazy."

"Do you think I'm crazy?" she asked flatly.

He got up to pour himself a glass of gin from the bottle of Bombay on the dresser. "No, I don't think you're crazy. I just wish you'd asked her a few questions."

"Well, I didn't. And by the way, you look damn fine naked."

He had to chuckle. "For a postmodern Joan of Arc, you sure have a dirty mind, lady."

She welcomed him back into bed. "Thank you very much."

But Alex would not let the matter drop. "So she's gonna go public, huh? Suppose she'll hold a press conference?"

"I have no idea. That's your domain, not mine."

"Careful with those 'Seinfeld' allusions, chica."

She laughed outright. "Damn, I've been meaning to ask you! Doesn't Walt remind you of --"

She was interrupted by the jingling of the phone. She snapped up the receiver. "Hello?"

"Hi, this is Matt Crowell, calling for Alex Trujillo. Is he available?"

She covered the mouthpiece with her palm. "A Matt Crowell for you. Do you want to take it?"

"Yeah, it's my editor."

She climbed out of bed, knotting her robe around her waist. Not wanting to eavesdrop, she went into the bathroom and took a hot shower. When she came out ten minutes later, a towel turbaned around her hair, he was still on the phone, all alertness as he scrawled into a memo pad bearing the Omni imprimatur. "Yeah. Gotcha," he was saying. "I'll get on it right away."

He hung up the phone. His expression was at once stunned and excited. "You're not gonna believe this."

"What?"

"The nuns contacted my editor. Cordelia Davis is granting me an exclusive interview."

Her blood turned cold. "No! Alex, you can't!"

"No? Watch me." He started to get dressed.

She grabbed his arm. "Alex, they'll destroy you! They'll find out about us, and about Natalie, and it'll cost you what you love more than anything else in the world, your work!"

"Listen to me, Jess. Don't you think all that's occurred to me? If I turn this opportunity down, it'll be somebody else's ass on the firing line. Apparently the nuns are more tuned in than I would have guessed. They know who in the press can be trusted to be fair, and there are a few others besides me."

She was not appeased. "Does your editor know about us?"

"No," he admitted. "I left your number, not your name, with the service at my hotel."

"Don't you think it would be fair to tell him?"

His jaw set stubbornly. "Jessica, I'm not gonna be scared away from this story. Especially when I have an editor who's willing to publish it in one of the three great newspapers in the country."

He started to hug her but she yanked away, angrily tearing the towel from her wet hair.

He drew her back, his eyes blazing. "Look. Don't we agree that in this case, the truth is a hell of a lot more important than either one of us? If I backed away now out of fear that what's happened to you is gonna happen to me, what kind of fucking journalist would I be? I'd be a shill, no better than the network pundits who've sneered at this story from the very beginning."

"Just be prepared, because I can already hear the play-by-play," she said harshly. "They'll imply I set up the interview, regardless of how much you and your editor protest to the contrary. They'll portray you as a man unhinged by his wife's recent suicide, a man manipulated by a disgraced and vindictive ex-legal analyst. Word will reach your editor just in time to pull the story from the front page, and you'll be lucky if you can find a job reporting on Elvis sightings for the *Weekly World News*."

"As long as the story makes it into print, let 'em say whatever the fuck they want about me." He glanced at his watch. "It's only three thirty Pacific time. I'll do the interview, write the story, and modem it back to LA just before deadline. It'll be impossible for anyone to yank it."

"And you don't think the other reporters out in Metairie won't sense something when you stroll right into the convent as if you lived there?"

"I made a couple friends among the cops today," he said, all confidence. "They'll help me work something out."

She shook her head sadly. "I think you're going to regret this."

She refused to kiss him goodbye.

Disheartened, she broke down and turned on the TV. No need for cable; the local affiliates were continuing live coverage from Metairie, even though darkness had fallen and from what she could tell, all signs of the morning's shooting spree had been obscured by night. But yellow police lines and rows of sawhorse barricades were sinister reminders of the evil that had taken place fifty yards from the Convent of the Blessed Virgin.

Police were still combing the area for evidence, announced a somber reporter clad in a trenchcoat. Even though the gunman was dead, ballistics experts were anxious to determine whether the weapon or ammo could be linked to other crimes, other neo-Nazi terrorist activities, including the bombing of the mortuary and the "assassination" of Sister Cordelia herself. And details were trickling in about the victims. Among the dead was a highly respected reporter from Mexico City; a mother of eight from Guatemala; a freelance photographer based in Atlanta. Most of the rest of the dead were New Orleans-area natives, many African-American. Two children remained in critical condition.

Against her better judgment she switched to CNN. Their coverage was appropriately grave and impersonal. The anchor and the reporter at the scene, good old Ann Magee, made only passing reference to Sister Cordelia, even though she was the reason over a thousand people had been gathered outside the convent in the first place.

When the phone rang again she turned off the tube. It was Gregg, worried about her safety. "I've been trying all day to get through, but all the circuits to New Orleans have been tied up. Just tell me you weren't out there this morning, Jessie."

"No, I was just getting up when I heard about the shootings." It seemed a benign white lie; what point was there in frightening him retroactively?

Especially when she knew she had a more portentous truth to tell.

"Thank God," he was saying. "Somebody should move those sisters out of there before another right-wing lunatic decides to bomb the place."

"At last you've deduced my true purpose in coming here. It's to persuade Sister Cordelia to take up residence at the Watergate."

He chuckled. "Talk about a building that could use a little sanctification."

She hesitated. "Gregg . . . "

"What is it, Jessie?"

"Speaking of bombshells, there's something I have to tell you. My name is probably going to be dragged through the mud again, maybe as soon as tomorrow. I'm afraid you might be embarrassed, so you'd better hear it from me first."

"Don't sweat it, honey. Everyone who knows either one of us doesn't buy the crap printed about you in the papers."

How tempted she was to let the matter go at that. But she felt honor-bound to warn him what was likely coming. "Will you hear me out?"

"Sure, if that's what you want."

"All right." She drew in a sharp breath. "A friend of mine -- a recent friend -- is as we speak interviewing Sister Cordelia. He's a reporter from the Los Angeles *Times*, and the interview is probably going to appear tomorrow."

He whistled, impressed. "An exclusive?"

"Yeah. Don't tell anybody."

"I won't. But what does this have to do with another impending pit-bull attack on you?"

"Because I know better than anyone the kind of smear tactics the mainstream media will resort to if you dare to imply there might be two sides to this story. They paint you as borderline psychotic. They egregiously invade your privacy, trying to dig up any dirt to discredit you."

"You're afraid that when the media starts smearing this guy, they're going to re-hash all that despicable bullshit they've been saying about you?"

Why was he being so damn dense? "In a way, yes. Because, Gregg, I have a feeling they're going to drag me in more directly." She thought of herself this morning, still in a state of benumbed ecstasy, strolling into the media enclave in search of Alex. He'd hugged her, kissed her goodbye, in full view of reporters she knew to be hostile to her. What fools -- what indiscreet fools they had been.

"Jessica, are you saying you and this guy are going to be linked romantically should the big guns take aim at him?" Gregg sounded pointedly uneasy.

"Yes. What better way to make him look like a charlatan than to make him out to be my dupe?"

He laughed uncomfortably. "Do I need to know whether or not any of it is true?"

"I don't know. Do you?"

Now was his turn to pause.

"I'm assuming you're still there?" she said at length.

"If this guy's your lover, I'd like to break his face for dragging you back into this crap all over again. Doesn't he know what you've already gone through?"

"By the same logic, you should want to break my face, too, since thanks to me, your name's been dragged through the mud. He's only doing what he has to do."

"OK. I'll consider myself duly forewarned," he said rather stiffly. "Take care of yourself."

He hung up shortly thereafter.

Jessica, still holding the receiver, spoke into the dial tone. "Don't tell me you have the goddamn nerve to be jealous!" Too bad she hadn't said as much.

Once again, she had dinner with Walt at the Napoleon House, but their conversation was tense. It was as if they were both trying too hard not to talk about the mass murders and how capriciously they'd escaped the line of fire them-selves. When he asked after Alex, she told him that he'd gone back to his own hotel to write a follow-up.

Yet all she could think about was the interview. Not just its inevitable ramifications, either. What would Alex ask Sister? What would he think? Would he leave her presence as convinced as Jessica of Cordelia Davis's sanctity, of her truth? Or would the investigative journalist in him detect some subtle but telling flaw in Sister's veneer, imperceptible to Jessica herself? A flaw that would save his own career as a respected, Pulitzer Prize winning reporter but destroy their love as sure as a deliberate cruelty.

To distract herself, she agreed to accompany Walt to a Bourbon Street jazz club, a smoky hole-in-the-wall where a Dixieland combo bopped and swung above clinking glasses and raucous laughter. Eerie how not even today's gruesome tragedy could dampen Bourbon Street's perpetual revels. Drunks still hollered and whooped; strippers still bared breasts and bottoms to leering applause; tourists in feathery masks and Jazz Festival sweatshirts still flooded street and sidewalk, reeling in and out of bars, peep shows, and voodoo parlors. In search of desire, or of temporary oblivion? She didn't know.

The musicians took a break, and Jessica and Walt were joined at their small table by a heavy-set brunette, around fifty, wearing glasses and a nicely tailored pantsuit. Walt introduced her as Lois Janofsky. "Lois is with Knight- Ridder," Walt added, giving Jessica a reassuring wink.

"So you're the famous Jessica Anders," Lois grinned, raising her vodka martini to Jessica. "God, you've got balls, girlfriend. Glad to finally make your acquaintance."

"'Balls, girlfriend'?" Walt mocked good-naturedly. "Sounds like some weird transsexual thing to me."

"Oh God, keep your voice down, or they'll be printing that next!" Jessica laughed as she shook Lois's hand.

Lois bummed a cigarette from Jessica's pack. "We're not all craven little shits, I hope you know. Why is it that once people hit the big-time, they lose what few scruples they had to start with?"

"That's a no-brainer, Lo. You don't make it to the top unless you're ethically bankrupt," Walt replied.

"Not true," Lois argued. "I went to journalism school at Missouri with Owen Shawn. Owen wanted to be the next Edward R. Friggin' Murrow. Look at him today."

"Who doesn't cut a deal, sooner or later, with the devil?" Jessica said. "But I've come to discover there are greater and lesser devils."

Lois nodded, considering it. "True enough."

"I'm not a martyr to this story," Jessica said. "We all know who the real martyrs are."

Now that the awful subject had been broached, Walt heaved a deep sigh. "All those people dead, for no damn good reason."

"The three-year-old was taken off life-support an hour ago," Lois said, removing her glasses and absently wiping them with a cocktail napkin. "Shit, I went to Catholic school K through twelve. If God was gonna raise somebody up from the dead, why the hell didn't He choose someone in a country with better fucking gun-control laws?"

"That's a great essay in and of itself," Jessica observed.

Lois brightened. "Thanks. I filed it three hours ago on the Net."

"See?" Walt said to Jessica in encouragement. "We hardcore newspaper people aren't quite the bottom-feeders that your ex-pals in TV are."

"Some of us aren't, at any rate," Lois rejoined, and Jessica wondered if the woman had seen the nasty syndicated piece with the Washington *Post* byline. "Look, Jessica. Someday your story will be told, and people will believe it."

"You're good to say so, Lois," Jessica said, "but it's not my story I'm worried about. I should be a footnote." She smiled wryly. "'I should have been a pair of ragged footnotes Scuttling across the floors of silent seas.'"

Lois laughed uproariously. "Oh, man, that's good! You can't put one over on an ex-English major! I did my honors thesis on Eliot."

Walt pretended to gripe. "Hey, if you girls are going to talk English poetry, I'm outa here! Anybody know how the Lakers did tonight?"

They stayed at the bar until after eleven, drinking too much, alternating between somber discussion of the "Sister thing," as Walt put it, and frivolous chat about sports and politics and child-rearing (Lois had a fourteen-year-old daughter who'd recently shaved her head and declared herself a Buddhist). Walt and Jessica walked Lois back to the St. Louis Hotel, then staggered two blocks east to the Royal Orleans.

"You're right," Jessica said, tipsy, as they climbed into the elevator. "She is so cool. I'm glad I met her."

Walt was swaying himself. "Lo is all right."

The doors slid open at the second floor. "Don' worry, I can make it," Jessica waved him off. "*Hasta manana*."

She stumbled a zigzag path down the corridor to her room.

"Where's the goddamn key," she muttered, rifling through her purse. She was just about to insert her ATM card in the narrow slot when the door flew open.

She'd forgotten she'd given Alex a second key that morning, before they'd set off that morning for Metairie.

"Whoa," he said, helping her into the room. "You've been out kicking up your heels, eh, muchacha?"

"No heels." Pointing down to her flat black leather ankle boots, she almost lost her balance.

He caught her. "My bad little Joan of Arc," he murmured, assisting her to a chair.

Remembering at once what he'd been up to, she struggled through the alcohol daze for clarity. Gradually he came into focus. Taut and troubled, a little drunk himself. "What?" she cried. "You have to tell me everything that happened!"

"We'll talk about it tomorrow." He refilled his glass from the now half-empty bottle of Bombay gin on the bureau. "Want a drink?"

"This is not fucking fair! I've told you everything, I repeated every damn word she said to me to you! Don't you dare hold back on me now, you bastard!"

At his silence, she turned fierce. Violence throbbed in her fingertips. "You chickened out, didn't you! You went in there with a fine-tooth comb and the horrible knowledge that if you wrote the truth, you'd become a laughingstock like me! You sold her out, and you sold yourself out, all to maintain your membership in a club of vicious liars and whores --"

She had leaped up to pound anger and betrayal against his chest. He seized her wrists roughly and forced her down on the bed. "Don't you get it yet? How can something that's supposed to be good turn people like you and me into what we are at this goddamn fucking moment!" He released her, his face contorted, and went back to the bureau to retrieve his drink.

Unnerved by his outburst, she sat up tentatively. She didn't feel drunk anymore. "I think it's you and me who are bad for each other," she said in a shaky voice. "Maybe you should leave."

"Fine, I'll leave. But first you have to hear me out. We skipped that part the last time you kicked me out on my ass."

Her hands flew up to cover her ears. "I don't want to hear you!"

He forcibly lowered her hands. "The die's cast, Jessica. The story's going to press at this moment. In a few hours, the early edition will be slapping against doorsteps all over southern California. It's probably already all over the Internet."

She looked at him in utter horror and disgust. "What did you do to her?"

He, too, regarded her as if she were a stranger. "Guess you'll just have to read about it."

Leaving, he slammed the door shut so thunderously the front desk called five minutes later, asking if there were a "problem."

Chapter 14

Pound pound pound! on her door.

Headachy and hung-over, Jessica glanced at the digital clock on the nightstand.

She blinked. Could it actually be ten a.m.?

"Just a sec," she called out, half-appalled to find herself in the same jeans and sweater she'd worn last night. She ripped the sweater over her head and quickly replaced it with a clean if wrinkled white linen camp-shirt she'd brought along as an afterthought.

The caller was Walt, nervous and excited and ebullient. "You see it yet? Christ, you must have seen it! They're doing their best to squelch it but it's too late, it's all over the wires and the Internet!"

Jessica's head spun. "What are you talking about?"

Walt was virtually swaggering. He thrust a folded newspaper into her hands. Eschewing the remote, he snapped on the TV, found CNN manually.

A sober panel was convened on "Burden of Proof." Even as she opened the newspaper, Jessica caught sight of a thin-lipped Suzanne Sheridan. "What I want to know is if this interview has been authenticated!" she pouted. "Trujillo might have made this entire story up out of whole cloth."

The camera cut to a shaken Bev Wallace in Atlanta. "I think it's more likely he was duped. Trujillo has a solid reputation as an investigative journalist."

"And a history of left-wing bias as long as my arm," Sheridan objected with a nervous giggle. "He did a series of extremely sympathetic stories a few years back about Shining Path, the ultra-Maoist Peruvian terrorists."

Jessica tore her eyes from the screen and opened the newspaper.

It was a first-edition Los Angeles *Times*. The headline blazed "14 DEAD, 23 WOUNDED IN LOUISIANA RAMPAGE."

In only slightly smaller type-face, a sidebar: "'GO FORTH, DAUGHTER OF GOD': SISTER CORDELIA SPEAKS OUT."

The dateline was New Orleans. The author was Alex Trujillo, *"exclusive to the Los Angeles* Times."

"Listen to these shitheads! They don't know what to make of any of this!" Walt exclaimed, shaking a gloating fist at the TV screen. He might as well have been a partisan fan at a Bulls-Knicks game.

Jessica scarcely heard him.

For here, in smudged gray newsprint, was Alex's testament.

"Inside the convent, the walls are papered and silent. A faint musty mildew smell mingles with the fragrance of dying flowers and incense. From the chapel, a prayer vigil can be heard, murmurs of supplication for the souls of the dead and wounded. Grief-stricken and bewildered, the sisters of the Convent of the Blessed Virgin are praying for the victims of a mass-murderer's spree less than a football field away from their sanctuary.

"Sister Cordelia Davis sits down to speak with me in a dim, austere room near the chapel. For all intents and purposes, she appears identical to the woman in the film clips from '60 Minutes,' and, I must admit, to the waxen figure borne to the altar of St. Louis Cathedral just over three weeks ago. Our paths actually crossed eight years ago, in San Salvador, at a memorial mass for Father Romero that I was covering for this newspaper. She looks to be the same woman to me.

"I ask her, point-blank, if it is true: has God, as she claimed inside St. Louis Cathedral, raised her, like Lazarus, from the dead, and if so, why?

"'God has raised me,' she says, in that quiet, musical voice revered by her followers. She is smaller than she appears on television, yet somehow less vulnerable as well. She maintains steady eye-contact throughout the course of our hour-long conversation.

"She insists she has no memory of the period between being shot outside the Louisiana death house and her ostensible resurrection three days later. 'It was just as if I'd awakened from a long sleep. So may it be for all of us, praise Jesus Christ.'

As for her skeptics, Sister Cordelia is reluctant to criticize. 'If the Lord intended to coerce people into believing, why bother sending his son Jesus Christ down here in the first place? The Lord gave us doubt, so we could know and appreciate the ecstasy of faith in all its fullness.'

"As far as yesterday's bloodbath outside the convent is concerned, Cordelia Davis observes, 'Each soul who perished is seated today at the right hand of the Lord. As for me, God has sent me a strong and clear message as to my mission here. If I am to stand for anything, it's for the struggle against violence and killing, be it in the name of the State or of personal vengeance. I believe the Lord brought me back not just to preach but to fight for the Word of his Gospel. Faith, hope, and charity, without which we would all be as resounding cymbals.'

"To fight? I press her.

"'Yes. To fight violence and intolerance and social inequity. For I believe that killing is the inevitable spawn of a fundamentally unjust society, where the divisions are too vast between rich and poor, white and black, and yes, as I've said before, straight and gay.'

"Then Cordelia Davis smiles. 'George Bernard Shaw wasn't a believer, but I'll always remember a line from his play about Saint Joan. Do you know it?'

"I shake my head, embarrassed by how little I'd retained from Freshman Lit at Stanford.

"But Cordelia Davis doesn't appear to hold it against me. She recites, 'Go forth, Daughter of God, go forth.'"

Jessica was in tears. She threw her arms around a startled Walt. "This is wonderful! He's so heroic I can hardly stand it." And she felt about two inches tall for having drunkenly accused him of capitulating last night. Small wonder he'd stormed off in a huff.

"He's got *cahones*, that's for sure," Walt agreed. "I tried calling him at the Richelieu but he's not in. Must have gone back out to Metairie."

Jessica was disappointed. She was anxious to congratulate him -- and to apologize for her unfounded lapse of faith in his integrity.

Walt was sneering again at the TV. "Look at the schmucks squirm. Hey, there's my old boss."

From a remote studio in Los Angeles, a silver-haired, patrician woman was identified as Gloria Bloom, a senior editor at the *Times*.

Paul Duncan, the moderator, asked her how the *Times* had obtained the interview.

"This is what tickled us," the editor said, smiling. "Apparently the sisters at the convent are on-line. The Mother Superior sent us an e-mail, in which she specifically requested that our reporter on the story, Alex Trujillo, conduct the interview. Apparently they've been following the news just like the rest of us."

"Nuns on-line," chuckled Randall Casper, the famed defense lawyer. "You've got to love it."

"Another question, Mrs. Bloom," Paul Duncan started, but interrupted himself. He clutched his ear-piece. "Wait a second. NBC news and Reuters are reporting that . . . that Alex Trujillo, who conducted the interview for the Los Angeles *Times*, is -- get this -- the boyfriend of former CNN legal analyst Jessica Anders."

"Shit," Jessica cursed. "Here we go."

"What does that goddamn prove?" Walt shouted at the console.

Gloria Bloom was obviously taken aback. "I'm virtually certain . . . that can't be true. Mr. Trujillo is a very recent widower, and his journalistic ethics are well above reproach."

"With all due respect to Mrs. Bloom," smirked Bev Wallace, "it looks like the pieces are starting to fall into place."

"Hold on," Paul Duncan said. "We've obtained from NBC a couple of still photographs taken yesterday after the shooting spree."

Juxtaposed side-by-side on the screen appeared two fuzzy shots of Alex and Jessica: embracing in the first, kissing in the second.

Duncan had Ann Magee on the phone. "Yes, Paul, Jessica Anders was briefly inside the media enclave yesterday. I saw her with that tall man, but I had no idea who he was."

Gloria Bloom's smile seemed frozen on her face. "I think we're all jumping to some rather hasty conclusions. I can imagine how emotional the scene in Metairie must have been for everyone there, including the journalists."

Walt interpreted for Jessica. "Gloria's pissed. She's really pissed."

Jessica collapsed at the foot of her bed, cradling her head in her hands.

Walt hastened to turn off the television.

The phone rang. "Want me to get it?" Walt offered.

"Please."

He picked up the receiver. "Yeah. No, she's not available. No, I have no idea." He hung up. "That was *Newsweek*."

Jessica grabbed the phone and asked the operator once again to hold all calls except any from Gregg Monahan or Alex Trujillo. "Damn, I knew this was going to happen," she said to Walt. "Alex's credibility is going to be blown to all hell."

"Keep in mind they were already starting in on him before inserting you in the picture," Walt reminded her grimly. "Bringing up the series on the Shining Path, suggesting he's a Marxist sympathizer with a political axe to grind. You know he had to see this coming, and stubborn asshole that he is, he decided to weather the storm."

But Jessica hardly heard him. She was thinking that maybe the time had come for her to return to Washington. Her continued presence in New Orleans could only complicate Alex's attempts to salvage his credibility, not to mention guarantee that she herself would be hounded all over again. "Walt, I think I need some time alone. Thanks for bringing me the paper and everything."

"No problem. See you later."

Alone, she slowly re-read Alex's interview with Sister Cordelia. His reporting was honest but dispassionate, as it should be. He avoided injecting any particular editorial slant. He asked the right questions, let Sister make her case, and then left it to the readers to form their own conclusions.

And for that, he was being pilloried.

Once again, the media was diverting attention from the subject of the story to the reporter. The panels would turn to dissecting Alex's possible motive and agenda, slurring him by innuendo and half-truths. The *Times* would start diplomatically backing away from him. And by nightfall, his privacy would be destroyed; his face would be as well-known to most Americans as that of the President; and a hard-won career would be in shambles.

She, of all people, had the script memorized by heart.

When the door clicked open, she leaped up, initially frightened.

Alex walked in, looking grim but oddly unruffled. His eyes were dark with anger, but with something else, too: *resolve*.

She dashed into his arms. "I'm so damn proud of you! Can you forgive me for all the bullshit I flung at you last night?"

He guffawed dryly. "Last night seems like pretty small potatoes. Besides, we were both drunk." He patted her bottom. "Sit down, Jess. I need to talk to you."

They sat down side-by-side on the bed. He clasped her hands. "Just as you predicted, my editor is royally pissed off at my failure to mention I was involved with you."

"You did the right thing, Alex! The truth would never have been published if you had."

"Well, that's water under the bridge. The *Times* is now leaning on me to go on fucking 'Nightline' and CNN and all those other goddamn quote, unquote 'news' shows. It's not that they're so freaked about the attacks on my integrity -- it's theirs that's got 'em sweating."

"Oh, Jesus. I wouldn't wish that circuit on my worst enemy."

"I can't blame them too much, Jess. They're standing by me -- so far -- and the paper's ass is on the line, too. All the same, I'd sooner feed my mother to the shark pond at Sea World than even pretend to make nice with those bastards who went after you like fucking hyenas salivating over road-kill."

She kissed his cheek. "Forget about me. I want you to do everything you can to salvage your reputation, and the integrity of the interview. I don't care if you tell the whole world I'm just a crazy lady who's been stalking you." She smiled crookedly. "Hey, seriously, that just might work!"

But he didn't smile back. Instead, he released her hands abruptly. "You think I could live with myself if I sold you down the river like all the other leeches and whores who dare to call themselves journalists?"

"Not even if I asked you to?"

"Especially not then."

She got up to grab her cigarettes. By now, she knew there was no point in arguing with him. "OK. What *are* you going to do, if anything?"

"Like I said, I owe the *Times*. I've called a press conference for three this afternoon. I'm gonna read a statement, then take questions." Now he rose as well, and put his hands on her shoulders. "Jessica, I want you to be there with me."

She was horrified. "You must be out of your mind!"

"Listen to me. Don't you realize by now that no matter what I say or how I say it, the Powers That Be are going to spin it to fit their fucking agenda? I can 'no comment' until I'm blue in the face, 'cause I'll be damned if I'm gonna lie. I'm gonna go down in flames over this one, baby. Why don't we at least do it together?"

"But . . . but if I just go back to D.C. and crawl into the woodwork, you might still have a chance! Even if they manage to blow you out of the water with the interview. Shit, Geraldo survived the Al Capone vault story!"

"I'm not Geraldo, thank God. And the next time you go back to D.C., I'm going with you."

Her heart felt ready to burst she loved him so. At once reckless and deliberate, his courage was devastating to her. "If we do this, our lives will never be the same," she whispered.

"Sure they will. Sooner or later another White House intern will get laid, and we won't even make it into a 'Jeopardy' category a year from now."

The press conference was to be held in the ballroom of the Riverside Hilton. Alex and Jessica slipped out through the back of the Royal Orleans and caught a cab. Dreading the public scrutiny, Jessica chain-smoked and rued not bringing any of her sleek designer suits with her to New Orleans, after all. It was too late to do anything about her impulsively crayoned hair, but she was sure she would have felt more confident in a Richard Tyler pantsuit than in the black turtleneck, jeans, and leather swing-coat in which she was currently clad. Alex didn't seem nervous at all. Wearing his usual Levis, casual long-sleeved shirt buttoned to the top but tieless, and suede jacket, he looked no different from yesterday save for the flinty purposefulness in his eyes.

Amazingly, not a single camera operator was staked out in front of the Hilton. Jessica guessed that Alex was as yet still sufficiently anonymous -- a circumstance bound to end in an hour's time -- that interest in catching him offguard as he strode into the hotel was minimal. And, of course, none of the journalists and photographers waiting in the ballroom would dream he'd be accompanied by Jessica.

Just after three they entered the Grand Ballroom, hand in hand.

Jessica was blinded by the detonating flashbulbs; at one point she actually needed to shield her eyes, despite her dark glasses. Alex stepped up to the podium, where a cluster of microphones was perched like a hardware bouquet. Then he turned back to Jessica. "You want a chair, or are you gonna stand?"

"I'll stand in back of you, even though it makes me feel like a politician's wife."

Though they spoke in low voices, away from the mikes, reporters seated in the first row overheard, and several laughed. Whispers of "what did they say? what did they say?" rippled through the ballroom.

And the network cameras bore in upon them.

Alex turned back to the assembly. "As you can probably guess, I'm more used to being out there with you guys than up here. I'm going to make a short statement, then I'll take questions from you -- my colleagues."

Nice move, Jessica thought. Scanning the room through her sunglasses, she was heartened to see Walt Haberman and Lois Janofsky in row four. Even amid this nest of vipers, they had a couple of friends.

A reporter from ABC stood up. "Before you begin, Alex, will Ms. Anders be answering any questions?"

"That's entirely up to her."

Jessica remained deliberately impassive.

"OK," Alex said. "The first thing I want to put on the table is the following: My friendship with Jessica Anders is none of anybody's damn business, and has no impact on my reporting. No -- let me correct myself. After seeing how this woman, a legal scholar and commentator whose ethics and professionalism have never been called into doubt --"

Nervous rustling amid the assembly. Jessica, aghast, wanted to rush over and drag him away from the podium. But it was too late. Just as he'd said last night, the die was cast.

" -- after seeing Jessica hung out to dry and even smeared by many of my colleagues in the media, just because she tried to raise the point that no one can yet prove or *dis*prove Cordelia Davis's apparent resurrection, I became all the more determined to cover this story as fairly and as honorably as possible. Last time I checked, that's the obligation of every damn one of us in the so-called legitimate media. To present the facts, without bias, whether or not they agree with the way we personally see the world. I think there's been precious little of that going on since this story broke just over three weeks ago."

Jessica saw the expressions of many reporters, including the man from ABC and Ann Magee of CNN, move from skepticism to barely veiled hostility. Walt, in the fourth row, looked ready to leap up and cheer.

"OK. Now that I've gotten that off my chest," Alex said, "here are the facts surrounding the circumstances of my interview with Cordelia Davis. Late yesterday afternoon I was contacted by my editor at the Los Angeles *Times*, Matt Crowell. He informed me that he'd been contacted via electronic mail by Louise Dumas, Mother Superior of the Convent of the Blessed Virgin. Sister Cordelia Davis wanted to arrange an interview. I went out to Metairie immediately, spoke with Sister Cordelia, and except for a few incidental comments, what was said is what was printed this morning in the LA *Times*." He folded notes he hadn't even glanced at, and tucked them into his shirt pocket.

Three dozen questions chimed in at once.

"C'mon, you guys, you know the dance," Alex chided.

NBC's Larry Bender got the first shot. "Alex, what exactly do you mean by 'a few incidental comments'?"

Alex arched an eyebrow. "You want examples? OK. Like, 'hi, how are you.' 'Nice to meet you.' 'Goodbye.'"

Again, nervous laughter at Alex's light sarcasm.

Ann Magee stood up. "Did Cordelia Davis indicate to you she was aware of your relationship with Ms. Anders?"

"No. Walt?"

"Are you convinced, at least in your own mind, that the woman you met with was in fact Cordelia Davis?"

Leave it to Walt Haberman to come up with the afternoon's first honest, fair question, Jessica thought.

Alex responded thoughtfully. "It's like I wrote in the interview. To me, yes, she looked and sounded like Cordelia Davis. I had no reason to question her sincerity." He shrugged. "Make of that what you will."

The briefest of silences gave way to a decidedly nastier line of inquiry.

"Did you think to ask her if she'd be willing to submit to a polygraph?" challenged a woman from the New York *Times*.

"No, I didn't."

"Didn't it strike you as a bit of a coincidence that of all the reporters covering this story, she explicitly asks for you to do the interview?" This from a callow legal correspondent from MSNBC.

"I have a healthy enough ego to think my writing's been among the most balanced in covering this story."

The legal correspondent wore his incredulity on his sleeve. "Don't you think that's a little naive?" he followed up. "Two days ago, the nun makes her first public appearance since the so-called funeral to come out of the convent and talk to a woman who just happens to be your girlfriend!"

The room hummed with muffled, derisive snickers. Alex refused to acknowledge either the last point made or the twittering. "Next question?"

"Isn't it indeed the case that despite the fact your wife died less than a week ago, you flew out from Los Angeles to New Orleans the same night of Miss Anders' very public encounter with Sister Cordelia?" a *Newsweek* reporter baited.

Jessica, sickened, saw Alex darken. But he held his temper. "Actually, it was the night after. But I can assure you, we haven't been colluding, as you seem to be implying, on perpetuating a hoax."

"What about your personal track-record of covering stories from a perspective favorable to Marxist political ideologies, especially in Latin America?" rejoined Ann Magee. "Doesn't that make you a somewhat biased party, particularly given Sister Davis's ostensible remarks, quoted in the interview, about struggling for social justice?"

"I'm not gonna get combative with any of you," Alex said coldly. "But these aren't questions, they're statements that just happen to end with question-marks."

"Leading questions," Jessica said softly from behind. "You're only allowed them on cross."

He tossed her a brief smile.

"What did she just say to you?" demanded Larry Bender.

"She's offering me legal advice, in case this preliminary examination is bound over for trial," Alex snapped.

"May I ask a question?" Lois, standing, waved her arm.

"That's what we're here for," Alex said.

Jessica saw a vein in his temple throbbing. How he was continuing to maintain his composure she couldn't fathom.

Lois nudged her glasses. "Why, Alex, do you think most of us in the media are treating you now the way we've been treating Jessica for nearly two weeks? You've got blue-chip credentials as a journalist, just as she does as a legal scholar. Why are we all treating you like a couple of cranks?"

Several reporters turned around to glare at her. A few others softly hissed.

"What's your name?" Alex asked gently.

"Lois Janofsky. Knight-Ridder. And I don't give a damn how many dirty looks I get for asking."

"In answer to your question, Lois. *That* just may be the real story here."

"What, the trusty old 'right wing conspiracy' theory?" scoffed the New York *Times* reporter.

More snickering.

"Look," interjected Christine Hewitt of *Time* magazine. "We're getting a little off-point here! Alex, if it were one of us who'd interviewed Sister Davis, and you were on this side of the podium, wouldn't you be asking a lot of the same questions?"

"Not a lot. Some," he conceded.

"Let me put it this way," she went on. "Let's pretend it was not Cordelia Davis but, I don't know, Reverend Charles Ingraham who allegedly arose from the dead. And the only interview he grants is to a conservative journalist from the Washington *Times* or the *National Review*. Toss into the pot the fact that the reporter's dating the only person Reverend Ingraham is known to have approached and spoken to in public. Wouldn't a few alarm-bells be going off in your head by now?"

"Maybe. But I'd make damn sure I had facts to back me up before I started slinging around completely unfounded innuendo." His anger was growing. "Are we getting anywhere with this?"

"I have a question for Jessica," Ann Magee announced.

He shot the woman a ferocious look. "I don't think

so --"

But Jessica gestured to him subtly. "It's OK." She removed her dark glasses and joined him at the podium.

"What did you mean the other day when you told me, live on CNN, that you were right and we were wrong?" Ann said, almost saccharinely polite. "And why did you yourself proclaim to columnist Debby King that you believed Sister Davis to be a fraud?"

Jessica felt calmer just knowing Alex was no longer in the hot-seat, if only for the time being. "I came into this story with an open mind, Ann. No more, no less. I never anticipated that an open mind would be perceived as subversive."

"Answer the question already!" someone complained loudly.

"Fine," Jessica said. "I believe in evidence, and I've seen none to suggest Sister Cordelia isn't genuinely resurrected. I only told Deb King what I did out of a temporary failure of nerve. It's not fun having most of the country thinking you're a raving lunatic."

The MSNBC legal eagle sneered. "So you're stating that you believe Cordelia Davis to be the genuine article -- a modern-day Lazarus."

Now the snickers turned to outright chortles.

"Yes, I do," she replied clearly. "Laugh at me if you like. But I'll never be afraid to speak what I believe is the truth."

"Have you ever been under the treatment of a psychiatrist or licensed psychotherapist?" shouted a reporter from *US News & World Report*, prompting laughter and even scattered applause.

"Are you and Alex recruiting for your cult of the Resurrected Death-Penalty Foe?" taunted another journalist.

"Because, let's face it, that's what you two are up to. Promoting a political agenda -- anti-death penalty, anti-capitalist -- by trying to foster the utterly preposterous notion that this nun came back from the dead through divine intervention!"

"You talk about evidence, Jessica," Ann Magee added. "You both have admitted political views that jibe with those of Cordelia Davis. What evidence can you offer that either one of you is free of ideological motivation?"

Alex took Jessica's arm. "Let's get out of here," he mouthed.

"Last question! Last question!" boomed CBS's Jeremy Kaplan, even as Alex and Jessica were leaving the podium. "When it's finally proven how the hoax was engineered, will either of you be prepared to issue a statement?"

Alex started to raise a stiff middle finger to his journalistic colleagues. "Don't," Jessica warned. "It'll be the last nail in your coffin."

As usual, he ignored her advice and did it anyway.

Chapter 15

Outside the Royal Orleans, a small but vocal group of hecklers awaited. They jeered and chanted "Bull-Shit!" as Alex and Jessica climbed out of their cab and hurried into the hotel.

Not a single pilgrim was in evidence.

Bystanders in the lobby gawked, but said nothing.

Jessica and Alex didn't exchange a single word themselves until they were safely behind the locked door of her room. And even then, their conversation was forced. "You want a drink?" Alex said, picking up the bottle of Bombay.

"No."

Abruptly he set down the bottle. "Me either." He pulled her to him and began kissing her roughly. They tore off each other's clothes like predators. She dug her nails into his back while he sucked at her breasts until she cried out in a paroxysm of pleasure and pain. She scratched at his face like a cat as she rode violently on top of him. Her orgasm was a banshee shriek. He dragged her onto the floor and pounded into her, crushing her, spilling into her until he fell back, sated.

Simultaneously they burst into soft yet uncontrollable laughter. "Oh, God," Jessica gasped, "this is so damn . . . kinky." She was literally clutching her sides.

"What . . . makes you say . . . that?" He was laughing so hard he could scarcely get the words out.

"Oh Jesus, you should see yourself! I scratched the hell out of your face!" She sat up, struggling to get a hold of herself.

"Hey, it's just like the song goes, girl. It's the end of the world as we know it, and I feel fine."

That got her laughing all over again.

Still chuckling under his breath, he tugged her to her feet. "Come on, let's take a shower."

Under the hot, relentless spray, they kissed and laughed and laughed.

Finally, once they were again dressed, the shared fit of desperate and defiant gaiety abated. "What are we going to do," Jessica sighed, plaiting her wet hair into two loose braids.

"Christ." He exhaled smoke.

A sharp, triple-rap on the door sounded.

"That's Walt," Jessica said, recognizing the knock. "Just a sec!" she called out. She hastened to make up the rumpled bed.

Alex strolled over to the door and admitted not only Walt, but Lois Janofsky into the sanctuary. Alex shook Lois's hand warmly. "I'll never forget what you did for us today," he said.

Lois waved him off. "It's a sick world when you're praised simply for not being an asshole."

"Jeez, what happened to your face?" Walt asked worriedly. "A lynch-mob catch up with you outside the Hilton?"

Alex gingerly rubbed the longest of the fingernail scrapes on his cheek. "Hate to disappoint, but this came courtesy of *mi amante loca*," he said wryly.

Walt and Lois looked a little embarrassed, but Jessica laughed. She got up and gave each of them a quick hug. "What happened today -- happened. And Alex is right. You were great -- both of you."

"You hear anything yet from Crowell or Bloom?" Walt asked Alex.

"Nah. I imagine they'll be faxing me my walking papers. You guys want a beer?" He sauntered over to the minibar.

"Trujillo, how the hell can you be so cavalier?" Walt demanded.

Alex twisted off the cap of a Heineken. "I call it being a realist, man."

Lois accepted a Diet Coke. "Looks like you did the nun a bigger favor than you thought. I just got word half an hour ago that she took advantage of the feeding frenzy at the Hilton to slip away from the convent, escorted by Father Salazar of Managua."

"You're kidding," Jessica said, excited. "That's great!"

"Who's Father Salazar again?" Walt asked Lois.

Alex, who looked vaguely troubled, replied. "One of the leading liberation theologians in Central America. He was a close advisor to Daniel Ortega before Ronnie's dirty little secret army overthrew the Sandinistas."

"He's also one of the Church's top moral authorities on the death penalty," Jessica added. "He gave the commencement address at Georgetown a few years back." She smiled dryly. "Listen to us. We sound just like the politically-motivated zealots we're supposed to be."

"You mean, you're not?" Lois joked.

Jessica fetched herself a bottled water. "Alex, now that Sister Cordelia's likely on her way out of Louisiana, I need to get back to Washington. I'd like to leave as soon as possible."

He nodded, though his expression had become a mask she couldn't read. "Go ahead and book us a flight. I just need to get my stuff from Le Richelieu."

Jessica turned back to Walt and Lois. "Walt, you've been an incredible friend to me --"

"No speech-making," he stopped her. "Someday we'll all sit down over nachos and a pitcher of margaritas and ask ourselves if any of this really happened."

"All right, then. Lois, take care. When my son hits fourteen and wants to pierce his tongue, I'm going to call you up for advice."

"God bless you, Jessica," Lois said, sounding as if she meant it.

"He already has," she replied quietly.

"OK, I'm outa here," Alex said, grabbing his suede jacket. "You guys want to play bodyguard for me the eight blocks back to Le Richelieu?"

"Jeez, that's a pathetic thought," Walt said.

"Come on," Lois nudged him. "Think how it'll look on your resume."

Jessica used some of her frequent flier miles to upgrade their seats to business class, which she trusted would afford them relative privacy. For once, luck was with them. The nine-fifteen flight to National Airport was only half-full, and none of the other passengers paid them any particular notice.

It was only once the plane was airborne that Alex disclosed to her the content of the fax that had indeed awaited him at his hotel. "They nailed me for just about everything. My 'unprofessional conduct' at the press conference. 'Failure to adhere to the highest standards of journalistic ethics' -- that, I believe, was in reference to my bringing you along. My 'inadequate efforts to defend the integrity of the interview.'" He signaled to a passing flight attendant for a second cocktail.

"I wish I hadn't agreed to come," Jessica said. "It just gave everybody more ammunition to fire your way."

The flight attendant placed a fresh miniature bottle of Tanqueray gin on his tray. "How're we doing on tonic?" she asked brightly.

He held up the almost-full can of Canada Dry. "Fine. Thanks."

"How about you, ma'am? Are you ready for another Cabernet?"

"No, I'm still working on this one. I would like some coffee, though."

As the flight attendant headed for the galley, Alex emptied the gin into his plastic cup. "Jess, they would have stuck it to me anyway. I talked briefly with Crowell. The *Times* has been under siege since the paper hit the stands, hours before the press conference. Editorials blasting them for printing the interview without verifying its accuracy are going to appear in tomorrow's New York *Times*, the *Post*, the Chicago *Tribune*, even the fucking *Wall Street Journal*. I was dead meat from the moment I filed the story."

"Do you regret it?"

He didn't answer immediately.

"You know, Alex, it's OK if you do. I'm sure that somewhere in the back of your mind, you were hoping against hope that your honesty and good faith in doing the interview would carry the day. I know I was hoping that for you."

"I don't regret it," he said, tensely swirling his drink. "I did what I believed in. I can live with that."

She still had the impression that there was something on his mind he wasn't confiding. She was about to press him, then thought the better of it. What if it were Natalie, about whose suicide he felt so guilty? Now his apparent callousness (or so she guessed he viewed it) was a matter of public record. She silently cursed that bitch from *Newsweek* who had taunted Alex for seeming to race to Jessica's side with Natalie barely cold.

Their plane landed at close to one a.m. It was far too late to collect Jordy from Gregg at his Bethesda apartment, so Jessica and Alex hailed a cab to take them to Georgetown. She half-feared she'd find the townhouse trashed by vandals, or at the very least a scorched cross on her tiny lawn, but her home was intact. She'd even inadvertently tripped her own burglar alarm coming in, forgetting to punch in the proper code within the allotted thirty seconds.

And then it struck her that something *was* wrong. No Jordan, no Vicky. She fought back tears. "Look, I'm going to check my messages," she said, trying to keep her voice from trembling. "Help yourself to anything in the fridge or bar."

But she bypassed the upstairs study and went directly to Jordy's room. She switched on the light. The sight of his empty crib, all the more pathetic for the much-loved stuffed bunny and polkadot turtle left behind, was more than she could bear. She collapsed into the rocking chair and wept into her hands.

She heard Alex come in, felt his hands massaging her shoulders. "I thought I might find you in here. It's OK, Jess. We'll get him tomorrow."

She swiped at her eyes with her knuckles. "It's just that . . . this is the first time I've ever come home and not found him here waiting for me."

"And it's gonna be the last time, too."

She managed a smile. "You know, for a fucking commie yellow journalist, you're a pretty nice guy."

He chucked her under the chin. "An *exhausted* fucking commie yellow journalist," he amended. "Let's go to bed."

"Best idea you've had all day."

He shot her an ironic look. "No shit."

As Alex's former editor had foretold, morning papers across the country carried withering front-page editorials ripping into the Los Angeles *Times* in general, and Alex Trujillo's interview with Cordelia Davis in particular. Trujillo's press conference the day before was routinely characterized as "bizarre," a grotesque and self-serving publicity stunt that virtually confirmed the reporter's questionable ethics. He was ridiculed for "parading out the equally dubious Ms. Anders, as though displaying a trophy a more conscientious journalist would stash in the attic along with last year's Christmas wrap," carped the New York *Times*. The dishier *Post* splashed Alex and Jessica's picture on its cover, under the sensationalistic headline "HUCKSTERS FOR JESUS?" Not to be outdone, the equally gamey *Daily News* featured the same photo from the press conference, with the caption "ALEX AND JESSIE: LEFT-WING CONSPIRACY OR LOONY LOVERS?"

Jessica awakened at seven. Leaving Alex asleep in her bedroom, she tiptoed downstairs, put on the coffee, and called Gregg. "Hi, I'm back."

Nothing.

"Gregg?"

"Uh -- sorry. I was working on this goddamn motion for summary judgment till about two in the morning. How are you?"

"Fine. You sound funny." More than just groggy. He sounded *guarded*.

"Jessica, we need to talk."

"What the hell is that supposed to mean?" she snapped, shakily lighting up a cigarette.

"Just that. Can you come over in an hour or so? I'm not going into work until this afternoon."

"This doesn't have anything to do with Jordy, does it?" she said suspiciously.

"Jordan's doing just great, Jessie. I'll see you around nine, all right?"

And he hung up.

"No. No. He wouldn't do that to me," she fretted aloud, starting to pace the kitchen parquet. "He just wants to lecture me about yesterday, about how rash and stupid he thinks I was."

"What's wrong?" Alex stood in the kitchen door, shirtless in jeans.

She jumped. She'd momentarily forgotten he was here. "Christ," she said, pressing her palm to her heart. "You scared me."

"And vice-versa. You look like somebody just kicked you in the stomach."

"It's nothing. Really. I'm just being paranoid." She picked up the coffee pot but her hand slipped, and she ended up spilling all over the counter. "Oh, shit!" She furiously began to sponge up the mess.

"For Christ's sake, Jessica, what is it?" He forcibly removed the sponge from her hand and led her over to the kitchen table.

"Alex," she said, her panic welling, "do you love me? I mean, really love me?"

He took her hand and kissed it, the hand that was still damp from mopping up spilled coffee. "More than you'll ever know, querida. What's bothering you?"

"I just talked to my ex-husband, and he sounded weird. I have this awful feeling he's going to try not to give me back my baby!"

"Did he tell you that?"

"No, but -- " She broke off, reassured by his calm. "You're right. I'm being crazy. Strong-arm tactics have never been Gregg's style. Not as a lawyer, not as a human being." She released his hand, and went back to finish wiping down the counter. "He probably just wants to impress me in his best lawyerly fashion with his disapproval. No doubt to assuage whatever residual guilt he still feels over dumping me for a twenty-five year old stewardess."

"Ah. That explains your uncharacteristic surliness last night when the flight attendant asked if you wanted another drink."

She glared at him. "I was not surly." She tossed the sponge in the sink. "All the same, Alex, will you go with me to Gregg's in about an hour?"

"As long as you don't think my being there might increase the likelihood of friction."

In fact, she guessed it might. But if there were even the most miniscule chance Gregg was planning to give her a hard time about handing over Jordan, her cause couldn't be hurt by the presence of her six-foot-two, hot-tempered lover.

Gregg was obviously surprised she had not come alone. Jessica made businesslike introductions. Gregg was cordial but cool, not just to Alex but to Jessica as well.

Jordy, dressed in red rompers, was crawling around in his playpen. Jessica scooped him up into her arms. "My baby, my darling baby!" she cooed, covering his downy curls with kisses. "Mama's missed you so much, Jordy!" She swung around to face Alex and Gregg.

Alex was smiling at her.

Gregg was not.

Jessica's heart began to race. "What? What the hell is it?"

Gregg turned to Alex. "I know this sounds rude, Mr. Trujillo. But I'd like to speak to my wife in private."

"Ex-wife!" she corrected hotly.

"Not for another three months," he rejoined.

"That's right, let's split hairs," she mocked. "And Alex stays."

"Look, Jess, it's no big deal. I'll go outside and have a smoke," Alex said.

"No you won't," she barked.

"Hey," Gregg said, tossing up his hands casually. "If you want him to stay, that's your call. But if you're going to get emotional, Jessie, maybe we should put Jordy down in his crib."

"No," she spat, clutching her child even closer. "Nobody's taking this baby out of my arms."

Alex shot Gregg a grave, warning look. "I'm sure no one is going to, Jessica."

Gregg ignored him. "There's no point pussyfooting around this any longer. Jessie, I don't think you should have primary custody of Jordan until all this hoopla has died down."

"You goddamn hypocrite," she hissed, frantically rocking the baby in her arms. "You swore you understood and supported me when I told you I was going back to New Orleans!"

"I did, and in a way, I still do," he said evenly. "I respect you for following your beliefs, though, granted, I sure as hell don't understand them or where they came from all of a sudden."

"That's real big of you, man," Alex said icily.

"You know something, Trujillo?" Gregg replied, regarding Alex with condescending patience. "You *are* part of the problem here. Have either of you seen today's papers? After that circus yesterday, you two have made yourself magnets for every wild-eyed, pistol-packing nut-case in the country. How could you be so arrogant and stupid, for Christ's sake?" Now he was growing emotional. "You both were right there in Metairie when that lunatic opened fire on the crowd. Thanks for lying to me about that, Jessie."

"Gregg, please," Jessica begged. "I'd lay down my life before I'd take even a remote chance where Jordan's safety is concerned. You know that's true!"

"If it will make any difference, I'll go back to L.A.," Alex said, his tone level. "You're right; it's my fault for bringing Jessica to the press conference. She didn't want to do it. She shouldn't have to pay for my error in judgment."

"Sorry, but you can't unring the bell," Gregg said, shaking his head in a show of apparent regret. "I don't question your sincerity, either one of you. You chose to offer yourselves up as martyrs to a cause you think is worthy. But there's no way I am going to allow my son's safety to be placed at risk, irrespective of the nobility of your principles. Sorry, Jessica. This is not negotiable."

"I'll go to some small town in New England!" she tried to bargain. "I'll change my name and cut off my hair, and I'll never see Alex again! You can have the baby every weekend! For God's sake, Gregg, don't do this to me!"

Alex lowered his eyes, anguished.

But Gregg was unswayed. "Do I have to repeat myself, Jessica? This is not negotiable."

"No!" she screamed, dissolving into hysterical sobs. "No!" The frightened baby in her arms began to shriek as well. "Oh, sweetie, I'm sorry, I'm sorry! I'm so . . . goddamn . . . sorry!" She sank to her knees, splashing him with her tears as she tried in vain to soothe him.

"You sonofabitch," Alex seethed to Gregg. "Look at what you're doing to her. She's lost almost everything. Are you going to take away from her the only thing left that matters?"

Gregg made no effort to disguise his contempt. "If it means keeping my son safe, yes."

"I'll take you to court!" Jessica threatened wildly.

"Under the circumstances, I doubt that very strongly, Jessica. You'd risk losing custody permanently, and I think you know it."

"How is that any different from what you're doing to me right now, you bastard!"

"It's a lot different. As I told you, I consider this a temporary arrangement. Five, six months from now, hopefully, this whole asinine Sister Cordelia debacle will be forgotten, and then we can rethink primary custody."

She staggered to her feet. "OK, that's reasonable, I mean, you've been entirely reasonable . . . "

Balancing Jordan on one hip, she made a mad, futile dash toward the front door of the apartment, a dash easily aborted by Gregg, who merely stepped in front of her and firmly removed the baby from her arms.

Alex looked stricken as Jessica beat her fists against Gregg's shoulder and keened like an animal snared in a claw-trap.

Gregg, holding the squalling baby at arm's length, turned to Alex. "If you actually do give a damn about her, Trujillo, do her a favor and make sure she gets some help."

She was inconsolable. He lit a fire and held her in his arms and tried to assure her that everything would be all right, but to no avail. She had no more words, no more tears; all she was seemed subsumed by her overwhelming sense of loss. At length, Alex appeared to realize there was nothing he could say to comfort her, and he fell silent too.

After an hour the fire was sputtering. He got up to toss in another log.

"Alex."

"Yeah, baby." He rejoined her on the couch, draping his arm around her.

"Don't leave me."

His face settled into by-now familiar, bitter lines. "I've fucked up your life every bit as much as those bottom-feeders in the media. The sooner I'm gone, the better your chances of working things out with Monahan." He refused to meet her eyes.

"You're wrong. Gregg's having the ride of his life on his goddamn high horse." She spoke dully, without emotion. Facts, facts, facts. "God knows, he may even be right. I've done this to myself."

"With a lot of help from me." He flicked his cigarette lighter furiously, generating only weak sparks. "Shit." He threw it down in disgust.

"I have matches in my purse." She fumbled mechanically in her bag and found a pack from Mr. B.'s Bistro, Royal Street, New Orleans.

He lit his cigarette. "Of all the stupid, fucking irresponsible things I've done in my life, nothing tops what I've done to you."

"Leave it alone. It has nothing to do with you."

"No? Who came to your hotel room the night of the funeral and delivered a speech crammed full of passionate bullshit about how a greater fucking good could be achieved by promoting the idea the resurrection was real? Who flew out here when you were trying to wash your hands of the whole damn mess because you knew you could lose everything if you pursued it? I guilted you and manipulated you into believing that anything short of direct confrontation was cowardly, and it's cost you your kid." Self-torment had aged him suddenly into an old man.

Jessica stared dumbly at him for a moment. Then she erupted. "Damn you! God damn you, you sonofabitch! How dare you make this all about you and your perverse need to torture yourself over Natalie's death! Do you get some kind of sick pleasure out of taking responsibility for other people's misery? I've never heard such patronizing, egotistical bullshit in my life!"

Taken aback by her outburst, he seemed about to retort, then caught himself. "This has been a nightmarish day for you -- "

"There you go patronizing me again!" she accused. "Do you really think I'm so weak-minded that your high-and-mighty influence could hold such sway? I went back to New Orleans not because of you, but because of *her*! Because I believe in her truth, I stood beside you at that exercise in the Theatre of the Absurd that was supposed to be a press conference! Not because of you -- because of *her*!"

Alex turned on her savagely. "Listen to me, you goddamn fool! Don't you see what everybody else has -- that she was manipulating us? That's why she picked you out of a crowd! That's why she chose me, of all reporters, to do the interview! Didn't it strike you as strange that she used that fucking press conference where we were both tarred and feathered on national TV as a convenient cover for her to hightail it out of town like a snake-oil salesman in the old west?"

Outraged and incredulous, Jessica slapped him in the face with all the force and fury she could muster. "That's a lie! A horrible, evil lie!"

She raised her arm to strike him again but he caught her arm roughly. "Get real, Jessica!" he challenged.

"*You* get real, muchacho!" she retorted, wrenching free. "She chose us because she trusted us, trusted our -- oh, yes, what were your lofty words? -- our 'honor' and 'integrity'! Now it turns out you not only don't believe in her, you don't believe in yourself. If anyone's a fraud, it's you. Go back to Los Angeles. I don't want anything more to do with you, a brilliant and beautiful man who believes in absolutely nothing!"

He didn't respond; he just slumped over the coffee table with his head in his hands.

She charged upstairs, past the nursery ordained to remain empty indefinitely, past the bedroom where the sheets were still rumpled from their fools' paradise sleep last night. She went into the study, wildly surveyed all the accoutrements of a career and commitment wrested violently away from her. Her framed diplomas from UCLA, Boalt Hall, Yale; the computer, fax, and laser printer; the answering machine with its twinkling red light; bookcases full of scholarly legal tomes and Law Reviews; the television, its nineteen inch screen a dull grayish-black eye that yet seemed to stare gloatingly back at her.

"I HATE YOU!" she screamed at all of it.

She suddenly remembered the baseball bat Grace had given her, half-facetiously, right after Gregg had moved out. "Keep it under your bed in case the bogey man breaks in," Grace had joked. A cheap Baltimore Orioles bat with a mass-produced Cal Ripken autograph. Jessica had tossed it in the linen closet near the second-floor landing.

She walked deliberately to the closet and found the bat behind a stack of Ralph Lauren towels. It felt heavier than she recalled.

She returned to the study. "You know what?" she said, as if addressing a friend. "I believe we could use a little ritual here." She fumbled through the books on the shelves, hurling them to the floor, until she found a King James Bible.

"Hmm, hmm," she said, flipping through the thin parchment. "Yes, I think this will do."

Holding the Bible in one hand, the baseball bat in the other, she read aloud from Psalm 41. "'By this I know that thou favorest me, because mine enemy doth not triumph over me'!" Dropping the book, she gripped the bat with both hands and crashed it first into the computer monitor, the fax. She pounded the diplomas off the walls before thrusting her assembly-line Cal Ripken like a battering ram into the television screen. "*Touché*, you sonofabitch!"

Glass shattered, wires sparked and fizzled, activating the smoke alarms.

Undaunted, she swung at the ruined TV again. "I'll kill you, you fucking bastard!"

Alex seized her from behind, lifting her off her feet, carrying her downstairs kicking and screaming to the kitchen. "Stay there!" he barked, grabbing the fire extinguisher she kept handy in case of overheated stir-fry in the wok.

Seated at the kitchen table, she pulled her knees to her chest and laughed triumphantly. "It's too late, darling! I've killed the shithead!"

In her hysteria she hadn't been able to tell him where her Xanax was. At first she fought his attempts to coax brandy into her, but then she grew weary of his nagging and accepted a couple of glasses. Soon thereafter came the tears and shame and recriminations. She didn't protest when he carried her upstairs to the master bathroom and turned on the faucet in the oval, faux-marble tub. "Do you want any of this stuff?" he asked, gesturing toward panoply of bath salts, oils, and fragrant organic suds.

She couldn't answer, so he dumped half a bottle of lavender foam into the rushing water. He helped her out of her clothes, and into the tub.

He sat cross-legged on the mat, his clasped hands pressed to his chin.

Slowly, the warm, sudsy water restored her to herself.

She massaged her throbbing temples. "Jesus," she said weakly. "I might have burned the damn house down over our heads."

"No. The sparks were all dead by the time I got there with the fire extinguisher."

Wincing, she couldn't bring herself to look at him. "Is that some kind of horrible, heavy-handed metaphor for you and me?"

"Not as far as I'm concerned." He sighed. "Jess, I'm sorry for everything I said downstairs. I didn't mean it. I was just so pissed at Gregg for taking your kid from you. I was lashing out at you, at everybody."

She bit back a sob. "I want so badly to believe that's true."

"It is."

"Because," she said, rocking herself gently, "the only way I can make sense of any of this is to trust that everything's going to be OK. That I'll get Jordy back. That I'll be a better person for having gone through this hell." She looked at him starkly. "Will you stick by me on this one?"

He leaned over the tub and kissed her, tangling his fingers in her hair. "Always."

"And you'll trust me?"

"As long as you leave batting practice to Tony Gwynn, yeah," he teased, amending, more somberly, "Yes, I will, and I do."

"I kept thinking of the father in *To Die For* … did you ever see …?" She brushed his face with her soapy hand. "It's all so crazy. Yet in the process of losing everything, somehow I found you."

"One hell of a consolation prize," he replied, his bitterness returning.

"Don't," she said firmly. "I need to tell you this, Alex. My heart is broken that Gregg's keeping Jordan from me. I'm going to get my son back, and when I do, I'll never forgive that pompous asshole for putting me through this."

"I'm glad you said it first. I thought the guy was a pompous asshole the minute he opened the door."

"Fine. Be that as it may. But here's the important thing, Alex, the part I really want you to listen to." She looked him directly in the eye. "I'm proud of you, and I'm proud of me. I'm sorry what we've done has brought such pain to both of us. But I know

I was acting on a moral imperative, and, bitter and cynical though you are, I think you know you were, too."

He clambered to his feet. "Hey, I gotta get my smokes. You probably could use one, too. Be right back." He hastened out of the bathroom.

But not before she'd noticed that his eyes were welling with tears.

Chapter 16

"I'm going to California for a couple of weeks." In her arms, Jordan slept, and she absently adjusted the blankets around his face.

Today's meeting with Gregg in Bethesda was markedly calmer than yesterday's. With her goal some kind of uneasy truce, this time she'd come alone. She apologized deeply for the scene she'd made, and warily, Gregg seemed to accept it.

"When are you leaving?"

"Tomorrow. I'll be in L.A. first, then I'm going to San Francisco to spend some time with my brother."

Jordan burbled drowsily, and she pressed his warm little face against her chest. One of her more profound disappointments had been her inability to breast-feed. There was nothing wrong with her, her doctor said; she just couldn't produce enough milk.

"Give Steve my best. Is he still with what's-her-name?"

"Shelly? Oh, no, she's long fallen by the wayside. Now it's Kris." She took a short sip from the Perrier he'd brought her. "Gregg, when I get back from the coast -- I want to have Jordan baptized. Please say you won't fight me."

He shrugged. "If it means that much to you, sure."

"Thanks. I thought Steve could be godfather, and you might want to ask someone from work who's Catholic -- maybe Kerry Doyle -- to be godmother."

He shook his head in mild bemusement. "This religious awakening of yours, or whatever it is . . . I've got to tell you, it blows me away."

"Don't worry. I've no intention of taking the veil."

"Obviously not."

She couldn't ignore his slight, snide undertone. "You surprise me. I'd have expected you to be thrilled I've found somebody else. It makes me less inclined to fantasize about separating Coffee-Tea-or-Me from her scalp."

"This has nothing to do with Doreen," he chided.

"True. Alex is much prettier."

"Come on, Jessie. You have to grant that you and Trujillo came together under extraordinary circumstances. Don't you wonder what kind of future you'll have once this Cordelia business finally blows over?"

"I'm sure we'll be just fine."

But she did wonder, she admitted to herself, as she drove back to Georgetown, pensive anyway for having to leave Jordy behind. It wasn't that she feared their love was predicated by a shared quest and equally shared persecution at the hands of those who would stop them. Rather, it was that their relationship undeniably had a dark aspect she'd yet to have leisure fully to contemplate. His heavy drinking concerned her, and she herself was drinking far more than usual because of his company. They'd had bitterer fights in less than a month than she'd had throughout her twelve-year marriage to Gregg. Their sexual passion seemed equal parts violence and desire. And perhaps scariest of all, she couldn't imagine her life without him, and she'd never felt that way about any man, not even Gregg in their giddy salad days.

She tried to picture them in a saner world, found she could not. Their former lives were irrevocably lost to them; it was not as if eventually she could resume teaching law at Georgetown and he could land a cushy job with the Washington *Post*. Even were Alex not in her life, the crystal ball would be cloudy.

Sister Cordelia's words returned to comfort her. *"Be strong, and have faith."*

What choice had she but to heed them?

The anonymity they had enjoyed flying from New Orleans to Washington was not to be the case on the American nonstop to LAX. Though Jessica pinned her hair up under a gray fedora and both of them wore sunglasses, no fewer than eight strangers approached them during the five-hour flight, requesting, amazingly enough, autographs. Jessica was sure most were mere curiosity seekers, but three people -- an elderly white woman, a college kid, and an African-American man in a natty three-piece suit -- wished them well and encouraged them to stand by their principles.

But once on the ground at Los Angeles International, they blended into the crowd again. After collecting their luggage from the carousel, they boarded a shuttle for one of the airport's parking complexes. "I can't believe you kept your car in long-term parking," she remarked as he tossed their bags into the back of his Jeep Wrangler. "Wasn't it outrageously expensive?"

"Trust me, it was probably the best money I ever spent," he said somewhat cryptically, slamming shut the hatch.

Unfortunately, it was four o'clock, the beginning of rush hour in L.A. The northbound 405 was bumper-to-bumper.

"Ugh," Jessica said, rolling down her window. Even late afternoon the air was pleasantly warm and dry. "I still don't know how people deal with this commute day-in and day-out."

He slipped a Miles Davis cassette into the tapedeck. "D.C.'s not exactly Mayberry."

"True enough. Hey, by the way, where do you live? Not that I'd have any idea how to get there."

"Silver Lake -- near Hollywood."

She nodded, sort of remembering. "When I went to UCLA, I had a friend who lived in Los Feliz, right down the street from Griffith Park. It's not far from there, right?"

He nodded. "Not quite as upscale as Los Feliz, though. It's funkier. Cool bookstores and bars."

Traffic was just as congested on the Hollywood Freeway. It was nearly an hour later that he turned up a narrow, hilly street and then made a sharp left into the driveway of a small, 1930s-style Craftsman bungalow. Though a garage remote was clipped to the sun visor, he ignored it and stopped in the drive.

Jessica hopped out. His was a pretty, unpretentious street of small houses and heavy tree-shade. In the fading sunlight she could still make out a hazy view of the downtown skyline, and, at the far western horizon, a hint of the Pacific Ocean. Hoisting her carry-on over one shoulder, she followed him, and the rest of the luggage, in through the front door.

"Have a seat in the living room," he said. "I'm gonna get a beer. I don't think I have any wine, but I'll check."

"That's OK. I'm fine."

She stepped into the living room, which was larger than she might have guessed from the apparent size of the house. An austere and attractive room, with plain hardwood floors and simple, geometric furniture mostly in shades of tan and gray. Above the fireplace hung a Diego Rivera poster framed in chrome. She skimmed the titles in one of the handsome, built-in bookcases; she'd always believed you could read a lot about people by their personal libraries and CD collections. For instance, if she spotted *The Bridges of Madison County* or the autobiography of Donald Trump, she'd have to assume he'd pulled a fast one over on her.

Nothing surprising, really. Maybe more Roland Barthes and Susan Sontag than she would have expected, but the majority, books on the media, on politics, on class struggle in Central America, she could have predicted blindfolded. Only a handful of

novels -- Russell Banks's *The Sweet Hereafter*, Thomas Pynchon's *Mason-Dixon*, Gabriel
Garcia Marquez's *100 Years of Solitude*.

Afraid she'd be caught snooping, she plopped down on the overstuffed beige sofa.
Atop the square, glass-topped coffee table were an ashtray, a month-old issue of *Sports
Illustrated*, and a packet of rolling papers.

And just in time, too, for Alex walked in with a Corona and a glass of white wine.
He handed her the goblet. "I can't vouch for this. My friends Nick and Leah brought it
over a year ago just after we moved in."

Uncomfortable by his invocation of first-person-plural, she promptly took a sip.
An OK Fume Blanc. "It's fine." Another sip. "This is a pretty room."

"The house was a real fixer, which is how I could afford it. We put a lot of work
into it. Ripped up the cheesy carpets and refinished the floors." He set down his beer.
"You gotta see the bathroom. Come on."

He led her down a short hallway. "Look," he said, throwing open a door. "Is this
so tacky it's cool, or what?"

She peered in, and had to smile. All black and white faux-marble and gorgeous
ebony tile, the latter of which she guessed was a recent renovation. A shiny black
porcelain tub on hideous claw feet. "It's really *Hollywood Babylon*," she said. "I like it,
though. It's so unapologetically Art Deco."

They went back out to the living room. And it was then that she realized he was
far more uncomfortable than she. In his own house he was as tense as a stranger, and she
intuited that his discomfiture had nothing to do with her. These were not his bachelor
digs. It was the home he had shared with his late wife Natalie, a home both clearly cared
about. Refinishing the hardwood floors, restoring the bathroom to its original grotesque
glory. It was here that Alex had caught Natalie in bed with another man, by her own
arrangement, if Renie's account was to be trusted. Was it here, too, that Natalie had died?

As if he'd guessed what she was thinking and wanted to distract her -- perhaps, distract both of them -- he snatched the rolling papers off the table. "You want to smoke?"

She shook her head. "You can if you want. But it's always made me kind of paranoid."

"Nowadays, how could you tell?" he quipped edgily, wandering over to the hearth and removing a plastic bag of weed from a vintage humidor. "Let's go out back. The smell sticks like crazy to these damp old walls."

The backyard was small, fenced on three sides. A redwood deck, also an obvious recent addition, overlooked a modest thatch of lawn. On the deck were a couple of white plastic chairs and, shoved to the side, a barbecue that looked unused since last summer. Jessica was starting to feel like an interloper.

Impatiently, efficiently, he rolled a joint, lit it. The acrid fragrance of marijuana filled her nostrils. He took a hit, offered her one, but she again demurred.

The sun was almost vanished, but vibrant wisps of violet and pink still streaked the western sky. "It's so beautiful," she said quietly. "You know what it makes me think of?"

"Uh-uh."

"Well, when I was an undergraduate, I went through this phase where I was just passionate about the French poet Baudelaire."

He nodded, though it was plain he was only half-listening. "*Les Fleurs du Mal.* Real cheery, upbeat stuff."

"Right. Anyway, I not only loved the poems, but I also felt compelled to read everything about him, about his life. He suffered a syphilitic stroke in a Belgian church. Talk about Catholic guilt."

"Yeah, I think I knew that." He took in another heavy draw on the smoldering joint.

Now she was almost entirely certain he wasn't listening at all. "He lost his speech. Aphasia. He could apparently understand everything people said to him, but he could only respond with this half-formed oath." Recounting the story more to herself than to him, she fixed her eyes on the pink and purple ribbons in the sky. "Nadar, the famous photographer, used to visit Baudelaire in the nursing home. They'd have these amazing conversations, even though Baudelaire could speak only this one nonsensical phrase, '*crenom*.'" She paused briefly to light a cigarette. "One day, they were having this heated argument over the existence of God. And Nadar, being a good nineteenth century freethinker, scoffed at Baudelaire, 'how can you possibly believe in a God or in an afterlife?' And you know what Baudelaire did?"

He didn't respond, nor had she expected him to.

"Well, Baudelaire raised his arm and gestured toward this brilliant, gorgeous sunset over the Arc de Triomphe. '*Crenom*,' he just said. I remember being terribly moved by that."

His face contorted in sudden, horrible despair, and she realized with a start that he'd been listening after all.
His chest was heaving.

Frightened for him, Jessica held her breath.

At last he exhaled wearily. "She died here, you know. Not here exactly, but there." He pointed toward the garage.

Jessica chilled. So that was why he'd left the Wrangler in the driveway.

"She washed down about fifty Valium with her old man's private reserve of Bombay Sapphire, went into the garage, and revved up the ignition on her fucking Saab. Let me tell you, chica, she didn't see any glorious sunsets over the goddamn Arc de Triomphe."

Jessica chewed nervously on her lower lip. "I'm sorry. I was being insensitive."

Now the sky was black; no glorious sunset lingered over the greater Los Angeles basin, either.

But Alex made no move to go inside. "She couldn't get in touch with me that night, because I was flying from New Orleans to D.C. to see you. So she called my sister Lily and just fucking screamed at her, 'Dead is dead!' Lily thinks it must have had something to do with my working on the Sister Cordelia story. Lily and her boyfriend raced over here, and guess what they found."

Jessica, shaken, fumbled for a response. "Renie told me your wife was pretty much a confirmed atheist."

Alex scowled. "What the fuck does that matter? So's Renie! So -- " He grew flustered. "What I'm trying to say is that all that crap's irrelevant. Natalie might have lit candles at daily Mass for the last ten years, and the outcome would be the same."

"Do you miss her?" Jessica asked gently.

"This goddamn house is haunted by her, if that's what you mean."

"It isn't what I mean."

He laughed wretchedly. "Struck mute in a Catholic church! That's pretty damn priceless, isn't it." He snuffed out the remains of the joint. "And, in answer to your question -- no, I don't miss her. If there's one thing I feel guiltier about than her death, it's that I can't even pretend to miss her."

Just as she got up to hug him, the doorbells chimed.

The callers turned out to be his sister Lily, accompanied by their mother, Rebecca Trujillo. Lily had heard on talk radio that he had returned to L.A., "and because you never pick up your phone anymore," she teased, "we decided to barge on over uninvited." Lily was a pretty, sparkling thirty-year-old, completing a doctorate in sociology at USC. Rebecca Trujillo was a greater surprise to Jessica, an elegant, handsome woman near sixty with perfectly coiffed chestnut hair and impeccably manicured nails. She wore a

Cartier watch, Chanel suit, and understated but expensive jewelry. She was as vivacious as her daughter; both had hugged Jessica on sight, as if they'd all known each other forever.

My God, I don't know him at all, Jessica thought, amused, as Alex crossly brushed off the displays of familial solicitude. "Look, we've had a long flight. I'll call you both tomorrow, OK?"

"You go take a shower and a shave," his mother scolded. Unlike Alex and Lily, she spoke with a strong Spanish accent. "You look terrible."

"We brought groceries," Lily explained merrily to Jessica. "Have you peeked inside his refrigerator? There's, like, a six-pack of Coronas and a shriveled cantaloupe they can probably whiff in San Diego!"

Jessica suddenly sensed that Natalie hadn't been living here for some time. That must have made her suicide seem to Alex all the more vindictive: she'd pointedly returned to the house they'd lovingly refurbished, to consecrate it with death.

She joined his sister and mother in ganging up on him. Swearing under his breath, he disappeared into the bedroom. Jessica helped unload the groceries, mostly deli stuff from Gelson's, fresh rolls and cold cuts and salads of marinated peppers and artichokes. A couple of very nice bottles of wine. They all made idle small-talk as they opened and shut the refrigerator and located clean glasses and plates in the dishwasher, but Jessica wasn't fooled. Lily and Rebecca were as curious about her as she was about them.

Rebecca was the more extraverted. "Such a pretty girl," she complimented, lightly touching Jessica's hair. "You're too thin, though, like Alex. It's no wonder, after what they've done to you."

Lily smiled. "Mom's ready to start up a petition. What for, I'm not exactly sure --
"

"This is America!" Rebecca snorted. "They can't do this to my son, or to this little girl so blessed by Sister Cordelia!"

Lily was uncorking the bottle of Clos de Bois chardonnay. "I can't believe Alex served you that ancient Fume. Don't tell me you actually drank it!"

"Don't worry, I have health insurance." Jessica accepted a glass of the Clos de Bois. "Lily, Renie O'Connor has spoken wonderfully of you. I'm so glad to meet you. And you too, Rebecca."

Rebecca gave her another quick hug. "You are a godsend to Alex, chiquita. After what he went through with that --"

"Mom, why don't you set the table?" Lily interrupted cheerfully, foisting into Rebecca's hands a bunch of fresh-cut flowers and a lead crystal vase. "No one does a centerpiece like you."

"Oh, Lily, you're mangling those!" Rebecca clucked, fussing over the flowers. Murmuring ruefully in Spanish, Rebecca took the foundlings into the small dining room adjacent to the kitchen.

Lily winked at Jessica. "That was the idea." Then the mischievous glint left her deep brown eyes. "Renie's told me a lot about you, too, Jessica. If anything good comes out of this nightmare . . . " Her voice drifted off.

"I love him with all my heart. Please know that."

Lily squeezed her hand. "He loves you too. You should have seen how distraught he was when he couldn't get in touch with you. The day Sister spoke to you. He was going out of his mind, and as scared as I was, I kept thinking, this is God's will. This is what will get him through that bitch's -- or to use my mother's word -- that *puta*'s final grandstanding play for attention."

"I'm not so sure it's good for him to be in this house," Jessica said. "He's acted really . . . bothered since we got here."

Lily leaned back against the kitchen counter and shook her head in disgust. "She did that on purpose, too. She'd been staying in West Hollywood with friends ever since Alex left for New Orleans. *La pobrecita couldn't* stand to be alone. But she knew Alex loved this house, so she had to ruin it for him."

Jessica felt uneasy with the casual bashing of anyone driven, for whatever reason, to commit suicide, much less when the subject in question had been wife to the man she adored. "She was obviously troubled. But there must have been something between them, at one time. Some kind of love, however dysfunctional."

Lily motioned for silence as she quickly checked on her mother in the dining room. "Mom? Don't forget, the silverware is in the china chest."

"I know, I know! You think my memory's shot since last time I was here?" replied Rebecca in good-natured exasperation.

Just to make sure she wouldn't be overheard, Lily switched on the radio on the kitchen counter, turned the dial to a local alternative station. A silken-voiced DJ named Adrian was introducing a set of Concrete Blonde. "Here's the deal," Lily said softly, sadly. "My dad split twenty-three years ago. Ran off to Venezuela because he couldn't make a success of himself here. Every once in a while he writes us -- usually to ask for money."

"I'm sorry. I had no idea."

Lily again checked to make sure her mother was occupied with the place-settings. "The money was always Mama's, but he might as well have left her without a cent. For years, Jessica, she was helpless. You have to understand her culture, and her generation. She'd done her best to be a good Catholic wife, and all of a sudden she was cast adrift. Alex was thirteen, and he was the one to pick up the slack."

Jessica refilled her wine glass. "I'm starting to understand."

"Don't get me wrong," Lily said, now busily unwrapping smoked salmon and placing the strips on a platter. "Mom's OK now. She has the boutique and her friends and her goddamn Catholic charities coming out of her ears. But that doesn't erase that five, six year period when she couldn't get out of bed, and Alex was making out the household bills and shopping for groceries and staying up until two a.m. on school nights to figure out our taxes -- " Lily swiped angrily at a random tear. "Jesus Christ! No wonder he grew up to be a frigging Marxist!"

But Jessica knew that Lily was trying to explain more than Alex's personal politics. Nor were these insights entirely welcome. Did he see her as simply the latest in a steady stream of shattered females in dire need of reclamation?

And was it any wonder he took such pride in restoring the derelict beauty of this 1930s house?

Lily seemed to guess what she was thinking. "Jessica, I wanted you to understand why Natalie was able to play him like a grand piano. I've seen you so many times on television. I've heard about you from Alex and Renie. You're strong. I have a feeling Alex needs your strength much more than the other way around."

Before Jessica could respond Alex strolled in, clean-shaven, hair wet. He patted Jessica's buttocks, then asked Lily in a low voice, "You think Mom can tell I'm stoned?"

"No, but just don't wolf down everything in sight as if you haven't eaten in six months, or she might get a clue." Lily grinned at Jessica. "My mother went to the 'Reefer Madness' school on the evils of pot."

Dinner was pleasant and uneventful. No one brought up Natalie or Sister Cordelia, though Rebecca Trujillo continued to fume about Alex's treatment at the press conference and his subsequent dismissal by the Los Angeles *Times*.

"Just forget about it, Mom," he said. "I was ready for a sabbatical anyway."

"I can't forget about it! They slandered your good name! How are you going to live?"

He snickered. "Jess here has bucks. She's prepared to accustom me to the life of a kept man."

Jessica and Lily laughed, but Alex's mother was not especially amused. "Was your first marriage in the Church?" she asked Jessica bluntly.

Jessica hastily wiped the smile off her face. "Oh. No, it wasn't."

"Good," Rebecca said with a satisfied nod. "Neither was Alex's. You two can have a wedding Mass."

"Mom!" Lily scolded.

"Covered live on CNN, no doubt," Alex quipped dryly, getting up to clear the plates.

Taking a hint from Alex's repeated references to jet-lag, Lily and Rebecca left not long thereafter. "Actually, I am kind of tired," he admitted to Jessica after they'd washed the dishes. "You ready for bed?"

It was only just past eight, but by Eastern Standard Time it was after eleven. But upon entering his bedroom, she became uneasy. It was ridiculous, she argued with herself; she hadn't thought twice about sleeping with him in the bed she'd once shared with Gregg. But Gregg had simply moved across town. Natalie had asphyxiated herself only twenty feet from her husband's bed. "You know what? I'm really not very sleepy. Would you mind if I went back to the living room and read for a while?"

He stopped removing his shirt mid-button. "It bothers you to be in here, doesn't it."

"A little," she admitted.

"Would you rather sleep in the study? It's not much bigger than a broom closet, but there's a couch in there."

"No, I want to sleep with you."

His smile was fleeting. "Well, that presents us with something of a logistical problem."

Now she felt more foolish than ever. "You're right. I've got to get past this, and as they say, there's no time like the present." She collapsed onto the bed, stretching her arms, her legs.

He sat down beside her and stroked her thigh. "So what do you say, Jess? You want to get married?"

She gazed up at him wistfully. "I think it would be redundant."

He tweaked her nose. "I mean, after your divorce is final."

"It would still be redundant."

He frowned. "I'm not reading you here."

She caressed his face. "Don't you see? We *are* married!"

He jerked away. "I've gotta be honest with you, Jess. It scares me when you talk like that."

Her turn for confusion. "But why? I don't understand what you mean."

He grabbed a cigarette. "When you suddenly go all mystical on me. It's -- well, I hate to say it, baby -- but it's kind of creepy."

She was hurt, but not up to another fight. Her lips pressed together, she snatched up a pillow and marched off to find the study.

He didn't come looking for her, either.

Had Jessica and Alex not been making a concerted effort ever since the disastrous press conference to avoid both print and broadcast media, they might have gotten wind of what *Newsweek* was planning. The issue that hit the stands that Monday, the day after the couple's return to L.A., bore a red strip above the masthead proclaiming "Special Report." Splashed on the cover was a photograph of Sister Cordelia, and big yellow letters trumpeting "The Truth Behind the Hoax."

The story provided one bombshell after another. According to the magazine's special investigation, the New Orleans D.A.'s office was preparing to file charges against the city medical examiner for falsifying a death report and possibly accepting bribes. Lawyers defending Brad Lefevre, the twenty-five year old white supremacist charged with Sister's murder, were clamoring for his release on bail pending an assault trial, and the D.A. was reportedly considering the request. Even sources close to the Vatican weighed in, revealing that Rome's own investigators had found that the so-called resurrection did not -- and could not -- pass Church muster.

Still unclear, however, was the matter of who exactly had instigated the hoax in the first place. *Newsweek's* investigative team suggested that a loose coalition of radical Jesuits from Central America, anti-death penalty organizations, and far-left activists had engineered the subterfuge, but so far, definitive proof as to the identity of the culprit -- or culprits -- was remaining elusive.

The lead story, several pages long, was accompanied by an extensive sidebar: "Sex, Lies, and Faith: The Bizarre Case of Anders and Trujillo." A grainy photograph of the couple standing side-by-side in the Cathedral just before the procession entered was juxtaposed with a clear shot of them at the press conference. While the authors concluded that Anders and Trujillo were more likely dupes than instigators of the hoax, the account wallowed in quasi-prurient details about their respective personal lives. Jessica's recent marital breakup. The suicide of Alex's wife, which occurred the very night an unnamed source confirmed Trujillo had boarded a Washington-bound plane. A desk clerk at the Royal Orleans told *Newsweek* about the night several guests complained about a passionate argument between a man and a woman in Anders' room. The clerk thought, but was not certain, that those complaints had poured in the very night of the massacre and Trujillo's interview with Cordelia Davis.

The argument, however innuendo-laden, was clear. Anders and Trujillo, addled by sex, were easy marks for exploitation by the shadowy confederacy determined to convince Americans that a politically correct miracle had taken place. "At last Thursday's surreal press conference, Anders' shrill declaration of faith in the 'resurrection' sounded pathetically sincere. The more circumspect Trujillo seemed, rather, a holy fool only for the integrity of the since-discredited interview."

Jessica, who'd slept poorly on the study's lumpy couch, was awakened at seven-thirty by a hodgepodge of discordant noises. Car motors rumbling. Brakes squeaking to a stop. A hum of voices calling back and forth casually. "Christ," she grumbled, forcing the pillow over her ears. "How can he stand to live on such a noisy street?"

Gradually she realized this was not the ordinary clamor of a busy urban morning. For one thing, the voices and cars sounded disconcertingly close. She tiptoed out of the study to peer through the living room drapes.

A small cavalry of satellite vans, minicams, technicians and reporters clustered in front of the house. "Test, test," a carrot-topped newsman, California-casual in shirt-sleeves, was barking into a KABC/Channel 7 mike.

Jessica leaped back from the window as if she'd received an electric shock, and hurried into Alex's bedroom. An empty glass on the nightstand told her immediately how he was able to sleep through the commotion outside. She shook him urgently. "Alex, wake up. The whole street's crawling with the goddamn media."

He snapped to alertness. "Jesus," he muttered, rubbing his brow. "Why the fuck now?"

"I'm almost afraid to find out."

"Hold your nose and turn on the tube," he advised.

Reluctantly she found the remote and pressed the "power" button. On the *Today* show, Katie Couric was interviewing a man and a woman Jessica promptly recognized as reporters for *Newsweek*. The woman had even attended Alex's press conference, and had posed the malicious question about his flying out to be with Jessica only days after his wife's death.

"How soon do you think it will be before the New Orleans D.A. actually charges the medical examiner?" Katie was asking.

"Our understanding is that it's imminent. You know, Katie, the New Orleans coroner's office has been implicated in corruption before, mostly relating to organized crime."

"Should we expect the medical examiner to be offered immunity in exchange for revealing who paid him to falsify the records and perpetuate the hoax?" Katie followed up.

Jessica snapped off the TV and folded her arms, as if to physically contain her simmering anger. "Do we need to hear anymore?"

"I wish I could get my hands on the motherfucker at the *Times* who leaked my address to the vultures," Alex said, tossing on jeans and a T-shirt. "What are they gonna do, keep us virtual prisoners in here until we go out and fall on our swords?"

"The bastards are going to hound us until we recant, or else look like fools refusing to!"

"I'm gonna get the whole story off the Net," he said, starting out of the bedroom but stopping to kiss her. "I missed you last night."

"Me, too. No more fights until you put a decent sofa-bed in the study."

She crawled under the rumpled sheets of his bed and tried to ignore the racket outside. It was dishearteningly obvious that *Newsweek* believed it had sounded the final knell on the Sister Cordelia story. All that was needed now was the punctuation mark of Alex and herself disgraced and penitent. But she knew that the originators of this latest passel of lies about Sister Cordelia extended well beyond a single, albeit influential, national news magazine. The nebulous Powers That Be had really hauled out their big guns this time, strong-arming the New Orleans District Attorney, the medical examiner.

Finally developing a single, coherent theory of their case.

Which had to mean one of only two things. Either they felt they were a hair's breadth away from killing the story for good.

Or --

A thrill of excitement swept over her.

Or they had reason to fear the story could *not* be killed, and more and more people were coming to believe.

She remembered the strangers who'd approached Alex and herself for autographs yesterday on the plane. Three had explicitly voiced support and encouragement, and even the others had treated them with respect, not derision. And those were eight people among two hundred on a 757. What if there were eight like souls on every plane? Even if only four percent of the population believed, that would add up to eight million, more or less --

Alex came back, shaken. "Looks like they've pretty much blown your pal Cordelia out of the water. Did a hell of a hatchet job on you and me in the process."

She shook her head firmly. "They're running scared. I don't care what they say about me." Then, recognizing the likelihood the magazine had printed the painful circum-stances of Natalie's death, she amended, "They still have no damn business invading our privacy."

He seemed mildly irritated by her equilibrium. "You know what they wrote about us? They implied we're a couple of pathetic, sex-starved losers who let our hormones get the better of our professional judgment!"

She tried to tease him out of his black mood. "I don't know, I kind of like the 'sex-starved' part." She lay back against the pillows and started to unbutton her pajama top. "You want to make up for last night?"

"Jesus fucking Christ, what's wrong with you!" he exploded, looking ready to strangle her. "Aren't you ever gonna wake up and smell the goddamn coffee? It's over,

Jessica! They aren't lying -- she *is* a hoax, she *is* a fraud, and you and I were fucking taken in by her!"

"Lower your voice," she said coldly, "or you'll give our friends outside cause for interrupting regular programming." She climbed out of bed and began fumbling through her suitcase for underwear, clothes.

"Jess," he despaired, "I've tried to hang with you on this one --"

"Bullshit. You thought it an impossibility from the beginning. I remember you telling me so after the funeral."

"I seem to recall you were pretty damn skeptical yourself!"

She spun around furiously. "I was, until I saw her, and she spoke to me. How can you, who talked to her, interviewed her, have the audacity to call her a fraud? I thought you'd be the last man on earth to capitulate to conventional wisdom!"

"Everything I wrote in that interview was the truth," he said. "I'll stand by it to my dying day."

"Then what is the big, fucking problem?" she screamed, forgetting her own admonition to him a moment earlier.

He seized her by the arms and shook her. "That day I interviewed her, I knew for sure it wasn't true. She's a human being, Jess. Flesh and blood. Just like you and me. This mystical aura you've been attributing to her -- it's all in your head, baby."

She jerked free. "I get it! That's why you were in such a foul temper the night after the interview. You were hoping she'd perform tricks for you, show you her stigmata, turn water into wine. Now, *that* would have been a story, muchacho. Definitely another Pulitzer. Poor Alex! You just couldn't make that old Kierkegaardian leap!" Clutching a bundle of clothes, she stormed into the bathroom.

When she emerged, he was slumped over the coffee table, smoking nervously. She was unmoved by his wretchedness. "I need to call a cab."

"Don't be crazy. You think that mob out there will let you anywhere near a cab?"

"I'm not Monica Lewinsky. I can shove my way through a wall of shutterbugs without the assistance of bodyguards."

"You sound just like a girl I used to watch on CNN," he said in a tone at once wistful and heavy. But he still refused to look at her.

He knew they were over, too.

Impatient, she located the Yellow Pages and ordered a cab. "What's the address here?" she snapped at Alex.

"1425 North Benton Way."

She repeated it to the dispatcher, who promised a cab in fifteen minutes.

He insisted on helping her bring her suitcases to the foyer. "I think it'll be easier on both of us if I don't watch you leave," he said, abruptly disappearing into the back of the house.

When her watch told her twelve minutes had elapsed since the time of her call to Yellow Cab, she squared her shoulders, picked up her bags, and stepped outside.

The expected flurry of flashbulbs, minicams, and hand-mikes were there to greet her. "Jessica, do you want to comment about the *Newsweek* story?"

""Are you at last willing to concede that the resurrection was a hoax?"

"I see you've got your suitcases. Have you and Alex had a falling-out about these latest revelations about Cordelia Davis?"

Out of the corner of her eye she spied a cab crawling up the hill. "This is all I have to say," she said. "Alex and I would both appreciate a little peace. This story has never been about us -- we've just been the messengers." She drew in a sharp breath. "And I stand by the message unequivocally."

They flocked around her as she pushed her way toward the cab. "Are you going to join up with Sister and her followers in the Imperial Valley?" pressed a reporter from KCBS.

Though she didn't know what the hell he was talking about, she answered impulsively. "As a matter of fact, yes, I am."

Chapter 17

Mindlessly, she had the cab driver drop her off at the LAX Hertz-Rent-a-Car. Hertz, out of habit, because they usually granted an ABA discount. At the rental desk, she filled out the proper forms and paid for the fire-engine-red Chevy Cavalier with a Chase-Manhattan credit card. At the last moment, she thought to request a map of Southern California.

The little Chevy didn't have much poop compared to her Land Rover, but it ran on gas and four wheels, and that was all that really mattered.

She veered onto the 405-south. She could pick up the 5 in southern Orange County, then the 805 in San Diego, which, according to her map, would take her to Interstate 8, and, eventually, the Imperial Valley. She wasn't sure it was the fastest route, but it looked the least complicated.

For the most part, she was driving against traffic, able to maintain a steady speed of seventy-five. She flew past miles of grotesque car lots, Los Angeles County's answer to the eastern blight of boarded-up factories and filth-belching smokestacks. It seemed like dozens of chintzy billboards heralded "Don Knotts Ford," but that couldn't be right, could it? Wasn't Don Knotts that scrawny plucked chicken of an actor who had played the ever-annoying Deputy Barney to Andy Griffith's down-home Sheriff Taylor?

In Orange County the sights became all the more surreal. An airport named after John Wayne. A gigantic silver monolith with "TACO BELL" inscribed penthouse-level.

An only slightly less impressive obelisk topped by the garish sign "AMERICAN ENTREPRENEUR."

Just across the San Diego County line, an obscenely swollen pair of concrete breasts hugged the coast, a mesh of wires strung from its nipples to canopy the freeway. The San Onofre nuclear power plant, maternal Chernobyl-waiting-to-happen against a gorgeous blue Pacific backdrop.

And soon, the international signs warning of pedestrians crossing the freeway. A cartoonish silhouette of a family, a harried father and mother apparently dragging a recalcitrant child by the wrist.

But the border checkpoint only obtained to northbound traffic. Jessica was therefore stunned at the sudden vista of brake-lights ahead of her on the 5 south.

So stunned she had to slam on her brakes to avoid rear-ending the Toyota Camry in front of her. Why the hell were armed United States marshals monitoring *southbound* motorists into San Diego?

Her heart was banging as she merged into the single-file of vehicles inching toward the checkpoint-in-reverse marked by orange cone-shaped pylons. The reporters in Silver Lake had tipped them off, or maybe it was the woman at Hertz who'd rented her the car. Yet as she rolled up to the squat stop-sign, an impassive, uniformed cop waved her through.

She sailed by, but she was shaking so convulsively she pulled off the freeway and into the first "Scenic Viewpoint" she spotted, a mile or so down the freeway. A couple of RVs, one with Utah plates, the other from Baja California, shared the tiny lot overlooking the ocean. A well-scrubbed white family -- two clean-cut parents, three rosy kids -- was posing each another for pictures against the ocean.

Jessica got out of her car, thirstily gulping the salty air. The wind whipped her hair in all directions, making it impossible for her to light a cigarette she didn't really want, anyway. Impulsively she tossed the whole pack into a trash can. Exorcising him.

"Excuse me, ma'am." The wholesome *pater familias* from Utah approached her, clutching his camera. "Would you do us a big favor and take our picture?"

"Yeah, sure. Let me just tie my hair back." She found a scrunchy in her purse and knotted it around her mane. The family, Dad's arm around Mom, the kids gap-toothed and giddy, struck a pose against the railing.

"Say cheese!" Jessica urged, mentally adding *pun intended*.

They all grinned, and she snapped the photo.

"Thanks so much," the man said.

"Thank you!" the kids chimed in unison.

Jessica handed the man back his camera. "Hey," she said as an afterthought, "do you have any idea why the marshals back there are stopping cars going south?"

"I don't think it's anything to worry about," the man replied, looping the camera's strap around his neck. "I heard they're just trying to avoid a media circus down there near the border. The only folks I saw who got pulled over were a couple of news vans with those satellites on top."

Jessica felt the blood drain from her face. "I'm sure you must be right," she fumbled. "Well, I'd better go. Enjoy your vacation."

She hurried back to the rental car and tore onto the freeway. Whatever was afoot in the Imperial Valley could not be stopped, so the Powers That Be were resorting to the next best thing: ensuring there would be no cameras.

An hour later she was in San Diego proper, heading east on Interstate 8. As she left the city limits far behind her, hotels and high-rises gave way to flatter buildings and more rolling terrain. Signs above the freeway tallied the miles to El Centro, Blythe, Yuma. She took a quick glance at her map. All right, she was nearing Imperial Valley, but she had no address, no freeway offramp. She'd been hoping she'd just stumble upon Sister and her followers, but if she kept driving east with no specific directions, she'd be across the Arizona border in another half hour.

She took the next offramp, pulled into a Mobil Station. It was self-service, but there had to be someone in the little kiosk that sold soft drinks, candy bars, and cigarettes.

The brown-faced kid behind the glass looked about fourteen. "I'd like a Diet 7Up," Jessica said, taking out a five dollar bill. "And can you tell me how to get to Sister Cordelia?"

The kid's heretofore stoical face lit up. In heavily accented English, he told her to bear ten miles east, then take the Holtville exit. "Then, senora, it's not like you're gonna miss it!"

Jessica, suddenly excited, took the soft drink but told the kid to keep the change.

Ten miles! Only ten miles! She was smiling without realizing it, occasionally chuckling under her breath as she sped along the narrow valley road onto which the Latino kid had directed her. In the lush fields tattery laborers toiled over rows of lettuce, melons, sugar beets. An occasional produce stand hawked fruits and vegetables via shabby hand-lettered signs.

The road sloped upward and around. Jessica screeched to a stop. To her left, what looked to be acres and acres of cars had turned the field into a colossal parking lot. Jessica backed up her car, pulled off the road onto the dirt shoulder, and climbed out.

She wound her way through the hundreds and hundreds of cars, not yet able to see beyond them, for the land sloped upward again. She saw license plates from all over the country and from most of the states of Mexico, too, with those sultry and lyrical names Sonora and Jalisco and Oaxaca. An enormous sense of freedom washed over her; she shook her hair loose as she neared the crest of the grade. Here was where she wanted to be. Where she was meant to be.

She reached the crest, and looked down.

The valley was teeming with a multitude of humanity, thousands and thousands, as far as the eye could see. She couldn't even estimate a number, she was so dazzled by the awesome magnitude of what she beheld.

Trembling with wonder, she clambered down the gentle slope, her sneakers deftly negotiating the terrain. She wove into the crowd inconspicuously, passing groups of people laughing and talking animatedly in English, Spanish, occasionally Italian. Dozens of tents had been pitched, and portable lavatories were also plentiful. Many of the pilgrims were barbecuing, the smoky charcoals and grills sending out savory wafts of burgers and hotdogs. Several people, crouched on their knees, were busily handpainting signs: "END STATE-SPONSORED MURDER!" "I AM THE RESURRECTION AND THE LIFE!" "BAN GUNS, NOT ABORTIONS!"

Then someone grabbed her by the elbow. "Jessica! I was wondering when you were gonna show up!"

It was Walt Haberman, wielding his cell phone and tape recorder, a 35-millimeter camera slung around his neck.

Thrilled to see him, she hugged him warmly, not even feeling his camera pressing against her collarbone. "Walt, it's so good to see you! How long has this been going on? Has the media covered it at all?"

He gave her a wry look. "Can't say I blame you for swearing off the news. As far as I know, there's nothing on TV -- I've only seen a couple camera crews, one from Tijuana, the other from a San Diego UPN affiliate."

"Walt, they're stopping media vans at the San Diego county border," she said. "But go on -- I need to know everything!"

He took her arm as they wended their way through the throng. "A handful of us from the wire services are filing stories. Our editors seem to be down-sizing our estimates of how many people are here, but at least the stories are making it into print."

"What's your estimate?"

Walt shrugged. "Sister Cordelia showed up at a little church in Holtville last Friday. When I got here yesterday, there were about fifteen thousand. Since then, I'd say another ten thousand have arrived."

She was vaguely disappointed. From her vantage point on the crest, she would not have been surprised to hear him number the followers in the hundreds of thousands. "Is Sister appearing to them?"

Walt chuckled. "Is she ever! She's organizing a huge protest at San Quentin -- I guess they've got an execution scheduled in a few days."

"I've been so out of it," she admitted. Cowardly, she added silently. "You hear about *Newsweek*?"

He nodded. "About a hundred copies were burned in effigy this morning."

"Wish I'd been here to see it."

"I bet. They sure did a number on you and Alex."

She said nothing.

"Oh Jeez," Walt said unhappily. "So that's why he's not here too."

"He doesn't believe."

"So? Neither do I . . . exactly."

She managed a wan smile. "'Exactly'?"

"Look, Jessica, as a Jew, I'm not particularly amenable to the idea the man upstairs chose a Catholic nun to get out the word that the Gun Owners of America are a bunch of assholes."

"Equal opportunity -- two thousand years ago, he picked a Jew."

"Wise guy." He feigned offense.

"Sorry. Go on."

"OK. But speaking as a reporter, I've seen a lot of things I can't make sense of. Not rationally, anyway. It's just too . . . strange."

They'd reached an empty, portable picnic table. Jessica took a perch on top of it. "'And therefore as a stranger give it welcome,'" she quoted distantly, remembering her doomed *Newsweek* essay, the rejection of which was her first real inkling of the mainstream media's determination this story not be told.

"Huh?"

"Never mind." She was feeling a little dizzy; too much excitement, she guessed.

Luckily, Walt appeared not to notice. "Don't you find it funny that given your high-profile among Sister's followers, everyone's leaving you alone?"

She placed both palms atop the table to steady herself. "Yeah, sort of."

"At dawn, when Sister Cordelia spoke to the crowd -- the Archdiocese of San Salvador has set her up with a podium and a mike and huge speakers -- she told everybody, 'when Jessica comes today, leave her in peace.'" He winked. "I'm assuming you two haven't been e-mailing each other."

At last the dizziness abated. "Alex thinks she's been manipulating us all along," she said bitterly. "Which can only mean he thinks I'm crazy."

"Maybe he really wasn't ready for the backlash against him over the interview," Walt said, squeezing her hand. "Here's a guy who's literally risked his life making sure he gets the story right, all of a sudden having his integrity as a journalist ripped to shreds."

She gnawed her lower lip, resolved she wouldn't cry. "Would it sound horribly selfish if I said that's not my problem?"

"No." And then he nudged her. "Look. Here comes your friend."

She glanced up and saw Sister Cordelia, in her plain dress and short veil, walking toward them as ordinarily as if they had all merely dreamed the assassination in Angola and the miracle at the altar of St. Louis Cathedral. The pilgrims blessed themselves as she passed by them, but the rabid hysteria of the mobs outside the convent in Metairie had been replaced by serene, matter-of-fact acceptance of her reality.

Walt was starting to step away, but Jessica held him back. "Sister, have you met my good friend Walt Haberman? He's a reporter with the Associated Press."

Walt waved nervously, but Cordelia Davis stretched out her hand. "I'm so pleased to meet you, Mr. Haberman."

Walt shook hands. "Likewise, Sister. Let me give you two some privacy."

Cordelia sat down next to Jessica atop the picnic table. "Has Mr. Haberman told you of our little operation here?" She sounded almost playful.

Jessica felt immediately comforted. "The protest at San Quentin," she said, nodding. "I think it's a wonderful idea. But how in the world will everyone get there?"

Sister smiled. "Didn't you ever see Spike Lee's movie, 'Get On the Bus'?"

Jessica returned her smile. "Of course. It's perfect." She thought of something. "Can I make a donation toward the cost of the charters?"

"It's all been taken care of," Sister said. "The Lord does provide, Jessica." Those huge eyes twinkled. "A good woman in San Diego who inherited a fortune from her late husband -- I think he owned a baseball or football team -- is underwriting us."

Jessica giggled. And then she found she couldn't stop giggling, and her giggles dissolved into shuddering sobs.

Cordelia clasped her in her arms and let her cry, rocking her gently. But she offered no words of assurance about the matters that weighed so heavily on Jessica's heart, and Jessica knew better than to ask.

Even as her tears subsided, she clung to Sister, resting her head against that frail shoulder.

"I want you to take very good care of yourself," Sister was saying. "No camping out here for you. I'm sure your friend Mr. Haberman would be glad to find you a clean little motel room not far from here."

Jessica raised her swollen face. "But why?"

Sister softly brushed away Jessica's tears with her fingers. "There's going to be opposition to our protest. More than usual. We'll need to be strong -- and vigilant."

Jessica swallowed hard. "Because of the media."

"Not just because of them. The man condemned to die was convicted of particularly loathsome crimes. He abducted and raped a twelve-year-old girl, hacked off her arms and legs, and left her in an alley to die. Which she did, though not for two months. She was just released from the hospital, fitted with her new prosthetics, when an infection set in, and the Lord, in His mercy, called her home."

Jessica winced. "I have a hazy memory of it. It happened about four years ago, right?" She recalled reading about the horrific crime in the paper, and telling Gregg this was one time she couldn't stir herself to decry a jury's decision of death.

And if she, a committed death penalty foe, felt that way, what could they expect of the execution proponents who far outnumbered the abolitionists?

Not to mention from a media united in their conviction that Sister was a fraud and her followers mindless dupes.

Sister Cordelia would be leading her faithful into the fire, and she wanted Jessica to know it.

"I'll be ready," Jessica told her.

"I know you will." Sister pressed her hand again, then slipped down from the table to mingle with others among the devoted.

Despite Sister's admonition, Jessica didn't want to leave the encampment. She'd lost sight of Walt, but that didn't keep her from milling among the disciples. She spoke with a middle-aged woman who'd driven all night from Denver to join the gathering. "My husband and kids think I've lost my mind," the woman chuckled. "I'm not even Catholic!" Then there was the young priest from Managua, who solemnly thanked Jessica for her long-term advocacy in the struggle to abolish the death penalty. A group of college students from the University of Arizona whose high spirits and humor reminded her of the kids from Tulane who'd given her a ride back into New Orleans.

She found all their stories interesting. Some had come to the Imperial Valley out of profound religious fervor. Like the woman from Denver, many were non-Catholics and a few not even Christian; they'd simply found the end of their spiritual searches in

Sister Cordelia. A self-professed "white witch" from Rhode Island told Jessica she truly believed the nun was an avatar heralding the imminent return to the matriarchal religious practices that had flourished in pre-Christian times.

And some of the pilgrims were still not exactly sure what they believed about the resurrection, but they were certain of one thing: the media, backed by powerful forces in government and organized religion, weren't telling them the truth. They'd come as much to protest the witch-hunts as to support Sister Cordelia. To this faction in particular Jessica was something of a heroine. When would Alex be joining them? they were eager to know.

"I'm not sure," she said, and moved on.

Just as the sun was starting to set, Walt tracked her down. "I'm under strict orders to escort you the Holtville Motel 6," he said. "I wouldn't expect HBO and a minibar if I were you."

"Sister corralled you on my behalf?"

"She nabbed me all right. You ready to hit the road?"

They took her rental car; Walt too was staying at the motel, and he figured they could just drive back to the grounds together tomorrow morning. "You and me at the same hotel," she observed, strapping into the passenger seat. "Just like old times."

"Calling this place a hotel is kind of like referring to Holtville as a bustling metropolis," he cautioned, pulling onto the road.

She leaned her head back, half-closing her eyes. "Are you going to follow this thing all the way to San Quentin?"

"I wouldn't miss it. This is the greatest damn story I've ever covered in my life. I'm not going to jump ship at this late date."

"Even if the AP stops printing your reports, now that goddamn *Newsweek* thinks it's outed Sister as a sham?"

"Hate to say it, but that could make this story even sexier. 'Why are thousands of people still flocking to an exposed charlatan?' Writing for the wires is different from being attached to one news organization. The New York *Times* and the Washington *Post* probably aren't going to pick up my stories. It's the smaller papers without their own news bureaus -- the wire services are their bread-and-butter, and vice-versa."

"Speaking of bread and butter, it's just occurred to me I haven't eaten all day." She straightened, trying to shake off the spell of drowsiness. "Does the Dew Drop Inn have a coffee shop?"

"There's a Denny's or something like that across the street."

The motel, a squat two-story complex of twenty-four rooms, was a far cry from the Monteleone or Royal Orleans; its swankiest amenity seemed to be an outdoor Coke machine.
But save for an ant or two in the bathtub, Jessica found her room sufficiently clean. She reapplied her lipstick perfunctorily, then she and Walt headed across the street to the coffee shop.

Walt ordered a hamburger and a beer, Jessica a club sandwich and iced tea. "What, you don't find the extensive wine list to your liking?" Walt teased.

"Actually, I thought about having a glass of wine, but . . . " She shook her head. "I've been drinking too much lately. I've picked up a lot of bad habits the past couple of weeks."

"What was it you said to me the night we had dinner at the Napoleon House? 'Pleasure must be paid'?"

"And so it must."

"Jessica, I can't tell you how bad I feel about you and Alex splitting up. Are you sure it's for good?"

She turned imploring eyes upon him. "Walt, I beg you, let's talk about anything except that, OK?"

"You mean that?"

She nodded.

"Be careful what you wish for," he joked weakly. "Here goes. Why do you think there's such a strong bond between you and Cordelia?"

"I don't think about it," she said in all honesty. "I just know it's there, and it's real."

She retired to bed early, and slept through the night. But she awakened at dawn, so queasy she wondered for one groggy moment if she'd gone off on a bender and had an alcoholic blackout last night. She staggered into the bathroom and dry-heaved over the toilet for a good five minutes until the nausea passed. "Ugh, God," she groaned, "what the hell was in that sandwich?"

It was only after she'd crawled back into bed with a tall glass of water that it occurred to her she might be pregnant.

She sat straight up, thinking frantically. When was her period due?

Last week. She'd forgotten all about it.

In the short time she'd been with Alex, they'd had sex -- violent and abandoned sex -- almost constantly. Unprotected sex. Not once had either of them raised the subject of contraception. Maybe he'd assumed she was on the pill. Which she hadn't been for nearly two years, when she and Gregg decided the time was right to try to have a baby.

But she could hardly lay full blame for this possible catastrophe on Alex. She was an adult woman, a mother, not an irresponsible teenager swept up in the throes of first love. Had Alex offered to use a condom, she probably would have discouraged him, for her body thrilled to the sensation of his seed spilling into her. Even now, the very thought of it sent heat rushing through her veins, between her legs.

Followed by a terrible sense of shame.

Here Sister Cordelia had chosen her, singled her out to walk alongside her on her noblest crusade. Sister, who clearly trusted that Jessica's courage in defending her, was steadfast and pure. What would Sister think of her if she knew how Jessica's commitment to the miracle had been framed until yesterday by a reality less miraculous, a reality of hours upon hours straining and panting in her lover's arms?

Pregnant or not, she had failed Sister. And Sister was too wise, too perceptive, not to realize as much one of these days.

Cravenly, she yanked the covers over her head and toyed with telling Walt she was sick, and unable to accompany him back to the camp. How could she face all those strangers treating her like a selfless paragon, the movement's foremost heroine after Sister herself?

But cowardice sat no better with her now than it had after she'd phoned in her bogus recantation to Debby King. She had no choice but to face Sister and the disciples. Should her venality come to light, she'd admit to it, confess all, and hurl herself at Sister's feet and beg for forgiveness.

She showered and dressed, slipped a note under Walt's door informing him she'd gone across the street for breakfast. She ordered cereal, juice, and decaf, forcing herself to eat. Until she knew for certain she was pregnant, she wouldn't decide whether or not to have an abortion. She suspected she probably would. But given even the slightest uncertainty, she supposed she'd better start eating for two, just in case.

Chapter 18

Shortly after arriving at the encampment, Jessica ran into another unexpected if welcome familiar face: Renie O'Connor, who'd arrived moments before with a small delegation of Stanford graduate students. "Jessica!" Renie embraced her extravagantly as if they were life-long friends. "I knew you'd be here -- I was just afraid I'd never be able to find you!"

The point was well-made; overnight, the crowd seemed to have swelled by another five thousand. Dozens of chartered buses were moving in as well, in preparation for the journey slated to begin the next day.

Jessica introduced Renie and Walt. "Renie is an old friend of Alex's and a recent one of mine," Jessica explained.

"Great -- then we have two of my favorite people in common," Walt said, obviously a little taken with Renie's dazzling smile and shiny, waist-length hair.

"Who?" Renie deadpanned flirtatiously.

Walt broke up.

Renie turned back to Jessica. "Lily says that you and Alex had a monster fight."

Jessica sidestepped the comment. "What are you doing here? I thought you were a die-hard atheist."

Renie flipped her hair. "Who knows what to believe anymore? I thought that maybe if I came down here and saw for myself what this is all about, I'll have a better idea." She grinned. "Besides, anything the Jeezoids on Christian Broadcasting bash as a quote, 'convocation of the unholy' has to have something going for it."

Walt reinserted himself into the conversation. "Why is that? The born-again contingent seems as hostile as the sitting Ayatollah. At least the Imam has a stake in calling Cordelia an infidel."

Jessica stepped away from their animated chatter. A tall black man in a clerical collar was distributing photocopies in both English and Spanish detailing the upcoming itinerary. Jessica accepted one, and scanned it. The buses would depart at sunrise. Disciples were asked to bring a single overnight bag; the trip usually took twelve hours, but "delays should be anticipated." A light lunch and dinner would be provided, courtesy of the Archdiocese of San Salvador, but pilgrims were encouraged to pack bottled water and snacks. Several buses would be available for those who wanted to smoke.

The execution of Donald Henderson was scheduled for just after midnight, the day after their arrival at the prison. Law enforcement and prison authorities were assuring them they would be permitted to assemble in peaceful protest, "so let's keep it on the high road, people."

"They're so well organized," marveled a thin man in an ACTUP! T-shirt. "This is gonna be the model for mass political protests for the next twenty years."

"What's so admirable is its simplicity," Jessica said. "No pyrotechnics, no Websites."

"Don't knock the Web -- that's how most of us heard Sister was down here to start with." He guffawed. "No need to remind you they weren't covering this place on CNN."

Jessica tried not to wince. Another stranger was granting her a special respect and credibility. She fought the impulse to tell him, to tell them all, how unworthy she was.

But then Sister Cordelia joined them, taking each of their hands. "I see our schedule agrees with you, Richard," she said to the man in the ACTUP! shirt.

"Thoreau would be proud," he smiled.

"You're looking much more rested today, Jessica," Sister said. "I'm glad."

As before, Sister Cordelia's touch, her presence, brought to Jessica an unfathomable peace. "I slept well last night."

"Good. Try for a repeat performance tonight. Tomorrow we all have a long day ahead of us." Sister touched her face lightly, then moved off to speak with other pilgrims.

At a convenience store in Holtville, Jessica, Walt, and Renie stocked up on Evian water, chips, and candy bars. Jessica's eyes lingered over an EPT box nestled on a small shelf amid Pepto-Bismol and Tampax. But Walt and Renie were at her elbow, and it was impossible to snap up the "home pregnancy" test without giving herself away.

She did toss into her basket vitamins and a calcium supplement. "After three weeks of debauchery, I'm going on a health kick," she told them.

"Penance," Renie teased her. "Not me -- where in this fine burg might I locate a six-pack of beer?"

"There's a liquor store around the corner," offered the clerk.

"Cool." Renie set her purchases on the counter and unsnapped her wallet.

Jessica grabbed a pint of low-fat chocolate milk. "This is about as decadent as I'm going to get tonight, folks. Sorry to be a party pooper."

She spent less than an hour in Walt's room, listening to him banter with Renie about the movement and the resurrection and the role of the media in quashing both. Renie and Walt seemed of like minds, smart, skeptical but willing to suspend disbelief in the absence of proof to the contrary. In short, they were just the kind of people whose access to the story the Powers That Be likely feared the most.

"You guys, I'm burning out," Jessica said. "See you at the crack of dawn."

Renie walked her to the door. "Lily says he's in a bear of a mood," she said quietly. "He won't tell her what blew up between you two."

"It was nobody's fault." Jessica was uncomfortable. "It's just like my other husband said. We were swept up in the drama of New Orleans, and we probably mistook the excitement for something deeper." She gave Renie a brief hug. "'Night. Good night, Walt."

Walt, poised discreetly against the far wall of his room, waved. "Don't let the bedbugs bite, Jessica. In a dive like this, you can't be too careful."

Jessica left, but the moment Renie shut the door she turned back to Walt. "Am I hallucinating, or did I just hear her say 'my other husband'?"

Another intense bout of morning sickness, pre-dawn, convinced her she'd saved twelve dollars bypassing the home pregnancy test.

Hunched over the toilet like one of the Scottish junkies in "Trainspotting," she retched painfully, bringing up half-digested Chicken McNuggets and streams of chocolate milk. She felt like hell. How could she possibly board a bus for a twelve hour ride?

"It's going to be over soon," she said unthinkingly. "I have to get through the next couple of days, and then it will be over."

It was a conviction she felt strongly, without understanding why. This pilgrimage to San Quentin was to be the test. Once it was over, she would then be free, finally free, to jet home to D.C. and make an appointment with her OB-GYN, to embark upon rebuilding burnt bridges with Gregg and reunion with Jordy.

Just a couple more days. A couple more days of drawing on reserves of courage and faith she feared were rapidly nearing depletion. Then she could go back to Washington and go to sleep for a long time, and when she awakened the entire mad journey begun the day Sister Cordelia was shot would turn out to be a bad, bad dream.

At the camp, the lines to board the buses were serpentine and seemingly endless. "Worse even than Splash Mountain," Renie complained, swigging from an AM-PM coffee. Supply was definitely insufficient to demand, and Father Salazar was busy on a cell phone, arranging for additional transportation.

Other priests and nuns circulated among the restless crowd, offering communion to those who would take it. "What do you do when the Body of Christ sticks to the roof of your mouth?" Walt cracked.

"It's been known to happen," Jessica replied, even as she stepped forward to accept the Host. She put the wafer in her mouth and blessed herself. An odd thought popped into her mind, prompted perhaps by Walt's quip: *The Doctrine of Transubstantiation rocks.* She wished she'd painted herself a sign proclaiming as much.

Walt and Renie noticed the unlikely sparkle in her eyes. "What do they put in that stuff?" Walt demanded.

She did feel strangely giddy, almost drunk. "The Body of Christ, of course! The literal, fucking Body of Christ!" She smiled broadly. "That's what Luther and Calvin rejected, narrow-minded little men that they were. How irrational, how superstitious to believe a few words of mumbo-jumbo could literally transform simple bread into a miracle."

Walt and Renie looked mildly disconcerted, but other pilgrims in earshot listened attentively. "Amen," affirmed an elderly black woman, crossing herself. She was swiftly echoed by half a dozen other disciples.

"More buses!" bellowed a sturdy nun through a megaphone.

The huge caravan of nearly five hundred chartered buses didn't set off from the Imperial Valley until nearly ten a.m. The passengers were buoyant; in many of the buses hymns were sung: "Make Me a Channel of Your Peace"; "Go Tell It On the Mountain"; "We Shall Overcome." Jessica, Walt and Renie found themselves in more secular company; except for half a dozen clerics from Central America and a trio of little Filipina nuns, most on this particular bus were college students, obvious curiosity seekers, and other members of the print media, both domestic and foreign, still following the story. Of these last, Walt knew several, which was how he, Jessica, and Renie ended up boarding this bus in the first place.

Jessica had no idea on which conveyance Sister Cordelia was riding, or whether she'd been among the first or last to board. She'd half-expected Sister to insist Jessica ride with her. That she hadn't filled Jessica again with agonizing guilt. She hadn't cared the least when the media publicly proclaimed her a fraud. But the very thought that Sister

Cordelia might have intuited the carnality that made Jessica so unworthy felt a much crueler kind of exposure.

Walt and Renie struck up a game of blackjack with a British reporter and a photographer from Tijuana, gambling with popcorn. Though invited, Jessica refrained from joining; resting her chin upon her fist, she gazed out the window, regretting the loss of rolling hills as they moved toward the city.

It wasn't until the 805 junction in San Diego that the first hecklers appeared, lining both sides of the freeway, wielding stiff middle fingers and incendiary messages. "WHO BRIBED THE CORONER???" "DEATH PENALTY FOR FALSE PROPHETS!" "SR. CORDELIA=THE ANTICHRIST!" Walt, Renie, and the others abandoned their card game to goggle out the windows. The Mexican photographer was busily snapping pictures.

The whirr of helicopters above sounded close. Traffic was slowing to a stop. "We'll be lucky to make it to San Quentin by New Year's, at this rate," someone grumbled.

Jessica could no longer bear to gape at the jeering protesters and their hateful signs. "I've got to pee," she said abruptly, getting up and moving to the back of the bus where a short line had formed outside the lavatory. She took her place behind one of the diminutive Filipina nuns.

The woman smiled up at her innocuously. "How are you today?" she said.

"Fine. And you, Sister?" Jessica feebly tried to mimic the nun's cheery nonchalance.

"Wonderful!"

The line inched forward. "Oh!" the nun said, startled her turn to use the facilities had arrived so quickly. "Will you hold this for me, dear?" She foisted a worn Bible into Jessica's hands.

OK, this has got to be significant, Jessica thought wryly, as the little nun disappeared into the tiny bathroom. She flipped the book open to where a holy card depicting Mary marked the nun's place. Just about smack-dab in the middle of Paul's Epistle to the Hebrews. Jessica cringed. Paul, who far more than any of Christ's Apostles railed against the sins of the flesh, like most converts overzealous and dogmatic.

She braced herself, scanned the verso. "Here we go," she muttered.

Chapter 10, verse 26: *"For if we sin willfully after that we have received the knowledge of the truth, there remaineth no more sacrifice for sins."*

Thanks, Paul, she thought with a grimace, I needed that.

She was about to shut the book when the holy card slipped out, and Jessica, in catching the little nun's book mark, happened to wedge it into the Bible's spine, blocking out the verso page but inadvertently emphasizing the recto, where Chapter 11 began.

"Faith is the substance of things hoped for, the evidence of things not seen."

She stared at the words, numbly at first. Then her heart swelled, though whether from grief or joy she could not tell. She re-read the verse several times until she had committed it to memory.

The massive caravan and the wildly virulent hecklers crowding freeway shoulders and overpasses compelled a reluctant national media to cover the event. None of the TV news networks was carrying the story live, but local affiliates throughout California were providing hourly updates, and the pilgrimage provided the lead on CNN's Headline News every thirty minutes.

For California, the procession was newsworthy if only from the perspective of traffic control. Commuters were advised to avoid the northbound 5, statewide, wherever possible.

Unfortunately, where the nation was concerned, it was a slow news day. No planes were hijacked. No new scandalous allegations had emerged from the House

Judiciary Committee's investigation of the President's private misdeeds. No Third World dictator was threatening to wage biological warfare against his neighbors.

Were it not for the cortege of buses rumbling north on the I-5, bearing no fewer than twenty-five thousand supporters of Cordelia Marie Davis, the national news would likely have led with the cocaine arrest that morning of chubby-cheeked Sandi Pendarvis, Olympic medalist in ice-skating and America's sweetheart, in a Tampa motel.

Swigging gin, he chain-smoked and tried to tear his eyes from the TV screen, but to no avail. Channels 5 and 13 in L.A. were staying with the story, even while the ABC and NBC and CBS affiliates were broadcasting soap operas and CNN's "Talkback Live" featured a heated debate over multicultural curricula in public schools. MSNBC had assembled a panel -- Caroline Bruckner, one of the two authors of the *Newsweek* hatchet job on Cordelia, and a renowned clinical psychologist -- to discuss cultic behavior that flew in the face of reason. A relative of one of the Heaven's Gate suicides wept on cue from a remote in Oregon, Illinois.

A little box in the upper right corner of the screen tracked the progress of the caravan on California's Interstate 5.

And suddenly, savagely he understood what had driven her to assault the TV with a fucking baseball bat.

All O.J., all the time. And when people lost interest in O.J., it turned into a game of fill-in-the-blank.

Except when the facts refused to jibe with the party-line, which was, of course, neither Democrat nor Republican but a perverse hybrid pandering in equal parts to popular opinion and smug perpetuation of the status quo. Guns didn't kill people, people did. The poor were lazy and unmotivated; look at all the successful minorities who had pulled themselves up by their fucking bootstraps. Peace and prosperity could be achieved only by tax-breaking the rich and funneling billions into Pentagon coffers.

And justice was vengeance. Locking up the crack dealers for twenty years and trying twelve-year-olds as adults. And for the most unregenerate, fry 'em in Florida. lethally inject 'em in Texas, gas the shit out of 'em in California. The more, the merrier.

He knew without needing to be told that she was among the pilgrims, that on one of those countless chartered buses she sat stilly, in quiet resolution. She'd never been particularly still or quiet around him; even those strange raptures to which she'd fallen prone since her first intimate encounter with Cordelia had a quality of violence about them. But on this day he somehow knew she was still and sad; and he'd never felt so goddamn cowardly in his life.

And it had nothing to do with politics.

The Imperial Valley caravan had yanked even the most desperate local TV straggler from his front yard. Too drunk to drive, he called Yellow Cab.

"We're experiencing thirty-to-forty minute delays," the dispatcher informed him officiously.

"That's OK. I just gotta get to the airport."

United had an hourly shuttle to the Bay Area; with any luck, he would beat her there.

Even before getting out of Los Angeles County, three of the buses had broken down. Two experienced run-of-the-mill mechanical problems. The third skidded into a freeway shoulder after one of its tires was blown out by a passing motorist with an air-gun. The bus was disabled, but no one was injured. The CHP apprehended the assailant within minutes, aided by the news copter overhead who'd tracked the sniper on film. The suspect was an Orange County teenager joy-riding in the family Mercedes Benz.

The vast majority of pilgrims were heeding Sister's advice to cling to the high road. But a few gave in to temptation and heckled the hecklers back, especially when the latter began hurling water balloons and rotten produce along with obscenities.

Along the so-called "Grapevine" in Kern County, a heavy, treacherous fog set in, not an unusual occurrence given the region and time of year. The caravan slowed to a thirty miles-per-hour crawl. The news copters, unable to negotiate the thick mist, trailed back to home bases in Los Angeles and Ventura Counties. An 18-wheeler operated by a sleep-deprived speed-freak plowed into the back of a Highway Patrol vehicle, gravely injuring one of the two officers and shutting down all but a single lane of Interstate 5.

Jessica missed all of it. She had fallen into a deep sleep, curled up in her bus seat, wrapped in a blanket. Walt, concerned, nudged her every now and then, only to receive the same mumbled response: "Go 'way."

"Do you think she's all right?" Renie asked Walt, glancing at Jessica as their bus crept along through the fog.

"I don't know," he replied. "I guess. She's not running a fever or anything -- I felt her forehead."

"God damn Alex," Renie cursed under her breath.

"C'mon. He's got his own bullshit going on, too."

"Stop the presses -- pun intended," Renie mocked. "I love Alex like my own brother, but as long as I've known him he's had his own bullshit going on. Look up 'Own Bullshit' in the dictionary, and there's Alex Trujillo's gorgeous mug staring back at you."

"'Trujillo's gorgeous mug' -- sounds like a special at Starbucks," Walt quipped, taking the cards from his pocket and shuffling them nervously. "You up for a game of gin?"

In her sleep, she smiled, and sighed. Again she stood at the altar of St. Louis Cathedral draped in yards and yards of white lace and satin. This time she wasn't alone; Grace and Renie and her brother Steve flanked her. The entire church smelled of incense and roses.

Oddly enough, CNN's Paul Duncan stepped out from the sacristy, clad not in the priestly vestments of alb and cassock but a folksy cardigan and colorful tie. He opened a gilded missal and recited sonorously, "'He that hath the bride is the bridegroom: but the friend of the bridegroom, which standeth and heareth him, rejoiceth greatly because of the bridegroom's voice.'"

"I don't get it," Jessica whispered to Grace. "Where the hell's my bridegroom?"

Steve, appalled, shushed her. "Jessie, we're in church!"

But Grace chuckled. "You Catholics are so hung up about sex."

Paul Duncan "ahem'd" reproachfully. "May I resume?" he baited.

Duly shamed, Jessica nodded for him to continue.

"'He must increase, but I must decrease,'" he orated.

A teasing, irreverent voice sounded behind her. "Then decrease, already. What a fucking windbag."

Despite Paul Duncan's solemn stare, she had to laugh. "I told you this whole thing was redundant," she teased back, as he wrapped his arms around her waist and kissed her neck.

Then Linda Tripp, the hound-dog-faced, grotesquely coiffured Judas from the Clinton-Lewinsky affair of two years before marched onto the altar, and shook an accusing finger at Jessica and Alex. "You two are hoaxes and liars, and I'm turning over everything I know to the OIC!" she thundered. "I have it on tape!"

Alex scoffed, but Jessica was frightened. She hurled herself at the foot of a statue of the Blessed Mother. "I'm so sinful, I'm so sinful," she sobbed. "Mother, forgive me!"

Linda Tripp sauntered over and spitefully shoved the statue off its podium.

Just as the plaster was crashing down upon her head, Jessica woke up with a start.

"It's about time," Walt said, with an uneasy chuckle. "Jeez, you were out for hours, Jessica."

"Yeah, and you missed the excitement of being stuck in ten-mile-an-hour traffic all the way up the Grapevine," Renie tossed in. "Was that Communion you took this morning laced with Seconal? We're almost in Oakland."

Jessica accepted the plastic bottle of Evian that Walt handed her, took a few deep gulps.

Dark and starless outside the window. No hecklers. Except for a faint, lulling music in her ears, all was perfect silence and clarity.

She smiled.

"Jessica, are you OK?" Walt leaned over her anxiously, picked up her limp hand. Warm, her pulse slow and steady.

Renie was on the verge of panic. "Why isn't she coming to?" she fretted, twisting her hair.

Jessica's blue eyes lit up with a sudden fire, illuminating her drawn, pale face. "I'm fine," she said serenely. "Not my will, but Thine, be done." Her arms floated outward to them.

Terrified, Renie screamed.

The bus driver screeched to a halt.

Chapter 19

They were on the 880, just south of Oakland. Not far from where the earthquake had pancaked tiers of concrete into a Dantesque vise a decade before. As the other buses in the caravan rolled on, this particular charter pulled off the freeway and into the parking lot of a Shell station.

Walt did his best to wave back the curious. "Is anybody here a doctor?" he bawled.

At first, no response. Then a priest from Guatemala stepped forward. "This is not sickness, my friend," he said somberly, in heavily accented English. "It's trance. She is best if we simply let it take its course."

"I've had about enough of this crap!" Walt protested, his arms flailing. "Trance my ass! This woman is --"

Renie, though ashen, motioned for him to be silent.

The priest approached Jessica, knelt down beside her, and touched the sign of the cross on her brow, throat, and shoulders.

She closed her eyes, sighing contentedly. "Thy will be done," she murmured.

Walt took matters into his own hands. He ripped open his cell phone and dialed 911.

Ten minutes later an ambulance screeched up.

Jessica, drowsy and distant and smiling, raised no protest as Walt and Renie escorted her off the bus and toward the paramedic van. Nor did she fight the EMT who eased her onto a stretcher and wrapped a blood-pressure cuff around her upper arm, his other hand gripping her wrist.

"BP's just on the low side of normal. So's her pulse rate," the paramedic barked at Walt and Renie. "What's the problem? Drugs?" Another paramedic hooked up an IV of saline solution.

Renie choked back sobs. "I think . . . she's having visions."

Alex had been in the Bay Area a little over an hour. The snarl on the I-5 had domino'd into a mad crush at the airport for any and all intra-state flights, and despite his willingness to accept stand-by status, night had fallen before he finally boarded an Oakland-bound Southwest 737. At the airport he rented a car and drove through Contra Costa County until he reached the Richmond Bridge, which spanned the east bay. Just on the other side was San Quentin, a massive concrete and barbed wire hell.

He knew he'd beaten the pilgrims to their sinister Mecca; according to traffic reports on the radio, the caravan was still two hours south of Oakland. During the seemingly endless afternoon trying to get a flight out of Los Angeles, he'd wondered a few times if he was going to make it. For once the caravan arrived in San Quentin, he'd have as much chance getting within five miles of the huge protest as negotiating San Francisco Bay in a rowboat.

The floodlights and satellite vans clustered on a rolling hill across from the prison complex were all too familiar. Alex got out of his car but he made no move toward the media enclave. It wasn't just that he'd been summarily stripped of his press credentials, and that everyone would know it.

In truth, he didn't want a goddamn thing to do with them.

He leaned against the car and lit a cigarette. He kept the radio on the traffic channel to monitor the progress of the procession. His eyes were fixed on the colossus of human misery across the road, a monument to how fucked up the world was, if you really thought about it.

He heard the inevitable rumble of rapidly approaching footsteps, and he averted his face from the bright lights. But he didn't stir. Why bother?

Someone shoved a microphone into his face. "Alex, are you here for the protest?" grilled a CNN reporter.

"Where's Jessica? Is she on one of the buses?" sneered another journalist.

Alex slowly exhaled smoke, refusing to look directly into the cameras. "I have no comment."

They kept at him, but to each query he responded with the same answer. After ten minutes they left him alone.

The emergency room doctor at Oakland Memorial confirmed the paramedic's preliminary findings. "I'll run a few tests on her, but I see no indication there's anything physically wrong with her."

Jessica, perched atop an examining table in a hospital gown, swung her legs lightly. A slight smile still parted her lips; her eyes were dreamy, her pupils dilated.

"What if she doesn't snap out of this?" Walt worried.

"Oh God," Renie said, shaking with fear.

The treating physician paged a psychiatrist. "Dr. Singh should probably have a look at her. He'll be right down."

Five minutes later, a swarthy, middle-aged man with salt-and-pepper hair appeared in the ER. Dr. Singh listened soberly as his colleague briefed him on the patient's condition. All Walt and Renie could do was stand back and wait, their eyes on Jessica, now gently rocking herself.

Dr. Singh stepped over to the examining table. "Hello, Jessica," he said in a soft, Indian accented voice.

"Not my will, but thine, be done," she murmured.

"Wait a second," Walt said, starting to step forward before Singh waved him back. "Aren't those the words Cordelia spoke in the church, at the funeral?"

Singh didn't appear to react. "Jessica, I want you to lie back and rest. Do you think you could do that for me?"

He helped swing her legs onto the table. She was pliant, resting back against a pillow that the attending nurse provided. Only then did Dr. Singh move away to address Walt, Renie, and the other doctor. "Barring an undetected neurological condition, which I agree, Tim, I see no sign of, she's likely suffering from some kind of dissociative disorder." He frowned. "Trance with religious content is extremely unusual in subjects with her background."

"The priest on the bus called it trance," Renie offered.

"Was the priest from Latin America?" Dr. Singh asked.

Walt and Renie nodded. "Why?" Walt said.

"In many other cultures -- Indian, Malaysian, much of Latin American -- trance isn't even viewed as a disorder," Singh replied, removing his glasses. "Even the DSM is antsy about dissociative trance disorder because it's so culture-specific." He paused. "Is Ms. Anders very religious?"

Renie started to protest, but Walt motioned her to remain silent. "As of late, yes," he told the doctor gravely. "Not fanatical -- I mean, she doesn't talk about it a lot. But she sincerely believes in Sister Cordelia's resurrection."

"I'd like to keep her here overnight, for observation," Dr. Singh said.

"Will she come out of it?" Renie demanded.

"In my limited experience, trance disorder rarely lasts more than a couple of hours. She may or may not remember the episode. We'll have to wait and see."

On the table, Jessica had fallen asleep, her chest rising and falling in slow, steady rhythm. The nurse double-checked Jessica's pulse rate, then covered her with a blanket.

As she was wheeled off, the nurse turned to Walt and Renie with a brittle smile. "Would one of you be so kind as to go through Ms. Anders' purse and locate some proof of insurance?"

The first buses rolled into San Quentin just after midnight. And then they just kept coming and coming, countless headlights on gleaming metal cylinders amorphous and eerie under the floodlights. Doors slid open and pilgrims streamed out, some smiling, some somber, as they pushed toward the prison gates. Alex stifled a fleeting revulsion and pushed his way into the crowd, accosting strangers, asking if they'd seen Jessica.

And still more buses were arriving, spilling out more human cargo. Alex caught a brief glimpse of Sister Cordelia before she disappeared into the ever-expanding throng.

Dozens and dozens of times he grabbed elbows and asked where she was. No one knew; they all assumed her bus had yet to reach San Quentin. Across the road, police in riot-gear poised near the media assembly, but the massive crowd was peaceful.

Counter-protesters were not expected until morning, as the execution of Donald Henderson neared.

Close to an hour later, he remained frustrated in his search for Jessica or anyone who'd seen her since leaving the Imperial Valley. One man assured Alex he'd indeed seen Jessica board one of the buses, so there seemed little chance she'd backed out of the protest at the last minute.

Alex was ready to wrest a megaphone from one of the smug, now ubiquitous cops. Virtually trapped amidst the teeming multitude, many of whom now held lit candles, Alex shouted her name at the top of his lungs.

At first, no one paid him any particular heed; he couldn't even be certain he'd been heard above the bee-like hum of twenty-five thousand voices engaged in quiet conversation or prayer. Shoving through the crowd roughly, he screamed her name again.

Someone tugged on his arm.

Alex spun around, hoping it was she.

A lanky youth shivering in a University of San Diego baseball cap cupped his hands over Alex's ear. "She was on our bus! She had to get off near Oakland!" he shouted.

Alex was alarmed. "Why?"

The young man shouted something back into his ear.

Alex was positive he hadn't heard correctly. "What?"

"I said, she went into some kind of trance and her friends freaked out! They called the paramedics!"

"Shit!" Alex swore viciously.

He didn't care how many startled pilgrims he nearly trampled in his desperation to get back to his car.

The fucking police had set up roadblocks. A sign had been erected announcing that the road was closed to all through traffic until six a.m.

Alex jogged over to the nearest cop. "Look, I gotta get to Oakland. My wife's sick, and I don't even know which hospital she's in."

Amazingly, the cop didn't give him a hard time. "Get in your car and I'll let you through."

Alex tore away from the open-air madhouse and sped for the Richmond Bridge. His white lie to the cop had left him feeling mildly queasy. He'd told the fib because a wife in trouble sounded more imperative than a girlfriend, but it also served to remind him of her bizarre declaration the other night. "We *are* married!" The way her eyes had glowed so goddamn beatifically. Why had it taken him this long to realize how ill she'd become from all this quasi-mystical religious bullshit? Jess was sick, and just as he'd done with Natalie, he'd conveniently managed to look the other way.

Well, if there was one thing for which to be grateful, it was that her "friends,"
whoever the hell they might be, had possessed the common sense to get her off that bus
and into an ambulance. Given the demeanor of the holy fools massing by the thousands
outside the prison, Alex would have expected Jessica's fellow passengers to break into
hymns and implore her to speak to them in tongues.

Once back in Oakland, he drove to the nearest police precinct. "My girlfriend's
been taken to an area hospital, but I have no idea which," he told the cop on graveyard
shift.

"Do you know if the EMTs were called?" the cop returned.

"Yeah, they were."

Yawning, the cop punched a few buttons on the computer. "Her name?"

"Jessica Anders."

The cop did a double-take, but refrained from comment as he typed in the name.
Moments later, he nodded. "Here we go. She was taken to Oakland Memorial around 0-
1700 hours."

"Thanks, man."

The fact that it was well past three a.m. did not deter him from speeding to the
hospital.

In the nearly empty lobby he was charging up to the reception desk, when, almost
unbelievably, Walt Haberman's voice sounded nearby. "Alex!"

Alex was stunned to see Walt rising from a shabby couch, on which Renie
O'Connor curled up fast asleep. Alex pumped Walt's hand vigorously. "How is she?
Don't tell me you guys were actually on that goddamn bus with her!"

"Thank God we were," Walt replied. "It was the damndest thing, Alex. She'd
fallen asleep, and all of a sudden she sits up with this spaced-out look in her eyes, and
starts reciting, over and over, 'Not my will, but thine, be done.'"

"Fuck," Alex said. It was about as bad as he'd suspected. "What does the doctor say?"

Walt scratched his stubbled chin. "Christ, I could barely tease it out. Some psycho-babble about dissociative trances and how rare they are in nice white girls from industrialized societies."

Alex rolled his eyes. "Yeah, that's real fucking helpful. Or is that just the latest APA buzzword for old-fashioned nervous breakdown?"

Walt gestured for Alex to join him on a couch across from the one on which Renie snoozed. "Poor kid, the whole thing scared her shitless. Scared me shitless, too."

Alex toyed with his lighter. He was crawling the walls for a cigarette. "I don't suppose there's much chance I can see her before morning."

"'Fraid not. They shooed Renie and me away as soon as they wheeled her out of the ER. I guess we could have gone to a hotel for the night, but what's the point? I know I wouldn't sleep a wink."

"They tell you how long they want to keep her here?"

Walt looked a little bewildered. "My understanding is that she's just in for overnight observation. The head-shrinker seemed to think come morning, she'll be good as new."

Alex scowled. "What a load of crap. This -- this fucking religious mania of hers is serious. It ain't going away overnight." He got up impatiently. "I'm stepping outside for a smoke."

"One more thing, Alex," Walt said, following him through the lobby doors.

"What?"

"I hope you don't go in there in a few hours and challenge Jessie about what she believes," Walt said carefully. "It kills her to think you think she's crazy."

Alex struggled not to grow defensive. "I won't be an asshole, if that's what's worrying you. But doesn't what happened tonight prove it's more dangerous to humor her?"

Jessica awakened at seven, head aching and stomach churning. She had a vague recollection of being brought to the hospital, a vaguer one still as to why. But she couldn't think about it now, not with her head pounding and her gut telling her a bout of vomiting was imminent.

The doctor, a half-familiar Indian man, strolled in. "Good, you're awake. How are you feeling?"

"Like hell -- I think I'm going to puke."

He swiftly placed a stainless steel bedpan next to her on the bed. "I'm not surprised. Are you aware you're in the early stages of pregnancy?"

She nodded, hunched over the bedpan, gulping air.

"It sheds a little light, I believe, on your dissociative episode. It might certainly have been provoked by all that raging hormonal activity."

The spell of nausea passed. Jessica fell back against the pillows, saying nothing.

"Was last night your first episode of that nature?" Dr. Singh inquired, as he casually checked her vital signs.

"Yes. And this is also not my first pregnancy."

"And if you have a third pregnancy, it will probably be very little like this one."

She despised doctors as a rule. "You won't tell my friends I'm pregnant, will you?"

"Now, Ms. Anders, I understand you're an attorney. I don't have to tell you the patient-doctor relationship is strictly confidential."

Typical patronizing doctor. "Sorry. Just checking."

He pulled up a chair to her bedside. "Do you remember anything about what you were feeling or experiencing last night?"

She frowned, which was a mistake, as the grimace aggravated her headache. "All I remember is this sense of peace, of surrender. It was like being inside of -- of, I don't know. The heart of light."

"You recall no fear, no distress?"

"No."

He scribbled something onto her chart. "In that case, I'm inclined to release you later this morning. It's none of my business whether you plan to continue or terminate your pregnancy, but I'm assuming you'll be consulting with your regular OB-GYN either way."

"I will." She pointed to the chart. "What did you write down about me? Paranoid schizophrenic?"

He chuckled. "Nothing that dire."

"Then what?"

He read from the chart. "'Dissociative Disorder NOS, single episode.' Do you want the code numbers too?"

"What does NOS stand for?"

"'Not otherwise specified.' It means, Ms. Anders, that your symptoms aren't congruent with the current diagnostic criteria for dissociative disorders."

"I don't know if I like the sound of that."

"Don't worry, Ms. Anders. In layman's terms, no, you aren't crazy."

She smiled, deciding he wasn't so bad after all.

Alex was furious with Dr. Singh's diagnosis. "This is bullshit! She's been acting weird for weeks. Unlike Walt and Renie, I've been around her constantly!"

Walt looked uncomfortable, Renie annoyed, as Alex berated the doctor.

"Weird in what way?" Singh asked, unruffled.

"Out of nowhere she'll come out with these cryptic, mystical platitudes. Let me tell you, Doc, it's fucking scary."

"Does she become agitated. or grandiose in her speech or gestures?"

"Well, no, not exactly . . . "

"Mr. Trujillo, Ms. Anders appears to believe, in her own mind, that she has undergone a profound religious experience. That doesn't make her delusional, even if we don't happen to share her beliefs."

Alex looked on the verge of losing his temper, so Walt eased him away from Dr. Singh. "Look, isn't the good news that she's OK?"

"That doctor doesn't know what the fuck he's talking about," Alex growled.

Renie joined the debate. "Maybe he doesn't, but you're going to make matters a lot worse if you rant and rave and the doctor boots your ass out of here. And don't you dare lay any of this crap on Jessica."

Alex tossed up his hands, disgusted. "Fine. And what do I do when she starts glowing like Joan communing with the saints, and insists on going back to that goddamn protest? Do I offer my services as chauffeur?"

"Just keep your big mouth shut for once," Renie advised. "We'll deal with the protest when and if it comes up."

Jessica picked at the typically repulsive hospital breakfast: rubbery fake scrambled eggs, melon balls that tasted more like their cotton counterparts, dry toast accompanied by miniature tubs of I-Can't-Believe-It's-Not-Butter and a teaspoon of grape jelly. And she'd never much liked plain milk; maybe that was why she hadn't been able to nurse Jordy.

She made herself gulp down most of it. She shuddered; milk just tasted so much like nothing. Thick nothing.

The door opened and she looked up, expecting to see Walt and Renie.

She was surprised and disconcerted to find Alex standing before her instead.

In moments he was leaning over the bed to kiss her. "You frightened me, Jess. I'm so glad you're going to be OK."

She regarded him warily. "Who called you, Walt or Renie?"

She saw that he was startled by her coldness. "Neither one. I flew up to be with you at San Quentin. Some guy on your bus told me what happened."

She was silent. It was the only way she felt she could avoid a fight.

"OK, you're still pissed. Jess, I'm sorry for what I said the other morning." He sighed. "I know it hurt you probably more than anything I could have said."

"You got that right, muchacho."

"Does it count for anything that I love you?" he said quietly.

The nurse stomped in. "Oh, I see we have a visitor." She bent over to retrieve the tray. "Are we all done?"

"Yes. But could I possibly have some chocolate milk?" Jessica asked, half-embarrassed at how childish she must have sounded.

"I'll have some sent up from the cafeteria."

Jessica tried to lighten the mood. "You know what they'll do, don't you?" she said to Alex as the nurse left. "They'll tack another seventy-five dollars onto my insurance tab and list it as 'special dietary requirements.'"

He had to laugh. "I should have known it would come to this. I'm in love with a goddamn lawyer."

Her unease returned. She loved him, too, loved him desperately, but his disbelief drove a wedge between them, one she feared was irrevocable. And something else; despite the ecstasy of the trance, she wondered if it were at its core a sort of spiritual consolation prize, a hard pill sugar-coated to save her from despair. For the trance had forcibly removed her from the pilgrimage. What could it mean if not that she was unworthy to stand beside Sister Cordelia at her moment of triumph?

And her violent love for Alex lay at the heart of her unworthiness.

She slipped her hand free of his to pick up the TV remote. At the snap of a button the mounted screen was filled with the image of thousands of joyous, defiant pilgrims holding candles and singing John Lennon's anthem "Give Peace a Chance."

Alex winced.

"Look," she said wistfully. "Have you ever seen anything so beautiful in your life?"

"Yeah. You."

She barely heard him. "The counter-protesters won't be able to get anywhere near them. If I were there, I'd be waving a huge sign that said, 'Hey, *Newsweek*, You Can't Spin the Truth.'"

"You're not planning to go out there?" His voice was very cautious.

She shook her head. "I'm not wor -- I'm not ready," she caught herself. "And besides, it's probably not even possible. They must have the roads blocked off by now." She lowered the volume on the television. "Nope -- for once, I'm going to have to content myself with being on this side of the TV screen. It breaks my heart -- but it just wasn't meant to be."

"Does that apply to us, too?" he said moodily.

"Can we not talk about this, at least for the day?"

"Whatever you want. Now, when the hell can we get you out of here?"

With Renie and Walt, they took a double room at the Oakland Hilton, where the travelers could freshen up and real food could be secured from room service. Jessica, poised at the foot of one bed, kept a close eye on the TV. Authorities were terming the congregation at San Quentin the largest death-penalty protest in the nation's history.

Because she refused to be subjected to specious network punditry, she stuck with the local stations, even if they did cut in for commercial breaks. Not that it wasn't jarring to have coverage of the solemn assembly periodically interrupted by hucksters for SnackWells and Velveeta processed cheese.

She apologized profusely to Walt for derailing his plan to see the story through. "You guys should have shoved me into the ambulance and gone on with the rest," she said to him and Renie. The latter had swept up her long hair in a towel, and seemed positively reinvigorated after a hot shower.

"Ah, forget it," Walt shrugged. "To be honest, I was starting to get claustrophobic around all those people. If I were out in the middle of that mob, I'd probably be hyperventilating into a paper sack by now."

Alex set down the phone. "Room service says it'll be about half an hour. I ordered beers for everybody. That OK?"

"None for me," Jessica said. "Dr. Singh told me not to drink for a few days."

"Cool -- more for us," Renie joked.

Alex sat down next to Jessica and draped an arm around her. She let herself lean into him for just a few moments, resting her head on his shoulder. Horribly enough, even now she wanted him; thank God for Walt and Renie's presence, or else she might have succumbed to temptation and lost her soul forever.

Abruptly, she got up to fetch a bottled water from the minibar, glancing out the window absently. Strange her journey had ended here: in a hotel room with the TV on, in the city in which she had grown up, the city in which her mother had died. After Georgetown had given her the axe, she'd resolved to come home.

And so she had, though hardly in the way she'd imagined.

With a start, she realized that Alex, Walt, and Renie were all staring at her in nervous concern. "Sorry!" she huffed. "I was just thinking!"

"You're sure you're OK?" Walt said.

"I'm fine. You know, this is a sort of homecoming for me," she explained, trying not to sound too irritated with them. "I grew up in the Oakland Hills. I went to law school just up the road in Berkeley. Sue me if I'm a little nostalgic."

Renie pretended to misunderstand. "If you're a little neuralgic?"

Walt and Alex chuckled, and Jessica mustered a dry smile. "Yeah, probably that too."

"You know what I've always wondered?" Walt said. "What the hell is dropsy, exactly?"

"Flopsy, Mopsy, and Cottontail's poor relation," Renie replied.

But Jessica no longer heard them. The commercial break had given way to resumed coverage of the San Quentin protest, and the camera was zooming in on Sister Cordelia.

Jessica was wrong; hecklers, numbering in the hundreds, had infiltrated the protest, but their efforts to shout down the protesters were futile. Sister Cordelia's Salvadoran supporters were busily setting up a microphone and oversized speakers to enable her to address the multitude. The cameramen from local affiliates shoved in a little closer.

Sister Cordelia stepped up to the microphone. Her large eyes shone, not with pride so much as purpose. "My brothers and sisters, my partners in the struggle for peace and justice." She spoke slowly, with quiet passion. "We gather here in a show of faith and commitment to the cause of nonviolence. Christian and Jew, Buddhist and Muslim, believer and nonbeliever, we stand united in peace, tolerance, and the hope for redemption."

Some of the pilgrims cheered, but most bowed their heads in reverence. "Fucking bullshit Antichrist!" shrieked a counter-protester, but Cordelia ignored him and continued.

"I am praying to the Lord that the governor will commute the death sentence of Mr. Henderson. I pray also for that innocent child tortured and killed, and for all victims of violence. But the Lord commands us to hate the sin and love the sinner."

"Bullshit, bullshit! Antichrist bull --"

"My brothers and sisters," she said, "hatred is so easy. It's the coward's way out, to point fingers and to demonize our fellow human beings, as if killing them steers us any further along the path of righteousness, the path toward truth. Christ called upon us to imitate his life, and here we are imitating the violent deeds we claim to despise.

"No, hatred is easy," she repeated. "Jesus Himself recognized that love is what's difficult. It's love that demands steadfastness and courage." A faintly impish smile curled her lips. "Listening to some folks preach our Lord's Word, you'd think He's just another hero from one of those action movies. An emblem of vengeance, not forgiveness. Of retribution, not redemption. Of punishment, not love."

"Amen!"

"Amen!"

"Motherfucking bullshit! Bleeding-heart bullshit!" A heckler had gotten his hands on a megaphone, and a scuffle erupted as several devotees tried to wrest the thing away. Two cops swiftly moved in to break up the fight.

If Sister was aware of the tussle, she didn't let it show. "Jesus embraced the wretched and the sinful. Jesus especially loved the poor. Who is this other Jesus invoked by the unrighteous to justify washing their hands of the poor, casting them into the gutter and telling them it's their personal responsibility to claw their way out? Who is this other Jesus who decreed AIDS is God's punishment for love? This other Jesus who advocates violence to pay back violence, this other Jesus who turns a deaf ear to the frightened pregnant woman unready or unable to bear a child?"

Now the applause was thunderous. Cordelia's secular followers were also the most passionately political, and their rapture rivaled that of their devout confederates.

Many cheered, and hugged each other.

"I'll tell you who this other Jesus is, brothers and sisters," Cordelia said, her voice rising. "He's the false prophet, conjured out of bigotry and ignorance and self-interest. That's not Jesus Christ. As one of our most beloved sisters might put it, that other Jesus is nothing but 'spin.' And we all know what this thing called 'spin' really is. Little lies employed in the service of greater lies. Not always evil, but always cowardly, because it fears the truth. And if it fears truth, it also fears love."

Sister lowered her head and crossed herself. "In the name of the Father, the Son, and the Holy Spirit . . . "

The enormous throng joined her in reciting the Lord's Prayer. Their collective voices drowned out the rumble of a low-flying turboprop Piper.

"Give us this day our daily bread," they were intoning at the moment the plane dive-bombed into the heart of the congregation.

Television screens nation-wide flashed two or three seconds of flames and smoke and confusion before the signal from San Quentin fizzled for good.

Chapter 20

In a hospital lobby in San Rafael, another vigil was being observed.

The national media had set up outside, where doctors briefed reporters hourly on the condition of surviving victims. Within the lobby, families and friends wept and waited. None paid any particular attention to the couple who sat silent and holding hands in one dim corner.

From the moment she heard that Sister Cordelia was alive, though in extremely critical condition, Jessica knew she had to come. Sister couldn't die, not this way, Jessica frantically told herself; so terrible an end would in-validate the miracle, awarding victory's spoils to the enemy.

After the horrific explosion, perhaps ten minutes elapsed before the first report came in about its cause: a pilot in a private plane had apparently undertaken a suicide dive into the crowd. Jessica and Walt had gasped and Renie even let out a short scream, but it was Alex who had broken into gut-wrenching sobs.

For hours, Jessica and Alex and Renie and Walt were poised shocked and rapt before the television. 72 people had been killed outright, over three hundred more injured, many severely burned. By mid-afternoon, the pilot had been identified: the reportedly distraught father of the child mutilated and murdered by Donald Henderson. An Air Force veteran, he frequently flew his family to and from vacation homes in Tahoe and Santa Fe in his eight-seat plane.

Forty minutes later had come word that Cordelia Davis was among the more seriously injured and had been airlifted to San Rafael.

Alex had turned immediately to Jessica. "I'll take you to her."

Now all they could do was wait. Jessica had begged a nurse to inform Sister Cordelia she was nearby. The nurse made no promises. Struck by heavy debris from the plane's on-impact explosion, Sister had suffered a concussion, broken ribs, and dire internal injuries, and had been rushed into surgery.

Some part of Jessica's mind recognized, in surprise, that Alex seemed as distraught as she, but her entire will was focused on the desperate necessity for Sister Cordelia to survive. They spoke very little, and what they did say was terse and inconsequential.

Just after seven a nurse crossed the lobby and addressed Jessica in a low voice. "She's asking to see you. Follow me."

Jessica leaped up. As she rode the elevator to the sixth floor, she anxiously asked the nurse, "How is she? Is she going to live?"

"The priest is with her now," the nurse said. "I'm sorry. She's not expected to make it through the night."

Jessica's hand flew up to smother a painful sob.

Sister had been moved to a private room at the far end of a corridor. A haggard priest was just stepping out.

Jessica fumbled for words. "Sister -- has she . . . ?"

He shook his head. "It will be soon, I'm afraid."

Jessica started to go in, but stopped and turned back to the priest. "Father?"

"Yes?"

"Please give me your blessing. I've sinned so terribly."

He made the sign of the cross over her bent head. "We've all sinned, my dear. We all need to pray for God's forgiveness."

Someone had lowered the lights in the nun's room. Jessica was nonetheless grief-stricken at the sight of Sister Cordelia hooked up to an IV and a heart monitor, an oxygen tube beneath her nose. Her breathing was shallow, her eyes heavy lidded, barely open.

Tears rushing down her face, Jessica hurried to Cordelia's bedside, careful not to disturb any of the medical equipment sustaining her waning life. Jessica touched Sister's cool hand. "Don't leave -- please don't leave," she whispered.

Sister Cordelia's lashes fluttered. The eyes she turned on Jessica were weary but serene. "I'm glad you came," she said. Her voice was weary and serene as well.

"Sister, I let you down. I love you and believe in you, but . . . " She cried all the more violently. " . . . but I never could with purity of heart."

"You're wrong. Love is always good, always pure."

"Not mine! You see, I --"

Sister gently interrupted. "You've been paying too much attention to centuries of lonely old men in Rome. The love of the spirit is no greater or less than the love of the flesh."

Jessica was startled. "You . . . you knew!"

"Your love for Alex, and his for you, gives me great happiness." She managed to give Jessica's hand a weak squeeze.

A wild joy befell Jessica. "You mean, it's not wrong to love him the way I do?"

"No, daughter. To love someone in body and soul is to love life. And the more we love life, the more we love God, who gave it to us."

Smiling, Jessica swiped at her eyes. "How could I have been such a fool!"

"It's human nature not to see the forest for the trees on occasion." A hint of the familiar twinkle glinted briefly in her tired and sunken eyes. "Now, before I go home to Jesus, I want to show you the rest of the forest."

Half an hour later Sister had fallen asleep, and though Jessica wanted to stay with her, the nurse urged her away. Jessica planted a soft goodbye kiss on the nun's clammy forehead and whispered, "Godspeed."

But the moment she left the room she began to run, sorrow giving way to hope, elation, clarity. She couldn't wait to see him, and tell him everything, even if he wound up thinking her crazier than a loon.

Clarity at last.

In the lobby, she scanned two dozen faces, none of them his.

He had left.

"No he hasn't," she said under her breath. She knew him too well; he'd just gone outside to smoke.

He certainly wouldn't be out front, where the cameras and reporters were swarming. She strode up to the reception desk. "Where would someone go to have a cigarette?"

The RN gave her a disapproving look. "There's a small patio just off the cafeteria," she replied crossly, gesturing over her left shoulder.

Jessica jogged through the overlit cafeteria, past grim doctors in surgical scrubs and tense visitors downing coffee and checking wristwatches. She pushed open a heavy glass door and stepped onto the dark patio.

He was hunched over a stone table, snuffing a Marlboro Light into a plastic ashtray already crammed with butts. He glanced up at her. "Is she . . . ?"

"Not yet. Soon." She sat down across from him. "Oh, Alex, I have so much to tell you!"

"Me first," he said firmly.

"All right." She figured she had better hear him out now; for after listening to what she was about to say, he was likely as not to summon a posse of men in white jackets from the psych ward.

Resting his forearms on the table, he looked directly into her eyes. "Whatever happened to you last night, Jessica -- well, it probably saved your life, and possibly mine and Walt's and Renie's too. I know you would have been right there next to Sister, and . . . " He faltered a moment. "Well, if you'd been killed, I couldn't have stood it."

"But that's what I'm trying to tell you --"

"Just let me finish. Everything you said to me the morning you split was right on target. After she first singled you out that day in Metairie, I envied the faith she'd inspired in you. When I interviewed her out there and felt nothing, I convinced myself that the problem was with you, not me." He lit a fresh cigarette. "You had an open mind and I didn't. I needed to be hit over the head with a fucking sledgehammer."

She struggled to keep her mounting hopes in check until she knew for sure. "Then hit me over the head with said-fucking-sledgehammer. What are you telling me?"

He exhaled a slow stream of smoke. "That trance, or whatever it was last night. She sent it to you, or made damn sure that God did. She singled you out one last time because she wanted you to live. And by doing so, she saved both of us."

Jessica was beaming. She reached across the table to clutch his arms. "You're right. She singled out both of us. Horrible all the people who had to die so that we could live."

"Yeah. That bothers me a hell of a lot."

"Alex, she told me why she singled us out."

He was struck by her urgency. "Why?" he demanded jaggedly.

"Kiss me first, and then I'll sing like a canary, as my friend Grace would put it," she teased.

Getting up, he yanked her to her feet and pulled her to him.

They kissed so hard it hurt.

Communion of faith or not, tenderness would never be part of their emotional repertoire.

"Alex," she said, her tongue absently savoring the droplet of blood on her lower lip, "I've been so dense. I felt guilty about the way I love you. I stupidly thought my sins of the flesh were the reason I couldn't go with her to San Quentin, were even the reason I'd lost you."

"Just like I thought losing you was my punishment for Natalie's suicide."

"None of it is true," she said. "Everything we've done has been worth it. That's what Sister told me." She smiled. "We're going to have a baby."

"You're kidding."

"I've known for a few days. I was scared. But then Sister told me what it really meant."

Suddenly he grasped her implication.

"No. No. You can't be saying -- " He didn't know whether to laugh or scream.

"It's nothing like that," she tried to assure him. "Not exactly, at any rate. Some things, at least, have changed over the course of two thousand years. Virgin births are definitely passé. And so -- God willing -- is martyrdom." They were living proof of both.

"I don't know, Jess. This is pretty fucking mind-blowing." And then, half-convinced he'd gone crazy himself, he laughed. "Why the hell would anyone choose us?"

"I kind of like it. A strident feminist lawyer and a Pulitzer-winning journalist with commie sympathies. Someone up there must have a bizarre sense of humor."

Now she was laughing too. Clutching each other, they swayed together like a couple of drunks high on Thunderbolt.

"Just one request," she gasped, covering his face with kisses.

"What's that?"

"No fucking cameras in the delivery room."

Cordelia Marie Davis was pronounced dead just after three a.m. A Vatican delegation arrived two hours later to claim the body. Despite her various apostasies outside San Quentin and the overwhelming proof her resurrection had been a hoax, Rome

still deemed her worthy of special recognition for her martyrdom in the fight against

capital punishment, a stoical Vatican spokesman explained to the media clogging the

hospital parking lot.

Her body would be flown back to Italy for private burial at an undisclosed site, the

spokesman emphasized.

The President declared a national day of mourning to commemorate the mass

slaughter of eighty-three death-penalty protesters and seven esteemed journalists who'd

been covering the event.

In New Orleans, the District Attorney's office regretfully announced that it was

dropping charges against the coroner for lack of evidence. The D.A. disclosed that

prosecutors had been engaged in secret negotiations with representatives of Cordelia

Davis, offering the nun immunity in exchange for her admission that the Chief Medical

Examiner had fraudulently pronounced her "dead."

"We were this close to making a deal," the District Attorney sighed at a press

conference carried live on CNN and MSNBC.

In Washington, D.C., Gregory H. Monahan, attorney-at-law, was stricken by an

excruciating kidney stone requiring brief hospitalization and several painful laser

treatments. His soon-to-be ex-wife Jessica was all too happy to lend a hand and reassume

primary custody of seven-month-old Jordan.

One week after the deadly suicide dive-bomb outside the San Quentin

penitentiary, a third teenager in that many years was charged with strangling her newborn

delivered in a high-school stairwell. The instrument of death, claimed Nassau County

prosecutors, was a violently severed umbilical cord.

Panelists on the TV talk circuit clucked and opined. A high-profile defense

attorney announced she was taking on the case of seventeen-year-old Kathy Broder.

The Nassau County D.A. countered, declaring the office would seek the death penalty in the event of a conviction.

Owen Shawn provoked his contentious panel into a vituperative debate. "I promise you," Bev Wallace was smirking, "the defense is going to parade out a veritable array of experts in junk science. I just hope that after O.J. and Louise Woodward, juries are sharp enough to realize the difference between reputable forensic pathologists and hired guns."

Leslie Everett, a striking brunette legal correspondent out of Chicago plucked by CNN as a quasi-replacement for Jessica Anders, begged to differ. "Bev, there is a mountain of legitimate medical research on postpartum psychosis. Just last year, JAMA published a piece on its alarming frequency among teenage mothers."

"That's such B.S.," complained career prosecutor Anson Nomura. "For every murderer, you can find two dozen experts willing to testify the defendant is suffering from some exotic physiological syndrome documented in a footnote in the *New England Journal of Medicine*. Give me a break, Leslie!"

Radical lawyer Dave Steiner blustered in. "Why's the D.A. seeking death, Anson? Isn't it to bully Miss Broder into pleading to a lesser charge, guilty or not, to save her own life?"

"Dave is absolutely right!" seconded Leslie Everett. "The D.A. is doing its best to intimidate a frightened teenager into admitting to a crime which she may not have committed! It's a textbook example of prosecutorial overcharging."

Bev Wallace rolled her eyes. "People, get real! The D.A. is hardly equivalent to KGB's Secret Police. They don't charge unless they believe they can prove the defendant's guilt beyond a reasonable doubt. Look at New Orleans. The prosecution had an airtight case against the coroner until last week's tragedy robbed them of their star witness. Even with the preponderance of evidence in their favor, they had to back-burner the case. That's what any ethical prosecutor would do, right, Anson?"

Anson Nomura nodded vigorously. "Right."

"That also might have indicated a fundamental weakness in the investigation," objected Leslie Everett.

"Or an under-the-table deal," added Dave Steiner.

Owen Shawn mugged impatiently. "I think we're getting a little sidetracked here. The question is, it seems to me, whether or not Kathy Broder's lawyers are willing to cut a deal."

In separate studios in Chicago and San Francisco, respectively, both Leslie Everett and Dave Steiner privately agonized over signed agreements stipulating they would never mention the names of Jessica Anders and Alex Trujillo on the air.

Chapter 21: Epilogue

"Hurray, you could get away for lunch," she smiled as he pulled out a chair across the table from her.

Because it was a weekday, she'd been able to secure a prime spot at San Francisco's elegant if borderline-touristy Cliff House. Their table had a stunning view of the Pacific, on this clear April day a brilliant turquoise; of the jagged rocks on which sea lions sunbathed and yelped. Having arrived ten minutes earlier, she'd delighted two-and-a-half year old Jordy by holding him up to the glass and pointing out the marine mammals.

A few other lunchtime diners glared at the slender blonde woman and tall, ponytailed man, not because they had the slightest idea who the couple were, but because they'd dragged two tiny, bound-to-bawl children along to this decidedly upscale restaurant. Why didn't people ever seem to leave their brats with baby-sitters anymore?

Alex chucked Jordan under the chin and kissed Stella's soft brown curls. "How you guys doin'?"

"They're both going to be ready for naps in another hour, so we'd better eat fast. I'm having the seared ahi."

"Sounds good. You want a drink?"

"One. I've no intention of repeating last month's fiasco. Round-trip cabfare between here and Burlingame's too damn rich for my blood."

"Well, I can't blow off the afternoon this time, so I guess the household budget's safe."

Stella was whimpering in her high-chair. Jessica leaned down to retrieve the favorite stuffed caterpillar from the floor. "Here you go, sweetie," she said, placing the toy in her fifteen-month-old daughter's chubby hands.

Jordan, meanwhile, had used the opportunity to scramble into Alex's lap the better to admire the sea lions lazing on the rocks.

Alex indulged the toddler's prattling. "Yeah, they are pretty cool, huh?"

"Oh, I forgot to tell you," Jessica said. "Big news -- Renie called this morning. She and Walt have set a date. The twelfth of June."

Impressed, he arched one eyebrow. "Good for them. Just don't tell your brother. Steve's a great guy, but if I have to endure one more of his less-than-subtle suggestions that it's about time you and I make it legal -- "

She scoffed. "I told you, just throw it back in his face. Shit, he's been dating Robin for a near-record eight months. For him, that's practically a silver anniversary."

Their shared and respective lives bore only the most cursory resemblance to what they had been two years before. Media interest in them had evaporated almost immediately, especially once it was established that neither had been in San Quentin the fateful afternoon of the massacre. They'd spent the months of her pregnancy in virtual seclusion at her Georgetown townhouse. Alex placed a few editorial pieces arguing against the death penalty in left-wing Spanish-language newspapers. *Mother Jones* actually deigned to publish an essay co-written by the couple, again, on the moral and legal imperative to abolish capital punishment. But in private moments, they both despaired over the prospect of ever re-gaining steady employment. Not even Jessica's well-invested two million dollar inheritance would be sufficient to sustain a family of four indefinitely.

Given their backgrounds as professional intellectuals, they were pretty much useless to the work-force at large.

Ironically, it had been Gregg who inadvertently pointed them in a direction leading out of the morass. Stella was two months old when Gregg disclosed his plans to transfer to his firm's Bay Area office. Though his wife Doreen was herself pregnant, he was concerned about the move's potential impact on his visitation schedule with Jordy.

Unwilling to part with her son for weeks at a time, which bi-coastal custody would necessarily entail, Jessica convinced Alex to move their household to San Francisco as well. It hadn't taken much coercion. He disliked virtually everything about the east in general and D.C. in particular. For him, too, California was home. Rebecca and Lily, of course, were elated he and his family would be only an hour's plane ride from Los Angeles.

Jessica's brother Steve called in a few favors owed him by management at the *Chronicle*, and Alex was hired as a copy-editor. Jessica knew he had to be frustrated with the nature of the work; composing headlines and jumps and proofing for the *Chronicle*'s relentless errata was a far cry from covering guerilla wars and populist uprisings in Latin America. Thus far, the paper had granted him a single byline when by chance, he'd happened to witness a carjacking just as he and Jessica were stepping out of a SOMA restaurant.

The story had been a mere three inches, and buried on page B6, at that. But he'd clipped it out and affixed it with a magnet to the refrigerator, underscoring the byline with a yellow highlighter: "*Alex Trujillo,* Chronicle *Staff Writer.*" It bothered Jessica every time she went into the kitchen, but he refused to take down the clipping, relishing its irony.

But the return to the Bay Area had turned out to be a propitious move for her as well. A former colleague of hers from the ACLU now taught law at the University of Santa Clara, and he vouched for Jessica when she applied for a part-time position. Hired as an adjunct professor, she taught core courses in Evidence and Criminal Procedure twice a week to first-years too stressed-out to take much interest in her past involvement with the Sister Cordelia affair. And though the law school was technically independent of the small Catholic liberal arts college, Jessica thought it significant that the university president, a Dominican nun, sent her a personal note welcoming her to Santa Clara.

With steady if unspectacular work, they invested the monies from the sales of their respective homes in Georgetown and Silver Lake, and bought a relatively modest house in the affluent suburb of Burlingame south of the City. Alex patently disliked living in so upper-crust a community, but they couldn't afford San Francisco proper and she refused to live in San Mateo or Daly City. He called her a snob and she called him a phony. "I haven't noticed you switching from Bombay to Vons brand gin, buster!"

The lone continuum linking their past lives with their present was the explosive quality of their relationship. Even her brother Steve, who privately admitted to her he liked Alex a hell of a lot better than he had Gregg, was somewhat appalled. "Don't you guys ever get *tired*?"

But Steve knew little of the wonderful ordinariness into which their lives had also settled. They had a three-bedroom house, two kids, an elegant Persian cat named Pat Riley and a neutered Labrador-collie mix adopted from the Humane Society they called The Big Eunuch, a wicked play on the nickname of ace baseball pitcher Randy Johnson. Alex played foam-rubber-basketball with Jordy for hours on end, and Jessica nursed Stella until the baby herself had to shriek her preference for bottle over breast.

They wore wedding bands, but thought the idea of applying for a license and going through a ceremony absurd and redundant. But they'd had both babies baptized into the Faith, Steve doing double-duty as godfather. Lily stood as godmother to Stella.

And they debated endlessly whether their kids would one day resent them for not having a TV. Jordy was already nagging them; every other weekend he spent hours watching cartoons at his dad's opulent house in Pacific Heights.

Alex glanced at his watch. "I'd better get back," he said ruefully.

While he settled the bill, Jessica was fitting Stella's struggling little legs into the stroller. Jordan clung to Jessica's shin, restlessly chanting, "Mommy mommy mommy."

A white-haired woman in a bright blue sweater and tan slacks arose from a nearby table to assist Jessica. "Oh, I'm so glad my kids are grown!" the woman exclaimed, helping strap Stella into her seat.

The woman's crinkled gaze lingered on Stella, on her little face with its rosy skin and wide brown eyes; she was unmistakably the child of her parents. Yet as Jessica was knotting a frilly lavender bonnet under the baby's chin, the elderly woman gently, inexorably, touched the tiny face.

"She's an uncommonly beautiful child," the woman said dreamily. "Such a beautiful child. You two must be so proud."

Stella gurgled and grasped the old woman's finger.

By now accustomed to the phenomenon, Jessica and Alex responded simultaneously. "We are."

Carrying Jordan while she commandeered the stroller, Alex walked her down the sloping hill to where the Land Rover (recently dubbed with California plates) was parked. The wind kicking up from the Pacific was fierce, and Alex tugged Jordy's knit cap over the toddler's ears.

He helped her buckle the kids into their car-seats. But he was suddenly loath to see them go.

Though her car keys were in her hand, he hoisted her up onto the hood of the Land Rover and kissed her.

Her arms wrapped around his neck, her legs around his hips. "Are you sure you can't play hooky this afternoon?"

"Better not. Seems to me we have a pretty fancy mortgage to pay."

"Shut up!" she laughed, pulling him closer.

Above their heads, gulls squawked, flocking madly as a group of tourists emerging from the Cliff House tossed them bits of sourdough rolls.

"Sign from God," Jessica pronounced. "If we keep hanging out here, we're going to get shat upon." She hopped down and yanked open the driver's side door.

Alex laughed heartily. "I stopped questioning your intuition a long time ago. See you tonight."

Curbside he watched her back out of the diagonal space. She blew him a kiss as she shifted into drive and sped away down Point Lobos Avenue.

He stood there until the Land Rover disappeared into southbound traffic. Only then did he strike a lit match to his cigarette and start back up the sidewalk toward his own car.

Life was good.

THE END

Coddon 302